An Unwelcome Arrangement

A Rose McDougal Adventure

By

Joe Benson

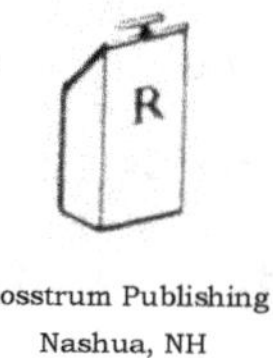

Rosstrum Publishing
Nashua, NH

Also available from Rosstrum Publishing

Non-Fiction

Fast Track for Caregivers

366 Tips for a Successful Job Search

Listen to the Cry of the Child

The Dave Maynard Spin (also in Large Print)

The Happy Heart Cookbook

Journey of a Beam

States Have Powers

Teacher Within the Coach (can be a textbook)

Fiction

Timberline

Dark Horizon

Death in Cedar Canyon

Missing

Pursuit

Tapping In to Murder

Lawless in Brazil

Dr. Lawless I Presume

Emotions in Motion (poetry)

Wind Castle (Large Print)

Dedication

This book is dedicated to Mary Benson, my mother. She provided the chief motivation for this book by suggesting I write a short story, something in the neighborhood of 100 pages. Thanks, Mom. I love you.

Joe Benson

Acknowledgments

Thanks go to God, who provides the health and energy necessary to get behind the keyboard and get to work.

Steve Burke, a professional writer who, from his home in Boise, Idaho, helped me at every step, even while busy working on a sequel to his book, *The Chieftains of Boston.*

Sister Margaret Gannon, in addition to being my favorite aunt, showed me an unrelenting desire to spread cheer.

Stephen Burke and Randy Hilfman spent untold hours polishing a very rough manuscript and serving as copy editors. Should the book find a measure of success, it will be the result of their direction.

Finally, many thanks to Joe Ross of Rosstrum Publishing. More than my publisher, Joe has been a coach (a necessary disciplinarian at times), an editor and has become a friend. He has encouraged me to develop this book into a series of books, thereby continuing to place Rose McDougal in one dangerous situation after another. Naturally, I agree with him.

Any stumbles and all errors are mine.

JB

An Unwelcome Arrangement

A Rose McDougal Adventure

An Unwelcome Arrangement is a work of fiction. Names, Characters, places and incidents are either the product of the author's imagination or are used fictitiously. Any resemblance to actual persons, living or dead, business establishments, events, or locales is entirely coincidental.

Rosstrum Publishing books are available at discount when purchased in bulk for premiums or promotions as well as for fundraising or educational use. Based on quantities, special editions can be created to specification. For details, contact the publisher.

Rosstrum Publishing
A division of The Border Company, LLC
8 Strawberry Bank Rd.
Suite 20
Nashua, NH 03062-2763
Rosstrumpublishing@gmail.com
www.rosstrumpublishing.com

Library of Congress Cataloging-in-Publication Data

Author: Benson, Joe
Title: An Unwelcome Arrangement: A Rose McDougal Adventure/ Joe Benson—
1st Rosstrum hardcover ed.
1. McDougal, Rose, fictional character. 2. Nashua, NH. 3. Drugs. 4. Benson, Joe.
5. Title. 6. Organized Crime 7. Fiction 8. Adventure

Library of Congress Control Number 2020951945
Manufactured in the United States of America
1 3 5 7 9 10 8 6 4 2

ISBN 978-1-62570-035-3
ISBN 978-1-62570-037-7 (ebook)
ISBN 978-1-62570-056-8 (CD for PC)

Chapter one

SMASH!

The driver's-side window shattered into a thousand bits, most of which fell inside the vehicle, thanks to Frankie's powerful fist. Sweet, toxic fumes came pouring out of the car's cabin, liberated and in search of another victim, another poor soul who would share the same fate as the unconscious woman who was sprawled out on the front seat. As Frankie withdrew his fist, which tightly gripped a rock, jagged ends of the remaining window cut his hand and wrist. Like a pincushion, small pieces of glass poked out from his right hand. Blood oozed from a dozen fresh cuts, a few rather nasty ones. For the average man, a slashed hand might have provoked screams of pain. But not Frankie. He felt no discomfort. His adrenaline rush was still peaking.

He leaned his head into a gaping hole which had once been filthy glass, squinting and holding his breath as he did. Immediately, he recognized the woman: Rose McDougal. She was the nice teacher who helped him one day after school. That was many years ago. Nowadays, Rose was the sweet woman who smiled at him, offering him sodas or hot dogs when he saw her at the baseball stadium.

Rose was sleeping, or so Frankie hoped. From within his mind came the hostile voice of Angie, that mean woman who managed the Dunkin' Donuts across the street, offering her morbid assessment:

> If she's alive, it ain't by much. My guess? She's dead. Now go stand over in the corner like I told you earlier!

Angie, who had been rude to Frankie an hour earlier, wanted only to cause him pain. Pushing Angie's image from his mind, he returned his attention to helping Rose. Frankie hoped it was only a deep sleep which had her motionless, but even someone like Frankie knew better.

He brushed the tiny pieces of glass off the door's armrest, then reached back into the cabin and wedged his hand under Rose's head and thick mop of hair, which covered the lock. By feel, he found it. For a moment, he had the lock in his grip, but it slipped between his moist fingers and her sweaty hair before he could yank it up. He tried again but could not get a firm hold. Frankie realized that finesse would not work.

"Sorry, Miss Rose," he mouthed.

Using both hands, he pushed her shoulders. She wouldn't budge. With his feet anchored on the pavement, his knees bent, and his chest pressed up against the vehicle, he pushed with all his might.

"Arrgh!"

Her body flopped onto the passenger side. With the lock free, he pinched it tightly and pulled up in a swift tug. He then grasped the door handle and yanked the door open. In an instant, the fumes and smoke, a mixture of carbon monoxide and burnt oil, engulfed him, nearly knocking him off his feet. He reached back for the door handle to steady himself. Any of the previous sweet emanations were gone. A deleterious stench was all that remained. He covered his nose and mouth with his bloody right hand. The coppery taste of blood made him gag. The sight of blood—never mind the taste of it—had always sickened Frankie. But the 32-year old knew he had to act fast; he had little time.

With his right hand covering his nose, he leaned into the smoky cabin and felt for Rose's collar. His left hand found it. He grabbed and pulled with all his strength. Her seatbelt was not fastened, which was good, but despite his feverish tugging, she barely budged. He would need both hands to pull her to freedom.

Ignoring the pain, he placed his injured right hand on Rose's left shoulder. Blood leaked from his many cuts, instantly staining Rose's T-shirt. Frankie squeezed hard with both hands and yanked. Her shirt began to tear at the neck, but he kept his grip and kept pulling. Her left leg got caught on something poking out of the floorboard. Frankie shot a glance at it but paid it little mind; he just kept pulling and pulling. Slowly, the hefty woman began to slide. He pulled harder, leaning his 250-pound frame backward and anchoring his legs.

"ARRGH!"

His last yank did the trick, and she was free of the cabin and its poisonous fumes. She flopped lifelessly onto the parking space next to her car. Though he had released her, Frankie was convinced: Miss Rose was dead. He dropped to his knees by her side and pounded furiously on her chest, a technique he saw on that medical show with the scary music, desperately trying to revive her. He could not leave her but knew that only someone who knew doctor stuff could help her.

"Help! Help! Over here!" he shouted, jumping to his feet. He began hopping up and down and waving his arms over his head. "HELP!"

Finally, others began to appear. A group of four men walking along Canal Street were drawn to his desperate cries. They turned off their designated course and broke in his direction, jogging, then running toward the Dunstable House parking lot. They drew to within fifty feet and stopped. Something about the scene didn't look quite right. Convinced it was some ploy to get attention, the four men, all toting sheathed umbrellas, shuffled off, scowling back at Frankie and the big woman sprawled on the parking lot. One of them mumbled something about adults not getting enough attention in their childhood.

Thankfully, however, Frankie's calls for help reached a more sympathetic audience. His pleas penetrated the inner sanctum of the Dunstable House, where landlord Jim Budzko sat in his humble apartment, watching Bob Barker warmly welcome a giddy, buxom blonde to his game show stage. As soon as Jim heard the shouting, he jumped up from the couch and raced outside. Upon spotting Rose, who was splayed out on the pavement, he called back to his assistant, who had sprinted out behind him, to go back inside and call 9-1-1. A minute later, five curious pedestrians arrived on scene. Before long, a small crowd had assembled in the Dunstable House parking lot.

Chapter Two

John Callahan and Jimmy Largy jumped out of their parked cruiser and hustled over to a group of onlookers who were gathered around a large woman lying on the parking lot, on her back. She appeared unconscious. A man on one knee was by her side. He was shirtless. Next to him stood a tall man with a crew cut. His right hand was wrapped in a cloth. The shirtless man was checking her pulse. Officers

Callahan told Largy, the junior officer, to see if the man giving aid to the victim needed any help while they waited on the ambulance. Callahan would deal with the crowd, which was growing.

As he made his way through the crowd, he heard the wail of an approaching siren.

"Step aside, folks. Step aside," Callahan said, gesturing with his arms. The crowd of bystanders did as instructed.

Callahan looked over his shoulder and watched as an ambulance turned off Main Street onto Canal Street. The shriek of the siren grew louder. The ambulance sped the short distance down Canal and whipped into the Dunstable House parking lot before slowing down prior to hitting a speed bump. The driver then cut off the piercing siren and executed a three-point turn, so that the back doors opened toward the accident scene. The ambulance inched back a few feet and then stopped. The driver EMT jumped out. The other came out through the back doors. He reached back into the ambulance and extracted a stretcher.

From the front, the passenger door opened. An attractive blonde woman stepped out. She walked to the rear of the ambulance but kept her distance from the medics.

Callahan watched her as she leaned against the corner of the rear bumper. She was strikingly beautiful, so out of place. She looked like no EMT or orderly he had ever seen. He couldn't keep his eyes off her. *What's she doing in an ambulance?* he wondered. *She ought to be modeling on a runway in New York.*

From behind, Callahan heard a man yelling at folks to get back. He pulled his gaze off the blonde and spun back to the crowd, which by then numbered in the dozens.

"Folks, keep clear. Got an emergency here!"

The EMTs pushed the stretcher through the gap in the crowd that Callahan made. They got to the unconscious woman and lowered the stretcher. Callahan watched as they instructed the shirtless man to come to the opposite side of the stretcher and hold it in place. He did. With the stretcher steady, both EMTs slid their arms under the woman's back and legs. As evidenced by the strain on their faces, it took great effort to get her onto the stretcher. The EMTs then locked her in place with straps across the chest and legs, before making the short trip to the back of the ambulance.

As she rolled past, Callahan noticed the woman's eyes. They were milky and distant, but at least she was alive. He took another look at the blonde woman, who stood back as the EMTs slid the stretcher into the ambulance. He squinted at the stitching just above a chest pocket on her white coat. From some fifty feet away, he could have sworn he made out the word *Doctor.*

Beautiful and smart? If she's got a guy, I hope he knows how good he's got it. He shook his head and headed back to his partner.

"John, this is Mr. Jim Budzko. He's the landlord here at the Dunstable House," Officer Largy said as Callahan and Budzko shook hands. "Jim knows the accident victim."

Largy nodded to Budzko, who slipped into a button-down shirt that had just been handed to him. Budzko turned his attention to Officer Callahan before beginning.

"Her name is Rose McDougal. She's lived here for about ten years, about as long as I've run the place." He looked up at the apartment building, as he fastened the last button of his shirt. "Never gave me any trouble, not one complaint against her. Always paid her rent on time."

"What about people coming by to visit her? Anyone you might consider out of place or even suspicious?" Callahan asked.

"None," Budzko answered, looking at both officers.

"No one appearing suspicious?" Callahan asked.

"No. I mean no one as in no visitors at all. Zero."

Callahan gave him a curious look.

"In the ten years she's lived here, I've never seen her with anyone inside or outside this building."

Callahan glanced over at his partner, who appeared perplexed. *Ten years and not one visitor? No family? Then who'd want to hurt her? Maybe we're not looking at a—*

Largy broke his train of thought, as a good partner is prone to do.

"Before you got here, I asked Mr. Budzko if one of us could take a look inside Miss McDougal's apartment, while the other looks around out here for a while," Largy said.

"Makes sense," Callahan said, then nodded back in the direction of the ambulance. "Look, the *Telegraph* is here. Right on time."

"Hmph," Largy said, shaking his head. "How about I stay out here and take a look inside the car." He glanced at the ambulance. "I'll wander over there shortly."

"That's a good idea. I mean, if you don't mind me saying," Budzko said looking at both cops. He then pointed to the ambulance. "That big guy with the crew cut was the one who pulled Rose from her car. He was the only one on the scene when I arrived."

"Sounds good, Jimmy," Callahan said to his partner.

Largy was reaching for a rear door of the vehicle when Budzko called out to him.

"The hero, I guess you might call him that, is named Frankie," Budzko said, before pausing. "He's . . . well . . . not entirely there, if you know what I mean."

Callahan understood. With the press in close proximity, an officer shielding someone who might be challenged or dim-witted would be useful.

"Why don't I head over to the ambulance first," Largy said. "That's Popovich from the Telegraph. A real pest, that one. Anyway, I'll check around the car after."

"Good idea," Callahan said.

"If you're finished before we are, we'll be in apartment 4D. Top floor," Budzko said.

Callahan followed closely behind Budzko down the fourth-floor hallway. His first impression of the Dunstable House was a sense of desolation. The interior was dark and dirty. A moldy stench hung in the air. The foul smell complemented a detritus of scattered litter on the first floor, up the stairwell and where he and Budzko now walked.

No wonder she never had visitors, Callahan thought.

A bug-encrusted light bulb, suspended from the ceiling inches above Callahan's six-foot stretch, swung listlessly a few doors down from apartment 4D. Plodding ahead, Budko pointed to a tripping hazard. Callahan looked down and saw what looked like half a toilet seat, but he didn't stop to confirm. He stepped over whatever it was, took a few more steps and stopped next to Budzko, who stood in front of apartment 4D. He fumbled with a set of keys, silently cursing the poor lighting.

"I keep reminding myself to get another damn light up here," Budzko said, shaking his head. "I swear this old place will be the death of me."

Callahan grunted, keeping his eyes down the hallway behind them. Being jumped by some ex-con drug addict in a place like this seemed possible.

"Ah, here it is," Budzko said, holding up the key as if it were the winning Lotto ticket.

He guided the key into the slot, twisted it twice before finally earning the click. He grabbed the door handle and turned it, but the door wouldn't budge. It was stuck.

"Damned humidity. Gotta get WD-40 for some of these doors."

Budzko lowered his shoulder and drove it into the door while turning the knob. He put so much force into the door that when it blasted open, he stumbled and fell face-first onto the linoleum floor of the kitchen. Callahan hustled in behind him. He extended a hand and pulled Budzko back onto his feet. Budzko groaned as he brushed off his shirt and pants.

"Lemme guess, a shot of WD-40 on some of these old doors, huh?" Callahan asked, grinning.

"That's right. Something else to add to that growing to-do list," Budzko said, steadying himself.

Callahan's first impressions of the woman's apartment were no different than the rest of what he had seen inside the Dunstable House: depressing and dark. The apartment was small. He guessed it to be about 600 square feet. The few pieces of furniture she owned were dilapidated and appeared dirty. A battered, steel garbage barrel, the likes of which one might find in a prison mess hall, sat under a windowsill behind the kitchen table.

"I'll check the bedroom," Budzko said, pointing to an open door.

Callahan nodded, "I'll look around out here."

Budzko turned back to Callahan before entering the bedroom. "Should I be looking for a note of some sort? Maybe a suicide note?"

"Anything that looks out of place and, yes, any sort of handwritten note," Callahan replied.

"Got it," Budzko said. He then stepped into the bedroom and out of view.

Callahan walked into the living room, a room equally as small as the kitchen and dining area. Its contents left little to be desired. There was a 13" rabbit-ear-antenna TV which rested on a two-foot-high TV stand. A grimy couch, covered in stains, and an old wooden chair were flush against the wall. Under all the crappy furniture was a repulsive shag carpet. Age had not served the carpet well. Callahan began his search with the couch.

Not only was the couch unsightly, it reeked of rotten meat. Her couch was the kind of repulsive thing one might find at the end of a driveway, its owner begging for someone—please, for God's sake—to take it far, far away. Of course, no one would. About the only thing it was good for was target practice.

Callahan held his breath and lifted its pillows. He searched behind the couch and under it. He found nothing. He walked over to the TV stand and pulled it away from the wall. Dust bunnies, a bottle cap, a cobweb and a few dead flies greeted him. No letter. No suicide note.

Suicides aren't supposed to hide their notes.

"Nothing in the bedroom or bathroom," Budzko announced as he walked up behind Callahan, causing him to jump. "Sorry 'bout that."

Callahan waved a hand, dismissing it. "Nothing out here," he said, as he pushed the TV stand back against the wall. He then made his way into the kitchen. He pulled open the cupboards and drawers. Budzko followed behind him.

"I checked under the bed, lifted the mattress and pulled off the sheets. I found nothing," Budzko said. "I checked the chest's drawers and the nightstand. Nothing suspicious. No notes or letters."

"Anything in the bathroom? Pills? Pill bottles?" Callahan asked, as he rifled through the kitchen drawers.

"Nope. No medicines of any kind," Budzko replied. He then checked the refrigerator. "And nothing in here, Officer Callahan."

"Well, I guess that covers it," Callahan said. "Thanks for letting me in here and thanks for the help, Jim."

Callahan shut the final cupboard and was about to leave the apartment when, from the corner of his eye, he spotted an edge of a crumpled piece of paper poking out from a gap between the garbage barrel and the wall. He looked over to Budzko, who had followed Callahan's eyes to the same piece of paper.

"Give me another minute, ok?" Callahan asked.

"Of course," Budzko said.

Callahan walked over, adjusted his weapon belt and lowered himself to his knees. He inched the barrel away from the wall. The paper slid to the kitchen floor. He picked it up. As he stood up, ligaments in his knees popped. He smoothed the letter on the kitchen table. Budzko walked up behind him to get a close look.

It was a typed letter, riddled with black scribbles, though still legible. Based on the many scribbles and a few small tears, the letter had not been well-received. Through the scribbles, Callahan read the brief, carefully worded letter.

Dear Ms. McDougal:

Thank you for your interest in the vacant teaching position at Dr. Crisp Junior High School. Your resume is well-written. Your references wrote of your teaching acumen in glowing terms. Clearly, your exemplary performance as a substitute teacher is undeniable.

However, I'm sorry to inform you that I cannot offer you a position at this time. Furthermore, State budget cuts have forced us to significantly reduce our pool of substitute teachers. You were one of the substitutes that we had to let go.

In the meantime, I wish you the best of luck with your goal of becoming a full-time teacher. If you wish to be added to our quarterly newsletter, which posts any teaching vacancies, please contact my secretary, Miss Eileen Dirubbo at 885-5544.

Sincerely,
Andrew C. Frazie
Superintendent of Schools

Chapter Three

Doctor Karen Bedard took the proffered card from Officer Largy and glanced at it. She had heard that it was considered polite to look over a business card before placing it into a pocket or purse. She smiled at the officer, then slipped his card into her breast pocket. He smiled back but seemed distracted by something behind her. She turned around and noticed a handsome man holding a small notebook. A badge of some sort was pinned to his shirt and he wore a Pirates' baseball cap. He stood in the vicinity of the ambulance.

"Well, I better get to work," Karen said, pointing at Frankie. "His hand looks pretty bad."

"Yes, of course," Largy said smiling, before looking back in the direction of the ball-cap-wearing man. Largy appeared suspicious to her as he gazed at the man. That was when it hit her. The badge, notebook and a police officer's suspicion? He was with the press, she concluded.

"Thank you, officer," Karen said. She then gestured to the reporter. "Don't worry about him. This isn't the time to comment on what we think took place. He can wait for the final diagnosis, just like everyone else."

"I appreciate that, doctor. He's a reporter with the Telegraph. He's good, but can be a damned pest," Largy said.

"I hear that's the case for the good ones," she said.

"Pretty much," Largy said. "Anyway, I need to take a look around your patient's car, then get inside and see if my partner found anything. Thanks again."

Karen watched as Largy walked across the parking lot toward the old Chevy belonging to the woman who lay on a stretcher in the back of the ambulance.

Chapter Four

Callahan sighed. He picked up the letter and folded it in half. He rubbed the back of his head and sighed.

"Talk about a kick in the nuts," Callahan mumbled.

"And patronizing as hell," Budzko added.

Callahan was about to slip the letter into a Ziploc bag when Largy arrived. Largy took a step into the apartment and stopped. He looked around.

"Spartan living for sure," he said. "But at least it doesn't smell like the puke I saw in the stairwell."

"That's nice," Callahan said, rolling his eyes. "How's it going outside?" Callahan asked.

Largy gave him a rundown. First, the pesky reporter never got near the crew cut guy. That was good. The blonde doctor treated crew cut guy's injured hand. That was good. Finally, one of the medics came over to the car asking forensics about any contraband. That was standard operating procedure. All in all, nothing special. And that's always good.

Largy concluded. "I stuck around until the medics loaded crew cut guy into the back of the ambulance with the woman."

"Good. The last thing we needed was someone who, for all we know, is mentally challenged," Callahan shot a glance at Budzko, "getting duped by the press into concocting some fantasy about what happened in that parked car."

"I just met Frankie today, but it's plain to see something's not right in his head. If that reporter had gotten to Frankie, there was no way he'd have been able to walk away with a 'no comment,'" Budzko said.

The two officers nodded.

"How about up here? Find anything," Largy asked.

Callahan handed him the letter.

Largy unfolded it and read it quickly. "Jeez. That superintendent sure has a way with words. What an asshole."

"My thoughts exactly," Callahan said.

"Think this may have been an attempt at suicide?" Largy asked.

Callahan shrugged his shoulders and said nothing.

"I went over to the car when forensics arrived. They checked inside the cabin, the trunk, everywhere. Nothing out of the ordinary. No pills, bottles, no weapons of any sort," Largy said, adding, "And no evidence of foul play."

"They'll dust for fingerprints. Since Frankie's the one who pulled her out, as you said," Callahan looked at Budzko, "we'll need to get Frankie's prints today." Callahan pulled out a notebook from a breast pocket and scribbled a reminder. "As for Rose, they'll check her for any bruising or any kind of foul play when she gets to the hospital."

"Forensics will be able to differentiate the bruising that Frankie caused with possible foul play?" Budzko asked.

"If they find more than Frankie's prints, then yes. And thanks for mentioning that. We'll need to get a statement from Frankie as well," Callahan said, nodding to Largy.

Callahan jotted down another reminder, then turned his attention to Budzko.

"Before I forget, I appreciate your help today, Jim. You and Frankie probably saved that woman's life. We'll investigate this case like any other, and regardless of its conclusion, you guys did great."

He and Budzko shook hands. He then looked over at Largy and pointed to the letter that his partner held.

“To your earlier question, yes, I think suicide is a possibility.”

Chapter Five

Karen pulled out a pack of Spearmint Gum and popped a piece in her mouth. She looked around to find the reporter, the "damned pest" as Officer Largy put it. He was nowhere to be found. She walked over to check on her medics. Both were inside the ambulance. Lou was checking vitals, while Harry, the more experienced EMT, fiddled with dials on the equipment mounted above where the woman lay. He held a ventilator in his free hand. Karen walked up to the open ambulance door.

"How's your patient doing, Harry?"

Harry made a final adjustment on a dial, then turned and answered. "She's barely conscious, doc, but she's stable. Heart rate is low and her breathing is shallow."

Karen nodded. "Got room for another back there? A guy with an injured hand. His bandage is field dressed. I'm worried about infection."

"Sure. Plenty of room," he said, then nodded in the direction of Rose's car. "Forensics is here. Before we go, I'm going to see if they found anything."

"I'll work on the guy with the injured hand, then we can take off," she said, then made her way over to Frankie.

As she approached him, he appeared even bigger. His muscular frame resembled that of a linebacker. From a few feet away, she had to crane her neck to look up at him. He had massive, powerful hands, the kind of hands that could bend metal. Yet while he appeared intimidating, there was something disarming about the man who stood in front of her.

He had a boyish face, free of wrinkles and any stubble. It looked to her as if he had never shaved, though she guessed he was in his early thirties. Adding to an adolescent image was the Pirates jersey he wore. Complementing the jersey were a pair of Red Sox shorts and high-top Converse sneakers. He was clearly uncomfortable in the presence of the few remaining onlookers. He fidgeted with his hands and circled slowly on his feet. But what struck her most was the way he appeared to be talking out of the side of his mouth, though to no one in particular. No one paid him any attention.

She took a close look at the bandage wrapped around his right hand and halfway down his forearm. The bandage was a shirt sleeve. It was blood-stained and needed to come off. His cuts would need to be disinfected before they became infected. She walked up to him and stuck out a hand. At first, he looked suspicious, but then he accepted. They shook hands.

"I'm Doctor Karen Bedard. I'd like to help you with your hand."

"Hi, Doctor. My name is Francis, but most people call me Frankie!" he said, singing it out. He shifted uneasily on his feet, nodded and then mumbled something inaudible.

She was taken aback. That was not the voice she had expected from such a strapping fellow, but it supported the elements of a childlike persona. She shook her head and smiled at him.

"Frankie, I've got stuff in the ambulance that'll clean up your hand."

She led him to the back of the ambulance, where she found Harry inside working on their patient. He had just returned from meeting with the forensic officers. He reported that they had found no contraband inside or around the vehicle from which the woman had been extricated. Karen thanked him and then told him she would take care of Frankie's right hand. She asked him if they had reported back to the ER. Yes, they had. They informed the ER that their patient was stable and that her vitals showed improvement. The ER was ready for them. Karen told him that she needed five minutes to work on Frankie. She then grabbed a first-aid kit mounted on the inside of one of the rear doors.

"Let's get a look at that," Karen said, turning her attention to Frankie and unwinding the bloodied shirt sleeve. Bits of glass protruded from his right hand's knuckles. Covered in blood, some of the smaller pieces were hard to see at first. A few shards of glass had been driven rather deep into his skin between his index and ring fingers. *Poor thing*, she thought.

Then she remembered the gaping hole, some eight inches wide, blown right through the driver's side window just above the door handle. His hand must have smashed that thing at full speed.

Forget his hand. Poor window.

Regardless, his right hand needed attention. Even if his face didn't show it, there was no way he didn't feel the sting from those cuts. She withdrew a bottle of hydrogen peroxide, strips of gauze, bandages and white tape. She set those items aside and pulled out a pair of tweezers.

"Try to keep your hand still, Frankie."

She got down to work on extracting the many bits of glass. Through it all, Frankie never complained. As she withdrew two sizable, razor-sharp glass daggers from between his fingers, he silently winced. She put the glass into a zip-lock bag, in the event the police wanted physical evidence. That done, she reached for the peroxide.

"This may sting a little," Karen said, holding his wrist and lowering it at an angle. She then poured the peroxide over his bloody hand, eradicating any would-be infections. Along its path down Frankie's hand, the peroxide scoured exposed nerve endings. Most men would've whined. But not Frankie. He shifted uneasily, that was all. *His mother would have been proud of him,* Karen thought.

"Very good . . . there we go." She dabbed the many visible cuts and patted down his hand with a fresh white towel. That done, she placed strips of gauze over the cuts. She layered additional gauze over the nastier ones, holding them in place as she reached for her bandage wrap.

"That's it. Just a minute more." She looked up and smiled at him, making him blush. "I think you're going to need stitches with two of the cuts, but we'll take a closer look at the hospital and decide. Sound good, Frankie?"

Frankie nodded. She began wrapping below his wrist. As she did, she interrupted Lou, who was checking the patient's pulse rate. "How's she doing in there?"

"Pulse is weak. Only inching up slowly," Lou said, placing her wrist over her chest. "I'd like to get going if we could, doc."

"Ok. Just about ready."

Lou glanced down at Frankie and nodded at Karen.

"Frankie, are you okay riding in the back? The medics will take care of you," she said.

"My mom took me to the hospital once when I hurt my knee really, really bad. But this doesn't hurt at all," he said, holding up his hand and flashing a big, toothy grin. "You've been so good to me. You're my favorite doctor!"

"Please call me Karen," she said, smiling. She made her final wrap of the bandage between Frankie's index and middle finger, pinning it over his palm. "We've got to get going. We don't want your mom to worry, so we'll call her once we get there."

Frankie's smile disappeared. In its place came a frown.

"Ma's going to be so upset with me," he shook his lowered head. "I spilled her coffee. She needs her coffee."

Karen considered an encouraging answer, but decided against it. She slapped the back of the ambulance.

"All set, Harry," she said.

Harry took a few steps to the back, then placed a foot on the step below the door and extended a hand to Frankie, helping him into the ambulance. He led Frankie to the vacant bench across from Rose and helped him get comfortable. Harry checked to ensure the stretcher was locked. It was. He then told Frankie to hold the mounted rail above the bench. Frankie nodded and Harry jumped out, shut the doors behind him and made his way to the front, entering on the driver's side.

Karen was reaching for the passenger door when she heard a man call out from behind her.

"Ma'am . . . excuse me, ma'am. Just a sec."

Karen turned around and wasn't surprised by what she found. It was the reporter, *the pest*, as Officer Largy put it. He stood in front of her with a pen in one hand and a mini-notebook in the other. He might have been only handsome from a distance, but he was striking up close. He had deep blue eyes, tanned skin and dimples, which accentuated his smile.

None of which matters, since we've got to get moving, she thought.

"Hi, I'm Dave Popovich with the Telegraph," he said, extending a hand. She noticed him eyeing the stitching above her breast pocket.

"Listen, I don't have time—"

"It's a pleasure to meet you, Doctor Bedard. Is there a first name?"

"Yes," she answered snappily. "It's Karen, but none of that—"

"Look, I'll be brief. I heard the wail of the sirens while standing in line at Dunkin' Donuts," he said pointing across Canal Street. "I ran over here and noticed the blown-out driver's-side window, then spotted Frankie O'Brien with a shirt sleeve wrapped around his right hand."

"Wow. You are really good," Karen said mockingly, then looked at her watch. "But you're out of time."

From inside the cabin, Harry tapped the horn. Karen held

up a finger. She needed a second.

"I know Frankie. I've known him a long time. I see him at every Pirates game. I'd never take advantage of him. Never. You might've noticed that he's . . . well, he's special, you know?" Dave paused briefly. "Anyway, he had something to do with what happened today and I'd love to hear his story. Maybe you'd let me get in the back and—"

"In the back? Are you serious? This isn't some carnival ride. If I approved a stunt like that, I'd be fired on the spot," she said.

Harry tapped the horn again, holding it down a little longer. She reached for the door handle as she shook her head. Popovich was undeterred.

"Can you arrange something? Maybe a meeting at the hospital?" His eyes pleading as he spoke. "Frankie and his mom don't have much to celebrate in their lives. I know this for a fact. This could be something really good for both of them."

Karen opened the door. Before stepping up into the cabin, she turned around to address him.

"In the back of the hospital there's a black dumpster near a large sign marked loading and unloading. Be there as soon as you can. Frankie doesn't need the ER, but he needs to call his mom. You'll have ten minutes. Tops."

Dave smiled and thanked her.

Chapter six

Hearing Frankie's voice brought tears of joy to his mother. That made Frankie very happy. So too did the fact that she never asked about her morning coffee. She had been so worried about where he had been that it must have slipped her mind. But the relief in her voice was short-lived. As soon as Frankie told her that he was in the hospital, her panic returned. She began firing questions. The rapidity at which she asked them was too much for him to process. He couldn't answer a single one.

"Which hospital, Frankie? What's the address? What happened? Are you hurt? Is there a doctor close by? Can I talk to him?"

Thankfully, Doctor Bedard was close at hand. When she overheard the panic in his mother's voice, she gently tapped Frankie's arm and gestured for the phone. He handed it to her and lowered his head in shame. Karen patted his shoulder in support, then turned her attention to Frankie's mother.

"Ma'am, I'm Doctor Bedard. Your son is just fine. There's no cause for concern," she said.

"Thank God! Thank you, Doctor," she said, the terror in her voice all but gone. "I've been worried sick."

"He's got a few cuts on his right hand, but those will heal in a jiffy," Karen said. "And please, call me Karen."

"What a relief. Thank you so much, Karen. I'm Claire."

Karen told Claire that she and Frankie were at St. Joe's Hospital and that she could come right away, if she wished. She told Claire that the receptionist would direct her to the ER, where she would find Frankie. Claire thanked her again and told her that it would take her twenty minutes to get there. She would leave immediately.

Karen rested the phone in its cradle and walked over to Frankie. His shoulders sagged and his head was hung low.

"I'm sure you heard your mom. She's very relieved," Karen said.

"But when she sees me, she's going to remember her coffee," he said, barely lifting his head to speak. "I bring her coffee every morning and it makes her so happy. Frankie let her down today."

"I bet she's already forgotten about the coffee. And when she hears the good thing you did today, Frankie, she's going to be so proud."

Which reminded her. They had a rendezvous with that Telegraph reporter, Dave Popovich. He was probably outside waiting. But before she put him in front of a reporter, she wanted to make sure he was comfortable with it.

"Frankie, there's a man who wants to ask you about what happened today. He wants to hear about how you helped save that woman. He says he knows you from the Pirates games. Would you be okay talking with him?"

Frankie lifted his chin. A big toothy grin spread across his face replacing the frown. Karen's optimism and her mentioning the Pirates flipped his mood from gloomy to cheerful.

"Yes, Doctor Bedard. I would very much like to talk to him. Frankie loves the Pirates!"

Doctor Bedard led Frankie down a flight of stairs to the basement. He followed closely behind her down a long, shadowy hallway. Scant light came from the laundry room behind them and the double doors ahead of them, which led to the rear parking lot. Otherwise, it was dark. Doctor Bedard had told Frankie that the meeting outside would have to be brief, because his mother would be arriving soon. The thought of seeing his mother made him happy. He knew he couldn't keep her waiting.

If I'm not there when ma arrives, then she'll forget the good thing I did and be angry at me, he thought. *And then she'll remember the coffee.*

Frankie fought back an urge to beg that they go back upstairs and to wait for his mother.

Karen pushed open a door near the loading deck, holding it for him as he walked outside in the bright sunshine. He shielded his eyes from the sun's glare off the many parked cars. Karen walked him toward a black dumpster. Next to the dumpster stood a man wearing a Pirates baseball hat. Frankie recognized him instantly. He walked over, smiled at the man and offered his hand. He spoke excitedly.

"I'm Frankie O'Brien and I know you from the baseball games," Frankie said, rigorously shaking Dave's hand. "You sometimes buy me a soda, sometimes even a hot dog!"

"It's a pleasure to see you again, Frankie," Dave said. He then looked over at Karen, who tapped her watch and held up eight fingers. "Listen, I won't take up much of your time. I know your mom is on the way and eager to see you."

Frankie's smile disappeared. He shook his head. "I hope she's proud of me and not mad. Frankie made a big mistake and dropped her coffee on the sidewalk."

"After she hears what you did today, I'll bet she forgets all about it," Dave said. He pulled out a notepad and pen from a breast pocket. "Frankie, can you tell me what happened this morning?"

Frankie was nervous, but he knew he could do it. He politely waited until Dave had his pen ready before beginning. Initially, his words came out at a feverish pace. Sensing Dave's confusion, he slowed his cadence, which allowed Dave to keep pace with pen on paper. As his anxiety eased, his speech sharpened and his words became understandable.

Frankie arranged the events chronologically, beginning with him seeing smoke coming from the car and ending with Doctor Bedard bandaging his right hand. In the end, Frankie delivered a captivating story, one which portrayed a selfless, courageous act. Yet not a shred of it was fiction. Frankie was raised to only tell the truth. He was incapable of exaggeration.

As he wrapped up his story, he noticed Dave and Karen nodding and smiling at him. It made him feel good.

They like my story. They're proud of Frankie. I acted like a big boy.

"Frankie, that was incredible. You saved that woman's life," Dave said.

Karen walked over and tugged on Frankie's arm. "Yes, you did and people are going to read about it." She glanced at Dave. "But now, we've got to get going. Your mom will be here any minute and I need another look at those cuts on your right hand."

"One last question?" Dave asked.

"Make it quick," Karen replied.

Dave leaned in closer to Frankie. Frankie could smell something on his breath. It smelled like the adult drinks. He hated the way they smelled. He took a short step away from Dave.

"First, you cut up your hand really bad. Then you exposed yourself to a poisonous gas. Were you ever worried about your own safety?" Dave asked.

"No, Mister Dave. Frankie was worried about Miss Rose. Miss Rose sometimes buys me sodas at the baseball games, sometimes even a hot dog. She's so nice to me, like you are."

Then Frankie paused. His eyes grew distant as he reached back into his memory. "When I was in school—"

Karen cut him off, tapping a finger on her watch. "Frankie, we don't want to keep you mom—"

But Frankie wasn't finished.

"In school, bad boys always pushed me and were always mean to me. They always took my lunch and tried to pull down my pants. They were really bad to me."

Karen forgot about the time, and Dave slid his pen back in his pocket. They looked at Frankie expectantly.

"One day Miss Rose helped me with the bad boys. They punched me in my face. It hurt me bad and I fell down. They tried really hard to pull my pants down. But Miss Rose fixed them!"

Frankie was now beaming, his eyes wide with excitement. "Miss Rose pulled all three bad boys off of me and pushed the biggest bad boy against the wall. He was so scared he peed his pants! And . . . and . . . and the other bad boys ran away like scaredy cats."

Frankie laughed so loudly that he staggered, nearly falling onto the cement loading dock. When his laughing fit ended, he continued.

"Miss Rose helped me to stand up. She got my lunch bag and we walked to see the nurse. I was okay. I thanked Miss Rose and told her she was so nice to me. She said the bad boys would never pick on me again. And they never did."

Chapter seven

Claire ran up to the reception area. She stopped to catch her breath. She was directed to a heavy metal door. She pushed past the door, walked a few steps and stopped. She had made it to the emergency room receptionist desk, the area where she was told she would find her son. She opened the crumpled, moist note. Frankie was in room D. She was frustrated that she could not immediately find the correct treatment room.

First the damned road construction on Route Three and now this. How is someone supposed to know where to go?

She looked up to the ceiling and sighed. She needed a nurse. In Claire's experience, a nurse would be inclined to help her; a doctor might not. She looked right and then left. There were no nurses to be found. She noticed that some rooms had letters, others labeled for departments or other functions. She stopped to catch her breath.

Please tell me I'm going the right way. I swear if I end up—

Just then, she felt a tap on her shoulder. Startled, she spun on her heels. She was relieved at what she found: a short, heavy-set nurse with black hair and a bright smile.

"Sorry to frighten you, ma'am. Can I help you find someone?" she asked.

"Yes, thank you. I'm looking for my son, Frankie," Claire said. She pulled out the crinkled note and opened it. "He's in room D."

"Frankie is your son?" the nurse asked.

"Yes, he is," Claire said, confused by the question.

"You must be very proud of him," she said.

"Proud? I'm not sure I understand what you mean."

"Oh, you didn't hear about what he did today? Well, I'm sure he's eager to tell you." Rebecca said. She turned and pointed down the hallway. "He is in the third one down."

Claire stood silently for a moment. *Proud?* She thanked the nurse, then hustled off to her son's room.

She covered the distance to Frankie's room in no time, sprinting into her son's room at full speed. Claire ran so fast that she was unable to avoid colliding with two police officers who were on their way out. The collision sent her to the floor. Shocked, the officers offered their apologies and assistance.

"Woah! I'm so sorry, ma'am. I didn't see you coming," Officer Callahan said rushing over to help.

He bent forward and extended his left hand to help her up. His partner came around to her side to assist. Claire thanked the officers and then apologized for her dramatic entry. She brushed her pants.

"I'm sorry. It's just been one of those days—"

Then it hit her. *Police officers?*

"Officers, is my Frankie in trouble? Is he here in this room?"

"No, he's not in any trouble, ma'am," Officer Largy said smiling. He then pointed to the portion of the room which was closed off by a curtain. "He's doing just fine."

"We needed his fingerprints for an investigation," Officer Callahan added.

Claire was even more confused. "Investigation?"

"Long story short, your son saved an unconscious woman from a car full of poisonous gas this morning," Largy said.

"We're going to check out the woman now," Callahan said. "We'll check her for bruising and so on. We'll check her for other fingerprints, besides your son's. Just standard operating procedure."

Claire's eyes grew wide. "You don't think that my son had anything to do with . . .?"

"With the woman who was trapped inside a car full of carbon monoxide? Not at all," Callahan replied.

Claire breathed a sigh of relief.

"We know that Frankie came along after she ended up in the car," Callahan said. "Anyway, we'll leave you to catch up with your son. As my partner said, he did a really good thing today. Far as I'm concerned, he's a hero."

Claire thanked the officers as they left. Despite the growing sense of calm, she still felt uneasy, which concerned her. If she exuded any anxiety, then Frankie would know. What's more, not only was he in tune to her feelings, he often felt responsible for them. If he detected any shred of anxiety, he would feel responsible.

God knows, he's been through enough today already.

She wanted him to see her relaxed and under control. She walked to the back of the room and stopped in front of the curtain. She then drew in a deep breath and slowly drew the curtain open. What she saw brought a smile to her face. Frankie sat on the edge of a bed next to a woman holding a clipboard. Both were smiling.

Frankie looked up and saw his mother. His eyes lit up. He held up his right hand, complete with black stitches and ready for a fresh bandage.

"Ma, ma, it didn't hurt!" he boasted.

Upon seeing her son's toothy smile, Claire ran in and hugged him. Tears of joy streamed down her face. She could see for herself that he was fine and in no pain. A giant weight had been lifted.

The blonde woman walked over and introduced herself as Karen Bedard, the doctor with whom she had spoken earlier. The two shook hands. She then gave Claire a rundown of the events, filling in parts of Mr. Budzko's account, which the two police officers had just shared. According to Budzko, Frankie had saved the woman's life. If not for Frankie, she would have died inside a car full of poisonous gas.

"The cuts on his right hand mark a very heroic act, Claire," Karen added.

"Now I get it. A few minutes ago, a nurse mentioned something about me being proud. Then, the police officers, who I literally ran into, called Frankie a hero and said he saved a woman's life," Claire shook her head. "I feel like I'm dreaming. It doesn't seem real. You're telling me the same thing? Frankie saved a woman's life?"

"Yes, he did," Karen said, then added. "And at great risk to himself."

She grabbed the free end of the bandage and began wrapping from the middle of Frankie's forearm in the direction of his right hand, which he held up as if swearing in before testifying.

Just then, Karen's supervisor, Doctor Botanger, arrived. He looked distracted. Frankie waved at him with his bandaged hand. Botanger dismissed Frankie's greeting and brusquely introduced himself to Claire, then scribbled something on the bottom of a form which Karen had handed to him.

"Thanks Karen. Don't forget the incident report," he said

eyeing Frankie suspiciously.

He handed the form back to Karen and was off without a word. Karen waited until he was out of the room before pulling out a pad from a jacket pocket. She wrote out a prescription for pain medicine which Claire could pick up at the hospital's pharmacy.

"He may not need them all, but don't let the pain get to be too much before taking the meds, okay?"

As Claire and Frankie got up to leave, Karen reminded Claire to take Frankie back in three or four days so she could remove the stitches. Karen gave Frankie a big hug, reminding him how brave he had been. After a quick stop in the pharmacy, Frankie and his mom were on their way. It was twenty after eleven. Just about lunchtime.

"So, my hero son, I'm betting you're hungry," Claire asked, her right arm wrapped around his left arm as they walked out of the hospital.

"Oh, yeah Ma, am I ever!" His thunderous proclamation caught the attention of an old woman traipsing along behind a walker. She flashed Frankie and Claire a friendly smile; the two returned the sweet gesture in kind. Then, out of the blue, Frankie remembered his morning's chore. The coffee! He cast his eyes down in shame.

"Oh, Ma. I forgot to tell you. I spilled your coffee and . . . and then I threw the bag down . . ."

Claire reached for his hand and stopped him. She turned and looked up at him. His head was hung low. As she studied him, her eyes began to moisten and a tear formed.

"Never mind that, son. That's not important."

She wiped the tear with the palm of her hand and looked up at him. She then gripped his forearm tighter. "Frankie, look at me," she said gently. He obeyed. "I am so very proud of you."

Frankie shuffled his feet uneasily, looking around the parking lot as he did. "Yeah," he whispered, moving his eyes to gaze out onto the traffic on Main Street.

"I'm so proud of the man you've become." Her eyes glistened with fresh tears.

"Yeah. Today was good, Ma," he answered, his voice barely audible.

"It was very good, Frankie." She wiped away tears and smiled. She stood on her tiptoes and kissed her son on his cheek. Frankie needed to tilt his head so that she could reach.

"Thanks, Ma," he replied, shifting his attention to a monarch butterfly which floated by.

"So, I was thinking that maybe we go to Friendly's for lunch," Claire grinned, knowing full well his response. Friendly's was his favorite restaurant, better than Shakey's Pizza or the Ninety-Nine. "Sound good to you?"

Frankie turned to face his mother, his eyes wide. "Friendly's? Really? Oh yeah! And . . . and . . . can I have a sundae, Ma?" he asked anxiously. "Only after I finish my burger, I know . . . I know. But, then can I? Can I, Ma?"

"Of course you can, Mr. Hero." She stroked his crew cut with her right hand, just as he loved. "I'd say you've earned it."

Chapter eight

Dave waited for the pedestrian signal before crossing at the Main and Hollis Street intersection. He was three blocks away from *The Telegraph.* He left his car back at St. Joe's, so that he could enjoy some fresh air. Dave enjoyed walking. Walking helped him organize his thoughts as he prepared to write a story. If a thought occurred to him, he could stop, pull out his notebook and pen and scribble away. He couldn't do that while driving, especially when the thoughts and ideas came in droves. Which was exactly how they came following his brief interview with Frankie.

In under ten minutes, Frankie delivered a gem. Most of it cogent, parts of it unintelligible babble. However delivered, Frankie's account confirmed Dave's gut feeling as soon as he saw the smashed window and Frankie's injured hand: something heroic had taken place, something worthy of being his paper's lead story. Where Frankie's wording was not clear, Dave would consider the context and fill in the gap. Dave's talent and flair for the dramatic would bring the story to life. Dave Popovich never equated interpretation as fabrication, not when so many renowned writers employed exposition so brilliantly. It was all part of the timeless tradition of storytelling. With just a touch of creative expression, he could bring Frankie to life as a superman. What could possibly be wrong with that?

Dave knew just enough about Frankie's situation to know that he and his mom could use a break. He knew the two could only benefit from the lavish praise a much-heralded story would bring. Dave also knew that if it came down to it, Frankie was not capable of disputing the finer details with his editor. Hell, he wasn't sure Frankie could even read. As Dave would discover later, there were no witnesses leading up to the actual rescue of Rose McDougal, whose name Doctor Bedard had provided. In the end, it came down to blending Frankie's account of events with a dose of literary embellishment.

He stopped and pulled out his notebook and pen. He scribbled a few more notes on a blank page. He was well on his way to making a hero out of Frankie O'Brien. He was convinced that, when he dropped his print-ready draft in his editor's in-box, Frankie would stand out as a storybook figure. His untidy scribbles were essentially a string of action words woven into high drama, one which would come to be known as Nashua's greatest rescue ever. The Telegraph's headline on September 7, would go on to read: Hometown Hero Saves Woman's Life. Dave Popovich would not have had it read any other way.

Chapter nine

Unlike Frankie, Rose's hospital stay was anything but short-lived or restful. Her roommate, whose bed sat to the left of Rose's, was a pallid and wizened 80-year-old woman. Her shallow breathing, interrupted by uncontrollable coughing fits, chafed Rose beyond belief. When the old biddy wasn't hacking up a lung, she rambled on nonsensically.

While Rose's stay did nothing to improve her spirits, she might have derived some measure of comfort knowing that her forty-minute encounter with a cabin full of carbon monoxide had created quite a buzz in the hospital's neurology department. That she was still alive after spending a lengthy amount of time inside a car full of the deadly gas was stupefying. Throw in the fact that she had suffered no apparent brain damage, according to the preliminary tests, her case was a "medical miracle," her intake nurse declared.

On the ride to the hospital, Rose had lapsed into a prolonged coughing fit. The nurse told her that her lungs had filled with smoke from the car engine's burning oil. It was the smoke, which had stymied the effects of the poisonous gas, and the fast actions of Mr. Francis O'Brien that saved her life, she was told.

"Had it been only carbon monoxide, Mr. O'Brien wouldn't have noticed anything out of the ordinary with your car," the nurse had said, adding, "No one would have. Carbon monoxide is invisible."

When Rose awoke on Tuesday evening, it was Dr. Levesque, along with Dr. Lanzara, who stood by her bed. Their sterile, white coats added some brightness to the otherwise dim room. Their matching expressions, grim and foreboding, were not what Rose had hoped to see. Having survived a brush with death, she didn't need any additional bad news. She struggled to push herself up into a sitting position. Whatever doom the two planned to deliver, she didn't want to take it lying on her back like some helpless chump. Unfortunately, sitting up proved to be a challenge with an IV poking into her arm.

Nurse Margo Olaf, the head nurse, just happened to have been passing in the hallway outside and noticed Rose's flailing arms in her peripheral vision. She strode into room 411 where, on the left side of the room, her patients' beds were. She walked right up to Rose's side and placed a firm hand on Rose's shoulder. She handed Rose the bed's remote control, which was on a cord and clipped to the bed frame. She then gave Rose a five-second tutorial on its use: press this for up, this for down. That done, she stormed out of the room without a word. Rose picked up the remote and pressed the arrow for up. Slowly the head of the bed inclined. Rightly situated, Rose set the remote aside and turned her attention back to the doctors.

Dread, rooted in an unfamiliar feeling of helplessness, washed over her. So, this is how it ends? Not at a time—or in a car—of my choosing, but in some disinfected, bleach-smelling hospital, lying in a bed next to Old Woman Wheezy?

"Might as well come out with it, docs. I'm screwed, aren't I?"

Dr. Lanzara's pursed mouth relaxed. He turned away from her hopeless gaze and repressed a laugh. Dr. Levesque, a seemingly humorless man, didn't even crack a smile.

"No, Miss McDougal, you're not 'screwed,' as you suggest. On the contrary, I believe you're going to be fine." He laid his clipboard at the foot of her bed before folding his arms. "I'm not sure if you realize, if any of us realize," he said glancing over at his colleague, "just how lucky you are to be alive."

Having regained his stoic posture, Dr. Lanzara cut in. "I've been a neurologist for over twenty years and I've never heard of, let alone treated, a case of carbon monoxide poisoning quite like this." He removed his glasses before slowing his speech for effect. "Your situation, Miss McDougal, is simply unprecedented. Bottom line—it's a miracle."

"I don't follow you, doc. I don't get—"

Dr. Lanzara cut her off. "Your car's smoke, the product of burning oil, literally saved your life."

Dr. Levesque nodded.

"And to think I was just about to trade it in. For years, I was convinced that ole shitbox of mine had contempt for its occupants, myself included. Now you tell me it saved my life. Boy, was I ever wrong," Rose said, chuckling.

Neither doctor laughed.

"We estimate you spent approximately forty minutes in a car full of mixed carbon monoxide and smoke from burning oil and, yet, somehow survived. After twenty-five minutes, even a man or woman of your, um, size"—Lanzara looked over at his colleague, avoiding eye contact with Rose— "should be dead. And certainly, after twenty minutes, we'd expect to see extensive brain damage."

Lanzara turned his attention back to Rose. "Further, I'd assess that you inhaled over 200 parts per million of the deadly gas. By any measure, you shouldn't be here."

Rose frowned. *If this haughty prick drops one more reference to my size or uses "measure" again, I'm going to jump outta this bed and—*

"What's more, we don't foresee any long-term brain damage. Perhaps none at all. However, just to be sure, I scheduled a CAT scan for you." He grabbed his clipboard, flipping back a few sheets covered with scribbles and unintelligible data. "It's either for tomorrow or Thursday . . . and I see . . . yes, there it is. It's scheduled for tomorrow."

Dr. Levesque chimed in. "Here again, we believe the MRI is essentially a formality at this point. We just want to be sure there are no lingering effects."

Rose sat quietly, taking it all in. She gazed out the room's only window, which was close to the right side of her bed. Bright sunshine splashed the tops of nearby buildings. She wondered what other tests might be in the queue.

"Quite frankly, you're all the chatter in St. Joe's," Lanzara said.

"I aim to please," Rose joked. "Since I seem to have done my part, and been a good sport, any chance I can get outta here tomorrow after that M-something-or-other is over?"

The two doctors looked at each other. Dr. Levesque sighed, and shook his head as if to suggest he was dealing with a foolish child.

"I'm afraid that's not possible. We're going to need you for observation and additional tests for another three days or so," Levesque explained. "Plan on Thursday. At the earliest."

Rose sighed. "Wonderful."

She slumped her shoulders and regarded the needle that pierced her pale skin. She glanced over at Wheezy, who rasped on in the neighboring bed. Rose wondered how many more needles she would have to endure. She tried another hand at humor, hoping to disarm the doctors.

"I don't suppose I get a vote in the matter?" she asked with a smile.

"No, you don't," Levesque answered. He turned briefly to Nurse Olaf, who had reappeared at the door, before focusing back on Rose.

"Be sure you get your rest, eat what's brought to you and follow Nurse Olaf's orders. She'll be managing your care for the remainder of your stay," Levesque looked over at Olaf and grinned. He then moved to conclude the visit. "Any other questions for myself or Dr. Lanzara?"

Rose grimaced, looked out the window and shook her head solemnly.

"Very well." Dr. Levesque picked up his clipboard. He turned to Lanzara. "Shall we?"

Both doctors turned to depart. Before Dr. Lanzara reached the door, he stopped and turned back to Rose.

"I almost forgot. There was no ID on you when you were brought in. No wallet, nothing. Is there family we could call? Maybe someone you'd like to call yourself?"

"Hmph," she grunted, dismissing the very notion. "Family? No, no one local."

"Well, wherever they are, I'm sure someone would like to know that you're okay," Levesque said.

"Not really," Rose said, imagining her mother getting the word, and then freezing up and having no idea what to do. She never did, which was why she had stayed with the same asshole for forty years. *A good part of the reason my life is so fucked up . . . and why I'm lying in this fucking bed.* Rose tried to banish those thoughts. She hated feeling helpless, but could not control it.

"Miss McDougal? You all right?" Lanzara asked. He approached her bed, looking concerned.

"Thanks for asking, but I'm fine. And nope, no family. Only one worried about me would be my buddy, Vic, who owns Kegler's Den," she said, smiling and waving a hand. "I'm pretty sure I have an open tab there."

Neither laughed. Dr. Levesque studied her curiously.

"That aside, when do I get to eat?" Rose asked. "A woman doesn't get to be, as you put it earlier, this size by accident. Besides, I hear the food here is really good. Actually, I hear it's to die for." She snorted.

"I'll bet that's just what you've heard," Levesque said, grimacing at her. "Anyway, we'll leave you in the capable hands of Nurse Olaf."

He looked over to Olaf, adding, "I'm sure you have something special for Miss McDougal, don't you?"

Olaf winked at him and said, "Of course, Dr. Levesque. Something very special."

Dr. Levesque wheeled on his black leather shoes and was out the door in an instant. Dr. Lanzara shrugged his shoulders to Rose, then nodded to Olaf before leaving.

As she soon discovered, Rose's dinner options ranged from bad to terrible: franks and beans, chipped beef (a/k/a mystery meat) or liverwurst. In the end, she chose the mystery meat and spent the next two hours pushing instant potatoes—cold and lumpy—and brownish-purple beef-flakes mixed with crunchy bits, that looked like cereal, around on her tray. Oh, what she would have given for a pizza from Espresso, one with mouth-watering cheese and thick sausage liberally spread across an oven-fresh, sixteen-inch pie. Alas, she would have to settle for what amounted to little better than prison food for the next three days. As she pondered that thought, Wheezy prattled on about some Sweet Henrietta and her fruit cellar. Her fruit cellar—where jams and homemade pies thrived—sounded like a nice place to visit. Better than St. Joe's Hospital anyway.

Rose opened her eyes. The room was silent. Wheezy lay motionless under her covers. No more irrational babbling about jams and pies, at least not now. Rose couldn't remember having fallen asleep, only that she didn't touch her dinner and was now famished. A yellow sticky-note with the command *BE READY FOR PILLS AT 4 AM* was propped up against a perspiring glass of water. She wondered what that battleax Olaf would do if she grabbed the cup of damn pills from her hand and chucked them out the window. She laughed imagining the look on Olaf's face. Rose dismissed the thought and looked up at the clock, which was perched above a blackboard. Written in white chalk was RN Margo Olaf as the shift supervisor.

In front of her to the left and mounted high on the wall, the room's black-and-white TV cast faint light into the otherwise dark room. On it, a split-screen image showed the presidential contenders, each addressing large audiences. Governor Reyes was in Georgia; Vice President Cartwright was stumping down the road in Lowell.

She was shaking her head at the TV when, suddenly, she saw something move out in the hallway. A shadowy form slipped through the darkness and stopped in the open door of her room.

Only the vague outline of a tall man was visible. Rose gripped her pillows, pushing herself up to a seated position. Suddenly, the man spoke.

"Yes, would be a shame indeed."

Rose gasped and nearly leapt from the bed.

"Though his boss didn't push the big red button, who's to say Cartwright won't," he said, then stepped in the doorway. "You know, Rose, we can't be starting wars overseas, not when we have so much to clean up here in our own backyard."

Rose cleared her throat, her voice delivering a rusty reply. "No, no . . . of course not."

He smiled at her, then stepped into the room and under the pale light of the mounted TV, where the news team had moved from the presidential race to lamentations about the Red Sox.

He stood less than ten feet away. Though faint, the light highlighted his features. Even under his tweed coat, Rose made out his athletic build, square shoulders and flat stomach. He wore pressed slacks and brown leather shoes. His pale skin was unblemished. His black hair was thick and perfect. Here was a man who would never fret over a receding hairline. A confident smile matched his suave brogue. His eyes were twinkling, studying her carefully. In the grip of his powerful right hand, he held a dozen elegantly wrapped red roses.

"Where are my manners?" he said and stepped toward the bed. "My name is Patrick. Patrick Donnelly."

"I'm—"

"You're Rose McDougal," he said. He extended his hand and offered her the roses. "These are for you. I was so worried when I saw the news."

Rose accepted the bouquet, struggling to keep her hands from shaking. She croaked out a thank you. The roses were full and fragrant.

He knows me. How the hell does he know me?

Donnelly gestured to a chair near her bed.

Rose nodded, her eyes locked on his. He undid a jacket button and then sat down. He inched the chair closer to her bed. He was within arm's reach.

He could choke me to death with those hands. Those hands could do what that damn car couldn't.

"So, nothing to say? Not curious?" he asked, shrugging his shoulders.

"I'm not sure that I . . . that I understand," Rose answered. She was not only scared, but confused.

"How about 'Thanks for the roses. So tell me, Patrick, how is it that you know me?'"

"Well . . . yes, I suppose that's—"

Patrick reached across the bed, squeezed her hand and winked at her. "That's a damn good place to start."

He stood up and began pacing around the room. He walked to the open doorway and peered out into the dark hall. He then walked over to the edge of Wheezy's bed. His expression suggested a mix of curiosity and revulsion as he momentarily observed her. Satisfied, he walked over to the room's only window and gazed out at the black of night. He checked his watch, then turned to her. After what felt to Rose like an eternity, he spoke.

"My dad saved your dad's life some thirty years ago."

She gave him a perplexed look.

"It happened in a South Boston bar called Mikey's. Your dad came in piss drunk, grabbing for chairs to stand up straight, asking for the toughest guy in the place. Said he wanted to scrap."

Rose sat up and shifted in her seat. She felt an uneasiness in her stomach that always struck when her thoughts turned to her father.

"Well, he got the toughest man all right: the bar's owner and one-time amateur welterweight champ, Mike Fleming."

"Mike must've hit your dad a dozen times. He would've ripped him apart had my dad not intervened," Donnelly said, adding, "My dad saved your father's life."

Rose shook her head in disbelief. "This Mike must've been pretty tough, because my dad was a big guy."

Donnelly dismissed her comment. "We had your dad stitched up, gave him some pills and brought him back to your hotel room. I came along with dad. That was the night I met you and your mom," he said. "And you, Rose, look the same. You haven't changed a bit."

Look the same? What's that supposed to mean?

She hated it when someone commented on her looks, however intended. She was no longer as afraid of Donnelly as she was pissed off at him.

He continued. "Needless to say, your dad was gracious. Offered my dad money, a favor, anything to repay his debt."

He turned away from her and walked back to the window.

"In the end, we accepted his offer for a favor. Well, a series of favors, actually. These favors amounted to a number of tasks which your dad performed in support of my dad's business interests in northern Maine. Close to where you lived, if memory serves me," he said, turning around and smiling at her. "Anyway, we kept your dad on the rolls for a couple of years and then let him go when my dad's company folded up shop in Limestone. In the end, your dad was dependable and proved his worth."

Couple of years? When was this? she wondered. During her childhood, her father worked at a furniture factory outside of Houlton. When he wasn't working, he spent much of his time drinking with co-workers.

Or making my life a living hell.

She never once remembered him offering to help her mother with the chores, let alone any yardwork like most men did. He was a lazy slob who enjoyed sitting in his recliner yelling at the sportscaster on the radio or ordering his daughter to bring him another beer. Shiftless and selfish? Yes. Dependable? No way.

"Wait a minute. Are we talking about the same Jack McDougal? You're telling me that *he* was dependable? I don't get it."

Donnelly paused for a moment before answering. "Yes, he did. You see, Rose, because when it came to working for my dad, failure was not an option."

Rose grunted and then considered replying with that quote from the movie The Godfather: "I made him an offer he couldn't refuse." She refrained. As she pondered a more thoughtful riposte, Donnelly walked back to her bedside.

"Enough of all that," he said. He pulled the chair close to the bed and sat. "All things considered, you appear to be doing well. You seem to be in good spirits. Your color looks normal." He reached over to the nightstand and picked up a yellow note. He silently read the command Olaf had written on it. He laughed aloud. "Maybe it's the medicine."

Rose slumped her shoulders and looked away from Donnelly, casting her gaze down to the tiled floor. Donnelly followed her eyes.

"You survive a brush with death, a cause for celebration and relief, and yet you're down. Something isn't right with you, love. Something that's troubling you greatly."

Rose shrugged her shoulders, keeping eyes cast low.

Donnelly leaned in toward the bed. He reached for her hand and squeezed it gently. "Seriously, Rose. What gives?"

"It's nothing really," Rose said, then slowly lifted her head. She looked at him through sad eyes. "I mean, who wants to hear some stranger's sob story?"

"But we're not strangers," Donnelly said. Then with empathy in his voice, added, "I'd like to think we were friends."

Rose lifted her head, as he leaned back in his seat and slipped a hand inside his jacket. He withdrew a golden flask, undid the cap and tipped it in her direction.

"Thanks, but I never touch the stuff," Rose said.

"Suit yourself," Donnelly took a long pull from the flask, then closed his eyes and tilted his head back. A smile spread across his face. "Mmm, it always hits the spot."

Donnelly folded his arms across his chest, closed his eyes and leaned back against the chair. He remained like that for a while.

Rose watched him with mild curiosity. She had no idea where this meeting was headed, but she knew that it wasn't out of the kindness of his heart. Men like Donnelly didn't stoop to visit a commoner like her. That is, unless they wanted something.

Men like Donnelly, who were blessed with good looks, money and power, ran with people like themselves. In Donnelly's case, some of those people were criminals. It was patently clear to Rose that whatever "dependable" service her father provided to Donnelly's father, it was illegal and supported a criminal enterprise, one that he always sought to expand. That's when it hit her—he was here to recruit her into the family business.

She decided she would simply ask him what he wanted. She needed to take control of the impromptu soiree. Wanting nothing more than for him to leave, she decided that she would listen. After she nodded her head and listened attentively, she would politely refuse and wish him well. But before she had a chance to enact her plan, he sat up and interrupted her mental rehearsal.

He opened his eyes and ran his fingers through his thick, black hair. He turned to her and smiled, his eyes full of compassion. She couldn't remember the last time a man so handsome ever smiled at her in such a way, if at all.

"Again, why the long face? Seriously, I'd like to know."

He spoke with such sincerity that she couldn't pull her eyes from him. Gone was any chance she had to put the kibosh to whatever he had in store. She was trapped, putty in his powerful hands.

Her defenses lowered, she opened up and told him everything. She told him about how certain she was that she would finally get a full-time teaching position. She told him about the gushing letters of recommendation, her wealth of experience in the classroom and her shining resume. And then came the rejection letter and its arrogance and patronizing tone. She told him about the shock she felt, the sadness and then the anger that the letter evoked. Not only was she not selected for the vacant position, she had been fired as a substitute teacher. Adding insult to injury, she would soon be saddled with hospital bills.

"Tell me, what kind of person could possibly write a letter so condescending and mean-spirited?" Rose asked him.

Donnelly took a second swig and then sealed the flask before placing it back inside his jacket. He studied her expression for a moment.

"I want to help," he said at last. "And I won't take no for an answer."

Rose lifted her chin, her eyes widening. "Help? Mr. Donnelly, I couldn't possibly accept. I appreciate your sympathetic ear, but I'll make do. I always have. When I get out of this, this hospital prison, I'll find something—"

He placed his right hand on her shoulder. Her eyes reflecting back the sadness and desperation she could not hide.

"Rose, your dad helped my dad in a time of need. Helping you in your time of need is the least I can do."

Rose opened her mouth to object, to thank him one last time, but graciously decline his offer to help. But as she looked into his eyes, she knew the matter was settled. Further discussion was not necessary nor would it be accepted. There was no escaping her end of the Mephistophelean deal that she had just entered.

He stared at her, then began to slowly shake his head. A thin smile spread across his face. He removed his right hand from Rose's shoulder and placed it on his lap.

"My offer to help you is not up for debate. My offer is final." He spoke slowly. "I may ask a favor of you one day, but that's another day. Today, you need my help. You have no job and no hope for anything good."

He looked around the room and gestured to the medical equipment behind her bed.

"When you return home, Mr. Budzko will have a double-wrapped envelope for you. He'll be told that it's from your cousin Billy. Budzko will be told that the contents are important family documents and that the letter must not be opened nor tampered with."

As he spoke on, Rose began to feel queasy and light-headed. Her pulse began to race. Her stomach churned and groaned. Her legs were burning up under the thin bedsheet. Her eyes began to water and her vision became blurry. She touched her face. It was hot and wet with sweat. Then, all of a sudden, she had to vomit. It couldn't wait.

She shot up in the bed, leaned over the bed's guardrail and began grabbing blindly for the wastebasket under the nightstand. Except it wasn't there.

Dammit! Where is that goddamned thing??

She flailed some more before feeling a hand on her shoulder. She looked up and saw the fuzzy outline of Donnelly. He took her hand and placed it on the rim of the wastebasket.

Rose lowered her head into the wastebasket and threw up. She panted and spat residue. Almost immediately, she needed to go again. She squeezed her eyes shut and puked. After the third time, her stomach was empty.

"There you go, love. Atta girl," Donnelly said in a nurturing tone. "You'll feel better real soon."

He took the wastebasket from her and placed it back near the nightstand. Rose leaned back in the bed, her head coming to rest on a metal rail above the pillow. Her eyes were closed as she took deep breaths.

Donnelly sat back down. He wasn't finished.

"Now then, where was I?" He tapped his chin. "Ah yes, your landlord."

Rose turned her head slowly to look at him. Though her vision was still blurry, she could make out the smile on his face. He spoke cheerfully as he concluded.

"Rest assured, Mr. Budzko will not let us down," Donnelly said, then winked at her.

The feeling of nausea, which Rose thought she had licked, began to return. She reached for the glass of water. Before she could get to it, Donnelly pulled it away.

"Tsk, tsk, tsk, my love. Drinking water after one has vomited will only make matters worse."

Chapter ten

Rose sat motionless, still in a daze. She pondered her new arrangement with Donnelly, wondering how many such messages, like the one she had just received, had he delivered in his career. But in knowing, what difference would it have made? Ultimately, it didn't matter. She figured that having seen the story about her accident and having recognized her name, he saw an opportunity, the prospects of advancing his personal interests through a series of "favors."

She looked over at Wheezy, who lay motionless under a sheet and blanket.

"Lucky old gull," Rose muttered.

Tucked under her covers, Wheezy hadn't made a sound nor moved an inch since Rose last checked on her. That had been an hour ago. A lot had taken place in the past hour. A lot had changed in Rose's life. *Perhaps forever.* Before they could get a grip on her, Rose pushed the thoughts away.

She glanced up at the TV, which displayed dizzying, black and white static. Above the TV was the clock. It was almost two. Dawn would arrive in four hours. Things always seemed better in daylight, she told herself. She assumed there would be no sleep in her immediate future. Too much had transpired in the past thirty minutes. Too much drama, too much fear. But she was wrong. Within five minutes, Rose was asleep.

Bright sunlight filled the room, as Rose woke up after a long nap. It was 4:15. Though the morning's MRI had proven uneventful, the lingering effects of carbon monoxide poisoning, the stomach-turning hospital food, the endless ramblings of her roommate and, above all, the deal she had sort of agreed to the night before had taken their toll. Rose was miserable. She felt trapped. Believing she had nowhere to turn pissed her off, making her feel combative, something so out of character for Rose.

Outside her window, birds sang a tribute to the waning summer. Fair-weather clouds rolled harmlessly across the sky. She could hear the steady buzz of traffic on West Hollis street. The outdoor scene was pleasant enough, but it did little to lift her spirits.

On the other hand, a good cup of coffee might, she thought.

If nothing else, a cup of strong, black coffee would help pull her out of her funk. Strong coffee always fired the synapses in her brain. Thus, she was able to process complicated matters a lot faster and with a lot more clarity. Her unwelcomed arrangement with Donnelly required clarity of thought, the ability to conjure exit strategies, for instance. Sneaking down to the cafeteria to score a cup of coffee with Nurse Olaf on the prowl had little chance of success.

Well, then maybe that harridan, Olaf, can do something useful and fetch me one herself.

Rose fumbled under her sheets for the bed's remote and found the nurse call button. She pressed it. Then, for good measure, pressed it a second and third time. A moment later, a scowling Olaf appeared in the doorway.

"You buzzed?" Olaf asked. Her tone suggested that Rose should expect no TLC.

"Hello, Nurse Olaf. Nice to see you," Rose said, flashing an acerbic smile. "I'd like a cup of coffee, please. Black. And if one of your orderlies could get one from Dunkin' Donuts, then all the better."

"No can do, McDougal."

Nurse Olaf walked up to the side of Rose's bed and folded her arms and looked down at her. A smile of satisfaction touched the corners of her mouth. She went on to explain, somewhat smugly, that because of her sedatives, caffeine was out of the question. Rose was not impressed.

"Huh? Wouldn't caffeine be *exactly* what I need? You know, something to keep me from being in a Zombie state for days?"

"Nice try, McDougal. It doesn't work that way."

"Says you," Rose mumbled.

"No, says your doctors. Take up your gripe with them," Olaf said, then chuckled. "See how far that gets you."

Rose frowned, then regarded the four horse-sized pills in a

cup, which Olaf handed her. Each pill seemed to be looking right back at her. No amount of water would do much to help Rose swallow those monsters without a fight.

"So, when do I get to kick these pills to the curb?"

God forbid I have to keep swallowing these fucking things, Rose thought, before wondering how the f-word came to mind so effortlessly.

Olaf glanced down at the orders on a clipboard which hung from a hook on the bed rail.

"The doctor will re-evaluate as we move forward." Olaf shrugged her shoulders, smiling piously as Rose forced down her third and then fourth pill. "Who's to say? Maybe this weekend. Perhaps when those pills are no longer needed."

That bitch is enjoying her little power trip just a little too much, Rose thought, again wondering how the cuss words came to her so easily.

"How about a cup of decaf tea?" Olaf asked, smirking.

Rose rolled her eyes. "Sure. Why not."

Rose pressed the bed's remote, beginning the grinding ride to an upright position. Setting the bed's remote aside, she picked up the TV remote. Her choices were few. There were only six channels, and that counted PBS and some station playing the Boston Pops. No ESPN and no NESN. She settled on Channel 4, the NBC affiliate in Boston.

A few minutes later, Olaf re-entered the room carrying Rose's tea. The paper cup looked like a child's toy buried in her pudgy right hand, which shook as she strode into the room. Without saying a word—or asking Rose if she took sugar or milk—she placed the tea on the serving tray and turned to walk away.

Some hours later, Olaf checked Rose's vital signs then, speaking over her shoulder as she exited, announced that Rose had a visitor waiting.

"She's been waiting about twenty minutes, in fact," Olaf added, before disappearing into the hallway.

"What visitor? I didn't tell anyone I was here," Rose called out.

But she got no reply. Olaf was gone. Rose sighed and then reached for her tea. As she lifted the cup to her mouth, her visitor appeared. It was her friend, Flo Wilkins. She stood in the doorway. She looked terrible. Sleeplessness was splashed across her face, her eyes were sunken, her lips trembled and her bleached hair was an unruly mess. She was clutching her purse so hard that her knuckles were white.

"Oh shit," Rose whispered softly.

"You stupid woman! What on God's green earth were you thinking?!" Flo yelled, launching her first salvo.

Rose cringed, forced a smile and gestured with a finger to her lips. From down the hall, Olaf's squeak-squeak footfalls drew closer and louder.

Great. Olaf. All I need.

Olaf peeked into the room. "I see your friend has arrived. Well then, I'll allow you two to catch up." A condescending smile spread across her chunky face. "Oh, before I forget, I'll be coming around with dinner at six o'clock." Olaf made some "tsk" sounds. "A shame we didn't get that shipment in today. Anyway, it's gonna be boiled ham and green beans on your plate tonight, if I'm not mistaken."

Olaf squeak-squeaked down the hall, off to torture some other hapless patient.

"Well? Just what the hell were you doing in your car?!" Flo implored. "And don't tell me that the woman who called me the day before about some journey you were planning hasn't at least considered some other line of bullshit to feed her friend!"

Rose found the TV's remote and hit the mute button. Might as well come clean, she thought. Might as well level with her.

"Flo . . ." Rose sighed. She dropped her hands onto her thighs, which lay idly under the flimsy sheet. "I'm not sure where to begin."

"I'd say with the truth." Flo's eyes burned. She inched closer to the bed and loomed menacingly over her.

"Well . . . Flo, it just got to a point where I . . ."

Flo cut her off, though in gentle tone. "Where you couldn't stop, could you? You'd lost your way, Rose?"

Flo pulled the chair from next to Wheezy's empty bed close to Rose's. As she did every afternoon, Wheezy was off strolling around St. Joe's sporting nothing but her shabby robe.

Flo reached for her friend's hand. Confused by the turnabout, Rose let her take it.

"You'd lost all sense of self-worth," Flo said, speaking sympathetically.

Rose could see it in Flo's eyes. Her look suggested that she knew precisely what Rose intended to do on Tuesday morning. Rose figured Flo just wanted to hear it herself.

Rose sighed and lowered her head, eyes locked on a dust-bunny which drifted airily under Wheezy's bed.

"You might say that," Rose said.

"So even when you were ready to make a life change this so-called grand journey which you'd flaunted, you couldn't do it. You were obsessed."

Rose nodded and lifted her head. "I lost the will. I lost the desire to—"

"To quit," Flo said flatly. "You lost the desire to quit drinking."

"Huh?" Rose was perplexed. "Quit drinking?"

Flo answered for her. "It was your drinking. Go ahead and admit it," she barked, then glanced back at the door before continuing. "Sorry, that's my pent-up frustration coming out. What I meant to say was that your drinking nearly killed you."

"Is that what you think?"

"Don't play stupid with me, Rose," Flo replied, and then darted a glance back at the door. "What'd the doctors tell you, huh? I bet it was some cockamamie crap about fatigue and being overtired. Bet they never checked your blood-alcohol level."

"You lost me," Rose said, shaking her head. She was interested in hearing more of Flo's version of the story.

"Well, let me fill in the blanks," Flo said. "You get tanked early yesterday morning, no doubt to suppress a blistering hangover from boozing it up the night before. After zero sleep, you slip into your car—wasted and tired—to run off to only God knows where, probably to restock your liquor supply. But you barely have the energy to start the car, let alone drive. You're so drunk that you slump over the steering wheel and pass out. Meanwhile, all that booze is still pumping through your veins."

Flo folded her arms across her chest and, in a sanctimonious way, lifted her chin and concluded, "It's no mystery, Rose. It was the booze."

Rose tried her best to hide her baffled expression. *The booze? Seriously? She's never seen me drunk. Hell, I can't remember the last time I even got buzzed.*

Flo had no idea what Rose had intended to do. If Flo had rightly concluded that it was an attempted suicide, she would have paraded into room 411 with a team of psychiatrists, social workers and pastors. She would have been an absolute mess. The evening's brief verbal haranguing would have proven mild by comparison. But it got Rose thinking. If Flo thought the whole episode was a drunk-induced exploit, then what did the doctors think was the cause? Besides the carbon monoxide poisoning, if they had concluded anything else, they hadn't said, at least not to her. It was not until after Flo had left that Rose would discover the official version of her "accident."

"Well, are you going to just sit there and ignore me? Can't you trust your best friend?" Flo asked.

She sat down. Her eyes had grown moist and Rose could make out tears forming in the corners of her eyes.

"Come on, Rose. If you can't trust me, then who can you trust? We've been friends for too many years for you to shut me out like this."

"I'll never forget how you were there for me when . . ." Flo sniffled, turned her head and wiped away her tears. ". . . how you were there for me when Jerry passed. When I was a mess, a wreck . . . when I . . . when I didn't know what to do."

Flo broke down, sobbing heavily, her shoulders shaking. She dropped her head into her hands. Just then, Wheezy walked in, grumbling about her chills. Rose shot her a glance—gritted teeth and piercing eyes. Rose jabbed her index finger back toward the door that Wheezy had walked in. When she replied with a confused look, Rose jabbed again and fired an even uglier look. Wheezy apparently figured it out. Without a word, she turned and left. Flo missed the silent exchange.

At least the old buzzard has some sense about her, Rose thought.

She turned her attention back to Flo, wondering how to get rid of her. She was not feeling particularly sympathetic toward her friend. A craving for caffeine and fast food were her overriding desires. Still, she had to conjure up some show of compassion. Rose drew a tissue from a box on the nightstand. She then proceeded to spread a little bullshit.

"Yes, Flo, you're so right. Everything you said—every detail you laid out—was exactly how it happened."

Flo lifted her face up from the palms of her hands and took the tissue from Rose. Her eyes, red and moist, squinted and focused on Rose. Her sobbing trailed off. For theatrical effect only, Rose sighed and looked up, as if seeking answers from the greying ceiling panels. *Yeah, all that gushy shit about booze, sure, sure . . . yeah, that and I didn't get the God-damned teaching job, but I sure ain't telling her that.*

"It was the booze, just as you said," Rose confessed, then added, "I'm an alcoholic and I need help. No two ways about it."

Rose raised a hand up to her face, pretending to suppress anguish. She bobbed her head, squeezed her eyes and forced a tear. Adding to her performance, she brought her other hand up to cover her face.

"Oh Flo. I'm so, so very . . ." She choked out her words,

dropped her head and began to blubber.

Pathetic, she thought, wanting to laugh aloud. *Oscar-worthy? Not a chance. But if it gets her outta here, who gives a damn.*

"Oh Rose, my dear Rose." Flo got up from her chair and sat herself on the lip of Rose's bed. She leaned forward to wrap her thin arms around her friend. "I'm here for you, honey."

She gently stroked Rose's black locks.

Rose sniffled, pretending to pull herself together. Concern and pity were exactly what she had hoped to elicit, but Flo's reaction had the potential to go overboard, to become smothering. She needed an exit strategy. Regrettably, Nurse Olaf was her only hope.

As Flo stroked her hair and whispered promises of support, Rose stealthily felt for the bed's remote. It took her awhile but eventually she found it. With her head pressed tight against Flo's chest, she blindly pressed all the buttons her fingers could find.

"You are my very best friend, Flo. Where would I be without you?" Her words came out muffled. Rose racked her shoulders, sniffled and wiped away imaginary tears.

Okay, Olaf, you old cow. The one time I need you . . ..

She pushed out a great breath, as if relieved, and leaned back against her pillows.

"Oh my Rose," Flo said with compassion and then leaned forward to embrace Rose. Before she could, there was a loud rapping on the door.

Olaf pushed the door open. Her face was flushed. Her burnt-red hair, pulled back in a bun, was rumpled, peeled strands protruded from under her white cap.

"You rang?" Olaf said, regarding the two with mild antipathy.

"Oh? I did?" Rose held her hands out and looked around, feigning surprise as she "found" the remote by her side. She pointed at the remote and shrugged her shoulders. "Well, look at this. I must've hit something or accidentally—"

"Whatever," Olaf snapped. "So, you're okay?"

"Since you mention it, Nurse Olaf," Rose began, seizing the opportunity and choosing her words carefully. "I'm feeling some sharp pain. Kinda serious. Maybe an 8 on a scale of 10." Rose winced and rolled her head back onto the pillow. If convincing enough, some morphine might follow.

Concerned, Flo looked to Rose, then to Nurse Olaf. "I think I should go." She got up off the bed and leaned down to pick up her purse. She looked back at Rose. "Now's not the time for my worries. You need to get healthy and regain your strength."

Olaf walked up to Rose's bed and reached for the pillows. She roughly fluffed them before putting them back under Rose's shoulders. The nurse noticed a pill remaining in a Dixie cup near the bed. She looked at Rose and shook her head in disapproval.

"I don't know how I missed that, but it's the last one for today, McDougal," she said, then smiled and shook the cup at Rose. "You can do it."

Rose frowned. She then reached for the pill and a glass of water.

"You know that you're not going to get better unless you follow the doctors' orders." Olaf added, regarding Rose with sarcasm. Olaf turned her attention to Flo.

"Ma'am, you're welcome to come back after dinner," Olaf said, then sighed and jabbed a thumb at Rose. "Seems this one has become a rather willful patient."

So much for that morphine drip, Rose thought.

"Thank you, Nurse Olaf, but I think it's best that I leave you two for the evening."

Flo leaned down and grasped Rose's hand. In just above a whisper, she said, "Remember, I'm your friend. We'll work through this."

Chapter eleven

Olaf grinned, relishing the moment. Since Rose had arrived, Olaf had begun to enjoy their playful banter. She refilled Rose's glass from a pitcher on the bedside table, as Rose's roommate, Gretchen Campbell, silently shuffled in. Gretchen, who looked exhausted, headed straight to her bed. Olaf watched her climb under the covers.

She needs to stop wandering so much.

Olaf wondered how many rooms Gretchen entered and how many patients she disturbed on any given day. Every afternoon, she would leave her bed and visit as many rooms as she could between one and five o'clock. Quietly she would shuffle from room to room, peeking in before entering. Gretchen was a kind lady who meant no harm. Most patients she visited didn't mind at all, some looked forward to her visits and stories about the legendary Henrietta, likely a figment of Gretchen's imagination, and Henrietta's fruit cellar. In a hospital full of lonely people, sometimes the company of another human, no matter the level of sanity, is good enough.

Olaf walked over to the sink.

"The good news is that your dinner will be ready in thirty minutes. Yours, too, Gretchen," Olaf said, her back turned on her patients. She drew a second glass of water for Gretchen, whose regimen of pills required five refills a day.

"Yeah, about that dinner," Rose began. "I'm not sure about that ham. In fact, I was thinking corned beef on rye, a bag—a big bag—of Fritos and maybe a few of the brownies you nurses hide in the break room refrigerator. Finally, I could sure use a couple of bottles of Bud, maybe from the stash you got tucked away."

A grin spread across Rose's face. "Cold bottles of beer, that is."

Olaf turned around to face Rose, drying her hands as she did. With no shortage of mockery, she shot back, "Sure, McDougal, I'll get right on that."

She walked over to Wheezy and plopped the glass of water on her bedside table, saying nothing, only pointing to the glass. The shriveled old woman's eyes remained fixed on the ceiling.

"Not even one beer?" Rose pleaded. "Listen, there's a twenty-spot in it for you if you can hustle down to Ron's IGA and grab me a six-pack. You don't have to tell a soul. It can be our little secret."

Olaf shook her head and flicked her eyes to the ceiling. She strolled over to the window. The day's light was fading. The traffic on Main Street had picked up some as more of Nashua's working class made their way home. She enjoyed sunsets and the calm they brought at day's end, as the doctors and visitors disappeared. She joined her hands behind her back and stood quietly at the window for a moment soaking it in. As she looked out on the city scene, she addressed Rose.

"You know, McDougal, this is going to work out fine, this thing between us. Seeing how you'll be here for days more." She looked over her shoulder. A grin spread across her face.

"Days?" Rose exclaimed, loud enough to capture Gretchen's attention. "What the hell happened to discharge as early as tomorrow?"

"Kinda came and went. You know, like that Mellencamp song about pink houses." Olaf laughed while keeping her attention on the approaching dusk outside.

Rose protested. "You can't do that. You're just a—"

"Just a what? A nurse? Oh, that's rich, McDougal, just rich," she said, turning her attention from the scene outside and onto Rose. "Who do you think keeps this hospital running when the doctors are off screwing around on the golf course . . . or on their wives? You think they spend hours on your case? Think they burn the midnight oil to work out some special treatment plan for Miss Rose McDougal? Or . . ." Olaf flipped a hand at Gretchen, "for her? You think Lanzara and Levesque studied the results of your EKG, or lab work or the slew of other charts? Not a chance. They glance over it, pretending to give a shit, then ask me what I think we should do. In your case, it was easy. Here's a woman who, at a minimum, was reckless and is now in search of a high. And yet there's more to you, McDougal. There's something else I can't put my finger on. I figure I'll need a few more days to make my own assessment about this little accident of yours."

Olaf shot Rose a glance.

Rose didn't appear to like the way she said "accident." In fact, Rose didn't appear to like any of it. Olaf wasn't finished.

"If the docs concur with my assessment, as they always do, then I'm gonna need a few extra days to work up a treatment plan." Olaf slipped her chubby mitts back into her pockets. "So, back to tonight's dinner, how about that nice plate of Spam ham and green beans? Play your cards right, and I'll throw in a juice box."

"Do I have a choice?" Rose said, lowering her head.

Chapter twelve

As hungry as she had been all day, Rose gave up. She couldn't look at it any longer, let alone eat a morsel of the food. The so-called food, which dominated the plastic tray which sat on the nightstand next to her, was an abomination. The greenish-grey gelatinous pile would've been rejected as an alternative to cannibalism by the starving, snowbound settlers trapped in Donner Pass. Colonial Era prisoners in New England were said to have revolted when served food considered not suitable for human consumption. Rose's dinner would've caused a riot. Her coagulating dinner smelled like burnt rubber and it shook like Jello when she tapped it. Crawling with slugs and termites, a slab of tree bark served *a la carte* would have been preferred.

Lucky me. I get a few more nights of this.

She was considering the likelihood of weight loss, a silver lining associated with a steady diet of hospital food, when she heard the squeak of footfalls out in the hallway approaching her room. A moment later, they stopped and her door was pushed open. It was Olaf, the callous nurse who had so gleefully delivered dinner hours earlier. She stepped into the room and crossed her arms.

"Come on, McDougal, eating one's meals equates to regaining one's strengths which means leaving here," Olaf said, flexing an arm and grinning. "Besides, don't you wanna be in the clean-plate club?"

Olaf was enjoying her power trip far too much. Rose gritted her teeth and fought back the urge to toss an insult at the curmudgeon nurse.

"I'd like to live to see tomorrow, so I think I'll pass." Rose said, looking dour at her untouched food.

"Suit yourself," Olaf said. She walked over and picked up Rose's and Wheezy's trays. Rose was surprised to see that half of Wheezy's food was gone.

Well, the old bat has courage, she thought. *That, or she flushed half of the shit down the toilet just to avoid a lecture from this nurse-witch.*

Rose watched as Olaf rested the trays near the sink under the TV. She washed her hands and then patted them dry with a towel. As she did, she addressed Rose.

"Oh, I almost forgot. You've got another visitor coming. Some guy named Vic. He called about thirty minutes ago." She looked down at her watch. "Which means he should be here any moment."

She turned to face Rose. "If I remember correctly, he didn't sound too happy. Well, anyway, enjoy your visit with Vic."

That's all I need now, Rose thought.

She opened her mouth to speak, to beg of her torturing nurse to deny all visitors, but it was too late. Olaf was gone and her friend, Vic, was on his way.

Vic LaRue was Rose's best friend. He was a hardscrabble Vietnam vet who owned Kegler's Den, a popular bar in Nashua. Tall, dark and undeniably handsome, his deep brown eyes had seen a lot of shit in the triple-canopy jungles straddling Vietnam's DMZ, which separated some Commie guy's north from some corrupt guy's south, according to the tales Vic told her. He had survived his 18 months of hell, earning medals for bravery. When he returned home, he started a family, earned success in business, and opened a bar which made him money hand-over-fist. By any measure, he had achieved the American Dream. Surviving the horrors of Vietnam, however, wasn't all he had to overcome.

Like Rose, Vic's childhood in Berlin, New Hampshire, was riddled with bad actors who peddled in misery. Chief among them was his psychotic mother. Rose remembered Vic telling her about the trauma of his youth. He recounted a night when he was only 13, a night he spent standing in a dark closet peering through a cracked door while his mother and her alcoholic boyfriend undertook their nightly ritual of verbal and physical abuse. The fighting normally ended when one of the two passed out. In the morning, they would make up. Except on this particular night, there would be no reconciliation the next day. The night would prove deadly. It would be Vic's last night in that house and his last in Berlin.

Vic's mom and her boyfriend had been drinking rotgut whiskey all day. Their fighting began just after dark when the boyfriend punched her shoulder, hard enough to spin her nearly around. Stunned, she charged at him. Her fists flying everywhere, she hit him in the face and neck. She pulled his hair and scratched his neck, yanking off his gold necklace in the process.

The loss of his prized necklace sent him into a rage. Screaming obscenities, he pushed her up against the wall, reared back his right fist and delivered a perfect roundhouse right to her nose. His powerful fist snapped the bridge of her nose. She fell to the living room floor, sprawled out and bleeding. She was dazed, but she was not down for the count. There was still some fight left in Vic's mom.

Picking herself up off the carpeted floor, she walked into the kitchen, grabbed her handbag and returned to the living room. She unzipped the bag, reached into it and pulled out a pistol. Without a word, she walked up to within a foot of her boyfriend, raised the gun, pulled back the hammer and emptied a clip of 9mm slugs into his chest. As he fell to the floor, dead, she casually headed for the kitchen and a cold beer. Vic never saw his mother again. He had seen enough.

Hearing the wail of approaching sirens, Vic bolted out of the closet, sprinted through the living room and shimmied down the apartment's fire escape with a backpack slung over his shoulder. The pack had been readied months earlier. Before he could become a ward of the state, Vic raced off into the cold, snowy night, eventually jumping a vacant boxcar on the Boston & Maine heading south, as far from his demons as the train would take him.

The sum of Vic's experiences helped him in spotting bullshit, something Flo was unable to do. Rose had it easy during Flo's visit. Day-to-day, Flo spent the bulk of her time fretting about her shiftless, reckless, twenty-two-year old son, Myron, who occupied space both in her house, and in her head, rent-free. Her incessant worrying about his latest shenanigans inhibited her ability to process things in a logical, dispassionate way. Asking Rose straight-forward questions as to the events that had transpired prior to her falling unconscious inside a car full of carbon monoxide would have never crossed Flo's mind.

Not so with Vic. He was not the type who would fall for some feigned display of dramatics. Conjuring up a cockamamie story as to why she was occupying a hospital bed after a brush with death would have been a waste of time. That was just as well since she was out of time. Vic had arrived.

Rose heard him down the hall at the nurses' station, inquiring about his "step-sister." One of the floor nurses, clearly smitten with Vic, happily led him to her room. Rose rubbed the sleep from her eyes, elevated her bed and smiled at Vic and the nurse as they entered.

With the sun long-since set, the room's only light was her bedside lamp. Rose's smile, intended to disarm and melt the icy stare with which Vic observed her, wasn't working. Vic wore pressed black pants, a black suit and black shoes, which sparkled in the gloom. His hair was slicked back. A red carnation, the outfit's only anomaly, poked out from his suit jacket's lapel. The lamp's faint light gently bathed him, exposing sharp, handsome features which cast shadows. He was as striking as she had ever seen him. But he did not appear happy.

He stood at the foot of her bed and regarded her for a moment. He then turned and thanked the adoring nurse, who smiled as she took her leave. After she left, he wandered over to the window. He stood with his back to Rose, his hands folded behind him. Beyond his vague outline, a black sky with a faint starlight was all Rose could see. She cleared her throat to speak. Her words came out in a squeak.

"Someone die?" she quipped, hoping that might take the edge off him.

"Someone should've," he replied. He pulled out a folded newspaper from his suit, turned and walked to the side of her bed.

"Read this," he said, tossing the paper onto her lap. He reached back into his suit, this time pulling out a silver flask. It was engraved with an anchor and globe and the words: SEMPER FI. He dropped the sealed flask onto the paper. Rose pushed the paper to the side.

"Take a sip of that. Consider it truth serum. In case you were curious about this get-up of mine," he said gesturing to his attire, "who expects someone coming from a funeral to smuggle liquor into a hospital?"

"You know I don't drink that stuff," she said.

"You do tonight."

She reached for the flask and frowned. She untwisted the cap and forced a sip. Instantly, she coughed. It was not what she had expected. Her mouth twisted in agony. It was disgusting.

"What the hell is this?" she gasped.

"It's called tequila. Take another pull. Go ahead," he ordered. "If you don't, I'll call in Nurse Ratchet. I like her. She's probably been terrorizing you. If so, I'm sure you've deserved every minute of it."

"How do you know about—?"

"Never mind that, just do as I said." He moved to the foot of her bed, his eyes showing no compassion.

The second pull was equally as repulsive. While she hated liquor in general, tequila was the one she most abhorred. Tequila was the culprit on that one occasion when she got sick as a result of imbibing alcohol. Just two shots had brought her to the floor, her head spinning before she barfed her guts up. That was over twenty years ago. For whatever reason, she must have revealed that event to Vic. Not surprisingly, he was using it against her today. Vic LaRue was a success in part because he paid attention to otherwise trifling details. Hence, the tequila-filled flask which sat menacingly in her hand.

"If you thought for a second that I would show up here with some sort of sympathy gift, then you obviously don't know me. And if you thought for a second that having survived your . . . your little goddamned stunt, that I'd come crying, then you're an even bigger idiot than you appear." Vic scowled. "Look at you there, trying to look pitiful."

He turned away from her and walked over to Wheezy to apologize for the ruckus.

"Ma'am, I'm sorry about this," he said, then looked over his shoulder at Rose. "As soon as I'm done with this one, I'll be on my way."

Wheezy's gaze was locked on some phantom object on the ceiling. Bits of saliva sat in the corners of her mouth. She then grinned, which spread her wrinkled skin like elastic.

"Sweet Henrietta invites you," she began, dropping her gaze from the ceiling and onto Vic, "to join us in her fruit cellar. Sweet Henrietta always made the best peach cobbler . . . with the finest peaches from Carolina. Oh, she'd be most happy . . . would be a . . . a real pity if . . ."

Her eyes moved back to the ceiling. The rest of her spiel eventually trailed off to soundless puffs of breath. Vic got the message: Wheezy was a nut job and didn't have the faintest idea what Vic and Rose were up to. Vic crossed the room and walked back to the window. And back on the offense.

"You may have fooled them, but you ain't fooling me." Looking out the window, he raised his right hand. "Go ahead and read that paper."

There it was in large, bold black print. It was the headline story.

HOMETOWN HERO SAVES WOMAN'S LIFE

Under the headline was a photo of Frankie O'Brien, his face locked in a toothy smile. She skimmed the article and found her name in a number of places. So, too, did she find the alleged circumstance which led to Frankie's heroism. The "accident," according to Dr. Levesque, whom the reporter, David Popovich, had interviewed hours after the rescue, was "the lethal amalgam of an overly fatigued, heavy-set woman and a car chock-full of carbon monoxide."

Heavy-set?! That's what's on the Telegraph's front page? The little prick! She had barely begun reading the article when she made a mental note to pay this Popovich a visit when she got out.

She scanned the rest of the two-page article, focusing on the dramatic and seemingly far-fetched valor. Then again, how would she know what was credible? She had been unconscious and flirting with death. That much she knew to be true. As for this Popovich, besides being an asshole, he sure had a flair for the spectacular. It pained her to admit it, but his writing was excellent. Excerpts of his lengthy piece read like an action-thriller:

> "Frankie O'Brien, who noticed the smoking car from across Canal Street, cast aside his personal well-being and sprang into action. Dodging the traffic on Canal, he raced gallantly to the smoldering car and quickly realized, at that fateful moment, that only he could rescue the bulky and unconscious victim from the jaws of an untimely death. With the car doors locked, he shattered the driver's-side window with his right hand; exploding glass tore and ripped his flesh. While bleeding and choking on the escaping poisonous gas, Frankie struggled mightily, but eventually dragged the large woman from certain death . . ." Later, while being stitched up in the emergency room, he modestly explained and brushed aside his heroism. "Rose is my friend. She's so nice to me."

On and on the gushing went. One might have expected such lavish accolades for a legend like Audie Murphy. But Frankie O'Brien? On the one hand, Rose was happy to see Frankie vaulted into the limelight. His deed, however heroic it had been, was likely to engender him some fame. That was a good thing. On the other hand, to a certain extent, it had come at her expense. The multiple references to her size pissed her off. Visibly disgusted, Rose pushed the paper off her lap and onto the floor.

"Okay, so you came here to tell me I have a weight problem?" she flippantly asked. Then, taking a swipe at his politics, she added, "Oh no, wait. I know what it is. You want me to reconsider my support for Reyes and straighten my ways before the election in November?"

"Don't be a smart-ass," Vic said. He walked over and snatched the flask off Rose's bed and took a pull himself. He slipped the flask back inside his jacket and pulled the chair up to the side of her bed. Vic glimpsed at the muttering Wheezy before sitting and turning his attention back to Rose. He took a more consoling approach.

"Look, you know I'm your friend, and that I've always been there for you," he said.

Rose nodded. She considered changing the topic to something more innocuous, like sports or taking another stab at politics, which had the potential to fuel an argument. Vic was a dyed-in-the-wool Reynolds fan. He loved the sitting president.

"You really let me down. Something was tearing you up on the inside, yet you decided not to come to me with it," he said. "Instead of reaching out to a friend, you tried the easy way out. You tried to destroy yourself."

"Vic, it's not wh—"

Vic held up the palm of his hand, cutting her off. "Please don't bullshit me. I'm in no mood." He paused for a moment. "I know what's going on and, dammit, I feel responsible."

"You do? I mean, you feel responsible for my intention to . . . well, you know . . ."

Rose was convinced he knew that she had planned to end her life. Armed with that insight, she knew what was coming: his plan to extract her admission.

"Yes, I do," Vic replied.

Rose broke eye contact with Vic and his deep, brown eyes.

"You didn't get the job. And, like you told me, you really expected to get it. All your dreams were shattered. You felt rejected. Lemme guess—someone in the school department uncovered some unfortunate incident from your past?"

"Well, there might've been something, though I never inquired," she said.

"There's no 'might've been' anything." Vic got up and walked back to the window, talking as he went. "You not getting the job isn't why I'm pissed off. It's not my place to be angry about that. What pisses me off is you not coming to me when you needed a friend."

"But you've got Cheryl, the kids, your bar. You've got enough going on in your life. You don't need some burden adding to all of that."

"Look, I know what you tried to do." Vic turned and walked back toward her bed.

"I've known you for 15 years. I've only seen you drunk once. I know you're no alcoholic but, given the bad news, I believe you intended to drink away your pain, until you were numb. You meant to send a message, a cry for help. And while you might not have intended to push it quite so far, you almost did. Guzzling booze and then getting into your car. How far did you think you'd make it? As for these doctors," Vic waived a hand, "what'd they think? You were just fatigued? What a crock. You wanted to get bombed and drive as far as that old jalopy would take you. Drive until you couldn't. And telling me you were looking for a change of scenery? What a load of crap. It wasn't about starting over. It was about running away." Vic took a breath. "You're damn lucky to be alive and not dead at the bottom of the Nashua River or wrapped around some telephone pole."

He sat back down next to her bed, checking toward the door. He ran his fingers through his hair and rubbed his eyes. From behind him, Wheezy began babbling about grass trimmings.

Incredible. Alcohol? Rose thought. *He has no idea either.*

"I'm sorry I snapped," he said, rubbing his hands together. "Just promise me that if you ever get to that point again, call me. Don't hesitate. And if you're unsure, call anyway, okay?"

Rose nodded, her eyes beginning to tear up. He had gotten his point across. Tucked under her sheets, with only her head exposed, she felt pathetic.

Unexpectedly, Vic cracked a smile. At that moment, Rose knew that the scolding was over. First, chew some ass, then close with encouragement and support. She was only partially right.

He got up and walked to the door, buttoning up his jacket.

"I'm your friend, the best one you got, or so I thought. Friends rally around one another, Rose. Friends are there for each other, especially during the tough times."

Vic reached for the door handle, then turned back.

"What if you'd landed in the obituaries instead? Then what? Then I'm left to wonder what might've been different if I'd have done something or said something. Left to wonder if I could've stepped in earlier."

Vic paused a moment, allowing his words to sink in. "You know, the whole world isn't out to get you. But if you ever find yourself feeling that way, you need to know that you don't have to go it alone."

Before leaving the room, he cast a stern look at her. "Don't you ever put me through this again."

With that, he was gone into the shadows of the hallway, leaving Rose with a heavy heart and a crushing guilt. Since arriving in room 411, she had adopted a blithe attitude about her "accident," attempting to minimize and make light of what she had actually set out to do in the first place. Just five days earlier, she decided to check out, once and for all. Never once did she consider the consequences. Never once did she consider the pain others might have borne as a result of her selfish choice. Flo and Vic had rushed to her bedside, baring their emotions, pain etched on their faces. All the while, she remained dismissive and insincere. She had been eager for them to take their leave, so that she could get back to her apartment and return to a life she had set out to end. As long as her friends didn't know the truth, why bring it up? Why deal with their anguish from a vulnerable, immobile position such as a hospital bed?

Fresh tears welled in her eyes. She realized that she had missed the whole point. Their grief was no imposition. It was the manifestation of their love, the love of a friend they could not bear the thought of losing.

Just how self-absorbed have I become?

She slipped deeper under the covers and began to weep. She raised her eyes to the ceiling, intending to reach someone she had not acknowledged since childhood.

"My God, what was I thinking?"

Chapter thirteen

After having tossed and turned for nearly four hours, Rose gave up. The likelihood of sleep was a myth. Her mind could not stop spinning. It spewed out terrifying images of what her unemployed life might look like. The most frightening of those images was that of a shopping cart loaded with shabby clothes crammed into plastic bags. Unfortunately for Rose, it didn't end with bags chockful of ragged clothing.

Scraps of cardboard lined the sides of what constituted her future home. Empty jugs of milk, for whatever purpose they served, rested on top of the many bags. A pair of shabby sneakers, tied to the cart's handlebar, swung gently in the air. Taped to the front of the cart was a flexible, six-foot pole. At the top of the pole was a bright orange, triangle-shaped flag, just like the one Rose had on the back of her bike as a child. Inexplicably, her Gramma Gannon's music box, Rose's only possession of any value, rested on top of a soiled denim jacket near the handlebar. She began to believe that pushing a loaded shopping cart, her home-on-wheels, from one bridge underpass to the next, was what lay in store for Rose McDougal, a penniless, unemployed substitute teacher.

Then she remembered there was an envelope waiting for her. That envelope, she had been told, contained enough money to keep her afloat for a few months. Enough for food, rent and other essentials. There would even be enough to keep her car on the road. Donnelly's insistence that her car be adequately maintained struck her as random, somewhat bizarre.

What difference does it make whether my car is in good working order or not?

The answer was obvious: because nothing is free. Everything comes with terms, especially when dealing with a man like Donnelly.

The memory of Donnelly's visit came roaring back. Before long, he would come to collect. Of that, she was certain. He would drop a marker. He would call in his chit. He would expect her to make good on her promise and do him a favor, one which would no doubt involve her car.

Rose couldn't remain in bed any longer. Lying helpless in a dark room as images of destitution and danger swirled in her head, she knew that she would go crazy if she didn't get up. She needed to get up and do something, anything. Maybe find something to quell the shakes. Maybe another shot of liquor.

God knows I need a drink.

For the first time in her life, Rose craved alcohol. Beer or liquor, anything would do. Then she remembered Olaf was still on shift and probably trolling the halls. What if Olaf found Rose sprung from her bedroom and rooting around in the doctors' lounge? Then what? Another week of sharing a toilet with Wheezy. Another week having to hear nonstop gibberish about canned peaches, grass trimmings or some other absurdity.

"Fuck it. I'm getting up," she mumbled.

Before she did, she recalled her photo-reconnaissance training in the Army. Proceeding undetected meant drawing back on Sergeant Jackson's instruction. She ceased all movement and slowly controlled her breathing. She was taking a tactical pause, a moment of motionless silence, before advancing.

Look, listen, wait.

Those were the three words which Jackson had drilled into her head.

Satisfied there was no one around, Rose slid the bedsheets down to her calves. She sat still, shut her eyes and listened. She heard nothing. Even so, she imagined that monster, Olaf, lurking in the dark hallway ready to pounce. Should she find Rose on the run, Olaf would be only too happy to dish out another—God forbid—forty-eight hours of hospital-life hell, just for kicks. As for the doctors, none of them would come to Rose's rescue, as Olaf is quick to point out. The doctors regarded Rose's survival as a medical miracle. Parlaying their involvement in her diagnosis and treatment had presented Rose's doctors with a golden opportunity to earn those coveted peer reviews should they decide to publish. Glowing reviews from fellow doctors almost always led to lucrative grants and other such boondoggles.

More probing, prodding and testing? Great idea, Nurse Olaf.

Extension approved!

A wretched soul like Olaf would take great pleasure in wielding her version of the hammer of justice on a willful and disobedient patient.

Wheezy's sudden hacking fit startled Rose, but it presented her with an opportunity. As she hacked away, Rose pulled her knees up to her midsection, while simultaneously pivoting on her posterior. Then, like an unleashed coil, she sprang from the bed, landing safely on both feet as Wheezy's coughing convulsions came to a grinding halt. The years of bodily neglect had not entirely destroyed Rose's athleticism and catlike reflexes.

Standing perfectly still, she closed her eyes and focused her faculties on sound alone. She heard nothing. If anyone was prowling out in the hall, then they were more disciplined than she. Slowly she opened her eyes and relaxed her body. Discipline and timing would get her to the doctor's lounge, and all the luxuries she sought.

Rose imagined the doctor's lounge as a lavish place, flush with adult libations. She pictured it adorned with overpriced artwork and opulent furniture. In such a setting, one found the best wines and scotches, Cuban cigars and that fancy cheese you spread on crackers, the kind which Ascot tie-wearing elites ate.

She decided that she would knock back a drink or two, then leave with a rounded plate full of that swanky cheese. She was famished. The hospital food had been severely lacking, both in appeal and portion size. But before she escaped room 411, she needed to find out what was outside that kept drawing both Vic and Donnelly back to the room's window.

She tip-toed over to the large, two-paned window and looked out into the night. Towering streetlights splashed sodium light onto East Hollis Street, where nary a car could be found. The streetlights provided just enough light to make out objects in the hospital's rear parking lot, which may have been what Vic and Donnelly had been looking down upon. What she discovered was unimpressive: three sedans, a dark-colored dumpster—might have been black, maybe blue—labeled BFI, a tipped-over shopping cart, scattered trash, and a large, heavyset orderly smoking a cigarette and leaning against the rear fender of one of the sedans.

She was about to turn away from the window and head down the stairwell to the doctor's lounge when the orderly walked away from the vehicle, revealing something else. It was a large cross with numbers and a name printed across the horizontal beam. At first glance it looked like another one of the ubiquitous signs declaring allegiance to some man running for office, except she didn't think it was promoting anyone at all. It was about five feet tall, its crossbeam about the same length. The cross tilted slightly to the left. It was propped up by an eight-foot wall of shrubbery, which separated St. Joe's rear parking lot and East Hollis Street. Having been hammered into the stony soil, the top of the cross was compacted; her 20/20 vision could pick up that much. With some squinting, Rose could make out the brush-painted, thick characters which ran the length of the crossbeam. It read:

Isaiah 44:22

She read the sign once, twice and then a third time. Something about the name Isaiah made her think of her past, something she may have been taught. Then she remembered. It was the name of a prophet, one she had learned about as a child attending Sunday school. But why was his name written on a cross, posted in some obscure parking lot where few would ever see it?

Probably one of those Jesus freaks put it there, she mused. They were the ones who wore white shirts, black ties, and cheesy smiles. They zipped around town on ten-speed bikes with backpacks full of pocket-sized Bibles slung over their shoulders. On two occasions, they knocked on her door, somehow making it up one of the Dunstable House's begrimed stairwells without being scared off by some unruly wino.

It seemed to Rose that it would have been easier to simply print the verse on a flier and hand them out door to door like those sports coat-wearing young men who zipped around town. They covered a lot of territory. Rose remembered having to listen to their spiel about her need for redemption. If she would only offer a small donation in support of their global mission, then they would ensure a happy outcome when she met St. Peter at the pearly gates. In the end, the salvation salesmen left her apartment sans donation. Rose opted to take her chances.

This is what drew them back to the window?

It must have been. There was nothing else out there. Perhaps Vic and Donnelly knew something about the prophet Isaiah. As a young child, Vic had been a practicing Catholic, but that all ended after his deranged mother filled her abusive boyfriend's chest full of lead. As for Donnelly, an Irishman, he would have most certainly been Catholic. In his case, however, only when Catholicism suited him.

She fidgeted with her hospital johnny's drawstring, while keeping her gaze on the sign below. Something about that sign reminded her of a soft-spoken nun who taught religion to her fifth grade class. Her elementary school years represented a time in her life where she still enjoyed moments of peace. As she stood looking down on the tilted cross, her thoughts slipped back to a happier place at a happier time in her life.

She was ten and had the world in her hands. She was trim, athletic and confident—as much as a preteen girl could be considered confident. She was a straight-A student who enjoyed school. Above all, she had her Gramma to support her every endeavor. Before they could creep in, Rose brushed aside the pain of her loss. She had no desire to rehash the years which followed her death. Gramma was gone. That was all there was to it. So too was the prospect of legitimate work. Her visions of being accepted as a member of Nashua's respectable society had been erased. Things were as they were and there was nothing that could be done to reverse course.

She turned away from the window. An adult drink was what she wanted, what she now craved. She took one stride toward the door when it hit her. She was not alone and she knew it. She sensed the presence of someone else, could hear faint breathing. She froze, lowered her head and closed her eyes, taking another tactical pause. Then she heard it again, gaining in intensity. Not breathing, but snoring. It was Wheezy. *Thank God.* Wheezy's agonizing gasps for air, a late-evening ritual before she hit deep sleep, had begun.

"No way that bag of bones lives another month," Rose muttered under her breath. "I only hope I'm not still stranded here when she goes."

When Wheezy's rasping finally decreased, Rose held her breath for another moment, just to be sure there was no other movement and sound. Only silence came in reply. Only a dizzying display of static on the TV accompanied Rose in the land of the conscious.

Feeling good about her situation, Rose slipped her hands in her pockets and casually walked to the door and into the hallway. Then she heard it, at first it was faint, only a soft shuffling sound. A split second later, she was blinded by an intense light. Rose could not see her, but she knew who it was without a doubt: Nurse Olaf.

"Just where the hell you think you're going, McDougal?" Olaf asked. Her flashlight disoriented Rose, who staggered backward, throwing her arms up in front of her face.

"Well?" Nurse Olaf demanded, flashlight in hand. "Thinking about springing this joint?"

Rose steadied herself. "Okay, okay. You got me." She held out her hands to block the piercing bright light. "Mind turning that thing off?"

Olaf lowered the flashlight to her side, but kept it on. Enough light splashed up off the polished floor to illuminate the outlines of her face. That was when Rose lifted her head to face her. She had never fully noticed Olaf's appearance, largely because she avoided any type of conversation with her. But Rose noticed it now. Olaf is one worn-out looking dame.

Nurse Olaf had a face, as Rose's father was prone to say, that could stop a clock. Bulldog cheeks, wrinkly skin, a snarl and beady brown eyes. Tufts of red hair pointed crazily out from under her cap. As Rose stood in silence, desperately trying not to stare, she noticed something else: Olaf looked like someone famous, some actress. Then it hit her.

That actress . . . the one who'd played Danny DeVito's mother in that movie where DeVito was trying to kill her. Throw Momma from the Train.

Rose suppressed a smile. Rose was no swimsuit model herself, but next to Olaf, she may as well have been Cindy Crawford.

"Think you can stonewall me, McDougal? Think that thug who stopped by last night can help you now? He can't. I'm in control of your future," Olaf said smugly, poking her own chest. "Listen, McDougal. I don't know what your deal is, why you're so messed up, but rest assured, I know your type. You ain't fooling me."

Rose remained silent and maintained an outward cool. Her racing heartbeat gradually slowed, allowing her to reflect on her current circumstances. Here she was in an empty hallway in the middle of the night, the head nurse having pinned her down. It was time to face the facts: she was busted. Her little stunt was going to cost her more time. Besides, what are a few extra days? At that moment, the thought of Donnelly and an envelope full of cash struck her.

Maybe when all is said and done, Margo and I can go barhopping with some of his money.

She laughed out loud at the thought. In an instant, the powerful white light was trained back on her face.

"You think this is some kinda joke, McDougal? How about another week in here? That sound funny? Another week of sipping cold pea soup littered with dandruff? How about struggling to get your chompers into a slice of stale, fungus-riddled bread? Don't think I can't make all that happen. Look, I'm here covering a shift so one of my nurses could enjoy a getaway with her husband. I do that kind of thing all the time. Hell, I'm here almost all the time."

Olaf eyed Rose up and down. "I ask you again—where did you think you were going?"

Rose kept up the game and stayed mum. Casually, she shrugged her shoulders.

"Not budging, huh? Tell you what, I'm gonna give you a final chance. I'm gonna ask you one last time. You're gonna tell me what you're doing out of bed and in the hallway—both serious infractions for one so sick, in such pain, that only morphine drips can provide relief." Olaf's smirk spread across her face.

"Tsk-tsk . . . hmm . . . imagine what the doctors will say when they hear about this. Never mind them: how about that dashing stud who crept in here and bribed me with a hundred bucks to get into your room? I doubt he'd be too pleased. Someone who packs a heater in a hospital doesn't fuck around. And if I understood correctly, he's your boss."

Olaf whistled and rolled her eyes in mock awe. Nearly a foot shorter than Rose, she stared up at her with a victorious grin.

"One last time, McDougal—what are you up to?"

Rose frowned. What's the point in resisting or lying? Instead, she chose honesty.

"I wanted a drink," Rose replied, her voice hoarse and scratchy. She looked down at Olaf with tired eyes and coughed. "A beer, maybe alcohol. Didn't matter. I wanted a buzz."

Olaf laughed out loud, really loud. And kept laughing.

Rose looked around anxiously for a moment before realizing that it was after midnight and she was with the head nurse, likely the only nurse on the floor.

"Booze? You tried sneaking away for that?" Olaf asked between cackles of thunderous laughter.

Rose's face blushed bright red. She was embarrassed. She hated feeling so small.

"Well . . . yeah, I did. So what?" she snapped, all of a sudden highly irritated.

Nurse Margo Olaf, the 51-year-old head nurse at St. Joseph Hospital, stopped laughing and turned serious. She placed a callused hand on Rose's shoulder and looked her in the eyes.

"If that was all you wanted, then why didn't you just say so up front? Come with me." Olaf began to walk off, adding, "Heck, maybe I can get something out of this deal."

Rose remained in place, confused.

When Olaf didn't hear footsteps in her wake, she stopped and turned to address her obstinate patient.

"By the way, that wasn't a question." Olaf gestured movement with the flashlight's beam before turning away and walking on. "Come on, McDougal. You might learn something."

Rose followed.

Chapter fourteen

Three flights of stairs, an endless hallway and five minutes later, Rose and Olaf were down on the first floor, entering a room through a heavy oak door upon which the words Doctors' Quarters were engraved in an elegant script. It was unlike any lounge that Rose had ever set foot in. It stood in sharp contrast to what she was accustomed to as an educator.

The teachers' rooms that she had visited were bleak places with sloppily-painted walls, grunge-smeared windows, scuffed floors and water-stained ceiling tiles. They were the kinds of places where you would find a prehistoric coffeemaker (if you were lucky to find a coffeemaker at all) with some brown-stained carafe sitting on some tilted end table between a couple of scuffed-up, mildew-plagued couches of some unsightly orange-red color scheme. Tucked off in a dingy corner littered with dust bunnies would sit a banged-up refrigerator, in which a couple of stale sandwiches, rotten fruit and some kind of powdered drink could be found. Regardless of the array of cheap furniture, in Rose's experience, there was one thing that most school Teachers' rooms had in common: that inescapable, nauseating smell of burnt coffee and cigarette smoke.

That smoking had been forbidden inside Nashua schools for many years didn't deter most teachers she knew. The very same teachers who would have levied a week of detention on a smoking student would, outside of the prying eyes of those same students, light up in the lounge without hesitation. Such was the case at Dr. Guidry's, where peeling black letters labeled FACULTY ONLY door led to a dreary, malodorous place where hypocritical teachers smoked away.

By comparison, the St. Joe's "Doctors' Quarters" stood in sharp contrast to the typical teachers' lounge. The "Doctor's Quarters", into which Rose walked, was opulent, palatial. Whoever was responsible for decorating this place had to have been given a blank check, Rose decided. She was tempted to ask Olaf if she should have taken off her slippers before entering. Rose was visibly awestruck. Her reaction was not lost on Olaf.

"Impressive, ain't it? Technically, I'm not supposed to be in here," Olaf said, as she made her way to the wet bar. Soft, warm lighting bathed the wet bar. A richly-framed canvas painting, featuring an Elizabethan-era rich kid playing a harpsichord, was mounted to the wall behind the bar. Olaf reached for the dimmer switch and dulled the lights. As she did, her eyes disappeared into shadows.

"Take a seat," Olaf instructed. "So, what's your poison, besides Bud? There's no beer in this place. The docs around here don't drink a working man's beverage."

Rose hesitated at first, then settled comfortably into one of the four auburn leather couches thoughtfully positioned among similarly colored recliners. The furniture display was no haphazard arrangement. Amazing what an unlimited budget could do, she thought. Initially, the cool leather chilled Rose's legs and butt through the hospital-issue nightie she wore. The chill was short-lived, but the sheer comfort of the lounge remained.

"You still with me, McDougal?"

"Oh, yeah . . . sorry . . . I'm not really a liquor drinker," Rose answered. *And until I landed in this hospital, I was never much of a drinker at all.* "I don't know. Surprise me."

Olaf said nothing in reply. Over her shoulder, Rose heard the clink of ice cubes in one glass, then another. The slow pour of liquor followed.

"I think you're gonna like this, McDougal," Olaf said. "Probably not the cheap shit you might've tried in your past, or the rotgut your buddies at The Stable drink." Olaf gave her a knowing glance. "It is The Stable, isn't it?"

Rose heard the opening, then the tearing of a plastic bag. Whatever the contents, they were being emptied into a bowl and, from the duration of the pour, a mighty large one. Apparently, Olaf had no qualms about being in here. She struck Rose as that kind of a woman: the no-nonsense kind who didn't really give a shit. She had what the old-timers called moxie.

Olaf came around from behind her, first placing two crystal glasses on the teak coffee table in front of Rose, both filled with a ginger-colored beverage. That done, she went back to the bar and retrieved an exquisitely designed clay bowl brimming with cheddar-flavored Bugles and set it next to the drinks on the coffee table. Olaf took the couch opposite Rose and flopped casually onto its rich comfort. Both were within arm's reach of the Bugles, one of Rose's favorite snacks. Rose studied the bowl; Olaf didn't. Olaf leaned forward and plunged in a hand, pulling out a substantial number before depositing them on the cushion to her right. Rose followed suit, extracting a smaller amount.

Olaf then snatched her drink off the table. She sat back onto the leather couch, took a sip of the superb whiskey, closed her eyes, and swished—almost gargled—the liquor before swallowing it. She breathed out in satisfaction. Gradually she opened her eyes, fixing her gaze on Rose. After studying her for a moment, Olaf spoke.

"McDougal, I can read you like a book." She took another, longer sip, nearly finishing the drink. "Like one of those pop-up books the brain-dead, MTV-addicted little shitheads like to read. Know the type, McDougal? You probably educated some of them."

Rose bristled. Being called McDougal had always been a pet peeve.

"Nurse Olaf, can I ask a favor?"

"Sure, McDougal. Shoot," Olaf answered, as she stood up to mosey back to the bar.

"Quit calling me McDougal. It's Rose. Heck, I'd prefer 'hey you' over McDougal."

"Something wrong with your name?"

"Rose? No. McDougal? Yes. Well, maybe. I don't know. It reminds me of my father, a real asshole." Rose shook her head. "But until I get hitched, I guess I'm stuck with it. And that ain't happening anytime soon."

Rose grabbed the ornate crystal glass, her right hand smothering it. She raised the glass to her mouth and downed the whiskey in one swig. It burned like fire and was disgusting. She fought off the urge to cough it up. Instead, through watery eyes, she tapped the glass on the table. "I have a second favor to ask: while you're up, Rose needs a refill."

A moment later, Olaf was standing beside her. In her right hand, she held her glass. Her left hand reached for Rose's empty.

"Okay, have it your way. We'll go with Rose. Since we're drinking, call me Margo." Olaf returned to the bar. A couple of clinks, two pours and she was back, an outstretched hand offering Rose round two.

"Rose is really your name? Nice name," Olaf said. She settled back into the couch's soothing grasp. "You know, this may come as a shock, but I liked you from the start, though I enjoyed messing with you. I knew eventually I'd warm up to your antics."

"Well, if the head nurse doesn't mind me saying, I couldn't stand you from the start," Rose said. She regarded the crystal in her hand. "With enough time and . . . what is this stuff, anyway?"

"It's a Macallan, and it ain't cheap," Margo answered.

"Hmph," Rose grunted. She gazed at her glass, "Perhaps I can be persuaded."

Olaf smiled.

"So it's Margo? That another cover? What about Olaf?"

"Nope. Both are legit. My husband's dad was Russian and so was my dad's dad. My father was born in Leningrad. When dad was seventeen, my grandfather decided it was high time to get away from that cocksucker, Stalin, the gulags and all the other joys of living in the USSR."

Rose nodded, impressed.

"So, tell me. How do you pull all this off?" Rose asked, gesturing to the expansive domain of the doctors' lounge. "I'd have been drummed outta Dr. Guidry if I even thought about sneaking into the principal's private office. And that place pales in comparison to this."

Olaf shrugged. "Who do you really think runs this hospital? The doctors?" She took another sip and a handful of Bugles, crammed them into her mouth. The sounds of a tree-shredder followed. Olaf was hungry.

"It's pretty simple, really," Olaf continued. "I keep them on the golf courses, or off with their mistresses, and outta this depressing place. For that, I get total access to whatever I fancy. Only stipulation? I use it when no one's around. That means when the hospital administrator isn't on the campus," Olaf said with gratification. She leaned across the table and lowered her voice. "And, at this hour, the only doctors around are interns and residents. They wouldn't dare come in here, except with one of the big-shots."

Olaf took a sip before continuing.

"Rose, you gotta understand—half these doctors don't know enough to get outta the rain. Yeah, sure, they're brilliant, they've spent years in higher education, but they've got about as much common sense as a chimpanzee."

"Hmmph," Rose grunted. "Seems like a darn good arrangement for you."

"Darn right it is," Olaf said, and then sat back, deep into the couch. She reached into the breast pocket of her violet scrubs and pulled out a pack of Marlboros. She lit a cigarette and tossed the snuffed match over her shoulder. It landed somewhere in the shadows, where eventually a vacuum would find it during the next cleaning. Olaf rested her head back and gazed up at the ceiling, watching her gray smoke rise and drift lazily.

Rose sipped her second whiskey. It was going down smoother than the first, but it was still a struggle. What she held in her hand was probably something Donnelly would have approved of. She held the glass up, reflecting briefly on her hospital stay. It had been a miserable last couple of days: doctors probing her; Olaf making her life miserable; an uncomfortable bed; disgusting food; a nut job for a room-mate; and some sort of favor, or favors, she would eventually owe an Irish crime boss.

No one forced you into that car on Tuesday.

Rose swept the thought aside. She was intent on enjoying the moment. She turned her attention back to her host.

"Thanks, Margo. I really needed this."

Olaf waved a hand. She then leveled her gaze at Rose, a touch of sympathy swam in her eyes. What she said next took Rose by complete surprise.

"So, why'd you try and do it, Rose?"

Rose swallowed and then faked a coughing fit, trying to mask her shaking hands.

"Why'd I try and . . . and do what?" Rose stuttered, forcing a smile.

"I didn't just fall off the turnip truck, remember? I'm not like those two doctors of yours parading around in their white jackets with stethoscopes, trying to impress their peers."

Olaf glanced off to the right at an enormous, polished oak-framed portrait, twice the size of her kitchen table. Rose followed Olaf's gaze. She was surprised she had not seen it previously. Featured in the center of this portrait were Doctors Levesque and Lanzara. Lesser doctors of lesser pedigree appeared smaller, their diminutive images flanking the two virtuosos.

"Come on. Don't make me ask twice," Olaf said, returning to the topic Rose had hoped she had forgotten. "I know you a lot better than you think."

Rose quickly chose a defense: obfuscation.

"Well, then, you of all people know that accidents happen. Even old ladies like you and I can fuck up," Rose replied, and then proceeded to lay the blame on the cause her friends had surmised. "Heavy drinking, no rest the night before, you jump in your car and then it hits you. I ain't as young as I used to be. Sooner or later, your body is gonna collect its due." Rose shook her head and shrugged her shoulders. "Could've happened to anybody."

Eager to change the subject, Rose tickled her near-empty glass. "Say, how about another round of the good stuff."

"Why'd you try to kill yourself, Rose?" Olaf sat forward, placing her hands on her knees. "I was suspicious the moment I read that so-called accident report. Fatigue? Bullshit. Anyway, when I got off work the other day, I drove over to your place and snooped around your car, something the police apparently failed to do. I looked underneath and saw the hose running from a hole in the muffler into the cabin under the floorboard."

Rose shifted her attention to the bar, then the door. She fidgeted uneasily, all of a sudden wanting to be anywhere but this place. Shrinking to the size of an ant and scurrying into the leather couch would have been welcome.

"You even managed to glue strips of cloth around that hose to ensure that every particle of carbon monoxide found its way to your inviting nostrils, all the while taking care to conceal the material from a casual observer. No doubt, you did your homework."

Rose smirked. She held her hands out in front of her, joining her wrists, suggesting she was ready to be cuffed. "Nice work, Sherlock. You got me. Guilty as charged."

There was a long silence. Olaf got up, walked back to the bar and mixed two fresh drinks. She returned a few minutes later and handed Rose a full glass.

Olaf sat down, took a sip of her drink and closed her eyes. She allowed the whiskey to work its magic, as it coated the back of her throat. She then raised her eyes to Rose.

"I tried doing the same damn thing, Rose. Only I got a whole helluva lot closer than you, and there was no one rushing to my rescue."

Olaf glanced back at the same portrait of the St. Joseph's doctors before taking another sip. A smile creased folds of worn flesh. Across the coffee table, Rose remained defiantly silent, her arms folded across her barrel chest. Olaf broke the heavy silence.

"It was so many years ago that I've nearly lost count. The images are still there, but they grow fuzzier every year. His image is still there . . ." Olaf smiled broadly. "Ever notice, there's always a 'he' somewhere in the mix? What is it with men, anyhow?"

Rose shrugged and managed the faintest of smiles.

"His name was Dick Thomas," Olaf began. "I can still see that movie-star smile and his perfectly-combed, jet-black hair. Dick was tall, athletic, funny . . . beautiful." Her brown eyes sparkled from within caves of skin as she spoke. "Dick had a scholarship to play basketball at Pitt that coming fall. He was two years ahead of me in high school. Nowadays, it would be a death spike to romance, but not so back then. It wasn't uncommon that the boy and girl would overcome the tyranny of distance, which a faraway college presented. So, before leaving for Pitt, when he slipped a promise ring on my finger, I felt in my heart that one day, he'd be my husband."

A shadow passed over Olaf's face. She took a long sip and then set the glass down on the table in front of her. She sat back, pulling her arms close to her chest before continuing.

"He left for Pitt in August. Just before he boarded the Greyhound, he promised to send me a ticket to come visit. Said he needed a few weeks to settle in first. I believe his words were 'three weeks, tops.' Well, for the first two weeks, he nurtured the relationship. He called a couple of times, sent a few letters. Keep in mind, phone calls weren't cheap back then, as you may recall. He affirmed his pledge to bring me to Pitt, which, as far as I was concerned, might as well have been on another planet. I was ecstatic. I was in love. Knock-the-wind-out-of-you kind of love. Meanwhile, my mother said nothing. I believe she knew it would never last." Olaf paused. "And she was right. Eventually, the phone stopped ringing, and Max, our mail carrier, started showing up empty-handed. Maybe you can guess what had happened: Dick had found another girl. Some gal from Indiana, someone older, smarter and probably a lot prettier than me. A week or so later, I got one of those letters. What are they called? Dear Johns? Maybe it's Dear Jen."

"Dear Jane. We write Dear Johns, we get Dear Janes," Rose offered, sympathy having replaced the hostility in her tone.

"Yeah. One of those," Olaf grunted. "I was devastated. I cried for weeks. I wouldn't eat; I wouldn't attend mass with my parents; I wouldn't go out with my friends. I stopped trying at school and I quit the band. I decided that I couldn't live without Dick Thomas."

Olaf took another sip. Her drink was almost empty.

"Because I couldn't live without this 18-year-old boy, who seemed perfectly content to move on without me, I decided to end my life. And you know what? After coming to that conclusion, it was as if a weight had been lifted off my shoulders. I actually felt relieved." Olaf looked squarely at Rose. "I'm willing to bet that when you decided to do the same, you felt a similar sense of liberation."

Olaf noticed a nervous look on Rose's face. She dismissed it and continued.

"Late at night on October 31st, after my parents had gone off to bed and our street was clear of trick-or-treaters and pranksters, I snuck out the basement bulkhead, walked around to the side of our two-level home and retrieved the twelve feet of rope and the stepladder which I'd hidden behind some shrubs earlier in the day. I'd already worked the noose's knot real tight. There was no way my skinny neck was gonna slip through. All that was left for me to do was to secure the free-running end around the massive oak tree which sat on the side of our house, the opposite side of the house from my parents' room. There was no light there. No one would see me and, if all went according to plan, no one would hear me, either."

Olaf paused briefly, staring at the melting ice cubes in her drink. From where she sat, Rose could have sworn she saw the lounge's cozy lighting playing softly off what appeared to be the glistening of a tear in the corner of her eye.

Olaf sniffled. "So, I did it. I never hesitated. I secured the rope, took the five steps up to the top of the wooden ladder, and then swung the noose end over a thick branch some ten feet off the ground. Just before I stepped off, I remember thinking, 'I'll show him. He'll be sorry.'"

She drained her glass, the ice cubes tinkling, then placed it on the table. Both eyes glistened with fresh tears.

"People wonder what it's like to be dead . . . or what it's like to die. As soon as I stepped off, I felt death approaching. I felt it coming fast. A choking pain was soon replaced by an almost numbing, heavy pull. I felt my body beginning to drift, my vision narrowed to a pinprick of light as darkness washed over me."

Olaf wiped both eyes before continuing.

"Then, out of nowhere, I remember thinking, 'No! No! Wait. I don't want this!' I must've been kicking my legs and grabbing at the rope, though I can't say for sure. All my flailing did no good; I was a goner. As darkness consumed me, my final thoughts weren't with Dick: they were with my mother. How would she ever get over this? How selfish of me to commit my mother to such unthinkable suffering."

Rose studied Olaf's moist eyes. She wondered what long-buried pain had remained dormant for so long. She leaned in toward Olaf.

"My mother's sweet face was the image I owned when I took my last breath," Olaf said, as she put both hands to her face, wiping tears from both eyes. "Thank God in heaven the story doesn't end there."

"The branch holding the noose snapped. I don't remember hearing the snap or falling. All I remember is sometime later—seconds, maybe minutes—waking up on the lawn, the branch behind me and the noose loosened around my neck. At first, I couldn't figure out how I'd ended up outside in the cold, lying on the damp grass in my pajamas. When the realization of what I'd done—what I'd tried to do—hit me, I began to sob like a little girl, my face buried deep in the cool, moist grass. After a while, I pulled myself together and decided to pretend the whole thing never happened."

Olaf wiped her eyes and nose with the back of her hand and then looked back at Rose. "Did I mention that my dad had fought in the U.S. Army during the war?"

Rose shook her head.

"Well, this was several years later, but dad was still experiencing severe depression, which had started when he returned home. As a young girl, I remember that he rarely spoke and rarely slept. It was all my mother could do to nurture and care for him. Knowing that her only child had just tried to commit suicide would've ruined her. So, after crying it out on the lawn, I gathered up the rope, undid the noose, tossed the rope in the garbage and went back for the ladder. As far as I know, no one noticed a thing. If my mother ever saw the bruises on my neck, she never said as much. As it happened, I had a cop-out for that. But even if she suspected something, I doubt she'd have ever asked me. In those days, mental illness, or anything that resembled it, was a stigma. You didn't seek help, especially if you were first-generation Russian. And you never aired out your family's dirty laundry, especially not to some psych doc. Heck, you wouldn't take such troubles to the priest."

Rose grunted in agreement. Rose knew a thing or two about families that kept their mouths shut about internal business.

"I went to bed that night, woke up the next day and never once wondered about Dick again. I never lost a wink of sleep over him." Olaf paused. "And I never saw him again, either."

Olaf slipped a hand into her scrubs and extracted a pack of cigarettes. She offered one to Rose.

"Haven't had a cigarette in years, but why not." Rose took the pack and pulled one out.

Olaf drew out her lighter and flicked it, as Rose leaned over and took the proffered fire. The first drag gave her a buzz, before it induced calm as it joined forces with the whiskey. The smoke pleased Rose, as had her engagement with Olaf. Hours earlier, the ruthless nurse was an enemy, cunning and shrewd. But that seemed an eternity ago. Rose rested back on the couch, took another sip of her drink and a puff of her cigarette. She watched Olaf casually tap her ashes onto the plush carpet. Which, of course, made it okay.

"I was too ashamed to talk about my pain, so I hid it," Olaf continued. "My only concern was with my mother. For months, I worried that, somehow, she'd find out. That maybe she already knew. After all these years, I still have no idea if she did, but still I wonder."

Olaf paused and stared down at her empty glass. Rose thought to get up and replenish their drinks, but she was too drawn to the story to budge.

"As for my dad, his life was spent reliving the nightmare of war. It was all he could do to keep himself together. Working six days a week, attending church on Sundays, along with the occasional social event, while maintaining an image of strength to all around him must have been exhausting. He never complained, though. The bloodbaths of Normandy and the Bulge forever altered his psyche. I suppose the memories faded and, over time, the nightmares recurred less, but the cheery, fun-loving man who set sail for Europe that summer was gone forever. I figured my problems paled in comparison, so I left dad alone."

Olaf pulled her gaze up from the floor and smiled at Rose.

"Thankfully, my story doesn't end there. Years later, armed with a nursing degree, I left Scranton and moved down to Richmond, Virginia, where I met Stanley Olaf, a Russian immigrant, who spoke with a funny accent and who, to this day, remains the life of the party. It was love at first sight, though not the physical, superficial type. It was better. He made me laugh, and he kept me smiling. And when he told his heartfelt stories, something he does to this day, he brought tears of joy. In the end, Rose, I married my best friend."

Olaf smiled, drawing from perfect memory.

"A year into our marriage, I gave birth to our son, Jacob. Natalie, my beautiful daughter, came two years later. They're both grown up, married and have moved out West: Jake to California and Natalie to Arizona. They're far away from Stan and me, but they're happy. Which makes us happy. Naturally, we meddle, as any parents would. During our last visit, Jake's wife, Cheryl, announced that she was pregnant. Knowing Natalie—and how competitive she is with her older brother—I suspect we'll get her good news before long. Of course, that means more trips, more time with the ones we love."

Rose listened, watching Olaf's every move with a growing

deference. Nurse Olaf was one impressive woman. At that moment, Rose predicted the start of a lasting friendship.

"You know, Rose, it wasn't what I thought I wanted, or could've hoped to imagine at age sixteen, but thank God it's what I've got today. I've come to believe that life presents us with what we'd never imagined on our own, something we'd never have expected. I suppose that's how it happened with me."

"Congratulations to your son, Margo. You must be very proud," Rose offered. She snuffed out her cigarette in her glass, stood up and extended a hand toward Olaf's empty glass. "In the spirit of celebration, allow me."

Olaf accepted the offer. A few moments later, Rose returned with both drinks in hand. She walked back to the comfy couches, offering Olaf her drink before settling happily back into the plush, inviting leather. She took a slow sip.

I could really get used to this, she thought.

"So why did I tell you all that?" Olaf asked rhetorically. "Because whatever it was you thought you wanted, thought you needed, you probably didn't. Whatever his name is—and there's usually some guy involved—he ain't worth it. You don't need some asshole pulling you down." Olaf waved a hand, then sipped her drink. "If I may, what was his name?"

"Jack." Rose answered flatly. "He was my dad. He ruined my life."

Olaf looked on.

Rose squirmed in her seat. The very thought of her father made her highly uncomfortable.

She paused before speaking. "He made me wear hair curlers." Rose rolled an index finger in her hair. "You remember the kind that came in an ugly plastic box, the kind that were an absolute bitch to roll and even harder to remove?" Rose shook her head. "Anyway, I hated every minute of dealing with those fucking things. Rolling those twenty curlers—and I was told that I'd roll every last one of them—took me over an hour. But what was I to do? Little girls live to impress their dads. So until I began to see him for the monster he was, I made every attempt to impress him."

Rose leaned forward. There was an intensity in her eyes, as memories sharpened.

"So, why the curlers, you may ask? Well, that had to do with his lifelong obsession with Shirley Temple, an obsession handed down by his father, who was another bona fide prick. You see, when I was young, I actually looked a bit like Shirley Temple, except I had McDougal hair: straight and black. Might be hard to imagine today, but I was a cute little kid."

Rose leaned back and grinned. Before continuing, she took a sip from her glass. "But then, life happened. As I got older, I got taller and I got bigger, which was another McDougal quality, or curse, depending on how you look at it. By the time I was eleven, I was tall, bigger than all the boys and girls in the seventh grade, never mind those in my fifth-grade class. Overnight, I lost any element of 'cute.' My size, strength and athletic ability allowed me to excel at sports, especially softball. And while playing sports beat getting in trouble like the pretty girls did, I wasn't his image of a complete daughter: beautiful, sweet, obedient, feminine and athletic. I wasn't anything to behold, and I was certainly not someone he could showcase like a trophy. He pretended to take an interest in my sports, but the sonofabitch only critiqued me. He never demonstrated any true support. If I went four-for-five, he'd asked how I could've possibly made an out against such a weak pitcher. If I hit a double, he'd berate for my lack of speed, saying that I should've made it to third. My mother, who silently hated my dad, never went to any of my games. Only he went." Rose lowered her head drawing on painful memories. "I'll never forget him badgering me from the stands. The only voice I could hear was his: that pig-like squeal, loud and clear." Rose glared at the glass, disgust in her eyes. "God knows I hated that man."

"And that squealing voice?" Olaf submitted.

"Yeah, especially that squealing voice," Rose replied. She took a quick shot, finishing off what remained in her glass. Before she could ask, Olaf was up. She took Rose's glass for a refill. A moment later, the warm timbre of Diana Ross's soft, sweet midrange came from overhead speakers.

"Every story needs some sort of background music," Olaf said. "From what I've heard, this one may suit you."

"There's no denying that voice. You gotta love The Supremes," Rose said, before returning to the topic of her dad. "Know what the damn thing was about that squeal of his? And I mean it was a high-pitched squeal. The damn thing was that the asshole was six foot six! He sounded like a little bitch when he got pissed, which might've been funny to someone else, but it wasn't funny to me. The onset of that squeal always preceded some titanic tantrum."

"You said he 'was' six foot six," Olaf said interrupting Rose's thoughts. "You mean 'was' as in 'off to see the spirit in the sky'?"

Rose swigged from her refreshed glass. "Yup, the asshole is no longer among the living. He's dead. Worm food now." She raised her glass in a mock toast. "To the man who did nothing but sow misery and pain. My only wish is that he knows that he is positively not missed."

Olaf lifted her glass slightly before following Rose's lead and taking a sip of her own.

Rose broke into a coughing fit, when some of the whiskey slipped down the wrong pipe. She hammered her chest, which remedied the matter. "Excuse me . . . whoa . . ." Rose let the hacking fit run its course. "I'm not used to whiskey, let alone anything more than a beer or two." She coughed a final time and then rubber her mouth before continuing. "Sorry about that. Anyway, I got the word from Mom. She told me that he died at the Goldenrod up on York Beach. Know the place? It's somewhat of a tourist trap. They make taffy and it's usually packed in the summer."

Olaf nodded. "I know the Goldenrod. I love the place. When the kids still lived at home, Stan and I would take them to York Beach for two weeks every summer. York Beach was a magical place back then, especially for our kids, who loved the cold water, building sand castles and devouring the Goldenrod's saltwater taffy."

"I only hope that when he kicked the bucket the place was crowded and that spectators huddled around his cadaver to get a good look," Rose said, chuckling at her own twisted brand of humor.

"I think I know the answer, but I'll ask anyway. Did you go to the funeral?"

"Hell no. I didn't go. I didn't want to see the man ever again. Not even the satisfaction of seeing him pumped full of embalming fluid lying lifeless in a coffin would've been worth it. It would've taken a whole lot more than him choking to death for me to go. Still, mom begged me. Said it would be a good chance to catch up with cousins and aunts and uncles I hadn't seen in years. I told her I'd think about it, but never bothered to call and tell her no. You know, since I left Maine, I can count on one hand the times I've called or visited with my mom."

Olaf sat back.

"Mom became a passive spectator after I turned eleven. And when my Gramma died when I was fifteen, Mom checked out altogether." Rose paused and looked up at Olaf. "I didn't mention my grandmother, did I? She was the one person who stood up for me."

Rose swirled a finger in her drink, watching the melting ice cubes swim in a lazy circle. She would not resurrect the pain of Gramma Gannon's loss, not tonight. Working through the memory of her prick of a father was hard enough.

"But this isn't about her. It's about him," Rose said, refocusing on her dad. "I will never forgive the man. When I couldn't be what he wanted—cute, thin, cheery, athletic and obedient to a fault—he set out to destroy me. The more he laid into me, the more I ate. By age fifteen, the verbal abuse was a daily event and I put on quite a few pounds. It pissed him off to see me packing on the weight. Since I enjoyed riling him up, I ate more. By sixteen, I was a pretty big girl. By that point, swatting a softball was about all I could do well."

"Back to your mom for a second," Olaf began, with a pinched look of frustration on her face. "She stood by as he abused and tormented you?"

"Yes. More or less," Rose replied. "Unlike Gramma, my mother never took up for me. She was afraid of him. As far I know, he only hit her once. That was a day I'll never forget. It was such a petty thing. All she did was politely disagree with him." Rose looked down at her hands, which fidgeted in her lap. "We were at a Ho Jo's up in Limestone. We'd finished dinner and I wanted dessert. Go figure, a kid wanting to have dessert after dinner, huh?" Rose looked up at Olaf and grinned, then lowered her eyes before continuing. "Before I can finish even asking for the damn sundae, the asshole says no, never bothering to look at me. He said I didn't deserve it. Said I was getting too porky, or something like that. Well, that's where mom stepped in. She told him that I'd been doing well in school, finishing my chores and so on."

Rose looked up and saw concern spreading across Olaf's face. It seemed that Olaf knew exactly where this was going. Rose took a deep breath, looked up to the ceiling and then exhaled.

"He didn't hesitate. He spun in his seat and smacked her across the face. The sonofabitch hit her so hard that it drew a trickle of blood from her nose." Rose lowered her eyes back on Olaf. "It was humiliating for her. I remember watching her fight back the tears. From that moment on, she kept to herself, rarely spoke and stayed the hell away from him. She became absent."

"Hmph. A real tough guy. Beats his daughter and wife . . . and in public no less," Olaf said, her voice elevated. "I'll bet you couldn't wait to get out of there."

"Damn right I couldn't. Years later, immediately after graduation, I skipped town and headed out west. I ended up in a commune in Carmel, California, where I began living a life in squalor. I slept in a tent, smoked joints and bad-mouthed my country a little. Full disclosure, Margo, I only smoked weed, not the hard-core stuff like most of the others. Weed was enough."

Olaf interrupted her. "Didn't we all do those sorts of things back then, Rose? Hell, I was considered an old-timer and I still rolled the occasional jay. I sure as hell wasn't gonna miss that party," Olaf snorted. "Say, when was it you left for California again?"

"1962."

"Ah, nice. You got there early. You beat the rush." Olaf raised her glass in admiration. "Sorry. Please continue."

"So, while living at the commune, I meet this trust-fund kid, Thorton, a guilt-ridden product of some high-society family of industrialists from Sausalito. I fell in love with him. So much so that I even had images of settling down and raising a family with the guy. A month or so later, I catch him with another chick, and then another after that. Turns out he'd been banging half the female population there. And from what I recall, there were a lot of females living in those tents."

Rose sipped her whiskey before slipping her hand back into the bowl of Bugles.

"Anyway, Mr. Moneybags screwed me over, and so did his successor, some Argentinean who knew about five words of English. So, I left the commune and headed north to San Fran. Same thing happened with guy number three." Rose paused to address her hunger, tossing a few of the Bugles into her mouth. "All the while, I could see my dad's shit-eating grin, that pig-squeal reminded me over and over again how fat, useless and clueless I was. I could hear his voice in my head: 'No wonder they dumped you. Look at that ass of yours. You need a shoehorn to squeeze into those pants you wear.' Shit like that. Not even California was far enough away from his reach. I doubt anywhere would've been. After the third guy, I told myself that I was never gonna let another man get the best of me. To date, I've toed the line on that promise."

"No man since the guy in San Francisco?" Olaf asked.

"Nothing significant. After that third strike, I put aside the pursuit of love and signed on with Uncle Sugar. At age twenty-six, I set out to be all that I could be. I figured, what would be the most appalling career choice I could make, from my dad's perspective, that is."

Olaf started to laugh, slapping her chubby thighs. "You crack me up, Rose. You joined the army? And during the height of the war no less!"

"Not the height, no. This was toward the end of the conflict. The drawdown had already begun. But I wouldn't have cared if they had sent me over. I was looking for something risky."

"Really? What'd they do instead? Hand you an apron and stick you in the mess hall?" Olaf got up and poured new drinks for them both, then returned to her seat.

"Nope, not after I flattened my basic training classmates during pugil-stick training." Rose shook her head, remembering it all like it was yesterday. "Just before we graduated, our drill instructor pulled me aside and introduced me to a Special Forces sergeant who'd spent a couple of years in the bush wreaking havoc and killing Commies. Came home with three Purple Hearts and a couple of Bronze Stars, he did. His name was Sergeant First Class Ervin Jackson. Tough as nails was Erv, though I didn't dare call him by his first name."

"Not with a résumé like that, you didn't," Olaf said. "Your highness, or at least sir, might have been more fitting."

"Not sir. Not for someone who worked for a living, he'd remind us. He was Sergeant or just plain 'Sarge'. Anyway, Erv took a chance on me. He taught me photo reconnaissance, taught me how to sneak around in Indian country armed with a camera, a pistol, and an escape and evasion plan."

Olaf gave Rose a funny look. "Indian country?"

"Sorry, Army-speak. It means bad-guy territory. Anyhow, it turned out there were a few slots available for women to do photo recon under cover inside the Soviet bloc. For all I know, there may still be a few today. Erv instilled discipline and a little more toughness: I needed both. I stayed on for four years, but never went anywhere outside the States. All in all, it was a good gig. Sometimes, I wonder how things may have turned out if I'd have made a career of it." Rose grinned. "Then again, I was never much at taking orders."

"Little seems to have changed." Olaf smirked. "Yet through it all, you never could shake off your father's poisonous hold."

Rose shook her head and lowered it.

"Of course, he'd heard I'd made it through recon school, the first woman to do so since WWII, I might add. I sent just enough info on a post card to Mom, assuming she'd leave it laying around for him to find. I took satisfaction knowing that it had to piss him off to no end. Hell, maybe it contributed to his heart attack years later.

"When I left Fort Bragg, North Carolina, I moved up here. I didn't know what else to do. I got involved in teaching because the Army had also trained me to be a drill instructor, something I did during my final six months in uniform. I enjoyed teaching, but with only an associate's degree, it was nearly impossible to land a full-time gig. To make up for the shortage, I worked at a car wash during the summer." Rose shrugged her shoulders, then, feigning a smile, looked up at Olaf. "But lucky me, one day I'll have the honor of running an errand or two for a handsome Irishman. You met Mr. Donnelly the other night."

Olaf gave her a knowing nod. "I did and I suggest you steer clear of him. He's a dangerous man. He's nothing but trouble."

"The purpose of his visit was," Rose paused, considering her words, "let's just say, wasn't just to check on me. I'll leave it at that."

"Setting him aside, I'm not convinced teaching suits you best. I'll bet restaurant or office management, which pays much better, would make you happier. Given what you've shared, you strike me as a natural leader. You might think that you enjoy teaching, but just how happy have you been these last several years?"

Rose shrugged her shoulders. "Seriously? Managing a restaurant? I don't know the first thing about management, let alone restaurants. I am, however, a damned good teacher." She lowered her head and waved a hand. "Not that it matters now. I'm unemployed, with no hope of working anytime soon. Unless doing favors for a 'dangerous man', as you put it, equates to a job."

"Rose, the time for me to make my life-changing decision came to me in my teens. Your time to decide has arrived. You've got choices. Your time in the Army, though many years ago, can open doors to something rewarding. Doing the bidding of a mobster like Donnelly will land you in prison."

"I don't think you quite understand, Margo," Rose said. "Donnelly didn't come here for a discussion or to get my buy-in. He promised money, something that'll keep food in my fridge and my ass off the streets. I get it, he's dangerous, but I don't see anyone else lining up to help me get through the next few months."

Margo cut her off, smiled, and raised both hands to lighten the mood. "Listen, you're a resilient woman. Whatever arrangement you have with Donnelly, you'll find a way to keep it short. You'll find legitimate work, something rewarding. And as for that full-time teaching gig, you didn't need that damn job any more than I needed that eighteen-year-old jock with the perfect smile." Olaf tilted her head and paused for a moment, as a smile crept across her creased face. "Though that perfect smile also came with a nice, tight ass."

Olaf broke into a laugh and Rose joined in. They laughed for a while, enjoying the moment. Their laughter and newfound affinity were the brick and mortar of a freshly cemented friendship, one which would stand the test of trials yet to come.

After a moment, Olaf spoke again. "It took me years to get to where I am today. Despite my rugged exterior, the shell that most people see, I love who I am." She paused momentarily. "Sooner or later, you gotta let the hate of your dad go. I think that's what is holding you back." Olaf sipped the last of her whiskey and then shifted gears. "Do you pray?"

Olaf's question took her by surprise. It rekindled the image of the sign out in the parking lot. Rose was about to ask about that when she heard a door open and footfalls outside, somewhere in the hallway. Olaf heard it, too.

"Party's over, I guess?" Rose asked, gesturing to the door.

Olaf looked down at her watch and pressed a button to brighten the face.

"That outside? Nah. Five after four. My nurses upstairs don't shift change until eight. As for the doctors, unless they're prepping for a surgery, the earliest they show is seven. Probably just the cleaning crew, and they won't come in here this early." Olaf winked.

"So, we got a little more time, then?" Rose asked.

"We do indeed. Plus, I think a final round's in order, seeing that as of five minutes ago I'm officially off-duty."

"Count me in," Rose said.

"Let's call this round 'one for the road'—me going off-shift and you going home."

Chapter fifteen

Jim Budzko heard the crunch of gravel outside as a car entered the Dunstable House's back parking lot. He pushed the recliner's lever to the upright position, and then reached for the TV remote which sat on the coffee table in front of him. He pressed a button switching off game one of a doubleheader between the Red Sox and the visiting Indians. It was another meaningless game in another forgettable season. The annual "September slide" had begun in August when, after being swept by the Orioles in a four-game series, the Red Sox found themselves seven games behind the Yankees. It wasn't long before the Fenway Faithful were intoning the well-worn phrase: better luck next year.

He stood up and walked over to the living room window and cracked the window's blinds with two fingers. Bright sunshine entered his shadowy apartment. He turned his head away and rubbed his eyes to adjust to the light. He turned his head back and squinted through the crack in the blinds. It was Rose, just as Jim expected. She stood leaned over the opened passenger side window chatting with the cab driver. After their short discourse, she opened the back driver's side door and reached inside. She extracted a large paper bag. Printed on the bag was *Ron's IGA*. Holding the bag under her left arm arm, she shut the door with her hip. Jim heard her thank the driver. He then pulled his fingers from the blinds, immediately returning his apartment to its customary gloom.

He felt bad that he had been away when she had called earlier looking for a ride. He would have happily left his superintendent duties to go and pick her up. He had always liked Rose. She had never given him an ounce of trouble. She paid her rent on time and was always polite. But there was another reason he wished he had been around to take her call. Picking her up from the hospital would have given him a chance to have spoken to her sooner. Far more important than an exchange of pleasantries, there was something he needed to get off his chest. It was something that troubled him greatly, so much so that he hadn't slept a wink in two nights. Nor had he eaten. The very thought of food—of meat—made Jim sick.

The cab's speedy departure distracted him, pulling him from the disturbing memory of what had taken place two nights ago. He heard the shuffle of Rose's sneakers on the gravel outside. A moment later, the back door squeaked open. Heavy footfalls came next as she began her trek up the first of three flights of stairs. He stood listening until he could no longer make out her steps. He rubbed his left hand with his right, being careful not to apply too much pressure. He could rub only so long before the pain set in.

He desperately wanted to sprint out of his apartment and bound up the stairs behind her. He would welcome her home. He would ask if her stay in St. Joe's had been a pleasant one. She would smile and give an answer, appreciating his concern. Jim would then get to the point, addressing the matter which had his stomach tied in knots: the two men who had come to his apartment unannounced, two men who claimed to be her cousins. He would ask her if they made a habit of showing up unannounced at someone's apartment wielding weapons. He would ask her if this should concern him. He imagined her reaction, one which he so hoped to see.

She would slap her knee and laugh so hard that she would almost fall to the floor.

"Concerned about those two buffoons?! Are you kidding me?"

Thus relieved, he would sit silently as she explained away their intimidating presence as nothing to be taken seriously. She would go on to tell him that her cousins were aspiring actors who, though in their forties, kept alive the dream of making it to the silver screen and starring in a mobster blockbuster. She would go on to tell him that they dressed up like hit men, weapons and all, just about every day. There was nothing unusual about it. They dressed like that to their kids' dress recitals. They dressed like that when they went grocery shopping or when running any errand, she would add.

"Look, I know it's not normal," she would say in a comforting tone, before reminding him, *"but it's just an act. That's all."*

Jim would smile and nod, offering her examples of people he knew, even a few friends, who seemed to live their lives as if they were always on camera. Rose would nod. People like that were a dime a dozen, she would tell him. One could find them anywhere. Jim would thank her for her time. Reassured he had nothing to worry about, he would return to his apartment and get some much-needed sleep.

Jim took the final swig from the day's tenth beer. He shook his head wondering how he could have been so easily shaken. For the most part, the two men were harmless, no different than anyone else desperate for attention. Just two men who had not given up their Hollywood dreams. Two men playing make-believe. Their aggressive posture? Their threats? Just an act.

His more inquisitive subconscious mind begged to differ.

Just an act, huh? Two men show up unannounced and walk into my apartment uninvited, opening their coats to show me their pistol grips. Two men who claimed to be Rose's cousins, one who spoke with an Irish brogue, hand me an envelope to be delivered to her when she returns from the hospital. Two men who threaten me with physical pain should she not receive the full contents of said envelope. Two men who threaten more than just pain should I attempt to interfere with the important business they planned to conduct with Rose in the days ahead. These two men were just acting?

Jim ran four fingers through his hair. "Gotta get it together, Jimmy. Take a breath. Rose will have an explanation. She'll clear it all up."

He checked his watch. It was 3:50. He decided he would head up to her place in 30 minutes. The time would give him a chance to unwind some, maybe knock back another beer or two, perhaps a bite to eat. He closed his eyes and rubbed his left hand on his hip. Then again, he had no appetite. The mere thought of food—*of cooked meat*—repulsed him. He could handle a few more beers but decided against a snack. Before heading up to Rose's apartment, he needed a distraction.

He walked back into the living room and switched on the TV. Game one of the twin billing against the Indians had ended in a loss for the Sox. With the loss, they had fallen to third place and were now thirteen games behind the first-place Yankees. As Jim listened to the post-game recap, he watched as fans got up from their seats and made their way to the exits, some opening umbrellas as a heavy rain began. He wondered how many would be back for game two.

"Come back and watch them lose again and fall further behind the Yanks and get soaked in the process?" Jim said chuckling. "I'm sure they've all got more important things to do."

He was on his way back to the kitchen when it hit him: important things. *Important business.* Suddenly, the memory of the two men came roaring back in haunting clarity.

The younger, taller man with perfect black hair, the one who was clearly in charge, had promised important business with Rose in the days to come. He told Jim that he should expect to see a lot of "Mr. C", the shorter, comely looking man who stood next to him. Mr. C confirmed his boss's pledge with a nod. Then, in his own brogue, Mr. C warned Jim that if Rose did not receive the envelope and its contents that his jaw would be shattered so badly that he would spend the rest of his life sucking his meals through a straw.

As to the details of their future business with Rose, the two men offered little, only that it would be handled professionally. Mr. C advised Jim to keep to himself and ask no questions of Rose. "Our business with Rose is of no concern to you," the man in charge had said. And should he decide to interfere with their business, Mr. C had an answer: "You'll wish that you'd have never been born."

Then, the man in charge intervened. He led Jim into the kitchen and was directed to a seat at the table. The two men told Jim that they liked him. They told him that he seemed like an honest man, one who could be trusted to keep his mouth and stay the fuck out of their business with Rose. But how could they be sure, they wondered. In their line of work, sacrifices demonstrated loyalty. Jim was asked to make a small sacrifice, to give up something which would prove his loyalty. After ten minutes of negotiations, some of which was a series of pleas, he offered his sacrifice.

Before leaving the apartment and stepping out onto the parking lot and into the warm, muggy night, the man in charge walked up to Jim, coming to within six inches of his face. With his sharp blue eyes locked on Jim, he slipped his hand inside his coat and pulled something out. "If you disobey me, then I will find out and I will come back," he said. Eyes still on Jim, he reached down and took one of Jim's hands, opening it up and placing the Polaroid in its palm. "Your sacrifice is appreciated, but so was his. Unfortunately, he didn't remain loyal. This is what was left of him."

How many aspiring actors traipsed around with envelopes flush with cash? The answer was zero. Actors on TV or in the movies might have, but that was because they were only acting. It was make-believe. The two men who had come to visit Jim a few nights earlier were not actors. Their menacing presence and their threats were not make-believe. They were members of the Irish mob in Boston, a criminal network with expansion plans into northern New England, a criminal network with cops, politicians and a handful of judges on the payroll who would help make that happen.

In the end, Jim decided that he didn't want Rose to see him. He was ashamed. He didn't want to risk the chance that he might speak to her, even just to welcome her home. Eventually she would tell the two men that her landlord had delivered her letter. Having been in the hospital where she had certainly been given meds, it was possible that she was still feeling loopy, disoriented and subject to misinterpreting things, such as the details of a conversation. Mistaking whatever Jim might tell her and then reporting it to those two thugs could spell trouble for him. And that was something that he was not willing to leave to chance. So, at 4:20pm Jim pushed the thick envelope under Rose's door, knocked twice and then walked away down the dark hallway. He walked as fast as he could, creating distance between himself and Rose's apartment and the haunting photo of a dead man, cooked beyond recognition, the last man who defied Rose's 'cousin.' It was an image that he feared that he could never outrun.

Chapter sixteen

Rose slipped into a fresh t-shirt. It was lime green with white print. The front of the t-shirt displayed a bulldozer approaching a pile of rocks. Granite State Paving was printed above the bulldozer. On the back was the number 9. The t-shirt was her old softball jersey, which the paving company sponsored. Of her many tees, it was her favorite. Wearing it somehow made her feel accepted, welcomed. Ten years had passed since she played on that softball team, or any team for that matter. She missed playing softball and the easy camaraderie that it stimulated.

She decided on a pair of sweatpants, which she kept in her dresser's bottom drawer. She bent down and grabbed the drawer's knobs. She pulled, gentle at first and then a little harder. But to no avail. The drawer wouldn't budge. She tried shaking the drawer before pulling. Still no movement.

Frustrated, she lowered herself into a crouch, leaned her shoulder into the dresser, gripped the knobs and then yanked. The drawer exploded open, flying off its rails and sending sweatpants, socks and underwear across the bedroom floor and Rose onto her back. The impact with the floor knocked the wind out of her. Stars briefly danced in her eyes. She remained on her back for a minute, and then slowly sat upright. She shook her head and coughed.

"Damned thing," Rose mumbled.

The explosion of clothes created three separate piles, the largest of which contained two pairs of sweatpants. She leaned forward and fished out her grey pair. She shook out the sweatpants and stood up, nearly losing her balance as she did. She gripped the dresser and closed her eyes, taking the time to regain her balance. Margo had warned her about trying to rush through even the simplest of things for a few days. After three days laying immobile in bed, her strength had been zapped. Of course, Rose's need for recovery didn't stop Margo from insisting that the two of them meet up at The Stable for next week's Thirsty Thursday. "That gives you a week to sort yourself out," Margo had said. Naturally, Rose agreed. The one good thing that had come out of her stay at St. Joe's was her friendship with Margo Olaf.

Rose stepped into the sweatpants one leg at a time, leaning against the dresser for balance. That done, she slid into her flip-flops and walked into the kitchen. She loved her flip-flops. They were a perfect fit for her long feet. And on a hot, humid day, no other footwear would do.

She opened the refrigerator grabbed a can of Budweiser and set it on the counter. She reached back and pulled out packages of sliced ham and cheese as well as a jar of mustard. She placed the items next to the beer, and then opened her bread box. She popped the top of the Bud, took a swig of the cold beer. She took a second swig before making a sandwich. Whatever became of her ham and cheese on white, it would at least be edible. The same could not be said of the rubbish that Margo had so gleefully delivered to her bedside over the past few days. She smiled, as Margo again crossed her mind.

Talk about flipping the script. My mortal enemy one minute and, a few drinks later, my good friend the next.

As she sat down at the kitchen table to eat, she thought about that old dresser. It needed replacing. So too did the kitchen table, where she now sat. Rabbit ears and all, her TV, a relic from a bygone era, was on the way out. She needed a new recliner, or at least a chair of some sort to compliment her couch in what constituted her living room. Practically everything she owned needed to be replaced. *Yeah, so when is this shopping spree supposed to take place?* she wondered. One needed a job to replace dilapidated pieces of furniture.

While it was true she had no job, she now had a sizable chunk of cash, $5,000 to be exact. Stuffed into an envelope, the promised money had been slid under her front door while she was washing her face. She had heard two loud knocks, but by the time she got to the door, there was no one there. Rushing to get to the door, she hadn't noticed the envelope at first. It took her stepping on it and nearly twisting an ankle to discover it. The envelope was so swollen that she nearly twisted an ankle in the process.

The five grand was a mixed blessing. Holding it in her hand gave her a measure of comfort and security. But for the money, she would have been unable to pay this month's rent. At the same time, however, holding Donnelly's money made her anxious. To his credit, he had made good on his pledge to help her out. But she knew full well that it wouldn't be long before he came asking for her to run an errand. *More like errands with an 's,'* she thought. Errands which had something to do with her car, of that she was certain.

During his visit to her hospital room, the reference he made about her car seemed random, almost bizarre. Then came the letter she had just received. A piece of parchment paper had been wrapped around the 100 fifty dollar bills. On the paper was a typed note. The note included instructions on how the money was to be spent. Half of the note focused on her car.

> *Dear Rose,*
>
> *I hope this finds you well. As I told you, I'm only happy to help you get your life back on track. In your time of need, it's the right thing to do.*
>
> *The money will cover your rent, food and other associated living expenses for the next four months. $1,000 is to be set aside to ensure that your car remain operational. You will take your car to <u>Maffee's Garage ASAP</u>. You will have the <u>oil changed and the car tuned up</u>. If other repairs are needed, you will ask the mechanic to have them <u>immediately resolved</u>. He will fix them on the spot. Finally, whatever money remains is to be used as you see fit. Take some time to enjoy yourself. Get your mind off of your troubles for a while. Above all, rest up and regain your health.*
>
> *Until we meet again,*
>
> *PD*

Rose stood up and went to the refrigerator for her second beer. She popped the top and walked back to the kitchen table. She placed the beer next to the letter. She read the letter again, and then a third and fourth time. As if focusing most of his instructions on her car wasn't enough, Donnelly had felt the need to underline parts of it. More than that, he had written his vehicle maintenance diktats in a scolding tone, like she was some child who needed to be harangued into action.

She shook her head, folded the letter and then slipped it back into the envelope. She didn't like it. Initially just unusual, his repeated references to her car had become troubling.

She took a sip of her drink and closed her eyes. Setting her beer down gently on the counter, her mind began to spin with worries about Donnelly and what he had in store for her. What troubled her most was the unknown. While she had no idea what to expect, she knew for sure there would be danger. Would the danger involve drugs, weapons? Would the danger involve blackmail? An image of two faceless, Donnelly-guns-for-hire wiring her before meeting with a rival crime lord popped in her head. Other equally unnerving images came, as her imagination went into free fall. She needed to stem the turmoil inside her head. And fast. Left unchecked, the disturbing thoughts would cause a panic attack. She rubbed her temples, struggling to find a way to quiet the storm inside. Then it hit her. *Quiet the storm.*

Sergeant Ervin Jackson, the valorous Army Green Beret who taught her photo recon, offered a tactic designed to allay anxious thoughts: write them down.

"Ain't gonna be no time to find a shrink to clear your mind when you're on a mission, McDougal. Ain't no time outs, ain't no recess," Jackson had warned. Tapping his forehead, he continued, "When you need to quiet the mind, grab a notebook and pen and write down what troubles you. It'll clear your mind. It'll help you make sense so you can carry on."

She opened a drawer under the kitchen counter. Inside the drawer was her Yellow Pages phone book, an empty box of cheap cigars, a lighter, a Lotto ticket, a few pens and a notebook. She pulled out the notebook and a pen, and then began to write.

From the moment she had opened the envelope, she realized that the five grand he had given her was a business investment. It was seed money given to a newly acquired soldier, one who would be expected to earn it back and then some. Donnelly was far more than a gangster with a gun, he was the CEO of a criminal enterprise, a businessman at the core. He needed to be shrewd, deliberate and calculating when it came to his investments. Sure, five thousand might not have been much money for a guy like Donnelly, but he wasn't the type to write it off like some kind of charitable donation. An ambitious, competitive guy like Donnelly thrived on an expansion of wealth and influence. She scribbled a final sentence and then set the pen down.

So this is it. I am now a pawn in his game.

The knowledge of this fact did little to suppress the anxiety she felt before commencing her writing therapy session. If anything, her unease had grown.

But what am I supposed to do?

Fretting about the inevitable was a waste of her energy. She needed to come to grips that servitude to a dangerous man was in her future. As to when that would happen, she had no idea. Donnelly called the shots.

"Might as well live in the present and make the most of it," she said aloud.

She finished her beer, walked to the kitchen window and looked down on Canal Street. On the other side of Canal was the Nashua River, which flowed leisurely on the warm and sticky late summer evening. The waning rush-hour traffic allowed for other noises to compete for Rose's attention. Chirping birds, the rustle of oak leaves, canned laughter from a TV set in an apartment below and the dribble of a basketball all formed an impromptu evening chorus. Then from somewhere in the distance came the rumble of thunder.

"Not surprising on a muggy night like this," she said.

She leaned out the window. She craned her neck to the left. She could make out a corner of the illuminated sign above The Stable, one of her favorite hangouts and just a block away. She decided to head over for a few beers, and to spend some of the five thousand in a way that, as Donnelly had put it, Rose "saw fit." Deciding to go out made her feel better, somewhat in control. Her friend, Hank, owned the bar. It had been a while since she had seen him and it would be nice to catch up.

She walked back to the shoe box and took out a fifty-dollar bill. She crammed it into a pocket of her sweatpants. Fifty bucks was far more than she would need, but fifties were the only bills she had. Which reminded her, she needed to thank Jim Budzko for delivering the envelope. She walked into her bedroom, splashed on a little of her Poison cologne, all the rage with the female teens, before leaving.

Chapter seventeen

When Rose entered The Stable, distant lightning was splitting the night sky to the west and north, but the rain had yet to come. Twenty minutes later, a light rain began as the flashes of lightning became more frequent. Rose stood up to walk to the bar to get another beer. She had drunk her first one quickly, which was out of character for her. As she approached the bar, she spotted Hank, who was on his way into the kitchen. The Stable didn't have much of a menu, but Hank was smart enough to keep a handful of salty items like popcorn, pretzels and pizza at the ready. Such food made for more beer drinking, and more beer drinking built up Hank's coffers. Rose moved a stool so she could lean against the bar. She asked for a Pabst Blue Ribbon.

From behind the bar, an AM radio cracked and hissed, as lightning interrupted the WSMN post-game wrap-up. Despite pitcher Jim Herken's strong outing, the Pirates lost 2-0, their sixth loss in a row. Herken went the distance, notching his eighth complete game, but as had been the case all season, the offense sputtered.

"It's been that kind of year. When the pitching is solid, the hitting comes up empty," the WSMN broadcaster lamented. "At this point, the best we can hope for is fifth place."

Rose and the bartender, Ricky, looked up at the radio and shook their heads.

"But that means winning the final four games of the season," the broadcaster added, "No easy feat, especially when closing the season in Albany."

Lightning-induced static cut off whatever else he had to say. Ricky reached up and switched the radio off.

"That ain't happening. I got a better chance at making the Olympic synchronized swim team than the Pirates have at climbing out of last place," Rose said, turning back to Ricky who slid her second pint of PBR across the bar. She nodded her thanks as Hank walked out from the kitchen, a towel thrown over his shoulder.

"How 'bout our Pirates, Rose?" Hank asked, smirking.

Rose lifted her beer and offered a toast. "Here's to another lousy season, Coach."

Coach was Hank's nickname. Over the years, a number of his friends told him that he resembled the dim-witted, white-haired bartender from Cheers, who dithered behind the bar alongside Sam "Mayday" Malone. Hank liked the nickname, so it stuck.

"Excuse me, Coach." Rose drew back momentarily and suppressed a burp. "That one almost got away."

"Thanks for the decorum. Around here, that's hard to come by," he said, pointing at the drunk men shooting pool. One of the men was shouting something about dumb, blonde strippers.

Hank liked Rose the moment she had walked into his bar back in 1974. It was true that she could be a little rough around the edges, but she was honest. It was also true she had been in a fight in his bar a few years back. And it was true that she had started the fight, but only after what Rose said was a reasonable provocation. The man deserved the good old-fashioned whooping she rendered. Prior to the scuffle, Rose's opponent had been harassing Claire O'Brien, the spinster mother who had a 32-year-old challenged son, Frankie, still living at home. Rose's opponent had gone so far as to slap the glass of white wine from Claire's hand. That cowardly act was her trigger for action. In the end, the man suffered a broken nose and was forced to apologize before being shown the door.

Her choice to start a fight had been considered over-the-top to some who had witnessed it. But not to Hank. He felt that kicking that man's ass was more than appropriate. It was necessary. Having known her for many years, Hank knew that Rose had a soft spot for the weak and helpless.

Hank set another beer down in front of her and pushed a couple of bucks' worth of quarters across the bar.

"That one's on the house," he said, as he watched two young men wearing tank tops and shorts walk in. His bar was beginning to fill up. He liked that. Hank had learned that Nashua bars made their money in the "shoulder seasons"—fall and spring. The Cape and the Hampton Beach made their money in the summer; the ski resorts raked it in during the winter. So when a busy September night presented itself, he welcomed it with open arms. Don't stare a gift horse in the mouth, his father, a bar owner himself, always maintained. Hank looked back at Rose.

"Little hot outside tonight, ain't it?"

"More like stifling," she replied, fanning her shirt. She pointed to the quarters. "What're those for?"

"Mind juicing the 'box for me?"

"Not at all," Rose said, nodding.

She swept the coins into her open hand.

"I trust you with that jukebox, Rose," he said. "None of that rap music. You know I hate that crap."

Rose grinned. "Well, here's to wondering what songs I might choose."

"Is that right?"

"Well, lemme ask you. Do you like Blondie?"

"You mean Debbie Harry?" Hank asked.

"One in the same," Rose answered.

"Well, what's not to like? I mean, a beautiful face and a great ass." Hank pumped his fists and shook his hips.

"Grow up, Coach," Rose said, laughing. "Anyway, Debbie Harry sang the very first rap song."

Hank appeared confused. He squinted up to the ceiling before addressing Rose. "So Blondie is a *rap musician*?"

"No fooling you," Rose said, winking at him. She walked over to the jukebox and pumped in the quarters and dimes. Led Zeppelin's "Going to California" was the first to play. *So far, so good,* Hank thought. Led Zep was one of his favorites.

He watched Rose finish with the jukebox and then walk toward an empty table. As she sat, he wondered if she ever felt lonely, returning to an empty apartment every night. In Hank's experience, some people were better off remaining single, living their lives on their own terms. Being alone didn't necessarily equate to feeling lonely, he believed. In Rose's case, she seemed content being single. He always found her to be cheery, upbeat. But still he wondered. He had never seen her come in with a man, never heard her mention a date. *Has she ever had a boyfriend?* he wondered. Before he could give it any thought, he felt a soft tap on his shoulder.

"Are you ok, boss?" Ricky asked. He then pointed to the line which had formed in front of the bar. "I could use a hand."

Rose returned to her table, eased herself into her chair and sat back, soaking up the music. She took a sip of beer. Her thoughts turned to California and the dirty commune in Carmel which she had called home for nearly six years. It had been only eighteen years since she had left California, but it felt like an eternity.

Over the years, she wondered how things might have turned out if she had stayed. How things might have turned out if she had stayed with her boyfriend, Thorton Pressley, the trust-fund baby from Sausalito who possessed a contempt for his country and its long-standing institutions. Luckily for him, his money could outlast the draft. He could stay in school as long as necessary without having to flee to Canada in order to avoid Vietnam. While Rose was no fan of the Vietnam War, she had never ascribed to the ideologies of the revolutionary factions of the 1960s, many of which proclaimed their desire to topple the long-standing, traditional America institutions. Thorton, a true believer, believed violence was the only way to supplant the capitalist system with something, in his mind, more equitable. In the end, the differences between her and Thorton were too numerous to overcome. She wondered how he would have reacted had he discovered that she had left the commune to enlist in the Army. More than likely, he would have blown a gasket.

Rose took another sip of beer, her mind still on Thorton and what had become of him. She imagined him strung out in some pay-by-the-hour motel with a skanky hooker, his face buried in a mound of cocaine, while his wife, a thousand miles away in some tidy suburban neighborhood, shacked up with a 7-11 clerk who gave her the attention that Thorton didn't.

From a nearby table, a balding man with a thick moustache turned towards Rose and caught her glance. He smiled nervously before quickly returning to his wife, a mousy woman who was delicately sipping her beer. She noticed Rose looking back at her husband and gave Rose a critical look, then whispered something to him. Rose dully regarded her, figuring the woman's little secret had something to do with her clothes. Rose had become used to people looking at her disapprovingly. It rarely bothered her. She normally brushed it off.

Rose took another sip of beer, reached into her breast pocket and pulled out an El Producto cigar. Cigars were her second vice, one which she had acquired while pouring over Army manuals and cramming before written tests. She lit the cigar and leaned back, staring at the ceiling. The couple at the nearby table made her think about relationships. It was normally the man of the house who was the source of misery, just as it was with Rose's father. Men were the ones who started wars. When was the last time a woman started one? Cleopatra? Women were the victims of man's evil nature. Most women she knew were laydowns. They were weak, simply accepting their subordinate lot. Belittled by her father, Rose's mother had learned this the hard way.

Rose's ruminating on the past was cut short when she heard the bar's heavy wooden door open. The sound of howling wind came pouring in. The din of surrounding conversations was cut short. Only the voice of Robert Plant emanating from the jukebox could be heard. Three Nashua Pirates ballplayers—Jim Herken, a pitcher; Mike Ashcroft, the catcher; and Armando Benitez, the shortstop—walked in. Most of the patrons stopped what they were doing and turned their attention to the professional athletes. Armando, the attractive shortstop, seemed to garner the bulk of the attention.

Armando wore a white T-shirt, Girbaud jeans and black leather sandals. Flashy jewelry adorned his neck. His smile revealed brilliantly white teeth. He appeared jovial, yukking it up with his fellow teammates and accepting a hug from a young lady, who had cautiously approached him. He wore no wedding ring. Apparently, Benitez was no one's property.

Turning her attention away from the ballplayers, Rose took a puff of her cigar and exhaled a cloud of gray-purple smoke. The smoke drifted languidly towards the cheerless couple at the neighboring table. Miss Mousy wrinkled her nose as she waved a hand in front of her face. Rose winked at her, took another puff and then released a donut ring of smoke toward the ceiling. That was enough for the starchy duo. They grabbed their drinks and made their way to another table, as far away as they could go. Rose chuckled and leaned back in her seat, far enough back so that her shoulders rested against the dark-paneled wall.

Rose watched as the three ballplayers made their way to the bar. Many of bar's patrons stopped what they were doing and got up from their tables to shake their hands, clap them on the back or simply offer their well wishes. The players seemed to relish in their celebrity status. Rose turned her attention back to her beer and cigar. She reached for the cigar, took a puff and sent another cloud of smoke skyward. She grabbed her beer and leaned back in her seat, tilting back far enough so that her shoulders rested against the wall. As she swilled down the rest of her beer, she wondered exactly what it took to become a celebrity in a town like

Nashua.

A Double-A ballplayer playing ball in a big city could expect a life of relative anonymity. But Nashua was no big city. The three ballplayers, who now stood at the bar encircled by fans, would be recognized almost anywhere they went. This was especially true for Armando Benitez, the heartthrob shortstop who had spent five seasons with the Pirates.

Double-A ball didn't pay much, but it seemed to Rose that he enjoyed the perks: a flattering media and an adoring army of Nashua females. As a diehard Pirates fan who attended as many home games as she could, Rose watched how he charmed the press. He was a natural with any form of media, especially in front of a camera. Even though no one outside New Hampshire watched the ABC affiliate out of Manchester, it didn't matter. It was airtime. Along with Al Kaprelian, the whacky weatherman, Armando Benitez was a leading celeb in the state.

Chapter eighteen

"Benny, whatcha drinkin'?" Herken asked, using the shortstop's nickname, as he leaned against the bar while admiring a shapely brunette wearing a miniskirt and shooting pool. Benitez noticed her as well.

"Oh, you know," Benitez ogled her one last time and whistled, before turning back to Herken. "the usual: top-shelf rum. None of that cheap shit."

Hearing Benitez's voice, Hank wandered out of the kitchen. "You got it, Armando," Hank said, gesturing to Ricky to make it a double. "Tough loss tonight."

Benitez shrugged his shoulders and smiled. "Been that kinda season."

Coach Rogers had given them tomorrow off before their next series in Albany. A day off meant no strength training, no early-morning run. The three could stay out all night and spend the morning nursing hangovers if they so chose. An all-nighter sounded good to Armando. As he pondered an evening of barhopping, the heavy wooden door opened and Frankie O'Brien walked in.

Benitez recognized him instantly. He was the goofy guy who chased after foul balls and begged for autographs alongside boys who were young enough to be the doofus's own sons. He was no threat to Benitez, or any of the other ballplayers, but his antics were at best annoying and borderline disrespectful. Benitez recalled an event, a few weeks earlier, when he had barreled to the front of some line to score one of those ridiculous foam fingers. In the process, he knocked down a kid who could not have been a day over eight. The kid went off crying to his dad while the doofus snagged extra foam fingers. When ballpark security approached Mr. Doofus, he appeared scared and confused. He froze up. Security escorted him to the kid he knocked down. He offered the boy's father what appeared to be an apology, but Benitez didn't buy it. He wondered if the guy had some sort of mental deficiency, but didn't see the point of asking.

Who's gonna admit that they're retarded? Even if he had some kind of mental issue, Benitez didn't care for an adult-aged man who seemed to get off on knocking over helpless kids in order to get an autograph, a foul ball or a goddamned, fucking foam finger that could not have been worth more than fifty cents.

Benitez sneered at Mr. Doofus as he nervously walked in and stopped, his eyes wide and his head turning left to right. He was clearly out of place. But for his half-ass apology to the little boy, Benitez decided that he would have walked over and had a few words with him.

Instead of a confrontation, the shortstop walked over to the jukebox, slid in a dollar bill and selected a Terence Trent D'Arby tune; it was fourth in the queue. Benitez was a big fan of D'Arby, not only for his music, but for his sexual appetite. He had heard that TTD, as the artist preferred to be called, boasted about having sex with someone new every day.

Now that's a guy with some game.

Chapter nineteen

Frankie took two steps inside the noisy bar and stopped. Almost everyone he saw was drinking alcohol. That made him nervous. According to his mother, drinking alcohol resulted in bad behavior and troubles. Fist fights, car accidents and homelessness were but a few of the tragedies waiting those who overindulged. For Frankie, it was plain to see: many of The Stable's patrons could expect tough times ahead. In Frankie's mind, his mother was infallible and incapable of lying to him, which made her word the gospel truth. Armed with her wisdom, he wanted to tell everyone holding a beer or glass of wine or glass of whiskey to please stop. Alas, Frankie could never tell them all. But, as time allowed, he thought he might warn a few, but he needed to eat first. He checked his watch. His mother would be expecting him in an hour. It was time to order food.

He figured stopping at The Stable for a couple of hot dogs would end the growling in his stomach. Frankie hated when his stomach growled. It was embarrassing and made him feel like a little boy. He was not a little boy anymore and he sure didn't want any of the adults in The Stable to think so.

They're all drunk so they're not real adults, he thought.

Drunks could not be heroes, of that he was sure. But he was a hero, the nice reporter had even said so. The story that he wrote in the paper and what he watched on TV confirmed it. Little boys and drunks could never be heroes. Since he was neither a little boy or a drunk, that settled it.

As hungry as he was, however, he wasn't sure his mother would approve of him being here, not by himself anyway. Yet here he stood. Frankie pondered his dilemma for a moment: his need to eat versus being in a packed bar. In the end, he decided against going home and waking his mother, just to have her cook something for him.

Along with the rank smell of booze, Frankie smelled cigarettes, something else his mother constantly warned him about. A few men were shouting at the TV, some of their words were swears. Two women who stood by the pool table were drunk and wore very little clothing. They swayed on their feet. *Definitely drunk from alcohol,* Frankie thought. One of the women had her hand on some man's butt. She was slurring her words. The other woman, who wore a short strapless dress and looked trashy, winked at Frankie. It reminded him of that movie he watched as a young boy where the women winked at some man and lured him into her room to kill him with pills.

Frankie started to tremble, his smile began to fade. He desperately wanted to leave. He could fight off his hunger like a big boy, he told himself. He could leave the bar, avoid the seductive gaze of the trashy woman and eat tomorrow. He could skip a meal, just like a big boy would, he told himself. He almost left, almost walked right out the front door. Until he spotted his Nashua Pirate hero, Armando Benitez. That changed everything.

"Oh Jesus, that's all I need," Benitez mumbled, noticing Mr. Doofus from Holman Stadium smiling and waving a hand in his direction. Benitez nodded and waved back, then quickly turned his attention back to the jukebox and his music selections. He wanted nothing to do with the man-child, who had pissed him off more than once.

Hoping that Mr. Doofus would get the hint, Benitez turned his back to him. He then leaned down and pumped two quarters into the jukebox. He was scanning the records when he felt a finger tap his shoulder. Benitez didn't like to be touched, let alone tapped. He began to clench his fists, but kept his cool. Forcing a smile, he turned around to face Frankie.

"Hi, I'm Frankie! You're Armando Benitez and you play shortstop," Frankie announced. He was beaming. His body appeared to be trembling in excitement.

"Frankie, huh? You sure you're not Detective Colombo?" Benitez replied. He turned his back to Frankie, hoping a dose of sarcasm would end a meaningless exchange with a fan he could not stand.

"No, sir. I'm really Francis O'Brien, but everyone calls me Frankie. You can call me whatever you want because you're good at shortstop." The last part coming out as indiscernible, breath-less babble.

Benitez looked up to the ceiling and sighed. *Don't say anything. He'll get bored, run out of things to say and leave. Keep your mouth shut and wait him out.* He kept his back turned on Frankie and scanned for additional songs on the jukebox.

Frankie was undeterred. He had spent a lifetime speaking to people who had little interest in whatever he had to say. He never noticed their indifference, so he spoke freely. He was never capable of interpreting their evasion for what it was. He tapped Benitez on the shoulder again, this time harder. What he had to say was important and could not wait: it would help get the shortstop into the Major Leagues and on a life-sized poster, which Frankie would hang on a wall in his bedroom.

While Benitez concentrated on his sex hero, Rose finished the rest of her beer and burped, loud enough to catch the attention of a couple of uniformed mailmen sitting a few tables away. They looked at Rose and frowned before returning to their beers, bowl of pretzels and conversation.

"Sorry, guys," she said. "That one got away from me."

Rose frowned. She had always made an effort to comport herself like a proper woman, especially in public. She made a mental note to stifle any future belches using a napkin. Just then, lightning flashed through the bar's porthole windows causing Rose to jump in her seat. Thirty seconds later, thunder exploded and shook the bar's ceiling. A chorus of ooohs and aaahs followed. A bald, drunk guy holding a pool cue shouted "Hell, yeah!" The storm was minutes out. Moments later, the front door opened. In walked Frankie O'Brien. Rose was stunned.

Just what the hell is he doing in here without his mother?

That was all she needed to see. She decided it was time to go, and he would be going with her. The Stable was no place for Frankie. She would tell him to stay put for a moment while went and got her car. The drive back would give her a chance to thank him for saving her life. She walked up to the bar to pay her tab.

At the bar, she noticed Jim Herken, the Pirate's losing pitcher. She nodded at him; Herken nodded back. He then turned to Ricky asking for another round. Before he could draw the first pint, there was a shout, which was followed by laughter coming from a small crowd gathered near the jukebox. In the middle of that crowd was Frankie. Rose had waited too long to act.

Chapter twenty

Frankie tapped a third time. That was when the shortstop snapped. He spun on his heels and got nose-to-nose with Frankie. His fists were clenched and his eyes blazed. Frankie looked back at him, confused. The same fear Frankie felt when he entered The Stable began to resurface.

"Listen, Bendejo, if you don't walk out that door in three seconds, I'm going to throw you out myself!" Benitez declared.

Frankie shuffled back a few steps, one hand extended out. The other hand lifted toward his mouth so that he could chew on a few fingernails, a normal reaction when frightened. Stuttering was another one.

"I want . . . want to . . . to tell . . . you . . ."

Those who had heard Benitez shout began to gather around him and Frankie, sensing the likelihood of a fight. Never one to shun the attention, Benitez decided to showboat a little. He started to mock Frankie.

Benitez waved his arms around, wobbled on his feet and slurred his words. "You . . . you want . . . want . . ."

He heard the laughter around him, which spurred him on. "You want what? To tell me you're Mr. Doofus? Well, it's too late. I already call you that." More laughter, this time louder.

By then, Frankie was terrified. His eyes darted at the door. He wanted to escape, jump on his bike and pedal home to his mom. But he couldn't. There was a storm raging outside the bar. Unfortunately for Frankie, there was another storm brewing inside the bar. A group of drunk and mean men and women, who laughed and mocked him, were closing in. Soon, they had him circled. Frankie looked back at Benitez, who sneered at him and inched closer.

Frankie's eyes pleaded for mercy. All he wanted was a minute with his hero. *If only Mr. Benitez would listen and not be angry with me*, he thought. He wanted to help his hero hit better and make it to the Major Leagues. If only Benitez would take a minute to hear what Frankie had to say, then he would be happy and clap Frankie on the back. Maybe buy him a hot dog or give him an autograph. Frankie took a deep breath and tried again.

"Mister Ben . . . Mister Ben . . . Mister Benitez . . . You need . . . need to . . . to keep your shoulder . . ."

Benitez couldn't resist. He threw his hands up in the air and smiled. "Everyone hearing this? Listen carefully. I'm about to get hitting advice from this idiot here." He signaled Frankie to continue.

Meanwhile, the crowd gained a few more spectators. Rose was one of them. With some twenty patrons looking on, Frankie made a big mistake. He misinterpreted Benitez's mocking gesture as an invitation for a hands-on demonstration. Frankie walked up to him and placed a hand on his left shoulder. That was all it took.

Benitez spun on his heels, grabbed Frankie's hand and whipped him around. He thrust his left hand to Frankie's neck and squeezed. A muffled plea to stop was all Frankie could muster. Benitez wasn't finished. As hard as he could, he kicked the helpless Frankie in the ass. A rush of air escaped Frankie's lungs as he stumbled into two of the spectators, knocking their beers from their hands. They didn't seem to mind. They pushed him back into the circle's center. They were eager for more.

From the back of the circle of spectators, Rose watched the bullying unfold. She was infuriated by what she witnessed: a helpless man being humiliated by a professional athlete while grown men and women watched and cheered for more. She couldn't let it stand another minute.

She looked back toward the bar. Ricky, who had a line of patrons to serve, had his back to the action as he worked the taps. She couldn't find Hank. She figured he was probably in the kitchen. Music from the jukebox and the thunderstorm didn't help; both reduced the likelihood of either Ricky or Hank hearing the drunken cheers associated with Frankie's torment. It would be up to Rose to put an end to the shameful disgrace.

She tapped a few shoulders in front of her, in the hopes of getting up to the front. No one would budge. None wanted to give up their view of the fight. Rose decided on a more aggressive approach. She bumped her shoulder into the back of a man standing in front of her. The man turned around and scowled at Rose, telling her to get lost.

Dammit. He's gonna get his ass kicked if I don't get in there, Rose thought.

Getting to Frankie meant busting through the inner ranks. The polite approach wouldn't do a damn thing to help him. So she tucked in her arms, removed the cigar from her mouth, lowered her shoulder and then charged toward a six-inch gap between two men. She hit the two like a battering ram. One of the men flew out of his loafers, while the bigger one collided headlong into Benitez, who was sent crashing against the jukebox before landing on his ass.

What the fuck?

Benitez shook his head and blinked his eyes. He saw stars. His chest and butt groaned in protest as he pushed himself up to his knees. Sprawled out on the floor next to him was the man who had smashed into him. After colliding with Benitez, he had fallen onto a table, knocking it over and whacking his head on a chair before hitting the floor. The man moaned and rubbed his forehead. He was reaching for the chair's seat when a bolt of lightning lit up the sky. Benitez jumped, forgetting his aches and pains. A second later, an explosion of thunder, lingering for several seconds, drowned out the music. Benitez steadied himself, leaning against the jukebox for support, then turned back to the crowd.

He was met with encouraging eyes, eyes which pleaded for a resumption of the evening's entertainment. Two dozen spectators stared at Benitez, eager to swallow both him and Frankie back inside the fighting circle. Benitez spotted Frankie. His eyes showed fear, as he cowered next to a tall, large-framed woman. It was clear that Frankie wanted no part of it. Benitez began turning his attention back to the fawning onlookers when it hit him: that tall, large-framed woman. He snapped his gaze back on her.

Her, too?!

It was that strange woman he often saw at the ballpark, someone who frightened him the first time he saw her. She seemed to be constantly watching him, her penetrating eyes observing his every move. On one occasion, he spotted her during a game trying to blend in among the younger fans who were after an autograph. But like the retarded guy he was about to pummel, how could a woman her size blend in with a group of kids? She looked back at him with determination in her eyes. Benitez realized that he would now have to deal with her as well.

Rose pushed aside some woman who tried telling her this scrap was none of her business. She went straight for Benitez, who was leaning back against the jukebox, breath-less. What was left of Rose's cigar was back between her clenched teeth. It might have been stubby, but it was still functioning. She strode up to him and leaned down into his face. He squinted as the cigar smoke clouded his vision.

"Hey, asshole," Rose said. "You got a problem with Frankie, then you've got a problem with me."

Benitez stood erect. He slid against the jukebox and away from Rose. He forced a smile and sued for peace.

"No problemo, Senorita." He brushed at his shirt. He offered Rose his right hand. "Let's chalk this up to a misunderstanding, shall we?"

Rose looked him in the eyes, then regarded his hand. She was about to shake it when she remembered Frankie. She turned to find him. He was now sitting, his head buried in his hands. He was crying.

"You and I ain't square until you apologize to my friend over there, Benitez," she said, pointing at Frankie.

"Me apologize to him? Seriously?" Benitez shook his head and scanned the surrounding crowd. Groveling glances came in return.

"No way, Senorita," he said, poking a finger at Rose. "You go tell your retard friend over there that he is the one who owes me an apology."

Rose felt breath on her shoulder. She turned to find the pitcher, Jim Herken, less than a foot away. He then placed his throwing hand on Rose's shoulder and, with his syrupy-slow Southern accent, suggested that she "show a little courtesy and walk out that door" before she found herself "riding on the pain train."

Rose tilted her head to the right, eyeing the ringed fingers which rested on her shoulder. She dismissed it for a moment and then turned her gaze back on Benitez. A flash of lightning, briefly distracting a few of the bystanders, lit up the sky outside.

"I got no beef with your pal. Just you," she said. "Do him a favor and tell him to take a hike."

"Do *him* a favor? Oh really?"

Benitez chuckled and then crossed his arms. From outside came the low rumble of thunder.

She heard Herken softly chuckle before gripping her shoulder harder. Rose turned around, her eyes now burning. Slowly, she removed her cigar from her mouth, its hot end glowing red, and issued the pitcher a warning.

"You have exactly three seconds to get your hand off my shoulder."

Smiling arrogantly, Herken looked over at Armando and then scanned the rest of the crowd. "Oh yeah, what are you gonna—"

That was as far he got.

Moving like lightning, Rose grasped Herken by the throat, then forcefully mashed her cigar into the stunned man's open mouth. The business end of her stogie found his tongue. A sizzling sound announced the cigar's demise, but it had done its job. The pain was intense enough to elicit a high-pitched scream out of the big pitcher. He fell to the floor, his eyes closed tight. He could no longer speak, only moan.

"Ya fucking monstah!" a blonde woman from behind Rose shouted. She took a stride toward Rose, raised her glass of booze and splashed it across Rose's face.

Rose wiped her eyes with the palm of her hand. "That was a dumb thing to do," she announced. Her eyes blinked away the sting,

The blonde then spat on Rose, her loogie hitting Rose square on the nose.

"And that was even dumber, Missy." Rose rubbed off the loogie, then leaned down and snatched two beers from a nearby table.

Benitez was the first to fully retreat, as he noticed Rose's face turn a shade of purple. Standing at a safe distance, he held out his arms, his palms down, in a gesture indicating the need for calm.

Rose paid him little mind, instead focusing on the little blonde. As Rose raised her hand to strike, she felt a sharp tug from behind her. It was Mike Ashcroft, the Pirate catcher. he strode over to Rose. His breath came in wheezes.

"Ma'am . . . that's enough . . . I've never hit . . . hit a woman before, but I'm not above it. You've caused enough trouble here. I think . . . think it's time you leave."

He spoke aggressively, but his eyes displayed his true intent: he wanted calm restored in the crowded bar. He glanced down at Herken, who was propped up against a support beam in agony. Someone had brought him a pitcher of ice water, which he tried pouring slowly over his tongue. Most of the water ended up on his shirt and on the crotch of his jeans. His eyes watered and he whimpered through a swollen tongue with a sinister burn on its tip.

"I ain't going anywhere. Not until you—and your buddy over there," Rose gestured toward Benitez, "apologize to my friend, Frankie. And it needs to be sincere."

Ashcroft could not believe the nerve of the woman who stood in front of him barking out orders. Who gave her the right to decide the outcome of this mess? He was no longer interested in a truce. The sight of his pitiful friend sprawled out on the filthy bar floor pissed him off. But the nerve of this beast of a woman making her demands and challenging his manhood in front of a crowd, pissed him off more. He couldn't hold back. He took a wild swing at Rose.

He missed by a mile.

"Now that was stupid!" Rose barked and then struck the catcher across the bridge of his nose with one of the glasses of beer. The impact splintered the glass into shards, which cut Rose's left hand and Ashcroft's cheek and nose. The beer splashed into his wide-open eyes.

"Ahhh!" the catcher screamed, raising his hands to his face and rubbing his eyes feverishly. Blinded, he stumbled and then tripped over Herken's legs. He began a quick descent toward the beer-stained floor. Fortunately for him, a table slowed his plunge to the barroom floor. He landed without breaking bones, but his capacity to fight was gone. A couple of long-bearded bikers cheered for more fighting. A few more drunks joined the biker's chorus. Their cries for more stood in sharp contrast to the jukebox, which had begun a pleasant song about a groovy kind of love.

Benitez had seen enough. His friends had been reckless with that "big woman." Since they thought it necessary to lock horns with her, they could wallow in pain on the floor together. He hustled to the door, sparing them a fleeting thought before racing out into the downpour and into the back of an off-duty Yellow Cab.

Back inside, Hank had come running out from the kitchen when he heard a couple of drunks cheer loud enough after the second man had gone down. He surveyed the scene, one which he had gotten used to in his decades of running a bar that catered to Nashua's more rough-and-tumble crowd. This is exactly why you have liability insurance, his father maintained. As he had done at the conclusion of every fight and, just before calling the cops, Hank took charge. Two of his employees stood ready to help.

"Vinnie, help out these two," he said, gesturing to Herken and Ashcroft. "Brenda, the mop and broom, please."

Hank shook his head, hands on his hips, looking down on the two burly men who were being helped into chairs by a few of the more sober patrons.

No match for Rose, were you boys?

Someone found it fitting to play Lynyrd Skynyrd's "Gimme Three Steps" on the jukebox. That prompted some cheers. A boom of thunder outside brought on more.

"Okay, everyone. Show's over. Go back to doing what you were doing: shooting pool, dancing, telling lies to someone you're trying to take home. Nothing more to see here," Hank announced, and then added, "While you're at it, don't forget to tip your bartender . . . and, for God's sake, tip me. I own the damn joint."

Ernie Berube, a bar regular, booed, "Come on, Hank. That's the most excitement I've seen in this place in years. I missed the first guy getting decked. How about a redo?"

Berube laughed and elbowed his barstool neighbor, who stared blankly at his vodka tonic ignoring Berube's sophomoric sense of humor.

"I'm sure before you're dead, and I'm no longer cursed with your presence, you'll catch a few more fights, old man," Hank said, clapping is friend's shoulder.

Rose sat on a stool, just a few feet from the defeated ballplayers. She was winded. Her head lowered, she watched Brenda's broom sweep shattered glass into a neat pile. Rose's adrenaline rush had disappeared. Pain from her left hand, which she had wrapped in napkins, had begun to throb. Blood darkened the napkins in splotches. Her cuts needed stitches, but only if she decided to go to the ER. She thought about another beer but decided against it. Her downcast eyes caught the bottom of Hank's apron and the toes of his scuffed black shoes. She knew what was coming.

"I'm sure whatever those two said or did, they had it comin', right?" Hank spoke calmly, his voice lowered so that only Rose heard him. "Listen, a run-of-the-mill bar fight is nothing to get excited over. Want excitement? Try two years on a sub in the South Pacific and a steady diet of Japanese depth charges. Now that's excitement."

Rose remained silent, eyes fixed on the floor.

Hank continued. "I'm sure that your intentions were honorable, and I know this little display wasn't just for kicks."

Rose raised her head, a bead of sweat dropping from her nose. She found Hank looking down at her, a look of consternation on his face. She nodded and lowered her head again. Thunder rumbled gently and heavy rain fell, but the storm was winding down.

"Okay, so I didn't see any of this. Don't know who started it," Hank began. He turned and raised his voice, addressing the few remaining bystanders. "In fact, none of these folks saw much. None of them saw how it started, who said what and so on. Shit gets confusing in a crowded bar, ain't that right?" Head nods followed. "Naturally, none of them have anything to tell the cops." More head nods.

"I'll handle the cops." Hank looked down at Rose. "But your night in this little bar is over, my friend."

Rose nodded, her gaze still locked onto the floor. "Is Frankie still here?"

"No. He must have taken off after you flattened the second guy. I'm sure he'll be okay." He leaned closer to her and lowered his voice. "The cops'll be here any minute. And when they get here, it'll look awfully suspicious with two ballplayers sprawled out in pain while you tend to a bloody left hand." Hank cracked a smile and pulled out a dishrag from a back pocket. He handed it to her. "That must've been one vicious hook."

Rose shrugged. She was in no gloating mood. She took the proffered dishrag and stood up slowly, gripping the back of her chair for support. Her head pulsed. A headache, a real monster, was on its way. Her left hand now throbbed unmercifully. By the morning, it would thump like a bastard.

"Thanks, Hank. I owe you one." Her eyes were downcast. "A second one, I suppose."

"You owe me nothing. I know you took up for Frankie, just like you did for his mother. Despite the mess you made, your motive was honorable." He smiled. "But if you still insist on owing me anything, then stop by tomorrow and we can bitch about the Sox."

She smiled. He patted her on the back before heading back behind the bar to help out Ricky.

Chapter twenty-one

Whoop! Whoop! Whoop!

Rose smashed the snooze button, scratched her head and yawned.

"Damn thing," she mumbled.

She rolled back onto her side. A minute later, she was sound asleep. Seven minutes later, the alarm sprang to life. She smacked the snooze button again. She hit it a total of six times before finally sliding out of bed just before nine.

Yawning, she slipped into a pair of sweatpants and then stepped into her sneakers. She walked to the window and looked down on the morning landscape. White smoke puffed out from the tailpipes of cars stopped on Canal Street waiting for the light at the intersection with Main Street to change. Low, grey clouds hung in the sky above. The white smoke, grey skies and specks of drizzle on her window gave proof of a cold, damp morning.

She tugged open a drawer and pulled out a black sweatshirt. A white Maltese cross decorated the back. Below the cross was a listing of cities and dates. Written on the front, over a few Indian symbols, was *The Cult "Love."* She picked it up when The Cult came to play at the Orpheum in downtown Boston. The sweatshirt wouldn't provide much protection from the chill, but it wouldn't matter. She didn't plan on being outside for more than a few minutes. The need to satisfy her daily caffeine fix, one which only Dunkin Donuts coffee could fulfill, was the only reason she would leave her apartment on such a crummy day.

Though an unemployed school teacher, she was thankful to have enough money for her coffee and a couple of donuts in the morning, as well as a few beers and maybe a burger at night.

Provided she didn't go overboard, she had enough bread for the occasional evening of Bingo with Margo and Flo. Was it a life of leisure or even luxury? Not by any measure. Since returning from the hospital four weeks earlier, however, she had come to enjoy her daily routine. It wasn't exciting, but there was no stress, which suited her just fine.

Rose hustled across Canal Street back to the Dunstable House parking lot between a gap in the traffic. She carried a large cup of hot coffee in one hand and a bag of donuts in the other. The slick pavement made the crossing a challenge, but she was determined not to spill a drop of her coffee. She used to rely on the power of caffeine to give her that necessary boost allowing her to stay one step ahead of any disruptive student. Nowadays the caffeine served to keep awake long enough to make it through *Bowling For Dollars* before taking her midafternoon nap at around two.

She was a few steps from the Dunstable House back entrance when she remembered her winter coat. It was on the backseat of her car. She would need the coat tonight, so she turned and walked back out to the parking lot.

She had plans to meet Margo at Tortilla Flats for margaritas and tacos. It wasn't a long walk, eight or nine blocks, but she would need something heavier to combat the cold. The evening forecast called for heavy rain mixing with wet snow after dark.

"Not even Columbus Day and they're calling for snow. I swear one day I'm trading in all this snow and cold for warmth and sunshine," Rose mumbled, shaking her head as she placed the coffee and bag of donuts on top of her Impala.

She pulled her keys from her pocket and was reaching for the door handle when she heard footsteps approaching from behind. Startled, she spun around and raised her hands in front of her. She was pleasantly surprised at what she found—a short, dumpy man with rosy cheeks wearing a ski parka and a tweed Scally Cap.

He stood about ten feet away. His hands were tucked deep in his coat pockets, protected from the chill. He looked at Rose and smiled. She smiled back, any lingering fear having melted away. The man who stood in front of her looked a lot like Howard Cunningham from Happy Days, a show whose reruns she still watched. Then he spoke, sounding nothing like Richie's affable TV dad. He had an Irish brogue.

"Sorry, love. Didn't mean to scare ya." His soft eyes were fixed on her. "Patrick Donnelly sends his best."

In an instant, dizziness and nausea struck her like a sucker punch. Her stomach began to do cartwheels. As she lifted a hand to her mouth, she stumbled back against the driver's side door, grabbing the handle for balance. As if in a dream, Rose watched as the man took a few slow-motion steps toward her. His mouth moved, but she heard nothing.

Patrick Donnelly sends his best.

She shook her head. Her stomach flipped and growled. She was going to be sick. The man stepped closer. His face displaying concern. He gently placed a hand on her shoulder. His mouth moved, but again she heard nothing. She shook her head and held out a hand, pleading him to step back. She dropped to the pavement on her knees and barfed her guts empty. She leaned her head against the driver's side door, remaining in place as the nausea passed.

She spat residue of vomit onto the pavement, and then wiped her chin. She lifted her head slowly. Her vision was blurry. The man stood over her, his hand extended.

"Let me help you up, love," he said.

Rose reached for his hand. His grip was like a vise, not at all what she expected. He pulled her to her feet with ease.

Rose brushed her hands on her sweatpants.

"I'm sorry. I'm not sure what came over me. I never get sick like that. Maybe something I—"

His smile disappeared as he cut her off.

"Never mind that. Mr. Donnelly trusts that you're getting along well."

Rose felt the nausea creeping back.

"Well, yes. . . yes, I'm well. Please tell him that—"

"And he trusts you've taken care of your car." His eyes flicked toward her rusted Chevy. "I trust that's the case, yes?"

"I just took it . . . took it to check the tires and brakes. And, I had the oil . . . oil changed," Rose said, stuttering. She struggled to remember what else needed to be done. What she should have already had done. "Unfortunately, I haven't had a—"

"Had a chance to do what Mr. Donnelly asked you to do a month ago?"

"Oh, I will. Everything's running fine, but . . . but I promise I'll bring it to Maffee's tomorrow. And please tell Mr. Donnelly that if there's anything else he needs me to do, anything at all."

"Actually, there is," he said abruptly. "Mr. Donnelly is far too busy to tend to small affairs, as you can imagine, so he sent me here to ask ya for a small favor."

Favor. There was that dreaded word.

"Of course, sure . . . anything at all. Name it." Rose swallowed hard. She was doing her best to fight off the nausea.

"Wonderful," he said. There was a twinkle in his eyes. He gestured over his shoulder to a black Cadillac, parked across the parking lot. "I've got a dozen small boxes that need to be delivered up to Manchester in a jiffy. Will take you an hour, two hours tops."

"Sure thing. I can run them up sometime this afternoon. *Bowling For Dollars* comes on at noon," Rose smiled and shrugged her shoulders. "Call it a weakness of mine, but I'm addicted to that show."

The man shook his head slightly. "I'm afraid that won't do, love. The boxes need to be up in Manchester within the hour. Very much time-sensitive."

"Oh, well then . . . I . . . I suppose I should—"

"You should go to the back of my Cadillac and pull out those twelve boxes," he said. "Time-sensitive, remember?"

He reached into a coat pocket and pulled out a set of keys. With his eyes still on Rose, he raised the keys above his shoulder and pressed a button. From behind him came a popping sound as the trunk crept open. He smiled at Rose and nodded toward the Cadillac.

"There you go, love. Chop-chop."

A few minutes later, Rose was in her car. The engine was purring. The shaking and shimmying that had plagued the Chevy for years was gone. Warm air from vents on the dashboard blasted the windshield. The moisture on the windshield and windows had cleared enough to make driving safe. Rose was tuning the car's radio when the man suddenly appeared at her window startling her. She fought to control the shaking in her hands as she rolled down the window.

"Ok, three men will meet you at this address," the man said slipping her a folded piece of paper. He lifted his head and scanned the parking lot. "When you get there, you'll park your car, open the trunk and stand there. You do not speak to anyone. You will be told what to do."

Rose nodded, mentally walking through the instructions she had just received. She looked down at the folded paper in her right hand. She began to open it. Before she could, the man grabbed her arm. She looked up at him through big, round eyes.

"Not here," he said, staring at her. "Drive to the Howard Johnson Motel parking lot. Open it there, away from other cars.

Directions to your drop-off point begin at the Howard Johnson Motel."

She nodded. The fear in her eyes remained. "Yes . . . yes, sir."

The man took a step back from the window. His smile was back. He rubbed his hands and blew into them.

"You'll be back in a jiffy. Maybe in time for your bowling show." He chuckled, then turned serious. "So, have any questions?"

She swallowed. Yes, she had a question, one which had been eating her up from the moment he said the word boxes. She nearly kept the question to herself, something she should have done.

"Well, I couldn't help but notice a mailing and return address as well as a postmark on each box. Of course, that's none of my business," Rose said, forcing a smile and jabbing a thumb toward the back of the car. "Anyway, I'm curious as to what's inside those boxes."

A shadow passed across the man's face. The pause before he spoke felt like an eternity. He took a step closer and leaned forward.

"That is of no concern to you. What does concern you, however, is tomorrow. I will be back here," he said, pointing a finger to the pavement below, "tomorrow morning between ten and eleven. You will be in your car waiting before I arrive; your car will be running. From now on, you will refer to me as Mr. C. Do you understand everything I just told you?"

Rose nodded.

The man nodded back, a smile returned to his face. He took a few steps toward his car before stopping and turning back to Rose.

"Go ahead and make sure you're available every morning until I tell you otherwise."

He tipped his Scally cap to her. Then, he was gone.

Twenty minutes later, Rose was on Route 3 approaching Manchester. Gone from her mind was the question she had asked regarding the contents of the boxes and hostile response the man had given her. In place of her curiosity was a more pressing concern.

My God, what have I gotten myself into?

Chapter twenty-two

Jim Budzko sat at his kitchen table and gripped the phone, which still rested in its cradle. Between two fingers of his other hand, he held Officer John Callahan's card. He closed his eyes and rubbed his hand against his hip. He took a deep breath. Then, as he had done every day for the past two weeks, he mentally prepared for the conversation with Officer Callahan.

He would lay it all out for the cop. He would tell him about the night when the two armed men showed up at his apartment unannounced. He would save that report for last. He would begin by telling Callahan about the Scally cap-wearing thug, one of the two to pay him a visit. He had seen the man with Rose McDougal in his parking lot every morning for the past two weeks. He would tell Callahan about the boxes that were transferred from the trunk of the man's Cadillac into Rose's car. Naturally, like any good cop, Callahan would want details.

"Anything unusual about the boxes? Any markings? How many of them?" Callahan would ask.

"I watch from inside, so I can't really be sure. Some days he only brings a few; other days maybe ten, maybe more," Jim would say.

"And she drives off after the exchange?"

"Yes."

"To where?"

"I don't know."

"Ever consider striking up conversation with her? Maybe she'll come right out and tell you what she's been doing every day."

"Whatever it is, Officer, I'm sure it's illegal."

Jim would hear Callahan draw in a deep breath and then huff in frustration.

"I can't do much with supposition, Jim."

Jim didn't think the parking lot story would go very far, but the thugs showing up at his apartment for a surprise visit would. He would eagerly give Callahan the goods on that one.

First, he would go into detail on their threats, threats of physical pain should Jim utter a single word to the police about seeing either one of them around the Dunstable House in the days to come. And when they did come to his apartment building, he was to promptly open when they knocked and allow them the use of his phone, which had become routine. Before handing off the boxes to Rose, Mr. Scally cap, who Jim was to call Mr. C, would make a call. From the kitchen, Jim could only hear bits and pieces of what Mr. C was saying. Much of what he heard sounded like gibberish since it was likely in code. And if it was in code, Jim was certain that it was illicit business being discussed. Drugs? Very likely, and maybe worse. Jim would tell Callahan that before leaving his apartment, Mr. C always made a point to remind him of what happened to rats, to those who squealed to the police.

Real physical pain.

Jim imagined how the conclusion of the conversation with Officer Callahan would go. Callahan might commiserate, might offer Jim the promise of the occasional patrol car swinging by, but he could do little more. Like any good cop, he needed proof and evidence of wrongdoing. He needed to know what was being said on the phone and what was inside those boxes. That was evidence that Jim could not provide. But he did have proof of another crime, evidence linked to Mr. C and his partner.

Physical evidence.

Jim released his grip on the phone and wandered into the kitchen. Before grabbing a beer, Jim opened the freezer. In a Ziploc bag was his physical evidence, should he ever muster the courage to make that call. Inside that little plastic bag was his left thumb, severed by a meat cleaver.

Over the past several weeks it had turned a sickly shade of blue. It was right there waiting whenever he peeked in the freezer, which was often. "It is not to be removed," Mr. C instructed, adding that he would check on it every time he came by. Lonely and frozen in place, his thumb seemed to beg for company, perhaps a friend or two, which could be arranged. There were nine other plastic bags where that came from, the two men had warned. Go and rat to the police, Mr. C had said, and we'll fill up those bags quickly.

There would be no phone call today, Jim decided. Maybe tomorrow.

Her delivery locations were always in some dingy alley in downtown Manchester. The cardboard boxes she delivered were tightly wrapped with thick tape. Each possessed a mailing and return address as well as postage to make them appear genuine. On the off chance her trunk was ever searched by the police, they were simply packages she was sending to friends. Her instructions were simple: don't fuck with the boxes, drive the speed limit and not a one mile per hour over and, when making the transfer, never speak to the men you meet.

The three men in Manchester bore no resemblance to any run-of-the-mill businessmen Rose encountered. The men to whom she handed off the boxes did not wear suits and ties; they were not balding and portly, pasty-skinned and bespectacled, like the stream of men who walked on the sidewalk below her apartment on their way to Nashua Corporation or Digital. The men she rendezvoused with were unshaven and always looked pissed off. They struck her as the types she had seen lurking outside some of Nashua's seedier bars, the types of men who would fight over the most trivial of matters. The types who of men who owned rap sheets with offenses related to assault. The men she met rarely spoke. On most occasions, they grunted at her as they transferred the boxes from her trunk to the back of some dingy van.

Initially, Rose had considered asking Mr. C just how long her servitude was supposed to last. But after a few weeks he started handing her $50 for each delivery, she let it go. Donnelly's initial gift of $5000, which fed her and kept her in her apartment, along with the delivery stipend, had made the short period of time she spent in the presence of the three thugs almost tolerable. Extra spending money was good, so it never occurred to her to ask again about the contents of the boxes, nor did her curiosity tug at her hard enough to open one up herself. It would not be long before she would find out.

Chapter twenty-three

Rose accelerated as she turned left off Main Street and onto Canal Street. Horns honked and someone shouted a profanity, but Rose heard none of it. She increased her speed to forty-five miles per hour, despite being a block away. She glanced at the rearview mirror. When she looked back on the road ahead, she realized she was about to blow past the entrance to the Dunstable House parking lot. With both feet, she hammered the brake pedal. The brakes squealed and the car fish-tailed to the right and skidded to a stop inches behind a garbage truck. The driver of the car behind her laid on his horn and shook his fist at her. Rose checked her rearview mirror. The man's face was blood red. Spit flew from his mouth as he screamed. Since the windows of his Ford sedan were rolled up, only his young passenger had to suffer through the tirade.

"Jesus, that was close," Rose said.

But it wasn't the near miss with the garbage truck she was referring to. It was her brush with death in Manchester.

I shouldn't be here.

She shook out her hands and took a deep breath. The entrance to her parking lot was to her left, across the westbound lane of Canal Street. As she waited for a chance to cross the opposite lane, the trail of cars behind her began passing her on the right. Leading the way was the foulmouthed driver of the Citation. He made sure to slow down enough to lay on the horn and offer her two middle fingers. Rose paid him no mind as he passed. His empty threats paled in comparison to what had happened up in Manchester. A moment later, there was a gap in traffic. She released the brake and idled the short distance into the

Dunstable House parking lot. As she entered, she took a final look in the rearview mirror. No one followed.

Three hours after nearly being shot dead, Rose sat in her parked car. Her heart pounded in her chest. It felt like it could explode. She could not believe she had survived. If she had decided to lock her car, something she rarely did, then she would have been killed. She had defied one of Mr. C's orders, a very simple order not to speak to anyone.

How could I have been so stupid?

She had sworn to herself to never make eye contact with those men in Manchester, never mind striking up a conversation with them. Despite Mr. C's warning, she went ahead and did so anyway, going so far as to insult them. One of the men had become pissed off enough to draw his pistol and shoot at her. At least four times.

"Jesus, what was I thinking?" Rose dabbed sweat off her forehead.

The day's delivery had been no different from any previous delivery: go to the designated address (which was always an alley); deliver the boxes (or in this case, a single package) to the same bearded men; don't speak a word to them; do as you're instructed and then leave. The only difference with this delivery was her task to return with an envelope. When the leader of the three slapped her with it, she should have left and called Mr. C, figuring Donnelly would send one of his armed goons to go get the envelope. But that was too much to ask of the willful Rose McDougal. She felt it necessary to ask the three men if they had gotten the memo that beards were no longer in style. That didn't go over so well. The biggest of the three men, which placed him in the giant category, had pulled out a gun and began to count in broken English. That should have been her second clue to leave, to jump in her car and speed away. Rose ignored her instincts.

What the hell came over me?

The question wasn't necessary: she already knew the answer. When she looked into the eyes of the Russian thug, it wasn't him whom she saw. It was her father. It was her father she saw holding the gun hurling insults at her in front of the other two thugs, insulting her in a way her dad would have approved of. It was the memory of her father's ceaseless verbal abuse, his endless harangues highlighting her many perceived shortcomings. Though not planned, the routine delivery had morphed into a personal crusade, a chance for Rose to settle a score with a man long since dead.

Rose had parked her car near the opening of the alley where she was to link up with the three Russians. As they had done every day for the past two weeks, the men would come to her car and take the boxes to their van. However, today would be different. She had only one package to deliver. Today, there would be no boxes. In exchange for the package, they would hand her an envelope. When the transaction was completed, she was to return to her apartment and stay inside, never taking her eyes off the envelope until she met Mr. C the next day. Simple enough.

She checked her watch. It was almost two fifteen. She looked down at the package on the seat next to her. She got out of her car and walked to the back. She decided to wait where she could watch both the road ahead as well as the alley. She leaned forward and rested her hands on the trunk and waited.

And waited.

Her deliveries had typically lasted five minutes, and that included waiting two to three minutes before the Russians arrived at the designated transfer spot. Ten minutes had past and there was no sign of their van.

"Not like I got anything better to do," Rose mumbled under her breath.

She was about to go and pull a cigar out of her glovebox when she heard someone calling her from the alley. She knew right away it was the three Russian men. The accent gave them away. From somewhere deep in the alley, came a command delivered in broken English.

"You bring package here, big woman," he commanded.

Rose walked around her car and toward the alley, stopping at the entrance. She stood in the shadow of the two bricks which flanked either side of the alley. It felt a good ten degrees cooler than it had when she stepped out of her car and onto the street. About ten feet wide and at least one hundred feet long, the alley was dark and damp, as evidenced by what looked like patches of moss on the bricks. At its end, Rose made out the opening of another alley, which broke off to the left, into a deeper darkness.

There were four windows on each floor of both buildings. There may have been more, but four was all she could see. Even in daylight, the gloom was hard to penetrate. Thirty-two windows featured uninspiring views of the alley below. Of the thirty-two, light came from only three. Given the rundown appearance of the neighborhood, Rose assumed these were low-end apartment buildings she was looking at.

Yeah, no different than the shithole you call home, she silently told herself.

At the end of the alley, she noticed the vague outline of what appeared to a large metal box of some sort. It was black or dark blue, she wasn't sure which. She took steps into the alley, into a deeper shade. She squinted and made out the large, bright red letters on the front: BFI. It was a dumpster. Taking two more steps into the alley she could see a ring of trash bags in front of it and on both sides. Apparently lifting the dumpster's lid was too much for some of the residents. A detritus of newspapers, empty cans, food wrappers and other swill were scattered about. The amount of trash seemed to increase further into the alley. Just then she heard a sound of feet shuffling from somewhere ahead.

"Hello," Rose called out.

"Fat woman, get package," the same voice demanded.

She inched further into the alley and froze. She craned her neck to look into a doorway on the right, above of which a busted light was mounted. Nothing there. The voice came again, this time louder.

"You stupid? Get package."

The voice seemed to come from the smaller alley, which broke off at the end. From where she stood, she made out its shadowy entrance, but nothing more. It was time to exchange the package for the envelope and get the fuck home. She grunted and turned to walk back to get the package.

Fucking lunatics, she thought and shook her head.

She opened the passenger-side door and reached inside for the day's delivery: a package the size of a loaf of bread. She slammed the door and headed back into the alley, leaving the warmth of the sun. She walked about halfway down.

"Ok guys, let's get this over with," she said, her voice echoing off of the brick buildings which surrounded her.

A few seconds later she heard the same sound of shuffling feet, this time louder. Then, emerging from the small alley which branched off to the left came the three Russians. The walked in her direction. Not that she had ever seen them smile, but today they looked particularly agitated.

If they wanna hurl insults, then I can play that game.

The leader of the group, the biggest of the three, led the way. He walked to within six feet of Rose. From behind him, one took up a position to his left and the other to his right. Arms folded, the black-haired, burly and bearded men formed an impenetrable wall, well over six feet high. The leader unfolded his arms and pulled out an envelope from inside his coat. He dangled it in front of her and began to smile. Rose swallowed and inched back.

"No need for games, guys. Let's just do this," she said, fighting back the quiver in her voice.

The leader turned to the man on his left. "Maybe we take package from fat lady and keep envelope, yes?"

All three laughed.

"I don't think Mr. C would approve," Rose said suppressing the tremble in her voice.

"I don't give shit about that fat man or you, fat woman." More laughter from the other two. He waved the envelope in front of her face.

Rose felt the breeze from the envelope. His mocking gesture and the continued insults began to overwhelm her fear. In its place came a surge of hate and rage, the type of hate she had only felt for her father. Until now. But as pissed off as she had become, she was damned sure going to do her best to hide it. She needed to get that envelope. Since he wasn't about to give it up freely, she had to find a way to get it herself. That meant keeping cool and curbing the hostility.

She smiled and, at her own expense, pretended to laugh along with them in a measure of self-deprecation. She patted her belly with one hand and shrugged her shoulders, which garnered laughter from the three men.

"What can I say? Fast food is addictive," she said. She shook her head and patted her belly again. More laughter followed.

With her eyes still on the men in front of her, she bent her knees and placed the package on the ground between her and the Russian leader.

"Now, that's yours. Fair and square," Rose said pointing to the package. "We don't want trouble with Mr. C or Donnelly, so I'm going to need that envelope."

The men looked at each other and then, in unison, they looked at Rose, sneering at her. The leader took a step toward her. He extended his left hand and slapped her face with the envelope, slapping hard enough to leave a mark. The others laughed, as the leader pulled the envelope back and held it close to his chest.

"This stay with me, fat woman. I keep package and envelope." He inched closer and pointed to the end of the alley. "You leave now before you get hurt."

Rose saw red. She balled up her fists. She wanted to break his nose and watch his blood gush like a toppled fire hydrant onto the filthy pavement. She wanted to humiliate him, just as he had done to her. But she couldn't. Hitting one asshole meant dealing with the other two, both of whom would be ready to tear her to pieces. Meanwhile, the leader of the three gorillas wasn't done with her.

"Maybe you go to drive thru," he said gesturing to her stomach. "I can see you do drive thru, yes?"

All three laughed.

That did it. She had heard enough. She was done fucking around with them.

"Gentlemen, and I use that term loosely, it appears you have a problem. Well, actually you have two problems." She shook her head and continued in a condescending tone. "First, that envelope in your filthy mitt—mitt equals hand, by the way—is for me. That means I leave with it. Second, didn't you men get the memo on beards? They're no longer in vogue."

She looked at each individually, then folded her arms. "Are we clear?"

The leader was not impressed. His face had turned beet red. He tried more insults but stuttered so badly that he couldn't piece the words together in a way that could be understood.

Rose clapped her hands and congratulated him on his command of the English language, going so far as to suggest he pursue a career in film, just like Yakov Smirnoff, the goofy Russian actor who laughed like a donkey.

"Keep brushing up your English," Rose said jeeringly, "'What a great country!' Right, Yakov?"

All the while, he mumbled silently through gritted teeth. His black eyes swam in hate and his red face boiled. He turned his head to the left, finding an equal measure of hostility in his mate's eyes. Rose heard the crumple of the envelope in his grip. Slowly he turned his head to the right. As he did, she saw an opening.

She lunged toward him, snatched the envelope from his hand and jumped a few steps back, increasing her chance for a clean escape.

"Look at this," she said, holding the envelope in front of her. "Now we're even, asshole."

The man was stunned. He looked down at his empty left hand in disbelief, unable to believe that he had been bested by a woman. His mouth moved, but no words came out. His eyes shifted back and forth between his left hand and the envelope which Rose now held. But his shock was short-lived. In its place came rage, stronger than ever.

"Fat and ugly woman, you make big mistake." He unzipped his jacket exposing the butt end of a revolver.

Rose's heart began to hammer in her chest. She had taken it

too far. She began to inch backward, her eyes darting left to right. Slowly she turned her head looking down the alley toward daylight and safety. She saw no one walk by on the short stretch of sidewalk, nor did she see a car pass in either direction on the street. She moved her head back to face the monsters.

As if in a trance, she watched as the leader extracted his revolver, a Smith and Wesson .38 with a wooden grip. The polished grip shimmered in the alley's gloom. He held the gun by his side and began to count, edging closer to her. She trudged backward, her feet as heavy as cinderblocks. When his counting ended at ten, he cocked the hammer of his pistol and raised it. The other two pulled out their guns and approached Rose from both sides.

She had no weapon, not that it would have mattered. She was outnumbered by men who probably killed for sport. Without thinking, she slipped the envelope inside her T-shirt wedging it under her bra.

"Tell me, you ready to die, fat and ugly woman? Yes?" the leader asked. The other two stopped, raised their pistols and edged closer to their boss. "Because I'm good man, I give you three steps, like that song say. Three steps to door. Eh, fat woman, three steps, yes?"

As Rose was inching backward, her foot brushed up against something hard and big. She looked down and found a rock the size of a baseball, maybe bigger. How it ended up in a stinking alley didn't matter, but the fact that the misplaced stone might be her last hope did. Getting to it would require a distraction.

Faking a dizzy spell, Rose stopped and began to swoon. She bent her knees slightly, closed her eyes and raised a hand to her forehead to complete the ruse.

"What's matter, fat woman? No lunch today?"

The three men laughed. As they did, Rose watched the leader lower his pistol as he acknowledged the approving laughter of his comrades. With his pistol lowered and his focus on her distracted, she needed to act.

Rose slowly lowered her right hand and grabbed the stone, gripping it tight. Before the men could register her move, she raised her hand and hurled a perfect strike hitting the leader square on the nose. There was a cracking sound, followed by an impressive flow of blood. From somewhere in her subconscious, Sergeant Ervin Jackson shouted an order:

"No time to admire your handiwork, McDougal. You ain't that fast. Pick up your feet and run!"

She turned and sprinted down the alley toward the street, never looking back. From behind her, she heard cries of pain followed by the cocking of pistols. She was panting heavily as she raced around the front bumper and lunged for the door handle. Her hands shook. She was struggling to get the keys out of her pocket when she felt an explosion of hot air next to her right ear and the crack of a bullet. Immediately, a second and third shot came, both just as close.

"Jesus! They're *really* trying to kill me!" she cried. She fought like hell to get the door open, but it wouldn't budge.

"Goddamned door!"

Her heart leapt into her mouth and her hands shook. If she didn't get it open in the next two seconds, she would be shot dead. Her adrenaline surging, she yanked the door opened, dove inside and crammed the key into the ignition. She turned it and the engine sprang to life. The fourth shot missed high. It struck a car parked across the street. Rose ducked below the dash, the envelope pinching her breast as she dropped the Chevy into drive. She hammered the gas, keeping her head below the dash. She clipped the parked car in front of her.

"Fuck!"

She lifted her head and steadied the car. She shot a glance into the rearview mirror. The three men were in the middle of the street. One was bent over, his hands resting on his knees. The other two had their weapons aimed at her car. Rose was still close enough to be killed. And they might have done just that had it not been for a kid on a skateboard, oblivious to the gunfire.

The Chevy fought hard to comply with her plea for more speed. She tilted her head in an attempt to minimize the chance of a head shot, which would kill her instantly. She shot another glance at the rearview mirror. She was shocked at what she saw. In the middle of the road between her and the men trying to kill her was a teen-aged boy holding a Walkman and riding a skateboard. He was ignorant of what was going on around him. His eyes appeared closed as he bobbed his head in tune with the music blaring through his earphones. Behind him, the Russians waved and shouted at him to get out of the way.

But the skateboarding dude heard none of their demands. He kept with the beat of his tunes and maintained his course down the middle of the street. Unknowingly, he saved the life of Rose McDougal.

Chapter twenty-four

Six days after her brush with death, Rose sat on her new recliner watching reruns of the Andy Griffith Show on her new twenty-four-inch color TV. Its picture was superb. In her lap sat a bowl of popcorn. A can of Coors, to wash down the buttery treat, rested on an end table next to her. Her left hand held the TV's remote control, while her right hand delivered popcorn from the bowl to her mouth.

Outside her apartment, the last trace of daylight had just disappeared. The past five days had been warm and dry with temperatures around 80 degrees. The long-range forecast called for much the same. Her window had remained open for nearly a week, allowing Rose to savor the balmy days and gentle evening breezes. From the large oak trees on the Dunstable House lawn came the sundown chorus of whistling bobwhites. She turned her attention to the open window, watching the silhouettes of the oaks as they began to sway in the breeze. She heard the soft rustle of leaves, those which had yet to fall, then felt the cool breeze on her face. She smiled.

To savor the moment, she reached down and pulled the wooden lever. The recliner tilted back another few inches. *Perfect,* she thought. She clicked the mute button on the remote control and leaned her head back, closing her eyes as she did.

Back in Mayberry, the dim-witted Gomer Pyle whistled a cheery tune as he pumped fuel into Deputy Fife's patrol car. Like Pyle, Rose didn't have a care in the world. Unlike the industrious Pyle, however, Rose hadn't worked a lick since nearly having her head taken off by a .38 caliber round. Since that harrowing day, there had been no parking lot rendezvouses. Which meant no deliveries. Life had been good to Rose McDougal for the past several days. The long stretch of Indian Summer and her color TV had made life even better.

She was on the verge of sleep when she heard the sound of a click behind her. The faint sound of footsteps followed. The footsteps were nearly inaudible. Only in the absolute silence could Rose have heard them. After a few seconds, the sound of footsteps stopped. Rose assumed the sounds came from out in the hallway, so she dismissed it.

"Someone stepping out on this beautiful night for an evening stroll," she said. She grabbed another handful of popcorn, then wolfed it down. She checked the clock on the wall. "Maybe I'll take one myself, maybe wander down to The Stable."

She adjusted the recliner to a position more suitable for eating, and less conducive to choking, and turned her attention back to the TV. She was reaching down for her beer when she heard a second click, this time louder. A few seconds later came the creak of footsteps, this time even louder. The click and footsteps did not come from out in the hallway, of that Rose was certain. They came from somewhere inside her apartment. She held her breath and slowly began to reach for the recliner's lever. Before she could, a voice greeted her. It was a voice she had not heard in weeks, one she had hoped to never hear again.

"Good evening, love," Donnelly said. His voice was just above a whisper. "How are you getting along?"

Rose froze. She opened her mouth to answer but couldn't speak. She heard the soft whoosh of his slacks as he stopped behind the recliner. The cushion above her head sunk as he placed his hands on the top of the recliner, causing the recliner to tilt slightly. She didn't dare turn to face him.

"Too excited to form the words?" he asked, then chuckled softly.

She felt his weight come off the top of the recliner as he pulled his hands away. Immediately the recliner jerked up to its original position. He came around from behind the recliner, the swoosh of his slacks preceding his appearance. A second later, he stood before her.

He wore a perfectly altered black suit, a light blue shirt and a solid navy tie. His hair was perfect, slicked back and glimmering from light cast from a lamp in the corner. The light accentuated the shine of his polished black shoes. In his hand he held over a dozen bright red roses. He held them out in front of him, smiling as he did. They were as pretty as any Rose had ever seen. The roses, his slouched shoulders and an easy smile lessened her anxiety.

"These are for you, love," he said.

He took a step closer and handed them to her. She pulled them to her nose. Not only beautiful, the bouquet possessed an enchanting, almost intoxicating, fragrance.

"These are just . . ." Rose looked up at Donnelly, then back at the eighteen roses. She brought them back up to her nose. "just magical. I've never seen flowers like this."

"Roses for my Rose," Donnelly said, winking at her. He gestured to the couch, which was a few steps away.

Rose looked up at him. She felt somewhat disoriented, almost like being in a dream. Donnelly leaned toward her, his hands folded over his waist.

"May I sit?" he asked.

She shook her head and snapped out of her momentary trance. "Oh, sorry. Umm, yeah. I mean yes, of course."

From down on Canal Street came the blaring of two car horns, followed by the angry shouting of vulgarities by one of the drivers.

Rose watched as Donnelly frowned and shook his head. He then looked at her with a look of disappointment. He got up and walked to the window.

"You know, some people never learn manners." He looked out the open window. "There's no reason to spoil a blissful October evening with such crude language."

Rose rested the flowers on the end table next to her. She reached for her beer and looked back at Donnelly.

"I'm sorry, Mr. Donnelly. Where are my manners?" She held up her half empty bottle. "Can I offer you one?"

"Thank you, but no," Donnelly said, shaking his head. "And please, call me Patrick."

Rose regarded her beer for a moment. It was half full, still cold and Coors was one of her favorites. Even so, she wasn't about to imbibe if her employer wouldn't.

"So, doing ok, love? Enjoying the break from work?" he asked, as he continued to watch the traffic.

"I do appreciate the break," she said. "I feel rested for the first time in a long time."

And I'd feel even better if you could extend this break of mine. Just don't stop sending me my allowance. I don't want to get off this gravy train just yet, she thought, wisely keeping those sentiments to herself.

Her heart raced as she watched his hands, waiting for one of them to dive swiftly into his jacket and extract a silenced weapon.

If he did, it would all be over in a split-second. Which might be better since she would not feel a thing. He was no more than eight feet away, plenty close for an experienced killer. She kept her eyes locked on him. He stood like a statue, hands folded behind his back. Eventually, he spoke.

"Believe it or not, I like that moxie of yours." He looked over his shoulder at her. She thought that she saw him smile, before turning his gaze back on the scene outside.

"As long as you remember who's boss and as long as you refrain from the wisecracks when you need to. In this casual setting, your juvenile brand of wit is almost refreshing."

Rose was confused. A minute ago, she was sure he was going to pull out a silenced weapon and pump a round into her brain. A minute later, he's complimenting her sense of humor.

Talk about Dr. Jekyll and Mr. Hyde.

He stood motionless for what seemed like an eternity. When he finally turned to her, Rose heard a gasp escape her throat. He casually walked back toward the recliner and cut off the volume on the TV before reclaiming his spot on the couch. As he settled onto the couch, Rose slipped her hands under the bouquet and between her legs.

"I'm impressed with how well you handled yourself last week."

He wasn't looking for a reply. Rose merely nodded. She began to rub her hands together, hoping that he wouldn't notice.

"Having the wits about you under fire to safeguard the money is impressive."

Rose slowed the fidgeting with her hands. She thought to ask how he knew such things, but she already knew the answer. Given the revelations he made during his visit to her in the hospital, she figured he had eyes everywhere. The details of the shootout in Manchester would have gotten to him quickly. Being omniscient, he would be asking about the money, the money which, as he put it, she had so valiantly safeguarded.

"Listen, I still have the money, the envelope. It's in the bedroom—" she began.

"You think I'm here for my money?" he asked.

"I promise I never spent a dime of it. I didn't even open the envelope. I swear."

"I have men whose job it is to collect my money. I don't deign to perform such petty tasks myself."

"So, you're not upset, not worried about—?"

"About the money? Not really. But you were. *You* were worried about my money."

Rose was perplexed. Patrick grinned, folded his hands behind his head and leaned back.

"For some, it's always about the money, Rose. Just ask your mum up there in northern Maine, or wherever she calls home these days. But for his money, why else would she have stayed with someone like your dad?

"Life is so fragile, Rose." He paused, leaned forward and then stood up. "The fact that you considered my money is exemplary. And all for what? Mr. C handing you a few extra bucks the next day?"

He regarded her for a moment, as if waiting on her reply. When it didn't come, he walked back to the open window. He placed his hands on the window sill and leaned his head outside. From above the evening breeze, Rose heard the sound of him inhaling the cool, fresh air. After a moment, he returned his attention to the business at hand. When he spoke again, his voice was elevated.

"Some might consider you insane, even stupid. But not me. I call it a selfless devotion to something beyond oneself. Your recon instructor taught you well."

How the hell could he know about Sergeant Jackson?

She opened her mouth to protest. Before she could, he spun around and raised his hand, silencing her. To her surprise, he was smiling as if he had just won the lottery. He slipped his hands into the pockets of his slacks.

I don't want this . . . No more, Rose thought. *God knows, I never wanted it in the first . . .*

"So here it is: there is a greater role for you in my organization. Your service as a delivery gal is over. I plan to put you in sales. Callow and edgy though you are, you have great potential. I'm going to put you on the road, expanding my business interests."

As he spoke, he began to pace between the living room and dining room. A magnificent ring on his left hand ring finger caught Rose's eye. Finely engraved, the silver ring bore the outline of Christopher Columbus. It practically shined, even in the dim lighting. She admired the ring briefly, before turning her attention back to what Donnelly was laying out for her, all of which was unsettling.

. . . I never wanted to have anything to do with this business. God knows . . .

". . . overcoming the competition, which is always fierce. So, what does that mean for you? Specifically, you will play a leading role in expanding my business enterprise to the north."

He let the words sink in for a moment. “Now this will require reliable transportation. So whatever you have not had fixed with that old shitbox of yours will be fixed tomorrow. No more holes in the floorboard, no more shimmying or whatever afflictions it still owns.” Donnelly raised his eyebrows as a show of concern. “I can’t afford to have an up-and-comer of mine stranded on the side of some road out in the sticks.”

Rose muttered thank you under her breath and then inquired about the travel. “When you say travel north, what do you mean? Like Canada kind of north?”

“Ah, the curious type,” he said.

He reached inside his jacket and withdrew a white envelope. He walked up to within a few feet of her, then tossed it on her lap. Rose glanced down at it, long enough to know it was a lot of money.

“Now’s a good time for you to ask me the obvious,” Donnelly said. His smile was back.

Rose wasn’t picking up his cues. She stared back at him, her eyes vacant.

“How about, ‘Thanks, boss. So, when do I start?’” Donnelly reached down and squeezed her hand before returning to his spot on the couch. “Ah, great question.”

“Patrick, you’ve already been too kind. The money to help for rent, for car repairs, for food and so on has been very helpful.” She forced a gracious tone, masking the fear she felt. “But as generous as your offer is,” she shot a glance at the envelope and his hand squeezing hers, then continued, “I just can’t accept. I mean, I appreciate your concern, the flowers and all, but I have to say no, thank you . . . no, thank you, sir.”

Donnelly’s smile disappeared. He studied her for a moment, seeming to uncover her true emotions. Placing his hands on his knees, he sat up straight.

“I wasn’t asking you, Rose. You don’t get a vote,” he said firmly.

Rose was terrified. There was no masking the fear that her face most certainly conveyed.

Donnelly repeated himself. “You don’t get a vote, love. You have no choice. This isn’t an offer. It’s an order.”

He leaned closer in his seat and slipped his hand inside his coat, exposing the butt end of his revolver. His eyes darkened.

He will kill me if I don’t cooperate. No question about it.

She croaked out a reply, rubbing her hands so hard she thought she could start a fire. “Well, since . . . since you put it that way . . . maybe there’s something in an office I could . . .

something more suited for me. Something clerical . . ."

Donnelly laughed.

"Clerical, huh? Don't count on it. No, you won't be riding a desk, you'll be heading north, to a place that will be revealed to you soon." He slapped his knee and stood up. "In the meantime, we're working on terms with your partner. We'll need to get him acclimated to working in New England." Donnelly winked at her. "He's a Southern chap, you see. He comes from one of the Carolinas. I believe his name is Bubba."

With furrowed brow, Rose stared at the bowl of popcorn on her lap, trying to make sense of the latest turn of events. On the muted TV, Sheriff Andy Taylor appeared to be scolding his son, Opie. Given the choice, Rose would have much preferred a verbal haranguing than her part in a Mephistophelian deal.

She looked up at Donnelly, bewildered, trying to muster some courage before replying. "Let me see if I've got this right. I'm going to have a partner named 'Bubba.' That's interesting. Must be a family name."

Donnelly threw back his head and laughed heartily. He began pacing back and forth in the small living room.

"More than just curious, you're funny. I like that." He stopped and looked down at Rose as he continued, "You seem to have a knack for raising my hackles. But, as I said, there's a time and a place for your brand of wit. I'm sure that your recon instructor—Sergeant Ervin Jackson—trained you right." He resumed his pacing.

His repeated reference to her recon instructor sent a chill up her spine.

Is there anything he doesn't know?

Donnelly stopped. A dark cloud spread across his face. Gone was the boyish, dimpled grin. His eyes displayed the very real promise of pain.

"I want you to consider me your present-day Sergeant Jackson. He wouldn't have tolerated disrespect, especially in public settings. I won't tolerate it, either. You'd do well to remember that."

He resumed his pacing and took on a cheerier tone.

"You'll be well paid for your performance and continued loyalty. Before long, you ought to have enough saved to get out of that beater of a car you drive."

He wandered back to the window. Lighting from the streetlights highlighted his hands, which he held in supplication. He continued with his terms.

"You will mentor Bubba. It won't be easy. Remember, he's a

Southerner, a Johnny Reb, as you Yanks might say. On the surface, he looks like a glimmering jewel of naiveté."

Rose sat silent, her thoughts spinning.

Jesus, tell me this is all a dream. Tell me I'll wake up and forget it all.

"But don't let his appearance fool you. He's been in this line of work for a while. He's a talented fella, one who fills his master's coffers. I suspect he'll teach you a few things as well. You two will eventually expand my clientele while protecting our recent gains." Donnelly turned to face her before continuing. "Now, you may be thinking, why am I and this Bubba chap doing the bidding of Patrick Donnelly? The answer should be obvious, Rose. Some slimy goombah from East Boston or trash-talking mule from Dorchester wouldn't do so well up in Yankee land. Two oversized, pasty lugs, such as you two, draw no attention. The average Joe will find nothing threatening about you and Bubba. You look harmless, even pathetic, which is precisely the image I'm after."

He let the words sink in for moment.

"So, there you have it." He reached into his coat and pulled out a golden flask. "What are your questions?"

Rose watched as Donnelly fondled his flask. She eyed the giving end as it delivered another swallow of what she assumed to be nothing less than the finest whiskey. He walked back to the recliner, holding the flask in front of him.

"But where are my manners?" Patrick asked, offering his drink. "I bet you'd love a nip, what with all this negotiating."

Rose accepted the flask and took a pull. She fought back an urge to cough as the liquor slid down her throat and into her stomach. It was warm and soothing. Just what she needed.

"Not to be a pest, but when you say up north you don't mean Canada, do you?" she asked.

Donnelly slipped his flask back inside his coat.

"No, not that far. I don't want you fretting about the 'where' just yet. Mr. C will be bringing you a letter which will provide all the details you'll need."

Rose tried not to show it, but she hated being kept in the dark. Which reminded her of one of Sergeant Jackson's many truisms. Jackson once told her that when it came to dealing with their frustrated voters, politicians all did the same thing.

"Treat 'em like mushrooms: keep 'em in the dark, and feed 'em shit."

She wasn't sure how long Donnelly would keep her guessing. What she did know, however, was that her anxiety would only increase the longer she had to wait. Guys like Donnelly were known to conduct a form of psychological warfare as a means of controlling their underlings. Subordinates needed to know who called the shots. It was exactly what he was now doing with Rose. She came to the conclusion that she would have to find a way to cope with her anxiety. She knew that peppering Donnelly with questions was no way to get off on the right foot. But there was something she had to get off her chest.

Notwithstanding the increase in pay, babysitting some hayseed named Bubba sounded like a drag. What if she hated him? Couldn't understand him? Which got her thinking.

"I look forward to meeting and, as you indicated, helping this Bubba guy," Rose said before lightening the mood with a stab at humor. "But in the event routine communication becomes a challenge, will I be assigned a translator? I mean, you did say that he came from one of the Carolinas."

Donnelly looked down at her. He was not amused, but he maintained an even countenance.

"I think your initial reply was more than sufficient."

Rose blushed, wishing yet again that she had kept her quick-to-the-draw yapper sealed. She watched him draw in a deep breath and his thin smile resurface.

"Believe it or not, this meeting has been a pleasure." He paused as he withdrew two black leather gloves from a coat pocket. "A great opportunity awaits you, Rose. Remember what I said: loyalty cannot be overstated. The same holds true with your physical health. I'll need you well-rested and full of energy next week."

Rose nodded obediently. Donnelly raised a finger and gave a final command.

"And don't forget to take that jalopy of yours down to Maffee's tomorrow. That rustbucket needs to be healthy as well."

He slipped on his gloves and flashed her a final smile. Then, like a vapor, he was gone, leaving her alone with her thoughts spinning.

Chapter twenty-five

The morning after Donnelly's surprise visit to Rose's apartment, a tall, blond man named Bubba drove north in the direction of the flyspeck town of Horseshoe, North Carolina. At his casual pace, he was still a good 600 miles away from his final destination. But he was in no rush; rushing was not his nature. He preferred using the secondary roads, avoiding the interstate any chance he could. Secondary roads gave him a chance to see the countryside and maybe meet a few locals along the way. Since he had left a day early, he could do just that.

Bubba Coslaw was a devil-may-care, go-with-the-flow kind of guy. On this journey, he decided that 250 miles a day, or about five hours of driving, would suffice. It would allow him time to see the sights, stop at a few diners and sample some local fare and maybe chat with a few townies. Someone suggested that he try sushi, but raw fish was a bridge too far for his palate. He thought he might stop in one of the bigger cities along the way. Maybe check out some fancy boutique and get his mama something real pretty.

As he drove north on Highway 17, bright sunshine blanketed the landscape, which had transitioned from cotton fields to an infinite sea of evergreens and mangroves. He had reached the Great Dismal Swamp, as dark and deep as any wooded area he had ever seen. The beautiful weather made the drive all the more pleasant.

He had checked the forecast before leaving. From his home in Burgaw all the way up to New England, the Weather Channel's Jim Cantore promised sunny and unseasonably warm weather. Trusting Cantore, he had peeled back the top of his red MG. Cantore's forecast was spot on. It was a bit chilly at four in the morning when he left, but it had warmed up swiftly. Under the bright sunshine, everything appeared in sharper focus. The forest was a deeper green, the sky a radiant blue and the sun a brilliant orange.

Bubba lived for rides in his convertible. The car had been a gift from his hero, Gary Busey, the rambunctious, hard-drinking actor from Arkansas. Bubba loved everything about Busey, from his stringy blond hair to his toothy grin and his booming laugh. He loved those qualities because they were ones which he shared with the actor. A goofy-looking blond himself, it was not uncommon for Bubba to be told that he resembled Busey, a comparison he cherished. It was no surprise that, when he and Busey met a few years earlier during the filming of a Stephen King movie outside of Wilmington, the two hit it off.

When the filming ended, Bubba got a lot more than an autograph. Besides a few pictures of he and Busey together, Bubba got quite a prize: the cherry red 1976 MG belonging to Uncle Red, Busey's character in the flick. Busey had told him that it was the least he could do for all that Bubba had done for him. As it was, Busey had plenty of cars—or, as he put it—money pits, sitting in his six-car garage back in Malibu. He didn't need another.

"Hell, between you and that moonshine-running uncle of yours, filming this horror movie ended up being a sweet deal."

When Bubba's friends commented on the nature of his Busey fixation, Bubba would always refer to the MG. After all, it was an actor of more than a dozen movies who had given it to him.

Bubba spotted a wooden street sign ahead. Curious, he slowed down to get a look. He eased the MG onto the shoulder. The wooden sign read Cooter Barn Road. Bubba popped open the glove box and pulled out a booklet of strip maps which AAA had prepared for him. He thumbed to page three, which covered northeastern North Carolina and southeastern Virginia. According to the map, if he went east on Cooter Barn, in two miles he would be in Lilly. He squinted down at the map.

"Not much there," he said.

By the map's reckoning, there were four paved roads. The size of the dot, placed at the center of the town, put the population of Lilly somewhere between 100 and 500. In this part of the state, that probably meant closer to 100. He would be lucky to find a McDonald's or Burger King there. And if a town like Lilly didn't have a fast food joint, then he didn't expect to find a place serving soft-shelled crabs, something Bubba was intent on sampling.

"Well, bound to be something up the road."

He folded the spiral-bound map and slipped it back in the glove box under a pistol. From the swamp, he heard crickets chirping a happy harmony. The sound reminded him of springtime on the farm. And life on the farm always reminded him of his father.

Bubba's father was both humble and generous. From his modest income, he did the best he could to provide for his family and their church. A part-time farmer and carpenter, he never earned a lot. When times were especially tough, Christmas gifts were hand-me-downs or home-made gifts made from cord wood or deer skin. During such times, meat on Bubba's plate was whatever game his father had killed. In the prosperous years, which were few and far between, Bubba recalled one Christmas spent in Fort Walton Beach, Florida. He cherished the memories of that Christmas. His father's hard work had made that vacation possible.

Bubba's father worked over twelve hours a day, five days a week. He spent most of Sunday volunteering at Friendly Community Baptist Church, which the family attended. On Saturdays, he taught Bubba how to shoot deer in the pine forests; how to fish along the banks of the Cape Fear River; how to jig a gator from a canoe; and how to stalk and trap wild boar. Bubba's father was an outdoorsman with no equal. But he could barely read.

He was an encyclopedia of nature knowledge, but a man of few words. About the only time he ever spoke was when he was sharing his knowledge of nature or his farm-related insights. Sadly, it had been a long time since he and Bubba enjoyed a conversation together. Nowadays, his father told him nothing. Dead for twenty years, Bubba missed his father dearly. The twenty years had not taken away the pain of his loss.

He thought of his father as he scanned the woods across the road. He imagined the game that the two could have hunted in that wilderness. Wild boar, black bear and deer, to name a few. Given a bow, a spear or a rifle, his father could take down any wild animal. His father's death might have ruined Bubba were it not for his mother and the close relationship they shared. As hard as it was losing his father, Bubba spoke little about it and rarely displayed emotion, certainly not in front of his mama. He needed to be strong for her. In the end, he mourned in private. After a few months of bereavement, he picked himself up and returned to his usual smiling and optimistic self.

Bubba shifted into first gear and gradually eased back onto Highway 17. Off to the north were high, wispy clouds obscuring the once-clear sky. The sunrise had been blood red, which made him think about a Farmer's Almanac axiom. "Red sky in morning, sailors take warning." His hometown of Burgaw, 155 miles behind him, might as well have been on another planet, given where he was going. As he had been told, his assignment would not be easy and there would be no shortage of danger. Of course, none of that was foreign to Bubba.

When he needed to be, Bubba could be a badass. Goofy grin aside, he had played the role of tough guy on many occasions. Not exactly the feigned image of a spry and cheery Amway salesman he outwardly displayed. Which got him thinking about his mama.

Bubba hated lying to his mama but breaking her heart with the truth of his profession. Well, that was something he would not abide. In the end, he told her what he had always told her before leaving on a business trip: Amway needed him to hit the road. His skills were needed elsewhere. The company needed him to train and develop more powerhouse salesmen like him.

To support this fiction, Bubba had actually signed up as a sales rep, freely allowing himself into the Amway enterprise and under the supervision of Bobby Delbert, a pedantic, small-minded busybody. Bubba could not stand the man. For his mother's peace of mind, however, he played the part. He even attended rallies at Delbert's house, where he bought boxes of soap, detergent and Amway's "Grade AA Coffee Creamer." He toted a box of pens, Amway bumper stickers and assorted mementos to complete the hoax. He went so far as to actually slap one of those detestable stickers on the fender of his MG.

When his mother saw him off, she watched him load three large cardboard boxes into his trunk. Printed on each box were the words PURE SOAP. Except there was not stitch of soap in those boxes. The boxes housed thousands of rounds of ammo and about a dozen ammo clips. He pledged to his mother that he would serve Amway well, promising to hawk his goods to naive Yankee families, hooking them "before they knew what hit 'em." The two laughed, and laughing made the imminent separation a little easier. As much as she hated seeing him leave, she was proud of her son's profession. In her mind, selling door-to-door was an honorable pursuit. Since he was successful in his trade, it proved to her that she had raised him right, raised him to be a man of integrity and character. That Bubba had concocted a sham to protect her was another matter. The thought of breaking her with the truth of his real business up north was something Bubba could not stomach.

"You were always so much bigger than this bug-splat town, Bubba Sunshine," she had said, ruffling his stringy blonde hair. "Some men go door to door selling vacuum cleaners or some botched-up version of salvation. Not my Bubba. My Bubba sells the stuff people truly need. That's why Amway needs you, even if it means leaving your mama and driving off to some strange land for God knows how long."

He promised to write and call as soon as he could, promises he had always made good on when away on business. He promised he would send money within two weeks. On this, too, Bubba had never failed to deliver. The odds of a Christmas visit looked grim, but he would do his very best and come home as soon as he could.

After hugging his mother and kissing her forehead, just as he had done at every goodbye, Bubba was off. He was off to do a job for a man he had never met in person and one he hoped he would never have to meet. Bubba's boss, Pico "the Castrater", who lived on a coral island south of Miami, owed Bubba's new employer a favor. All Bubba was told was that his new employer could be quick-tempered and that he was not a man to be messed with, much like Pico. Over the years, Bubba had served Pico well and had contributed handsomely to his coffers. Nothing would be different up north. Bubba had every intention of serving the New England boss in the same fashion: with efficiency, loyalty and, if need be, audacity.

Driving along and deep in thought, Bubba barely noticed the blue sign posted a few feet off the shoulder of Highway 17, shadowed by a copse of lofty pines. A cardinal perched on a tree branch surrounded the white text, which announced the first of eight states through which he would travel.

Virginia Welcomes You

"Hell yeah!" he hollered into the sky, clapping his hands. One state down, eight to go.

Wind whipping over the windshield tossed strands of his long hair across his forehead and eyes. He brushed them away. It was ten o'clock and he had been on the road for over five hours. The day's goal was Virginia's Tidewater region, and he was not far away. The highway's next sign read:

Newport News 40m (65km)

"That's good enough for one day."

Since he had initially planned on driving farther, he realized he now had time to kill. He decided an early lunch was in order, preferably soft-shell crabs. Whether the next town had them or not, he was stopping there to eat. He was famished.

"If I can't find it in . . ." Bubba squinted as he approached the town sign. "in Benefit, then I'll get me some in Newport News tonight." The matter of soft-shell crabs was settled.

He turned right onto Douglas Road heading east, toward the town of Benefit. Farms raced past on both sides of the road. He passed a Civil War marker and made a mental note to return to it, just as soon as he filled his belly. He had plenty of time to explore. Acknowledging his unintentional pun, he hoped his new gig would not involve any of that—killing.

His pa taught him that killing was only necessary for sustenance. His job as a drug runner taught him that survival justified killing as well. Luckily, he had only cut down two men in his eighteen-year career. Would there be a third? The thought had crossed his mind in the days leading up to his departure. Bubba had no qualms about killing again, if it came down to it. If the survival of him or his partner, whose identity was still a mystery, was ever in jeopardy, then he would freely pull the trigger.

Bubba slowed the MG down to thirty as he approached a sign informing travelers that downtown Benefit was two miles ahead. He glanced off to the left, where an older woman smiled and waved while holding a stack of mail in a sinewy hand. Immediately he thought of his mother and her sweet smile. Knowing the real purpose of his trip would have broken his momma's heart. That was something Bubba Sunshine simply could not accept.

Chapter twenty-six

The phone rang in the kitchen, waking Claire from a nap on the couch. It rang again. She sat up and rubbed her eyes as it rang a third time. Slowly she got up and shuffled toward the kitchen. Her legs were stiff from having laid on a couch shorter than she. The phone rang two more times as she crossed the kitchen. She grabbed the handset before it could ring a sixth time.

She yawned, holding the handset away from her, before speaking. "Hello."

"Yes, good afternoon. I'm Vice President William Cartwright. I was hoping to speak to Miss O'Brien."

Claire O'Brien breathed heavily, shook her head and looked out her picture window, eyeing nothing in particular. "Yes, of course you are. And I'm Wonder Woman."

"Ma'am, I understand this must seem irregular—"

"Listen, mister, if this is some kind of joke, then just stop now."

"Ma'am, this is no joke. I assure you I am who I say I am." Then Cartwright laughed, that hyena-cackle laugh of his. "I asked Dana . . . maybe you've seen my impersonator on Saturday Night Live . . . to stick to the jokes and let me take care of the campaign." Again came the laugh.

He kind of sounds like the vice president.

"Tell you what," Cartwright said, as if reading her mind, "if you don't believe me—and I can appreciate your skepticism—then call me back. I'll give you my office phone number, which is where I am now. I'm off the campaign trail for a few days. The boss needed me back in D.C. to work on a project."

There was a pause. "Miss O'Brien?"

Oh God, this is the vice president.

"So, it is you . . . I mean, sir. I'm . . . I'm awfully sorry, but you have to realize that . . . that it isn't every day . . ." Claire trailed off.

"Please. No apologies needed. I'm sorry to call you out of the blue." Cartwright coughed away from the phone before continuing. "Pardon me. I think I've got a cold coming on. I'll be glad when the election is past us. I think most Americans will be."

Claire was not sure how to reply. She was no dyed-in-the-wool political junkie, but she was no fan of Cartwright's party. While she appreciated the vice president calling, it wouldn't change her vote in a few weeks. Not to mention, she had a prickly sense that this call was another attempt to capitalize on her son's heroism. She tried to hide her growing frustration. She didn't do so well.

"Mr. Vice President, I suppose you'd like to toss my son on stage like some prop for one of your campaign stops. That's the reason for this friendly call, isn't it?"

He replied gracefully. "I won't lie to you, Miss O'Brien. I'm very impressed with your son's story. His selfless act is emblematic of our country's exceptionalism. However, I assure you that I'm not calling in search of a campaign gimmick or some stage prop."

Claire blushed. She had just shoved her foot in her mouth and probably pissed him off in the process. Worse still, someone was probably listening in on the call. She had heard Reynolds was a fan of not only nukes, but wiretaps.

Damn my temper.

A lifetime of protecting her challenged son from scammers and bullies had kept her forever on the defensive. Frankie being thrust into the limelight, and the genuine adoration which followed, should have taught her that everyone was not out to get him. His fame had proven there was a whole lot of good out in the world.

"Sir, I'm awfully sorry. I shouldn't have snapped like that. It's just that raising Frankie has . . . well, it's made me overly cynical."

Claire stopped herself before divulging more.

What am I saying? This is the vice-freakin'-president! Here I am wasting his precious time listening to some run-of-the-mill sob story. I need to apologize. And fast. Who knows who's listening in?

"Why am I telling you all this. I mean, I don't know about

your kids . . . I'm sure they're fine . . . and I'm sure you're really busy . . . and you don't have time for my rambling . . ."

"Well, Miss O'Brien—"

"Mr. Vice President, sir, umm, please call me Claire. I mean, please call me whatever you'd like, because you're the vice president." Her words came out at machine-gun speed.

"Very well. Claire it is." Mr. Cartwright paused momentarily before continuing. "First off, my kids are doing well. Thank you for asking. It's not them that I worry about—it's Don Garrett, my running mate. You've seen him on TV, I assume? I got my hands full with that one."

He laughed heartily, that trademark laugh which Dana Carvey had perfected on Saturday Night Live.

The president summons him to the White House, yet he has the time to call me?

"The purpose of my call is to invite your son to the post-election party up in New Whitby. No firm date yet. Barb is still working on that. Naturally, she and I would like you to be there with your son. We have plenty of room. Win or lose, the party is our way of thanking those who helped with the campaign. In addition, we're extending an invitation to some of those who have gone above and beyond in the service of their communities—firefighters, police officers, members of the military and ordinary citizens."

Cartwright paused for a moment. "Your son is part of this special crowd, Claire. Barb and I would be honored to have you both."

Claire's eyes watered and she swallowed hard. She squeaked out a reply. "We'd be honored to attend."

And so it would be that Nashua's newest hero would enjoy his fifteen minutes of fame for a while longer. As for Claire, this was another occasion substantiating her awakened faith in mankind.

Chapter twenty-seven

Rose stared across the threshold of the open door at a life-sized horse costume occupied by what had to have been a large man. Befuddled, she looked back down at the slip of paper in her hand, then at the number on the doorsill: it checked. Unless she had written something down wrong, she was where she was supposed to be. She looked back up at the horse's head, which stared at her. Its occupant offered no greeting.

"Gee, Wilbur, I must've missed the memo," Rose said, eyeballing the costume from top to bottom. "That or I'm simply in the wrong place. This is 168 Main, apartment 3-E, right? I realize I'm in the Odd Fellows Building, but isn't this a bit over the top?"

A faint giggle came in reply, but the horse didn't budge. It was as if it were cemented to the floor. Breaking the awkward silence, a woman's voice came from inside the apartment. Rose recognized it right away. It was Claire. Which meant Frankie was the equestrian greeting committee.

"Claire, it's Rose. Sorry to come unannounced," she called out.

"No problem. Just one . . . one sec," Claire said.

Claire came running up behind her son. Her breathing labored. She too was in costume. She held a wand, sported a wig and wore a dress which resembled Cinderella's.

Rose was perplexed, eyes shifting from the horse to Cinderella.

"Jeez . . . I really did miss the memo."

Claire looked down at her flowing white dress and then at her son. "All this, you mean? We dress up every year. You know it still remains one of Frankie's favorite days."

"But not as much as Santa Day and Easter. Except I get a bellyache on Easter," Frankie offered.

Still stumped, Rose shook her head gestured to Claire's costume. "Maybe I slipped and whacked my head this morning, because I'm not sure why you two are . . ."

"Dressed like this? You mean to tell me you really don't know?" Claire asked, then laughed. "It's Halloween."

"It is?" Rose looked down at her new Seiko, which confirmed Claire's assertion. "Hmph, so it is."

Frankie removed the horse-head. Chicken wire from inside the costume had imprinted thin lines across his cleanly shaved head. Trails of sweat ran down both cheeks. *Breathing inside that thing must be a bitch,* Rose thought. And the heat? Even worse. Nevertheless, it didn't seem to faze Frankie one bit. He flashed his toothy smile at Rose.

"Well, come in," Claire offered, stepping back from the threshold, guiding Frankie to do the same. "Given the occasion, I have candy to offer, or I can make you a plate. Frankie and I already ate, but I still have plenty of spaghetti."

"Oh no, thanks. I didn't come to burden you. I, um . . . well, I came . . ." Rose stepped inside the apartment and walked into the kitchen, where Claire and Frankie had retreated. She shifted uneasily on her feet, rubbed her hands and looked up at Frankie with tired eyes. "I came to say thanks. Thank you for saving my life. I should've come a lot sooner, and I don't know why I didn't." Rose looked down at her feet for a moment. "Fact is, Frankie, I wouldn't be alive today if it weren't for you."

Frankie nodded to Rose and handed the horse-head to his mother, who set it on the floor behind her. He peeled his right arm out from inside a sleeve of the gray costume, one of the elevated front legs. Hair on his arm was matted with sweat. He stuck his right hand out to Rose, who accepted with a smile. He shook her hand enthusiastically.

"Thank you, Miss Rose, for all the sodas, hot dogs and sometimes the ice cream. You're always so nice to me at the baseball games. Thank you for helping me when those bad boys tried to hurt me after school."

Rose would not find out until later that night, hours after Frankie had turned in, and after hours of drinking wine, that the last several weeks had been a heartwarming journey for Claire. The tears she had shed over wine, recounting the many experiences that she and Frankie had enjoyed, were tears of joy. As she explained to Rose, her belief in humanity had been rekindled.

She asked Rose about her own faith, curious to know after Rose's brush with death inside her parked car. Rose dodged the question and changed the topic back to Frankie.

"I'm gonna sound repetitive here, I know, but your son was Johnny-on-the-spot. If not for Frankie, I'd probably be dead."

Their marathon conversation rivaled the length of the one Rose had enjoyed in the doctors' lounge with Margo, whom Rose insisted Claire meet at The Stable in three nights at the next Thirsty Thursday. Though Rose had never attended one herself, she sold Claire on the prospects of a good time with friends. When she inquired about specifics related to "thirsty," Rose simply suggested that Claire need not worry, given the close proximity of The Stable to her apartment.

Through their night together, the women laughed heartily, sharing memories of misspent youth. It wasn't until after midnight when Rose got up to leave. Her new job required physical training, the likes of which she had not experienced since recon school. The pull-ups and sit-ups were torture; the running was worse. The shooting had been the only fun part, she had told Claire. Claire didn't ask Rose anything about her new job. That was just fine by Rose. She hated the thought of being mendacious with her friends.

The two women were still laughing as Rose stumbled into the empty hallway on the third floor of the Odd Fellows Building. As she slipped on her parka, she reminded Claire about Thursday night, stressing the need to wear her "drinking shoes." Claire promised she would be there. Rose was halfway down the long flight of stairs when Claire called down to her.

"Wait, Rose. Can we make a deal?"

Rose stopped, turning her large frame on the narrow steps, "Of course."

"I'm on board for Thirsty Thursday, but I need you to do something for me."

"Sure. Anything."

"That you join Frankie and me at First Church this Sunday for service at eight."

Rose swallowed. "Is that eight as in 'p.m.' or 'a.m.'?"

"As in morning," Claire said, a grin turning up the sides of her mouth.

The night before she left for Maine and her new job, Rose met her friends at The Stable for Thirsty Thursday. The night was warm and there was a full moon. They sat outside and listened to the chirping of crickets and the rustle of the few remaining leaves on an oak which loomed over the outdoor patio. They drank many beers and shared many stories. They laughed in a way that lifelong friends laughed. In short order, friendship between Claire and Margo was forged. The two made plans to get together while Rose was off on business, business about which Rose spoke little. The three enjoyed their best night out in a long time. But the gaiety was short-lived.

Chapter twenty-eight

"Four more fucking years," Rose muttered, while she stared at the election results plastered across the screen of a dust-covered, thirteen-inch black-and-white TV. The TV rested atop a banged-up dresser, which was made of the same shoddy, particle-board furniture which filled all the rooms of Captain Gordon's Motel on York Beach, Maine.

She could not do anything about the election outcome, but she damn sure was not about to sit and watch a gloating Cartwright with a room full of rednecks. She decided to take a walk down to the lobby and remind the receptionist to send her "husband" to the right room when he arrived, the very same "husband" who should have been here hours ago.

The room doors at Captain Gordon's Motel opened to Maine's often harsh elements, such as the storm which raged outside. Rose pulled open the door. Immediately, a blast of wind struck her. As she stepped outside, it was worse. Cold rain pelted her face and arms, adding to the misery. She hustled down towards the front office, silently cursing as she made haste.

Thanks to that stupid, goddamned hillbilly, I'm out here in this bullshit.

She made it to the motel office and grabbed the storm door handle and pulled. It would not budge. She pulled harder. Still nothing.

"Damn thing," she grumbled.

Repeatedly she pulled and tugged on the handle, but to no avail. It was either stuck or, for whatever reason God only knew, locked. She pounded on the glass door. She rubbed a hole in the moisture on the door and peeked in. There was no one to be found.

"Anybody in there? Hello. Somebody open the goddamn door!" Rose hollered, the wind dampening her shouts, inaudible to anyone who might have been inside the toasty reception area.

The frigid rain continued to blast her body. From her exposed neckline, cold water trickled from the soaked ends of her black locks down her back. It was a miserable, creepy sensation. She shook her head, sending sprays of water onto the door. She rubbed the glass again and peeked in. Just then, the owner, a frail, gray-haired man wearing spectacles, appeared behind the counter, having emerged from a hallway beyond her view. He was looking down at something in front of him. Rose waited a split-second too long to whale on the door again. As she raised her clenched fists, the man scurried like a mouse back down the hallway from which he had come.

"Dammit!" she yelled and then pounded a final time. "Hey!"

Wretchedly drenched, she silently cursed and turned to wander back to her room. Rose had taken a few steps away when she heard a click behind her, loud enough to be heard between gusts of wind. She spun around and took a step toward the lobby door. A frail woman, either the owner's wife or sister, poked her head through the pushed open door. A cigarette dangled from her mouth. Her shabby clothes were several sizes too big. For a moment, she seemed to regard Rose with suspicion, before realizing she was staring out at a guest.

"Ah, it's you, Miz McDougal," she said, her voice raised against the wind. "Kinda wet out theyah."

"No fooling you," Rose replied, walking toward her. "Just let me in, please. I'm freezin' out here."

Rose followed her into the reception area and plopped herself down on a plastic sofa. The withered woman's brother—or husband—smiled at Rose, then disappeared down a hallway behind the reception area. A moment later, he returned with a mug of hot chocolate.

Rose took the hot chocolate and thanked the man. She scanned the reception area. It was as tacky a place as she had ever seen. The room's contents included puke-green-colored plastic seats, a tilted, wooden coat rack and an old coffee table, held upright by strips of black duct tape. Resting on the table was an assortment of old magazines, including a *Yankee* magazine from June 1973. In a corner near the reception counter sat a grey waste basket. Affixed to the basket was a faded sticker of Smokey the Bear. It was stuck on the basket at an odd angle, its edges peeling back. But for the absence of ashtrays and yellowing walls, the reception area could've passed for a teacher's lounge.

She looked up on the wall and spotted a Mickey Mouse clock, which was at least three feet in length. Where does one find such an eyesore? she wondered. Who displays crap like that? Whose business did they hope to solicit? Ex-tenants from the funny farm? Rose kept her smartass comments to herself. She blew on the hot chocolate then took a sip. It was delicious. The clock, with all its visual absurdities, read 3:35.

Rose pushed aside a *Boy's Life* magazine and set her hot chocolate on the coffee table. She then asked the hoteliers about her husband, Bubba. Had the two seen him? From her visit earlier in the morning, she reminded them that he would be easy to spot: a big guy with a goofy accent, which was about all she had been given in terms of a description. The two had seen no such individual. They wondered if he might have gotten lost.

"So ya hubby, he knows where we ah? Ya told him before da Nubble, yah?" the shriveled old man asked, spectacles perched at the end of his nose. His thick Yankee accent was irritating.

"Yes I did. If you mean your hotel, the Captain Gordon's with an 'r,' then yes, that's what I told him." Rose spoke slowly, as if to a child. The man grumbled something inaudible to Rose.

The woman dismissed Rose's cheekiness, shooting a look at the man. At that moment, Rose decided the two were married. The woman said, "Well, ya know how men ah. Too proud to ask fa directions."

"That's probably exactly what happened," Rose said, then rolled her eyes, adding, "How I ended up saddled with a man named Bubba, I'll never know."

"After over fohty years with this one," the woman said, nodding to her husband while snuffing out her cigarette, "my muthah, who's on her way out, God love her, still hasn't forgiven me."

Rose smiled and wondered, not for the first time, if she had ever met a happily married couple. True, Margo bragged on her man, but she had never seen the two together. Vic and Cheryl? Same thing. Sometimes, Rose felt content in her single status.

Rose addressed the woman. "When he finally does wander in, please send him down."

"Shoe-ah will." She took Rose's empty mug. "So, what ya two gonna do fa suppah?"

Rose gave her a confused look.

"Supper?"

"Yah, ya know. What ah ya gonna do fa food? Not much open during the week, especially this time of da yeyah."

"Oh, I hadn't really thought about it. What do you recommend? Probably ought to figure that out for the next few weeks. Don't want to end up eating fast food in Kittery every night."

"'Bout da only place you'll find hee-yah is Above da Waves, down on Sho't Sands. That's ya best bet. Ya gotta stay off Route One headed no'th. Got some big pahty fa Cartwright up in New Whitby."

The desiccated woman shook her head, her face twisted in disgust. "Gonna stop all da traffic, but no one knows if he's gonna even be hee-yah," she moaned.

Thanks for reminding me, Rose almost said. She had left her room to avoid the post-election coverage; she didn't need any reminders. Even so, the woman's tip was a good one to keep in mind. She and Bubba didn't need to be near crowds, especially if they had large sums of money. The reference to New Whitby, a very affluent seaside town, got her thinking about work.

During her collections, she had overheard one of Donnelly's lackeys mention something about "moving the product" into communities like South Jefferson and New Whitby, places where old money had resided for generations and where new money was pouring in. Bubba's and her performance over the next few weeks, a trial run of sorts, so she was told, would determine their expanded roles in Donnelly's ambitious plans. Reliable service, such as the solo run she conducted last night, would put her in good standing for promotion.

And probably confine me to this goddamned work for life, she silently lamented, before turning her attention back on the woman.

"Near New Whitby, huh?" Rose asked.

"Ayuh, just up da road no'th," the woman said, pointing a finger outside in the direction of Route 1A. Route 1A paralleled Long Sands Beach and wound its way to the north in the direction of Maine's wealthiest communities. On last night's collection run, Rose had gone into Porter's Neck, one of Maine's wealthiest towns, but only long enough to break into the house of some trust-fund junkie and snag $10,000, the amount needed to put the guy back on the right side of Donnelly's ledger. Just enough money to keep him supplied for a few more weeks.

Rose thanked the couple for the hot chocolate and walked back outside. The rain had ended, but the biting wind remained. The slate-gray sky promised an even earlier darkness, one which was fast approaching. She rounded the corner to the ocean-facing side of the motel, where her $25-a-night room sat. Out on the bluff, she saw lights on inside the home which represented the evening's target. *Assuming the idiot shows up*, she thought.

"And if he isn't here in an hour, it ain't happening," Rose groused.

The house was about halfway down Cape Neddick. Along with other large Victorian homes, it straddled the high rocky cliffs, offering its inhabitants unfettered views to the south and east out over the churning Atlantic. On a clear day, the Isles of Shoals were visible. The subject house had lights shining from its first and second floors; the third floor, which the old-timers called the "widow's watch," was dark. During her morning's reconnaissance of the house, Rose spotted six college-aged adults: four males and two females. Over the course of two hours of spying, she counted eight cars come and go, none staying more than five minutes. Rose was certain that lots of money and drugs exchanged hands. Money in, drugs out.

It got her thinking about the "hub and spoke" business model, one which fit the legitimate and the illicit alike. In the drug business, the "hub and spoke" model made sense. The hub fed the many spokes. In turn, the spokes—large-volume dealers—supplied petty dealers, who then supplied the innumerable addicts across the fruited plain. It was simple: the hub and spoke relied upon reciprocity to thrive. Nothing rocket science about that.

Yeah, whatever. This shit still sucks. I'd walk away if I could. God knows I would.

She pushed wishful thinking aside and returned her focus to the target home. Its three inhabitants served as one of Donnelly's northern New England "spokes," and was supplied by the Lowell "hub." So long as the spokes paid him through the hub, and on time, Donnelly didn't give a shit what they charged their flock of devoted druggies. In this business, if you hustled, you stood to make a killing. As a "spoke," greed was your driving force. You never gave a second thought to screwing one of your faceless addicts in any number of boondock towns and villages. Those were addicts who, without access to cable TV and malls, and some without running water, were bored to tears and inclined to do just about anything to get that next high.

Those conditions didn't apply to those within the four walls of the target house. In Rose's estimation, none of them had struggled a day in their pampered lives. Polo shirts, pressed slacks, perfect hair and BMWs on their sixteenth birthdays. No hardship tours there. They were soft. So when taken by complete surprise and facing down the barrels of two handguns, they would crumble and do whatever was demanded of them. First, they would offer up the loot they owed, which was close to thirty grand. Second, they would toss out an apology for their month-long delinquency.

Just an honest mistake . . . please tell Mr. Donn—umm—please tell, you know, him, that we were gonna pay. Honest we were.

Rose had a good idea how tonight's raid would go down. She took her eyes off the house and shivered in the howling wind. She lumbered back into her room, shut the door and picked up the TV remote. She was glad to be out of the cold, but she was pissed at Bubba, cursing his name as she repeatedly flipped through the channels searching for something—anything—other than post-election coverage. Every channel she passed displayed a virtual tribute to the flogging that Cartwright had given Reyes not 24 hours earlier. Throngs of the faithful, waving to their new hero, William Cartwright, danced and shouted. Making matters worse was the celebratory blowout up in New Whitby that the Captain Gordon duo had mentioned.

"That's all I need," Rose grumbled. She kept flipping channels.

She paused on a station showing an elderly man delivering a soliloquy in French, his eyes cast down on a messy stack of papers. He was speaking uneasily from a corner of his sagging mouth. Again, she switched the dial, arriving at the very last channel—Channel 2, the NBC affiliate in Portland. The *Wheel of Fortune* was on. Something neutral like a brain-dead game show was a whole lot less appalling than watching country-club yuppies flaunting Cartwright's victory or some Canuck seizing while delivering some incomprehensible message. Rose made herself comfortable.

"S!" an ebullient, fat woman wearing a putrid orange sweater hollered after the wheel stopped. Her arms and belly shook like Jello when Pat Sajak announced that, yes, there was one "s." Instantly, she was $200 richer. And she could keep that $200 and earn more, so long as her next spin didn't land her on Bankrupt.

Rose smirked as she watched Vanna White stroll to the board to turn over the lit square. *Real tough job,* she thought. A nice smile, a trim, shapely body and a good head of hair was all it took. She shook her head, and then looked over at the bedside clock: 4:05. Bubba was now very late.

She despised being made to wait. Her blood pressure was rising once again. Fuck what Donnelly said. It might be a stupid idea, but she decided that whether numbnuts showed up or not, she was going to that house. She would get the money out of those little shits—beat it out of them if need be, drop it off with Donnelly's goons tomorrow at that rest stop in New Hampshire, and then make tomorrow's collection—with or without this Bubba character. The sooner she got through this probationary spell of making house calls, the sooner she could move on to the more lucrative stuff.

Or, should the gods smile down on me, the sooner I can get out of this goddamned business.

But she knew that was a pipe dream. Thus, survival became her overriding pursuit. With her time in a photo recon unit and Y-3's training, she would be at least prepared.

On TV, the fat lady spun again. The microphone attached to the collar of her repellent sweater picked up her labored breathing for all of TV land to hear. Narrowly missing Bankrupt, her spin landed on $800. Provided she picked the right letter, she was up to a thousand bucks, a tidy sum. One could spend a month dining at Golden Corral, likely the very place where this one probably grazed on a daily basis, and still have money left for untold rounds of Slurpees and sausage dogs at 7-11.

"Um . . . oh boy . . ." she balked, panning the studio audience with dread. What to choose? Her face had gone beet-red. Random letters were shouted. The audience members were not helping much, some by design. A gruff voice barked out "'Z,' no, 'Q' . . . go for the 'Q'!"

"Um . . . um . . . a Q?"

For the briefest of moments, Sajak paused and leaned towards her, as if encouraging another choice. The fat woman's bulging eyes searched the audience for clues, only stony silence came in return. Oh well, Q seemed as good a choice as any. She nodded, her chins quivering, affirming her choice.

"Is there a Q?" Sajak asked. The buzzer buzzed sharply. No Q.

Not in this puzzle, not in almost any puzzle, you moron.

Rose snickered.

She decided to have a beer. If she had to sit around waiting on shit-for-brains, at least she could enjoy a frosty libation, which the refrigerator was packed with. In total, she had schlepped in some three cases, along with chips, cheese dip, Twinkies, walnuts, Circus Peanuts and coffee. The food would cover her snacking, the operative word being *her*. If that cowpoke thought he was going to get any of it, then he had another thing coming. *He eats what he brings*. She would share a few beers, sure, but not the junk food.

She thought it best to keep the refrigerator stocked, since their time in Maine was open-ended. She and Bubba had the room booked through December 5. When she had checked in two days earlier, the best the old couple could offer was thirty days at a time, with the option to extend an additional thirty days. As for the costs, Donnelly didn't bat an eye. Twenty-five bucks a night was budget dust in his world. Donnelly had $1,000 wired to Rose, instructing her to spend the rest "as she saw fit." She cracked a beer, silently cursed her employer and then guzzled. The Schlitz was cold.

Outside, the nor'easter raged on. The rain had resumed and was now beating on the windows, while waves pounded the jagged rocks just a stone's throw away. Cold and blustery conditions were forecast for the next twenty-four hours. Saturday would bring sunshine and unseasonable warmth. A few months ago, she had begged for relief from the sinister heat, but when it came down to it, there was only so much rain and cold Rose could stomach. By the first week of November, winter had worn out its welcome.

She chugged the last of her beer and then got up to grab a second when she heard a rapping on the door. *Bubba?* Not one to take chances, she took three silent steps to her nightstand, opened its drawer, reached in and pulled out her .38. She held it tight against her damp jeans. Before she could issue a warning, the door was pushed open. She stiffened and then raised the handgun.

It was Bubba. It had to be him. Soaking wet, saddled with bags and miscellaneous crap, he grinned in at her.

"Howdy, ma'am."

The man who stood in front of Rose out under the roof's drip line looked exactly as she had imagined: big and goofy. At first blush, he resembled one of the actors from the TV show *Hee Haw*, one of those who wore a crooked hat and dopey smile, though "the dopey smile" description didn't narrow things down much. On closer examination, it was not so much a *Hee Haw* actor he favored, but some other simpleton from TV land. Then it hit her.

Jesus, it's Gomer-freaking-Pyle!

He could have been Gomer Pyle's twin, save the blonde hair.

What was that guy's real name? Newton? Neeley? Whoever he was, he apparently had some golden vocal cords. Whatever talents Bubba possessed, an intimidating presence sure was not one of them, something he would need to do a better job of developing over the next few weeks. Rose studied him like a dissected frog.

There he stood, as the gutter poured cold water on his hat,

his shoulders and all the crap he had stuffed under his arms: an olive duffle bag, a smaller gym bag, and two red Tupperware containers. He had a jack-o'-lantern smile with a gap between his front teeth. Wisps of soaked, blonde hair were matted to his forehead. His pale face was free of wrinkles; no scars or cuts she could spot. She would have bet a swim in the surf that he wasn't a day over thirty-five. He was tall and broad-shouldered. His brown, suede jacket, possibly ruined from being under the gutter's gush, protruded slightly at the waist. He had a bit of a belly, but he was no porker. He was a few inches taller than she. She guessed six foot three.

He's got height and size, but I'm gonna have to work on his appearance of naïveté.

Rose broke the silence.

"So, wild guess here . . ." Rose began, closing her eyes and placing index fingers on her temples like Johnny Carson as Carnac. "I'm betting you're the Bubba. The one who should've been here—what—four hours ago?"

"Yes ma'am, I am." His smile grew even wider, practically swallowing his face. From behind him, the howling wind pushed against his coat. If he was cold, he didn't show it.

"Aha. So, tell me Bubba. You got a last name?"

"Yes ma'am, I do, but I don't ever use it," he drawled, and then tipped his hat, spilling trapped rainwater from his hat onto the motel room's shag carpet. "Mama calls me 'Sunshine,' always has since I was knee high to a grasshopper (pronounced grass-huppa). Bubba Sunshine."

"Of course she does." Rose suppressed laughter. *You can't make this shit up,* she thought. "So tell me, with a name like Bubba, it must get confusing at family reunions, huh?"

Bubba's smile disappeared. He looked at Rose, clearly lost. "No ma'am. All my kin know who I am."

He was positively clueless. Suddenly, Rose was no longer amused.

I swear to God, if he's really a dumbass, then I'm outta here. Screw Donnelly and his threats. I never asked for—

"Um, permission to enter, ma'am," Bubba asked, his smile back in place. "I really need to pee. Been in that car forever."

Rose frowned and extended her left arm.

"Permission granted, Bubba Sunshine." She popped off a fake salute and followed it with a warning. "Come on in and do whatever you need to do, but don't put that soaking-wet crap you're carrying on my bed. Put it over there." Rose jammed a finger toward the bed behind her.

Bubba sprang into the motel room, unloaded his drenched items on the edge of his bed, and then placed the Tupperware on top of the dresser next to the TV, before sprinting to the bathroom. Rose shut the outside door behind him. A few seconds later, she heard what sounded like someone releasing the full fury of a fire hydrant against aluminum siding. It was deafening.

What the hell has he been drinking?

"Don't worry about shutting the bathroom door. I know the barn you grew up in didn't have one."

Rose walked over and closed it herself. From behind her, the same persuadable fat woman spun the wheel of fortune, bouncing a little before shouting out "X!" The predictable buzzer followed. No 'X' in this puzzle.

After washing his hands and swiping them on his damp jeans, Bubba emerged from the bathroom appearing satisfied. He smiled and nodded to Rose, who was sitting on her bed facing him. Her gun rested on the nightstand between the two beds. He plopped himself down on his bed and leaned back against the headboard, which banged roughly against the wall. He laced his hands behind his head, breathed deeply and shut his eyes.

"Ma'am, I gotta say—it's so good to finally unwind. Dealing with all them rude drivers back in Massachusetts was nerve-racking."

Rose rolled her eyes. "First-world problems, Bubba Love-Gun. Get over it."

"You're right. I just ain't used to it," he said.

"Never mind all that. Let's get something straight: I ain't no ma'am or missus or whatever you're used to calling women back home. I'm Rose McDougal or simply Rose, if your pea-brain is into the whole brevity thing. Nothing else. Pretty simple."

Bubba sat up. He'd earned her full attention. "Yes, ma'am . . . I mean, Miss Rose."

"You start in on that 'ma'am' shit and I'll slap the blond outta your hair. Got me?"

Bubba nodded obediently.

"Good. Now that we've got that established, how about a cold one?" Rose stood up and walked to the refrigerator.

"I'd love one," Bubba declared. "Been a lot of miles. Never knew how far Burgaw was from Maine. Oh, while you're at it, would it be asking too much if I can get two?"

"Yeah, sure. Why not." Rose reached into the refrigerator and grabbed another beer. She stood up, turned back to him and pointed at him with one of the cans of beer. "On one condition—that you're all ears and listening to me, until we leave here to collect the money. No stories about Dixieland and pig-picking or cow-tipping or whatever harebrained customs you practice. I don't wanna hear any of it until we've collected the dough and we're out of small-arms range. I'm not interested in your absurd musings. Understand?"

"Yes'm. Oh, and that'd be about thirty meters." Bubba pushed himself up and leaned back against the headboard, his eyes locked on the wall behind the TV. He looked almost as if in a trance.

"Heads up," Rose said, regaining his attention. "What's that about thirty meters?" She asked, tossing him a beer. After he caught the first, she tossed his second. He caught that, too.

"Thank you kindly," Bubba said, life returning to his sky-blue eyes. He cracked open one of the beers, putting the second in a coat pocket. "Thirty meters is what the law would consider effective small arms. With the right caliber handgun, you can drop a fellow from inside thirty with no problem. Beyond that, it takes shot placement."

"Is that right?"

"Yes'm. Pa taught me that as a youngster."

"Hmph," Rose grunted. "Pretty impressive, Bubba." She then shifted the conversation back to the night's job. "So, what are you carrying?"

Before he could answer, hard pounding and shouting from a loudspeaker outside, audible over the howling wind. Frightened, the two and ended their exchange. Flashlight splashed across the closed curtains. Rose looked anxiously at Bubba. She put a finger to her mouth, then pointed to the window. From the loudspeaker, the police issued a warning.

"It's the police. We've got you trapped! Come out with your hands up and there'll be no trouble."

More thumping on a door came from outside. *Could this doofus have been followed?* Rose wondered, as she crept toward the blinds with Bubba taking up the rear. The police officer kept yelling, urging the occupants to open the door and come out with hands up.

"We're not going anywhere!" screamed one of the police assaulters. "We'll bust the door down if we have to!"

How the hell did they know we were here?

Then it struck her. This was no coincidence. Slowly she turned to face Bubba. Her feelings of anxiety and fear were joined with suspicion and anger.

"You have anything to do with this?" She spoke through gritted teeth and jabbed a thumb at the door. "You better fucking tell me that you didn't."

Bubba jumped back a step. He tried to speak but only stuttered.

"Not here for five goddamn minutes and already the cops—or Feds—are swarming outside," Rose said. It was hard enough for her to keep her voice down, let alone grab her .38 and take his head off. *Day one with this idiot hayseed and I'm off to prison. For a very long time.*

Bubba pulled himself together. "Miss Rose, I swear to you I had nothin' to do with this. Why would I? I'm carrying unregistered guns and loads of ammo."

The demands outside continued. "This is your last warning. Come out now or we'll knock down the door."

Rose slumped her shoulders. Their game was up, before it even began. That familiar subconscious voice chimed in.

So this is it?

Rose gestured Bubba to get behind the door as she pulled back an edge of the curtains, just enough to get a look outside while remaining concealed.

There were four that she could see. Two were closer to the motel, while other two stood further back and held flashlights and loudspeakers. One of the two officers closer to the hotel held a service revolver, while the other held a pump-action shotgun. All four officers wore black outfits and Kevlar helmets.

Rose assumed the pump-action shotgun was for blasting the doorknob and breaching the room. She turned her head to Bubba and flashed four fingers; Bubba nodded. The two officers who stood further away began to approach the other two. They switched off their flashlights. All four were close enough that Rose was able to spot badges stitched onto each outfit over the breast.

"Well, fuck it," Rose muttered.

Her heart sank. For a split second the image of her detestable father and his shit-eating grin flashed across her mind. She could almost hear that godforsaken laugh and one of his well-timed insults.

Good job, Rosie. You know, prison might be good for you. The food sucks so bad that you might even shed a few pounds.

He would follow his insults with more of his maddening laughter.

"Bubba, stand back and put up your gun," Rose instructed. "I'm opening the door."

Just as she was about to turn the doorknob, more yelling came from outside.

"Down on the ground! Down on the ground!" one officer demanded.

"That's it . . . just like that. Now put your hands behind your back."

Rose turned to Bubba. The two exchanged perplexed looks. She reached for the curtain, this time pulling the edge back several inches. From what she could gather, there were two men, both with ponytails. Both were lying face down on the cold, wet grass. Each had a police officer's knee in the back, holding them in place. They would soon be on their way to jail. As for their crimes, Rose could not care less.

So long as it ain't us.

Rose let go of the curtain. It fell back into place. She exhaled deeply, bent over and put her hands on her knees. She looked up at Bubba, who was conveying his own version of relief. Color began to return to his face.

"Ok, well that's a relief," Rose said. "So, let's get back to work."

Bubba nodded and moved to his side of the room and grabbed his duffel bag, which he had placed at the foot of his bed. He unfastened its buckle, unzipped it, then stuck his right hand inside the bag extracting a locked black case. It was no bigger than a toiletry bag. Its key was attached to a bungee cord wrapped around his wrist. He unlatched the lock and opened the case and pulled out a SIG Sauer P226, a double-action, semi-automatic 9mm handgun. Whatever flaws ran up and down Bubba Sunshine's family tree, and however branchless that tree may have been, the man possessed a penchant for quality weapons, a similar passion for weapons that Rose had only developed after weeks of intense training with Y-3.

"Okay, High Speed, that's great. Whether you can use them or not, however, is an entirely different matter. Hopefully, we never have to find out," Rose said. "Shifting gears for a moment, let me lay down the rules for room 13."

Bubba set his weapons aside, placed his beer on the adjacent nightstand and paid strict attention to Rose, just as his handlers had instructed.

"First off, all the food is mine. It ain't for sharing." Rose pointed to a Styrofoam cooler under the window and continued. "The beer is a different story. You may indulge, provided you replenish the stash and provided you are willing to fetch ice in the lobby, should I feel the need for something stronger than beer."

Rose stood up and, with a finger, drew an imaginary line across the middle of their motel room floor. "Number two, you keep all of your shit on your side of the room, Mister Sunshine. Follow these two simple rules and you won't end up singing soprano in the Vienna Boys Choir."

Rose allowed him to let the words sink in. Bubba nodded and smiled, as if Rose's decrees and threat were some kind of puppet show. He guzzled the remains of beer #1 before reaching into his coat pocket and popping #2, then draining its contents like it was his job.

"Aah! That hit the spot." Bubba wiped his chin, and then got up and placed the two empties in the plastic barrel under the sink, on his side of the room. "What I wouldn't give for one more."

She got up and pulled out another Schlitz, cold to the touch. She turned back to Bubba and held the beer up like a trophy, allowing his eyes to behold the prize. Behind her, Pat Sajak was consoling the once-jolly, now defeated, tubby woman, whose final tally stood at a measly $100, just enough for the Greyhound fare to send her back where she came from.

"Ready to get down to business?" Rose asked. "And don't answer with 'Yes'm' either. That, too, has joined the ranks of the banned. Hit me with a 'Yes'm,' and you'll wear this beer can like a crown."

"Yes, Miss Rose." Bubba's eyes followed the beer's path as Rose underhand-tossed it across the room. He caught it across his body, one-handed. Bubba Sunshine had some decent reflexes. Rose noted that as well.

She pulled the spiral-bound from the drawer in the nightstand. She opened it on her lap and flipped a few pages until she found the notes she had taken earlier while conducting recon. She glanced down at Bubba, who held a pocket-sized notebook. With a pen at the ready, Bubba the Beer-Guzzling Wonder Boy was ready to take his own notes. She eyed the two monstrous Tupperware containers. She pointed her pen at them, balanced on top of the bed's pillows.

"What's inside those? Southern fare like ham hocks and fatback?"

"No, Miss Rose. In there is mama's famous cornbread. Every time I hit the road, she fixes me some." He patted the containers lovingly, and then looked back up at her like he had forgotten something. "Where're my manners?"

Bubba peeled the top off one of them. "You want a piece? You never did taste cornbread like mama's."

Rose shook her head. "Maybe later."

She sat down and got to work. She began detailing the evening's mission. She provided an assessment on the "spoiled motherfuckers" who occupied the target house. She briefed him on the vehicles which she had recorded coming to the house. She judged most to be small-time dealers. On a strip map, she identified possible escape routes should any of them get spooked or catch her and Bubba approaching the home. In Rose's estimation, the neighbors—the few who remained off-season—would prove to be nonfactors during the raid, assuming there was no gunfire or major commotion. Generally speaking, she told Bubba, New Englanders kept to themselves. On the same map, Rose charted their route to the target house, the vehicle drop-off, and their approach to the house by foot. Bubba nodded, only piping up to suggest they assault the house from the back porch.

"Ain't no way they're expecting trouble, especially on a night like this. The strong wind will help reduce the chances of us being heard," he said.

Rose nodded in agreement. They would hit the back door, which was nothing more than a flimsy storm door. It would be easy to bust open. Given his input, she was glad she had checked the back of the house as well. Rose decided that he would kick in the door, and she would enter first. As she did, he would provide cover fire, if need be. She insisted that he not hesitate in dropping anyone inside who pulled a gun on them.

Bubba sipped his beer and nodded.

"The mission is simple: we get the thirty grand and get the fuck out."

Bubba continued listening in silence, his eyes down as he scribbled away in his notebook.

"What could you possibly be writing?" she asked.

Bubba set his pen and notebook aside. "If I hear it, write it, then read it, I ain't ever gonna forget it."

"You know, you may not be as stupid as you look."

"Miss Rose, there ain't no one as stupid as I look," he replied, with a wide grin.

Rose rolled her eyes and put the notebook with her map back in the nightstand drawer. If all went well, they would come back and burn all documentation related to tonight's mission. She and Bubba polished off their beers. It was 5:50 p.m. It was time to roll.

"Okay, Bubba Sunshine, let's see if Donnelly is right about you. Grab your piece."

Bubba got up and pulled out an envelope from the same olive duffel bag, and then crammed it into a front pocket of his jeans. Rose noticed he was still grinning, almost smirking.

"What the hell is so funny? Wipe that grin off your face." It caught his attention, his radiant smile faded. She pointed to his front pocket, from which an edge of an envelope, revealing a post-marked stamp, poked out.

"What's that in your pocket?"

"Miss Rose, I never worry about nothin'," Bubba replied matter-of-factly. He tapped his pocket. "I never worry 'cause mama's always with me."

Rose sighed and looked to the ceiling. "Whatever. Let's go."

Rose slipped on her parka, picked up her .38, popped the magazine and rechecked it for ammo; she had a full clip. She then slipped it into a concealed holster sewn inside the parka. Bubba selected the stout Glock 17 and tucked it into the back of his jeans. He then grabbed the Browning Hi Power 9 mm, his personal favorite for the up-close affair. Skillfully he conducted a functions check. The pistol had no issues; it never did. Checking it was purely instinctive. That one fit nicely into his jacket's lower-right pocket. Bubba zipped the pocket and stood up. They were ready.

They walked out of room 13. Bubba shut the door behind him, jiggling the doorknob to ensure it was locked. They had a simple plan. They were well-armed, both with weapons and experience. In this business, it paid off.

Chapter twenty-nine

As Bubba went off to the men's room to clean up his right hand, Rose chose a table in the corner of the empty restaurant. It was one of three tables adjacent to a sliding-glass door which led to an outdoor patio. Most of the tables were arranged in a horseshoe surrounding a recessed dance floor. At the head of the dance floor sat the vacant DJ booth. Whether there was dancing in the immediate future or the arrangement of tables was simply a holdover from the summer, Rose had no idea, nor did she care. She heard a swinging door open from behind the bar and turned in her seat.

From out of the kitchen, a waiter, a scrawny man with greased-back black hair and a thin moustache, walked around the dance floor and approached their table. He handed Rose a menu; she asked for a second one, which he produced. She ordered a pitcher of beer—whatever he had on tap would be fine. The waiter disappeared. She glanced briefly at the menu, which proudly proclaimed *Above the Waves* as York Beach's premier summer hangout. Plastered across the front and back of it were a dizzying array of gimmicks:

Live Music Every Friday!
All-You-Can-Eat Steamers Saturdays!
Dealing the Drafts Thursdays!

And so on and so forth. As for the menu itself, it had seen better days. Its laminated corners were peeled back. She put it down. She would order when Bubba returned.

A couple of minutes later, the waiter arrived with the beer and two frosted mugs. He placed them in the center of the plastic table. Rose thanked him and let him know it would be a few minutes before they would be ready to order. As he walked off, she turned her attention to the black night outside. She wondered if the nearly vacant beach town would know such excitement as that which had unfolded not thirty minutes earlier. Not likely, though terming it "excitement" was a stretch. By and large, the raid went according to plan, lasting all of five minutes. The worst that came of it all was the gash in Bubba's right hand, which he earned punching it through the bathroom door. In the end, she and Bubba got the cash and a flurry of confessions from the groveling little shits. Not one to throw around compliments, Rose had to hand it to him: Bubba did well.

A peppering of house lights to the south illuminated Cape Neddick where, according to Captain Gordon's ripened proprietors, only one of four homes remained occupied after September. On the eastern point was the Nubble Lighthouse, which locals claimed to be the most photographed lighthouse in the world. On this windy night, it blinked its warning to mariners, just as it had done for over 100 years. There was something calming about a lighthouse, Rose thought, as she watched its periodic blink of white and red light. Across the street from the restaurant was the Short Sands parking lot and its army of coin-operated meters. The lot was empty. Rose had parked her Chevy behind the restaurant and away from Route 1A. The car needed to be out of sight for a while. Beyond the parking lot lay the Atlantic. Whitecapped waves slapped against weathered rocks, captured by light coming from the few occupied homes. Otherwise, the ocean was as black as tar, virtually invisible.

"I think I got it," Bubba announced from behind her.

Rose jumped in her seat. She caught her breath and then shot him an ugly look.

"What the hell is wrong with you? Sit down."

Rose scanned the restaurant. The skinny waiter and the cook, a chunky black man with a comb stuck in his hair, stood behind the bar smoking. They appeared to be the only employees on shift.

Bubba removed his coat, laid it on a table behind him, and then took his seat. Both pistols were tucked under his belt and underneath flaps of his flannel shirt.

"Sorry about frightening you like that. I figured you'd like to know that I put in two stitches for that cut." Bubba smiled, marveling at the handiwork on his right hand. The stitches were tight. An overpriced surgeon could not have done a much better job.

"Good for you. And good call bringing that first-aid kit you had in your car. We need to remember that each time we go out." Rose tapped the menu in front of him. "Now, pick something quick. I'm starving."

Bubba's thirsty eyes looked up at the pitcher of beer. Its sweat-stained exterior protected golden goodness, perfectly topped foam, and rising bubbles of carbonation that called to him. Yes sir. that Bubba Sunshine of North Cackalackee, can drink some beer.

"Thank you kindly," Bubba said, and helped himself to a glass. He chugged the frosty beverage with gusto. "Now that hits the spot."

"I appreciate the pitcher." He wiped foam off his lip. His smile suddenly disappeared, replaced with a look of mild concern. "But what are you gonna drink, Miss Rose?"

Rose snorted, then shook her head, grabbed the pitcher from him and poured herself one.

"Gonna need to pace yourself," she said.

She grabbed her menu and waved it at the waiter, pulling his attention away from his cigarette and his chat with the cook.

"Another pit- . . . no, make it two," she said, pointing at the empty pitcher on their table and holding up two fingers.

She looked back at Bubba. "Figure out what you want before he comes back."

Rose took a slow sip of beer. It was time to review the night, discuss what went well and what didn't. In Army-speak, she and Bubba were about to conduct a "hot wash." She sat back in her chair and folded her hands across her lap. It felt good to unwind a little.

"Listen, tonight went well," she said, then paused for a sip of beer. "But I think we—"

She stopped as the waiter approached, carrying two fresh pitchers of beer. He offered his regrets: only steamers, clams and burgers remained in the kitchen. Rose and Bubba both ordered the clam platter. It came with fries, hush puppies and hash browns. Bubba poured another beer as the waiter vanished. He was about to open his mouth when Rose began to speak.

"Like I was saying, tonight went well. There were a few things that I think we could improve upon," she began. She then proceeded to dive into the details of the evening's mission.

As she spoke, she leaned back in her seat, her head resting comfortably against the 1960s-era wood paneling behind her seat. On and on she went. Comfortable in her seat with beer in hand, she carried on about tactics and procedures. On and on about the need for communication. The need to maintain weapons discipline, as they had done earlier. The need for silence, stealth. As she continued, Bubba's attention began to fade.

Chapter thirty

Before long, his attention was lost, fully detached from her mission-parsing and meticulous analysis. His attention settled on a poster on the wall above Rose's head. It was a framed *Genesis* tour poster, some five feet tall. The headline announced a show in Portland scheduled for May 14. Tickets would sell quickly, the poster read. "So get yours today!" Bubba didn't know where Portland was and had never heard of *Genesis.* Of course, there was a lot about New England he didn't know. The same held true with his current job.

Short of what he had learned tonight, he knew nothing of Donnelly's grand plans, in which he and Rose were supposed to eventually play a significant part. During his brief time in Worcester, which he learned was pronounced without either of the two r's and two e's, he was provided with only vague details into the aspects of his work. He was told that Rose was no-nonsense and that he was to follow her lead.

"Listen to her and do what you do best. Collect our money. Do that well, and we'll have something bigger and more profitable for you two," said a man wearing an eye patch, who never gave his name.

He was given a thousand bucks, the address and directions to the motel he now called home, and nothing more. When he left Worcester earlier in the day, he was nearly as clueless as he was when he had left Burgaw the week prior. His gaze remained locked on the poster, a mild curiosity mixed with puzzlement.

Guess it don't matter much now about some concert that happened over five years ago. Wonder why they'd even keep—

Suddenly, something hard cracked him across his broad

forehead and snapped him back to the present. As he came to, he found a saltshaker in his lap. Rubbing his forehead, he looked up and saw Rose glaring at him.

"You hear a word I said, you fuckin' doofus?" she barked.

Bubba continued rubbing his forehead. Her aim was good. She hit him dead center. But he had earned it. She was right: it was not the time for daydreaming. In the short time he had known her, Bubba found Miss Rose to be no-nonsense, just as Mr. Eye Patch had said. When it mattered most, as it did earlier in the night, she was as cool as the underside of the pillow. She was unlike any woman he had ever known back in North Carolina. She was rough-an-tumble and a touch vulgar. But if tonight was any indicator, she could be trusted in a pinch.

"Sorry, Miss Rose. I lost my train of thought."

"Whatever," she said, frowning. "Listen, do me a favor and go juice the jukebox."

She thrust a hand into the front pocket of her jeans and pulled out a handful of change, which she had taken from her glove box after parking her car. She placed the quarters and dimes onto the table and then swiped them onto an open palm, making the space on the table needed for her basket brimming with her food as the waiter arrived. Rose pointed to where she wanted the food. The waiter did as instructed.

"Here. Take this. This ought to get us a dozen or so," she said, handing Bubba close to three dollars in change. "None of that country bullshit either. I got enough issues of my own without hearing about some whining cowboy's lost love or his broken-down pickup."

Bubba nodded and placed the saltshaker back on the table. His legs had fallen asleep, so he grabbed the table with his left hand and pushed himself up slowly. He shook out his legs, one at a time. He sauntered toward the bar area, where the Wurlitzer sat. The vintage jukebox was a good thirty years old but appeared to be in working order.

Coins clinked as Bubba's fingers moved expertly across the numbers and letters of the ancient jukebox. Seconds later, Frankie Valli and the Four Seasons—recorded decades earlier in a safer, more innocent America—replaced the silence with a desperate plea to his woman not to leave. Frankie confessed his regrets for cheating, as only his high-pitched tone could pull off. Frankie Valli was one of Bubba's mama's favorites. Ergo, it was one of his. A few moments later, Bubba was back at the table, drinking beer.

Rose took a sip of beer. "Don't get used to me complimenting you. It's not my style, but you did well tonight. And if this song is any indication, your music taste is good as well."

"Well, thank you for saying, Miss Rose. You know, I always aim to please my boss."

"Your boss? Is that what Donnelly's guy told you?"

"Yes, ma'am—I mean, Miss Rose." Bubba paused for a moment. "So that's his name? Donnelly? All I've been told is the man is Irish and that my boss owed him a favor. Anyway, it was one of Donnelly's guys who told me to keep my trap shut and just listen."

Rose nodded. She seemed to study him for a moment before replying.

"Well, he's right." Rose poured herself a beer and stuck her plastic fork into the pile of fried goodness, withdrawing a clam and then placing it into her mouth. "Like I said earlier," she said, slowly chewing her food, "tonight went well. Before we left, you were all ears. Don't change that. After the vehicle drop-off, you moved silently in the shadows. Good on you there."

Bubba listened intently, breaking eye contact only to sip his beer. Across the bar, brief silence preceded Jefferson Starship. Rose perked up and smiled: "Miracles" was apparently one of her favorites. She gestured to the stitches between the thumb and index finger of Bubba's right hand.

"As I said, we need to bring your first-aid kit before we roll. If either one of us gets injured, it'll be our only medical care." Rose shifted gears. "Now, regarding our entry, as we approached the door, did you have a plan for the breach?"

"No, Miss Rose. I wasn't sure which your strong side for shooting was. If we can get to a range, I bet we could work on our entries."

By and large, their dynamic entry was effective: swift and shocking. Looking down the barrels of approaching handguns, the five punks froze in place, while a sixth raced to a bathroom for refuge. He didn't find it.

Bubba took the pause in their discussion to stuff three hush puppies into his mouth, chasing them with the remainder of his beer. As he did, Rose, picked at her clams, taking her time to dip each into drawn butter, before devouring them. Bubba finished chewing and then spoke.

"Say, I don't mean to be nosy, but ya think you gonna be able to eat up all your clams? If not, I'll gladly help ya."

Rose placed her plastic fork on top of her impressive pile of heart-clogging food. She looked across the table at Bubba, flashing her own smile.

"Remember what I said about food back in the hotel room, Mr. Sunshine?"

"Yes, Miss Rose, I do."

"And what was that?"

"I'm to stay on my side of that room and I'm to stay away from your treats."

"Precisely," Rose said. "Well, the same rule applies when we eat outside of the room. Whether in my car, in a restaurant or wherever, Miss Rose's food is only Miss Rose's."

Bubba nodded, still eyeing her pile of clams. He had no idea fried clams and hash browns could taste so damn good. Fried chicken, fried turkey, even fried Twinkies? Absolutely. Those were the staples of any Southerner. But fried clams and hash browns? What a discovery!

"Well then, I reckon I'll do fine staying on my side of the table."

"Why yes, you will," Rose offered. She raised her glass in a toast. "Good job tonight, Bubba, but this game is only gonna get harder."

Chapter thirty-one

If it was money that mattered most, Rose thought, then tonight was a success. In her purse, she held $31,000 in cash, thirty of it to be dropped off tomorrow with one of Donnelly's lieutenants. The extra grand was an added tax to account for her partner's pain and suffering, as she had told the occupants of 65 Nubble. Staring down the barrel of a loaded .38 made the decision of giving up a little more than one owed an easy one to make. As for the possibility of police involvement, whatever concerns she and Bubba might have had were unfounded. After all, what could the so-called victims claim? *We've been robbed, officer. But please don't ask the reason why. And please don't look down in the basement, where you'd be sure to find coke-covered scales, syringes, bags of weed and stacks of twenties.* For a police force with little else to do other than snoop around, that would only invite trouble. Besides, police involvement as a result of three tattletales would prompt Donnelly's direct involvement leading to a most unwelcome outcome. And who wanted that?

Back in the hotel room, Rose sat in a chair close to the window overlooking the grassy area where their hotel neighbors had been arrested earlier. The light from their room illuminated the grass. It was wet, green and needed a trim. She contemplated the evening. Meanwhile, Bubba sat against his bed's headboard and drained beer after beer, all the while gazing at a rerun of *Bonanza* on the small, static-sprayed TV. The raid had been basic: minimal drama and no real threat. The contact had told her and Bubba that they should expect similar missions over the next few weeks with the same stated goal: get the loot and get the fuck out. Which was exactly what she had told Bubba before they set off. Rose reached down next to her chair and picked up her beer. She sipped it slowly. It's not invading homes and businesses, where drugged-up zombies or armed thugs may lay in wait, Rose thought. *It's the business that lay ahead. The business that Donnelly said little about, only that it would coincide with her promotion.*

In the raids to follow, she knew that each of those miscreants had a vote in the outcome. Even so, she was confident in her and Bubba's speed of action and surprise, talents that she believed would counter most any threat. No real worries there, she thought. However, the business that would follow, expanding Donnelly's enterprise and supplanting any would-be competitors, was another matter entirely.

Chapter thirty-two

The phone's ring startled Claire, waking her from an afternoon nap. She jerked in her rocking chair. Her cup of tea tumbled from her lap spilling the lukewarm drink onto her jeans. Harmlessly, the cup hit the wooden floor below and rolled under the chair.

The phone rang again.

"Shit. Another stain," she said looking down at her wet jeans.

"Ma, that's a bad word!" Frankie announced from his bedroom.

"Yes, Frankie, it was. Mom's really sorry." The phone jingled a third time. Claire stood up and walked off to the kitchen. She picked it up on the fifth ring.

"O'Brien residence, this is Claire," she said cheerfully, knowing that Frankie was listening. A pleasant voice greeted Claire.

"Yes, ma'am, I'm looking for Miss Claire O'Brien or her son, Frankie."

Didn't I just say I was Claire? She thought to say that, but decided against it. With Christmas coming, wasn't it nicer to try a little patience? She could have sworn that was one of Oprah's themes last week.

"I'm Claire," she replied. "How can I help you?"

"Well, my boss called you a few weeks back about coming up to the election party in Maine. He called you from the White House, if I'm not mistaken."

Claire remembered in an instant. She was referring to Vice President Cartwright, now President-elect Cartwright. "Oh, yes . . . yes, of course. How could I forget? And what a surprise that was." She delayed, as she scanned the room for paper and a pen.

Soon the woman would pass names, a dress code, etiquette pointers and so on. Alas, not a pen or scrap of paper could be found. *Dammit.*

"Ma'am? Hello?"

"Yes, hello. Sorry, things are crazy. I . . . I can't seem to find . . ." Claire's eyes desperately searching the room.

"No problem, I understand. I'm sure it's busy on your end. It's the time of the year after all. It's much the same for us here," the woman said, chuckling. "The president-elect keeps us hustling day and night."

"I'm really sorry, but I can't find a pen or piece of paper anywhere," Claire confessed.

"Don't worry about that, ma'am. The details will come in the mail," she said. "The point of my call is a follow up to the vice president's call. Consider this call a formal invitation. The President-elect and Mrs. Cartwright request you and your son's presence at the post-election party on Christmas Eve. We hope you can still make it."

Claire was speechless. This is really going to happen. Her mind raced as she considered what to wear. Did she even have something worthy? Where would they stay? How about Frankie? Should they bring Christmas gifts? Maybe there was a gift exchange, like a Secret Santa? Should she pack linens? It had been years since they had stayed in a hotel.

Claire started peppering the staffer with the questions as they occurred to her. The woman on the other end of the phone handled them with ease. A package, sent by registered mail, would arrive at their apartment within three days. In it, she would find everything she would need to prepare her and her son for the two-night visit to New Whitby. If they had any questions at all, she could call the toll-free number she would find on the enclosed business card.

"And the package will have a map? You know, like one of those AAA strip maps?"

The woman laughed politely. "No maps needed. We'll send a driver to pick up you and your son." Claire felt the woman's smile across the phone. "Totally stress-free travel."

Claire shook her head, and then turned away from the phone's mouthpiece as she called for Frankie. "Honey, come here. Quickly."

Frankie emerged from his room and slipped across the wooden floors in his long underwear, the smooth bottoms of his footies allowing him to slide effortlessly. When he saw his mother glowing, his jaw opened and his eyes widened. Claire was beaming like it was already Christmas Day, Frankie's best day of all. He became giddy.

"Ma, ask the guy if he knows Santa. Come on, ma, ask him. Or if it is Santa, then please . . . please tell him I'll be under the covers like every time he comes," he pleaded.

Claire held up a finger to Frankie, hoping he could suppress his questioning until the woman on the other end was finished. She turned her back on her son and pressed the phone to her ear. Outside, a bitter wind rattled against the windows, while tossing the winter's first snow flurries hither and yon.

"So, can we count on you and your son for the party?" the woman asked.

"Absolutely. We can't wait." She turned and winked at Frankie. "Oh, wait . . . there is one thing I have to ask." She dialed down her enthusiasm a notch. "And I feel really awkward asking."

"What's that, Claire?"

Frankie walked over to the window and plopped himself down in his little wooden seat. He sat silently, watching the snow dance across the white sky. Just to be safe, Claire lowered her voice to a whisper.

"We'd really like to see Santa. I mean, is that possible?" Claire winced, anticipating some polite rebuke or an awkward pause. There was no pause nor reproach.

"Well, it just so happens that jolly old St. Nick will be visiting the residence, as he does every year. He should be arriving around 10 p.m. We've made some special requests of him," she said in her best matter-of-fact tone. "Speaking of which, has your son written that letter yet?"

Ensuring her son's attention was still focused elsewhere, Claire continued. "He's written one for nearly thirty years, the same day every year. You've never met anyone who loves Christmas more than my son." Claire looked back at Frankie. He was motionless, his eyes peeled to the winter scene outside. "Maybe you're aware, but my son is—"

"An American hero? Yes, I am. His presence was a personal request of the vice president and Mrs. Cartwright." The woman spoke sincerely. "Your son will have a great time, Claire. You will, too. I promise."

Claire was at a loss for words. What did one say to such a marvelous invitation, one made with no conditions. In the end, Claire offered her sincerest thanks and a promise that they would be ready by noon on Christmas Eve for their ride up to New Whitby.

Later that afternoon, with the day's light growing faint, Claire walked down the hall to her son's room. She found him seated at the foot of his bed, leafing through a *Mad* magazine. At his feet were scattered baseball cards, more than enough for a game of 52 Pickup. The rest of the room was in a similar disheveled condition. Underwear and random clothing strewn about, a pair of jeans and dress socks in a pile by the closet, and a baseball cap wedged under an open window made up the bedroom scene. Why his window was open on such a blustery day, she didn't ask. She walked across the room and lowered it. She was about to remind him about the cost to heat a home when he suddenly piped up.

"Ma, what did Santa say?" he asked. He pitched the worn magazine onto the socks-jeans heap, eager to get the scoop on his hero.

Claire sat down at the foot of the bed next to her son. "He's expecting us in Maine. In fact, he's sending a helper to come get us on Christmas Eve."

"I thought Santa came from the North Pole, Ma." Frankie looked confused.

"Well, he does, but he has helpers all over the world."

"Did you ask him for anything, Ma? Like a nice watch, or a dress, or a mink coat?" Frankie said, his eyes growing wider, "Ma, ma, I can imagine you in a mink coat."

Claire rolled her eyes. A mink coat was a little too ostentatious for a woman of modest means. In cold weather, which was all but certain up in Maine, her ski parka would suffice.

"Santa doesn't need to bring me anything, son." She stroked the short bristles of hair on his head, just as he liked it. "This year, Mom has everything she needs."

She smiled and patted his knee. "I'm going to make dinner. How about franks and beans?"

"Yeah, Ma! They're GRRRR-EAT!" He declared in his best Tony the Tiger voice.

Claire got up and walked down the hall and into the kitchen, flipping on a switch as she entered. After a series of blinks, faded yellow light, filtered by cobwebs and years of dust, bathed the kitchen. She looked up and frowned at the light, making yet another mental note to clean it out. Maybe I could ask Dave, she thought. Speaking of whom, she could not remember whether she had returned his call from over a week ago. She made a second mental note: call Dave. Not right away, maybe in the next day or so. Or as time allowed.

Dave Wells was a nice man. Over the years, they had shared

laughs together, a few bottles of wine and even her bed on a few occasions. But there was no spark. Butterflies didn't dance in her stomach when he entered the room. It was a relationship that was not going anywhere. He was a friend, pleasant and kind, but that was it.

Maybe he and I need to talk. Discuss expectations, maybe.

She cut the gas on the stovetop. Two clicks preceded a faint pop and the circular blue flame. She went to the refrigerator to get the hot dogs. They were the Fenway Park brand, Frankie's favorite. In fairness to competing brands, he preferred any type of hot dog. She placed five of them on a plate, while reflecting on the day's pleasant surprise. Against the backdrop of the past few months, today's call should have seemed routine. Yet it didn't. How does one process an invitation to the president-elect's Christmas party?

"We're going to the president-elect's home in just over two weeks. We're going to his home in just over two weeks," she told the empty kitchen.

However, the man who would become the nation's president in six weeks wasn't the only celebrity politician who had reached out to her and Frankie in recent days. How could the surprise visit on the day after Thanksgiving have slipped her mind? The memory of that visit struck her.

First came Cartwright's call prior to the election. Then, a few weeks later, Governor Alejandro Reyes sent a glowing letter to Frankie thanking him for his selfless, heroic act. Other letters from other high-ranking politicians, and even a few actors and professional athletes, followed.

Claire emptied the can of beans into the heated saucer. As she did, she reflected on Frankie's gallantry. Though it had happened three months earlier, it proved to be the gift that kept on giving. The microwave dinged. The hot dogs were ready. In a minute, the beans would be sufficiently warm, but not too hot. Frankie could not stand having to blow on his food. Hot food was harder to swiftly shovel into one's mouth. Shoveling down one's food meant that a second helping came sooner, at least in Frankie's mind. Sometimes Claire wondered if he tasted the food at all. She had long ago given up on scolding him for his table etiquette, unless of course they were dining out. The celebration at the president-elect's beach house in Maine would be one such case where proper table manners would be compulsory.

Dinner was finished by six, which was too early to sit on the couch and settle in for the night waiting for the Christmas special which came on at eight. Frankie had read in the TV Guide that Frosty the Snowman was tonight's feature. Once the special started, he would be glued to the TV. Not much matched his persistence when it came to watching his favorite programs, especially the animated Christmas ones. But Claire, who was eager to get out of the apartment for a spell, had just the fix for her son: video-game stimulation. It worked every time, and this time was no exception; Frankie loved the idea. So, while Frankie pumped quarters into machines with the hope of achieving high scores, Claire would have a couple of beers. With an adjoining arcade, Leda Lanes and its cozy little bar seemed the right place. They would spend a half hour, tops. She promised they would be home long before Frosty became a real snowman.

Claire found a coin machine inside Leda Lanes. She exchanged a ten-dollar bill for quarters and handed them to Frankie. It was more than enough to keep him chasing after high scores on Galaga, Ms. Pac-Man, Tron, or any number of the addictive video games in the bowling alley's arcade. The forty quarters would buy her a half hour, maybe more if she was lucky. She didn't feel the least bit guilty conning her son. She needed a few adult beverages and, if it could be found, some adult conversation. As Frankie scampered off into the gaily adorned *Games Room,* Claire wandered into Kegler's Den. The scene that greeted her was uninspiring.

She counted a dozen patrons, seven wearing bowling shirts advertising some print shop in Hudson. The bowlers all sat on stools around the center bar, behind which two strapping men stood ready to pour, pop or mix drinks. Most of the barstool boozers looked as if they had just left a funeral. As far as she could tell, no one spoke. Surrounding the bar were a few couple-occupied tables. One of the couples sat at a table positioned in a dark, recessed corner. Overall, the bar's vibe was depressing, nothing like she remembered the last time she was there. To be fair, she reminded herself, it was close to Christmas, which for some was a depressing time of the year. Claire enjoyed Christmas, and the weeks leading up to it, but only because she was able to live the season's magic vicariously through her son. Were it not for Frankie, she, too, might have been hunched over a glass of whiskey and melting ice brooding solemnly at the bar or in one of the darkened corners.

She considered turning and walking out, maybe pumping a few quarters into a pinball machine in the *Games Room.* Instead, she decided on a beer. If, after one beer, she got tired of the scene, she would leave, find her son, and actually make good on her promise to be home long before Frosty the Snowman started. She walked up to the bar and selected one of the tall stools, one which afforded her a view of the door opening up to Leda Lanes. She wanted to be able to catch Frankie should he come barreling in.

She placed her right foot on the stool's lowest rung and grabbed the bar rail with her left hand. In a fluid motion, she pulled herself up onto the stool. At five foot even, Claire O'Brien needed props to reach higher places. Cautiously, she shimmied the stool under her weight, bringing it as close to the footrest as the stool's legs could get. Settled in, she looked up to find a tall, attractive man, one of the two strapping bartenders she had spotted earlier. He looked down at her. His perfectly combed black hair matched his dark eyes. He had a nicely chiseled face. Tendons in his forearms flexed as he gripped a towel. His shoulders were square and, from what she could gather, his stomach was flat. He was close to perfection but, alas, he was married. A gold band shined on his left ring finger. She pulled herself together to speak.

"So, I guess a beer? I don't normally drink beer. You know, all those calories . . ."

The bartender smiled. "Well, I have both regular and light beer. Three on draft, eight in bottles or cans."

"Oh, then in that case, whatever you recommend," Claire said, smiling back.

He turned to retrieve a pint of Bud Light that he had on draft. Somewhere, from one of the bar's dusky corners, the juke box came to life. Hall & Oates began to sing "When the Morning Comes."

Damn it. I am so out of practice. A hot guy looks at me and I start yammering.

He walked back to her. He slipped a coaster out from under the bar, slid it toward her and placed the beer on top of the coaster. Then he took her by surprise.

"You look familiar," he said, lowering his elbow onto the bar and resting a cheek in an open palm. They were now eye-to-eye. "Maybe you've been here before? Anyway, I'm Vic and this is my place. That big guy over there," Vic said pointing to a man punching keys on a cash register. "He's my manager, Dave. Even though I own the joint, he rarely lets me back here." Vic grinned, gesturing with his hands.

"It's nice to meet you, Vic. I'm Claire."

She sat back in her stool, slightly discouraged by the wedding band.

You know what they say about the good ones.

"You might've seen me in here with a good friend of mine. I guess you could call her that. She comes here all the time, though it's been over a year since I've been here." She blushed and looked away for a moment, rubbing her hands in her lap, discomfort over bringing up what always came up in a conversation with someone new. "I don't have much free time. You see, I have . . ." She paused for a moment. "I have a challenged son."

"I see. I'd imagine that free time is hard to come by," he said with what seemed to be genuine interest. He then looked around the bar and grinned. "Tell you the truth, as much as I love it, I'm not sure *this* bar is where I'd spend much free time, at least not tonight."

Claire laughed, and laughing made her feel good. Vic's charm had a way of melting away her inhibitions. *And of unclothing a woman*, she thought. She felt herself blush.

"It's never been easy, but I love my son more than anything on earth," she said, before drinking half her pint in one pull. The beer tasted good. More than that, it stripped away some of her bashfulness. "It's not like my friend, Rose, who has no children and plenty of time to kill. Or our friend, Flo, who seems incapable of controlling her nineteen-year-old hellion of a son." Claire paused and sighed. "Neither of those two can score boyfriends, so I guess hanging out with them only reduces my already thin shot at meeting Mr. Wonderful, doesn't it?"

"Wait a sec. What'd you say your friend's name was? Not Flo, the other one," he said.

"You mean, Rose. Rose McDougal. She's the one who suggested I come—"

"You know Rose? Jeez, sorry to hear that. Didn't know she had friends." Vic laughed and shook his head. "I'm joking, really. Rose and I go way back. She's a dear friend of mine."

"You're kidding?!" Claire exclaimed.

"Not at all. I've known Rose for many years," Vic replied, then looked back at Dave, who was busy running drinks out to the tables. "Say, you don't mind if I join you for a drink?"

Claire beamed. "Please do."

Vic grabbed a glass and filled it with Sprite. He took a sip, then a second.

"Speaking of Rose, have you heard anything from her lately?" he asked.

"All she told me was something about going away for a job in Maine and that she'd be gone until after Christmas. Said she'd write when she could, but I haven't received a letter yet. She called once. She sounded okay, but that was nearly a month ago. Have you heard from her?"

"She called me, too. Told me she was okay, though that was a few weeks back. Nothing new since then," he replied. "I've known Rose for almost fifteen years. She can be elusive." His voice trailed off and he cast his glance to the floor below. "I worry about her all the time."

"We've only recently become good friends," Claire said. "Rose was a substitute teacher for my son during his last year in school." She fidgeted with her hands, looking off in the direction of the bowling alley. "Well, the last year the state could support him at his age and all."

"She was really good to him. She took up for him when the other kids picked on him, which happened all the time. Come to think of it, she may have been the only teacher to have done so." Claire shook her head and grinned before continuing. "And in such a convincing fashion."

Claire sipped her beer and smiled, as if recounting a warm memory.

"For a mom with a special-needs son, that meant a lot to me," she added.

Vic nodded. "She's always had a soft spot for the underdog. Despite the exterior, Rose has a big heart."

"A softie, huh? Well, that wasn't my last experience with her," Claire said.

She asked for another beer. With any luck, Frankie would stay entertained long enough to let her finish her second. She wondered if he knew about the beating Rose took on their last night out together. Whether he did or not, she decided to tell him.

"Not sure if you'd heard, but she got beat up at The Stable. It was just before she left for Maine. Anyway, it was really bad. Two big guys, baseball players apparently. Well, those two thugs literally pushed me and Rose's friend, Margo, to the ground after pulverizing Rose." Claire studied her beer, watching the foam settle. "Two big guys against one woman. Real fair, huh?"

"The world is full of cowards, Claire. I've met my share. Like I said, she's got a big heart and is generally a good-natured woman. Another good quality of hers is her low tolerance for bullies. I watched her scrap with a bully one night in here," Vic said leaning across the bar. "I don't know who started it, but she kicked the living shit out of him. No one liked the guy. He was a real big mouth. Anyway, I had to pull her off him. If I hadn't, she'd have knocked him out. I got lucky that night—no lawsuits and only cursory police involvement. Turns out, the hotshot was too embarrassed to press charges. And he was too embarrassed to ever show his face in here again."

Claire was momentarily stuck on the image of Rose in a knock-down, drag-out fight before she changed the subject. "What do you think she's really doing up there in Maine?"

The reference to Maine must have triggered Vic's recollection. He snapped his fingers, his eyes widened.

"She did say something else before she left. I almost forgot. She stopped in here and said something about helping a friend get his business off the ground. Never said anything about Maine. I don't remember her mentioning a specific place, but she did say she'd be gone for a while. She said she wasn't sure when she'd be back."

"Business, huh?" Claire asked. Rose McDougal didn't strike her as someone who would be involved in starting a business. For one, she didn't seem to do well at kissing up to people. "No other details? Maybe the type of business?"

"Nothing more than it being a start-up. Maybe she's gotten involved with Amway," Vic offered and then chuckled. "Can you picture Rose sitting politely in some musty, crowded living room, motivating a bunch of Amway warriors to take to the streets and meet—no, surpass!—their sales quotas! Just imagine Rose McDougal selling laundry soap door-to-door."

The two shared a laugh and drank their drinks. Claire finished her second. Before Frankie wandered into Kegler's with his empty pockets, she enjoyed a third beer.

Chapter thirty-three

Jay Natale waited silently in a closet as a heavy woman skulked down the hallway, just a few feet away, moving in the direction of his living room. Jay was a heavy man himself and was doing his best to curb his labored breathing. Known in the underworld as the Candy Man, Jay was an excessively hairy fellow, making his shirtless appearance all the more repulsive. The closet's door was cracked open, just enough for him to notice that the woman held a pistol. She was not alone. Somewhere out of view, perhaps back toward the kitchen, her partner lurked. He had gotten only a brief glance at the woman's partner, but enough to know he was tall and had blonde hair. The woman's gun was drawn, raised to chest level, and pointing in the direction of her slow advance. For so big a woman, her steps were soft, as were her partner's. He soundlessly cursed.

Dammit. Where the fuck is the big, blonde guy?

Not knowing where her partner was, he was in no position to burst out of the closet and clobber the woman. The man might be somewhere in the kitchen, or a foot or two away on the other side of the door. He had no way to know for sure.

When the two entered, the Candy Man knew that it had not been just a couple of small-time hoods. The intruders were professionals; their movements rehearsed. Their entry, the jimmying of a credit card against an easily defeated lock, had been textbook: swift and practically soundless. Again, he silently cursed.

How the fuck could I forget the damn chain lock?

Thankfully, the break-in had not been entirely soundless. The faintest click from the sprung lock tipped off the drug dealer, who had been in the processing room, weighing and bagging his expensive product. The click of the lock gave him just enough time to spot the two as they slithered in before he could scamper off into the hallway closet.

The Candy Man peeked into the hallway and watched the woman pause before she entered the living room, turn around and point. Gradually, she lowered herself to a knee and then peered around the corner, her back to the closet. She was now vulnerable. The Candy Man was anxious to eliminate the trespassers, and he had just been handed a golden opportunity to do so. Before he could, however, he made a colossal tactical mistake.

He assumed that her pointing was a command to her partner to go back in the direction from which he had come. He assumed that he could leap from his concealed position, strike down the unsuspecting woman before she knew what hit her, grab her pistol, and then charge into the kitchen and cut down her stunned mate. Sadly, the Candy Man mistook his enthusiasm for a high likelihood of success. None of what his mind's eye scripted would follow. His drug-ravaged imagination, which promised him all the talents of a Marvel Comics superhero, precipitated an excruciating conclusion. He made his move.

As Bubba turned to cover Rose's movement into the living room, he watched the closet door ahead of him inch open. Just in the nick of time. From the open door emerged a shirtless man; his back was to Bubba. He was obese. He had a crop of dense black hair running from his neckline down to the crack of his ass. He wore his jeans low and was barefoot. He paused for a moment, appearing to size up Rose. In his right hand, he held a tire iron, which he was slowly raising as he crept forward. One effective strike to the head with five pounds of unbending steel would kill her. Bubba Sunshine was not about to let that happen.

Bubba raised his Browning and took three long strides toward Rose's would-be assailant. At the last second, hearing Bubba's steps, the man spun around, his eyes wide with fright. He was too late. Bubba swung the butt of his pistol down across the man's head instantly breaking his nose, a sharp crunch announced the fracture. Blood sprayed from his nostrils. The tire iron fell from his grasp, and he slumped to his knees before flopping onto his shaggy, round belly in a moaning heap, inches from Rose. She spun around, stumbled and then fell back onto her ass. For a second, Rose appeared disoriented.

"What the hell—?" she said, shaking her head. Spotting the fat man splayed out on the floor, and the tire iron he had been wielding, her shock was soon joined with anger.

Sonofabitch! Her initial thought was to empty the contents of her .38 into the back of his head. He deserved nothing less, since he had intended to eliminate her with a tire iron. However, killing him would get them no closer to the fifty grand they were assigned to recover. So, while the piece of shit, who had planned to call for the Grim Reaper, would be spared death, a most vicious response was still in order. Rose saw red; the bastard needed to pay.

Rose jumped to her feet and took a giant stride toward the man. She drew back a steel-toed boot and kicked him ferociously in the mouth. His head snapped back violently. He choked out a series of moans, spitting out a tooth in the process. Then, defiantly, he cursed at her, blood sailing from his twisted mouth. His insult, barely audible, had something to do with her weight. In the worst way, she wanted to kick him until he swallowed what teeth he had left, maybe even choking on the fucking things. But she restrained herself. She and Bubba needed the information that only this dirtbag possessed. Instead of extracting more teeth, she focused on the money. She looked up at Bubba and told him how things would go down.

"I'll keep shit-for-brains company. You're gonna get that money he owes us," she commanded, then sneered down at Candy Man. "And this one's gonna help us."

Rose stared down at the heap of a man. Somehow, he had managed to roll onto his back. He could barely breathe; hatred was plastered across his face. She leveled her gun so that its front sight was trained on his forehead.

"Finding the money won't be hard, Bubba," she said, keeping her gaze locked on the Candy Man. "Asshole here is going to tell us exactly where it is. Ain't you, asshole?"

Slowly the man elevated his right arm and bent it at the elbow. He rotated his hand so that Rose could clearly see his fist. He then unfolded his middle finger. That simple act incensed her.

"Real tough guy, ain't you," Rose said through gritted teeth. It was all she could do to hold back. "Keep it up because the beating I give you will be a life-changing event."

She brought up her right foot and lowered it softly into the middle of the man's protruding belly. She applied an increasing amount of pressure with her foot, then released. Puffs of air escaped his strained lungs. She pressed and released her foot as if pumping a car's brakes. She saw hatred in his dark eyes. Rose imagined the pain that he would have loved the chance to inflict on her. But it was Rose, not him, who held the gun.

"It'd be really easy to blow your head off," Rose said.

Rose reapplied her foot, gradually ratcheting the pressure while maintaining her aim on his forehead. She flashed a glance at Bubba, then back to the Candy Man. "Whatcha think? Should I pull the trigger and put an end to the suspense?"

"Yes, I do believe ya should," Bubba replied, his Browning also drawing a bead on the man's sweaty forehead. "Then again, this fella might deserve a second chance."

"For what?" Rose played along. "For trying to bash my brains in?"

"Good point, boss. But he just might be the only one here to tell us what we're wantin' to hear."

Rose nodded slowly.

"You have a point, Mr. Sunshine," she said. She then asked the fat man, "Say, how's it feel getting bested by a woman, one carrying quite a bit of freight, and a guy named Bubba Sunshine? That's gotta suck."

Pinned under her weight, he could only scowl. In his current state, words would be nearly impossible to utter and just as difficult for Rose and Bubba to comprehend. None of that mattered to her. One way or the other, she was going to get the location of the money.

"You're gonna tell us where the fifty thousand is stashed, and you're gonna tell inside of ten seconds," Rose commanded. She looked down at her watch. "Make that seven seconds. Tick, tock—"

A blood-choked ". . . not . . . yours . . . fuck you," was all he could muster.

Rose gripped her sweatpants with her left hand, fighting back a desire to blast him to kingdom come. If she did, however, they would leave without the money and would have a corpse to hide, a very large one. Donnelly could help with just about anything, but getting pinned for a homicide in a back-ass state like Maine? They would be hung out to dry. She could not afford to kill the puke, but he was going to pay.

"Wrong answer, asshole."

Her knees leading the way, Rose crashed square on the man's chest, delivering the full force of her large frame. A sound like snapped kindling announced freshly broken ribs; a sudden whoosh of air escaped his flattened lungs. Rose figured she had snapped three ribs, maybe four. She snagged the tire iron by his side and tossed it over her shoulder, where it shattered something made of glass. Not that he had the wherewithal to use a tire iron, but better safe than sorry.

"You won't be needing that," she said. The barrel of her pistol was now pressed up under his nose. Any shred of his defiance was gone. Terror danced in his eyes, eyes which bulged and danced between her and Bubba, whose Browning remained pointed at him.

"Good aim, boss. I bet ya got a couple ribs there," Bubba said.

"So, let's try this again," Rose said before elevating her voice. "The money, asshole. Where's our fucking money?"

Rose pulled the pistol back from under his nose and then belted his saggy face with her open left palm. The slap sounded like the report of a rifle, her left hand leaving its imprint across his flabby right cheek.

"Ullloooggaaa," he croaked.

"Ulugah?" Rose mimicked. "That a place? Never heard of it."

She slapped his jowly face again and then jammed the barrel back into his nostril, twisting it slightly. The man's eyes watered. He coughed and choked. Fresh blood seeped from his nose and mouth.

"Uuuhh . . . uuuhh . . ." the man gasped.

"That won't work either. Need something more specific." Rose shoved the barrel of the gun deeper into his nostril. She twisted it and pushed it harder. The pain was excruciating: it was written all over his face.

"In . . . in the . . . the . . . cl . . . cl . . . closet . . ."

He flicked his eyes in the general direction of the closet, the same closet from which he had launched his failed offensive.

"Oh, that closet?" Rose jabbed an index finger toward the open closet just a few steps away. "The same one you cowered in like a pussy?"

Rose grinned. She looked up at Bubba and nodded toward the closet.

"Ain't no one else in there waiting, is there?" she asked, and then snickered. "Of course not. No extra space with your fat ass in there."

Bubba stepped into the closet and switched the light on. It didn't take him long to find a leather satchel with a padlock. It was heavy. It had to be the money. A few old coats, hats and a pair of snowshoes were the only other items. By the looks of it, the lock would be a cinch, one he could pick with a hairpin. Absent a hairpin, a hammer would do the trick.

"Got it," he called out. "Gonna grab that hammer I saw in the kitchen."

"Great," Rose answered. She kept her attention on the fat

man below her. He was completely subdued and appeared resigned to whatever she had in store for him.

"That bag does have the money, *doesn't it*?" Rose asked.

Rose heard something thump on the kitchen floor, just before Bubba sprinted back. He held the open bag by both handles giving Rose a flash of its contents. Sure enough, it was teeming with Ben Franklins. Donnelly expected $50,000. The bag was bursting at the seams, but there was no way to know if they had scored the sum. They would have to count it later. It was time to get the fuck out.

"Go get the car. I'll take care of this one," Rose said looking down at the Candy Man. Bubba tucked his gun into his belt and slipped a shirttail over its grip. He then raced out into the cold, damp morning.

"You ain't gonna remember a thing, are you?" Rose asked the defeated man. Her tone was softer, but no less menacing.

The helpless man, not knowing what to expect next, stuttered something that sounded like no. While "no" was the right answer, how could Rose be sure he was telling the truth? How could Rose be sure he would not simply wait until the second she ran outside, grab his rifle, and squeeze off a few rounds as they hopped into her car. There was only one way to be sure that he would not: she had to knock him out. That would buy her and Bubba enough time to escape and put miles between them and the house. Later, he would awake with a monster headache and blurred vision. Trying to hunt them down would be the last thing on his mind.

From outside, Rose could hear the crunch of pebbles as a car careened up the stone driveway, its rumbling sounded like a Trans Am, nothing like her car, the one which brought them here, the one she had driven for the past several years, the one which belched smoke and shimmied like a sick mule.

What the hell is that outside? she wondered.

The car came to a skidding stop. She heard a door open and then slam shut. The car's engine remained running. Footfalls sped up the outside stairs leading to the front door. The same heavy footfalls echoed through the foyer. Unsure of what was happening, Rose jumped to her feet and raised her pistol, aiming it in the direction of the kitchen and the rapidly approaching footsteps. Whoever he was, he was sprinting. Her heart pounded. She cocked the hammer and locked her elbows to brace for the .38's kick. As she was applying pressure on the trigger, Bubba came around the corner. He saw the muzzle and threw up his hands.

"Whoa, boss . . . it's just me," he said between breaths. He bent forward and placed his hands on his knees. He waved an arm behind him. "Your chariot awaits."

Rose huffed. "You know you might've called out before racing in here."

"You're right." He stood up. "We can cover that later, but for now we gotta git."

Rose nodded. The time for a clean escape was narrowing. Screwing around at the crime scene dramatically increased your chances of getting nabbed by the cops. Or worse.

"Cover me," Rose instructed. She tossed her pistol to Bubba. Using both hands, she leaned down and grabbed greasy locks of hair from behind the Candy Man's head. She managed to get a solid grip. Her would-be assailant, so bold minutes ago, looked like a trapped rat. His eyes were loopy; his teeth stained red. Rose decided that it was time he took that nap.

She brought her face directly in front of his. Then with her hands gripping his hair like a vise, she made her sudden, violent move. She tilted her head back far enough to create a massive force and then, holding his oily mane, whipped her head forward, maximizing its impact onto his ruined face. Ground zero was his nose.

She hit him so hard that he fell back unconscious onto the carpeted floor. Rose figured it would be a long time before he returned to the land of the conscious. As an added measure, Rose grabbed his bare feet and dragged his 300-pound bulk back into the closet from which he had come. With great effort, she pushed him in as far as he would go, folding his legs at the knees. That done, she shut the door, raced into the kitchen and grabbed a chair. She propped the chair against the door's handle, another line of defense designed to give her and Bubba time and space. Even if he awoke in the next few minutes, he would have to work real hard to get out. Satisfied, she and Bubba sprinted out the front door, with Rose jumping into the passenger side of her revamped Impala. Bubba dropped the Impala's transmission into drive. It growled, begging for greater speed.

"He ain't goin' anywhere for a while," she said, then turned to check the road behind. "What do you think we scored? And, while you're thinking about that, what the hell did you do to my car?"

Bubba took his eyes off the road and peered into the satchel, tucked under his legs. He smiled as he lifted his gaze back on the road ahead.

"I'll bet it's way over fifty grand. As for your car, I replaced the muffler," Bubba declared. "Wait, you're just noticing that?"

"Noticing what?" Rose asked. *Muffler? Wasn't the mechanic back in Nashua supposed to handle that?*

"Noticing the purr of that engine, Miss Rose. Only took me an hour to replace," he boasted.

"No, I hadn't noticed until you drove it up to get us outta here. It sounds great."

Bubba shifted his right foot off the brake pedal and gently pressed the gas. The car idled smoothly between rhododendrons and other dormant shrubbery. Her old beater sounded like a muscle car in its prime, as it wove along a dirt trail toward Hooper Sands Road. From there, it was three miles to Maine Highway 4, which led west to South Berwick and on to New Hampshire. Once there, they could stop, find a safe place and count the dough. Until then, creating distance from the house was crucial. They also needed to maintain their vigilance as they drove. That fat slob stuffed inside a cramped closet might have been the only one in the house, but who was to say for sure. Maybe a doped-up addict sleeping upstairs? Or maybe someone out for a stroll in the woods who happened to notice an out of state license plate. While it was true that most people in rural Maine kept to themselves, it made sense to err on the side of caution, especially when transporting a hell of a lot of money. When they made it onto the road, what about a tail?

The car slipped through a copse of stubby pine trees before turning out onto Hooper Sands, an unpaved country road.

"Take a left," Rose said, as she consulted her strip map. She turned to look at the road behind. "Keep your speed at thirty."

Bubba did as Rose instructed. He seemed to know what Rose was concerned about: a tail. It was not rocket science, but if you wanted to shake a tail, then you had to have good situational awareness, enough to spot a pro. While he didn't seem to need Rose's direction, she was going to give it anyway. She was the boss and she was still amped up after her brush with death, amped up enough to crack him across the mouth if he got sideways with her.

Periodically checking the rearview mirrors, Bubba held the steering wheel at the recommended ten and two o'clock as they headed northward toward Highway 4. The highway sign—a simple black box surrounding the number 4—was a quarter mile ahead. Rose spotted the stop sign in the distance.

"Okay, when you get to the stop sign, bang a left and speed up to sixty."

"That's a big ten-four," Bubba said.

He was grinning and Rose didn't care for it at all.

She scowled at him. "Think this is funny, Gomer? We ain't in the clear yet."

Gomer had become one of Bubba's nicknames. According to Rose, his resemblance to Gomer Pyle was uncanny. She figured no sense in letting a good thing go to waste. Besides, like the affable actor, Bubba was the self-deprecating type who never seemed to take himself seriously. Only his work—and his mama—did he take seriously. Rose liked that about him, but she didn't like the thought of him getting lax. They now held a sum of money exceeding fifty grand. It served them both to remain vigilant.

"No, Miss Rose, I don't think anything is funny. Bubba, I mean, Gomer awaits further instructions."

"Smart-ass," Rose mumbled, then smirked.

She turned and looked out the rear window. Nothing suspicious. Hell, not a car as far as she could see on their westbound heading. South Berwick was just minutes away. As they drove along, a message caught her eye. It was painted on a sign propped up by wooden beams. The sign was a few feet off the road in front of the South Berwick First Baptist Church. Bubba saw it also. He slowed down as they passed. The message was rather catchy:

SEVEN DAYS WITHOUT PRAYER MAKES ONE WEAK

"You get a look at that, Miss Rose?" Bubba asked as they passed the church. He increased his speed to forty-five. "Not trying to pry, but are you a religious woman?"

She pretended not to hear the question. She stared at the outside world as it raced by, contemplating the seven words which, as arranged, were more than just catchy. The message appeared both powerful and cliché at the same time. It was a pun she had never heard before. Like so many catchy puns, she mused, this one was bound to fall from the "mildly interesting" into the "gone and forgotten" category. After all, what difference could a roadside slogan make?

After five weeks in Maine, Rose felt trapped in her ignoble profession. Every time she took on another job—as if she had a choice in the first place—she fell deeper into a lifestyle befitting the amoral. Today's mission was the twenty-seventh in less than six weeks that she and Bubba had been working together. There was no denying that they had gotten good. On the days when they didn't have a mission, they sharpened their skills. They would go to a pistol range; they would practice lock-picking; they would work on door-breaching; they would plan for the next mission. Except for their one day off, they had worked or trained every day.

In short order, the raids had become practically routine. The danger and the thrill, which at the outset had a physical component, eventually faded. Numerous missions had dampened the exhilaration. After their tenth raid, Bubba commented that most of the raid had been about as mundane as ordering take-out food. Powerless to resist it, her unwitting plunge into criminal endeavors had begun to feel permanent. She had become increasingly convinced that there was no exit strategy in this business. She was all but certain that the moment Donnelly had walked back into her life as she lay in that hospital bed, she was a lost soul. Against the backdrop of her illegal ventures, what good could a sign touting the value of prayer do for someone so lost as she?

With her full-time plunge into the underworld, gone was any trace of independence, any shred of getting out from under Donnelly's thumb. Gone were the days of deciding whether to pick up a part-time teaching gig or not. However mundane her previous life had seemed, the one she now lived was not of her own making. Her life had radically changed.

But not every mission had been dull. On five occasions, she and Bubba had faced weapon-wielding opponents, the most recent being this morning. She had been shot at twice, while her partner had been shot at five times, three in the last week alone. He handled it coolly, balancing his return fire with Rose's, in order to suppress the threat. Despite the thrill of those five missions, even the exchange of gunfire had become almost monotonous.

Still, it was more than whatever innocence that remained in her shabby life which Rose feared was gone forever. She feared the loss of her friends, friends like Margo whom she had only known a short while. Rose knew that if you didn't nurture a friendship, then that bond, like a neglected flower, would wither and die. Whatever had been a relationship between her and her mother had long since died, so she relied on her friends. She needed to know there were people she could count on for the weeks, months and, God forbid, the challenging years ahead. As a young girl, her Gramma had told her that there were few things in life which one got to choose. Chief among those few things were one's friends. It had been weeks since she had spoken to Flo, Margo or Vic.

Add Claire to that list.

At any point during the past several weeks, she could have called any one of them, at any time. But what would she have said? What could she have shared? And share any of it—the gunfire, the narrow escapes, the piles of drug money—with Flo? Bad idea.

"Hey Flo? It's Rose. Been a while. Sorry I haven't called."

"Rose? Is it you? Oh, thank God, it's you. Just where have you been? What are you doing? We're all worried sick. Vic, Claire and I . . . we've been waiting for word. God forbid something should've happened to you. You really need to put our minds at ease. You remember what I said in St. Joe's—"

"You're right, Flo. But listen, there's no need to worry. My job is pretty much humdrum, really simple work actually. Although, for what it's worth, I almost got my brains bashed in by a coke addict brandishing a tire iron. Two nights ago, I actually felt the pop of a .45 caliber slug as it sped past my face, nearly killing me instantly. Fortunately, my partner and I survived and got the money. Turns out, he's pretty good at this, too. And hey, the money's not bad, so . . ."

In the end, there was nothing to tell them that would not have sent them over the cliff with worry. And bringing Gramma into her thoughts? To what end? Best to just brush those thoughts aside and stay sharp on the job. Rose figured that forgetting about her friends and not thinking about her Gramma would keep her focused.

"Miss Rose," Bubba asked. "Don't mean to interrupt, but are you wantin' to stop somewhere and eat?"

She pulled her attention away from the decaying brick buildings and bare trees which they passed. She looked at Bubba as if waking from a trance. Then she remembered: what about a tail?

Her heart leapt. She spun in her seat. A Ford Ranger, with a middle-aged woman in the front and a teenage girl in the back, followed, two cars lengths behind. They were turning into a McDonald's. Not a tail. She gently slapped her face a few times. She then instinctively patted her coat pocket. Her pistol was secure.

"Sorry about that, Bubba." She smiled faintly and then looked back outside. She waved a hand forward. "No, not here. Let's go a little further," she said and pointed ahead. "New Hampshire is over that bridge."

The rusty bridge, built in 1936 during the Great Depression, spanned the meandering Salmon Falls River. The river snaked its way south, dissecting the states of Maine and New Hampshire on its way to the Atlantic. Once into New Hampshire, the land opened up from empty brick buildings into small barren fields. Neat tracts of Christmas trees flanked one of the fields. Some of the taller ones were sure to meet a chain saw before adorning living rooms in the days to come.

"Say, Miss Rose, look o'er there." Bubba pointed to the telltale bell imprinted on a sign high above town.

Hmmph, so Taco Bell has made it to Dover, Rose thought. Taco Bell delivered Mexican food in under five minutes. It was only three blocks ahead. Rose laid out the plan.

"First, we're gonna get our food at drive thru. We eat in the car. While one of us is eating, the other is counting the loot," Rose said.

She looked at the clock on her dash. It was showing just past eleven.

"After eating and counting, I'm going to find a pay phone and call our contact. He'll give us our link-up time. From here, it's a thirty-minute ride to the rest area."

"Taco Bell lookin' good, Miss Rose. It looks empty inside. Maybe we could find a table and—"

"No," Rose snapped. "We're eating *outside*, I said." She shot him an annoyed look. "You don't take this kind of money into a restaurant, not if you hope to deliver it all to your homicidal employer who expects every damn penny of it."

"I need to pee, but—"

"But you can hold it," she said, cutting him off again.

Bubba nodded, slowed the car and turned its steering wheel to the right. He put muscle into the turn as the Impala pulled into the Taco Bell parking lot, the area's only non-burger fast-food joint. The undercarriage of the Impala scratched as it entered the parking lot. Rose winced. Despite the recent repairs, she worried if her old beast had enough miles of life left before she could afford a worthy successor.

She scanned the parking lot. Three cars, likely belonging to employees, were in the back. Otherwise, it was empty.

"Where the hell is everyone?" Rose muttered.

Bubba idled into the drive-thru lane, stopping next to a speaker box. A few seconds later it squawked. A blasé teenager, smacking gum, greeted them. Her voice displayed indifference, which pissed Rose off. Bubba's indecision and dawdling pissed her off even more. Rose took charge. Her impatience and hunger pains hastened their orders: four beef burritos and two chimichangas. No need for beverages; they had their own.

"Did little Miss Princess copy all that?" Rose said into the speaker box.

Little Miss Princess got the order, loud and clear.

They drove up to window number two. Rose handed Bubba money from the stash of their stolen plunder. Bubba paid the gum-smacking teen in exchange for two bags of processed food. Bubba then drove the car into a rear corner of the parking lot, the nose of the car pointing out toward an exit. Rose took first shift as banker, carefully counting out the money in thousand-dollar increments, rubber-band wrapping each grand in a roll.

"So where is everyone, anyway?" Rose asked.

"Well, it is Sunday. I reckon, church."

"It is?" Rose had no idea. The days had blended together. "What's today's date?"

"December 11th," Bubba answered, never taking his eyes off his chimichanga, which dribbled mystery sauce from a small hole in the tortilla onto his pant leg.

"If I ain't mistaken, it's the second Sunday of Advent."

Rose noticed Bubba spying her food, as if his wasn't enough. She set the money aside for the moment and narrowed her eyes on him.

"You remember the two rules, don't you?" she said, a smile emerging. "Specifically, the one about the food?"

Bubba pulled his gaze from her food and looked up. "How could I forget?"

"So, you can be trained after all," Rose said and laughed. She then turned more serious. "I never did answer your earlier question, did I?"

She took a bite of her chimichanga, chasing it with a swallow of warm Schlitz. A moment later, she burped. It never occurred to her to apologize to Bubba. After a month of sharing a small hotel room on the beach, Bubba had heard worse. Just a few nights ago, she woke him from a deep sleep as she retched and gagged over the toilet, eventually recycling close to a six-pack's worth of cheap beer. As to the belching, she knew a guy who hung out at The Stable who could burp out half the alphabet. Apparently, the key to that feat was guzzling an insane amount of beer without stopping for a breath. That sort of crude behavior used to disgust her. But times had changed and so had she. She had grown to tolerate certain obscenities.

"Which question was that, Miss Rose?" Bubba asked.

"You asked me if I was religious," Rose said.

"Oh yeah. I nearly forgot," he said. "I didn't mean to be nosy by asking. I reckon that's a personal question, so I don't mind if you don't wanna share."

"No, no. It's fine." Rose sat back, resting a fresh beer in her lap and taking the last bite of her lunch, which had been most satisfying. "Sometimes I think I'm religious, but only when it suits me. At least it seems that way."

She took another sip of beer, then looked up to see a train of four cars pulling into the parking lot. Sedan-type cars, which carried smartly dressed boys and girls and their dapper dads and tidy moms. Members of society's legitimate class on full display.

Where I thought I was headed. For a moment, anyway, Rose quietly lamented.

"What are you? Protestant? Catholic?" Bubba asked. "I ain't seen too many Protestant types up here in the North."

Rose pulled her gaze away from the outside scene and answered him. "Catholic. Once upon a time, anyway."

"Oh, really? Y'all sprinkle, right?"

Rose looked at him suspiciously.

"What do you mean 'sprinkle'?"

"Well, my mama's mama said that Catholic pastors have those sprinklers and when one of them feels like wandering the aisles, he sprinkles his flock."

"That's priest, not pastor," Rose said. "And sprinkle? Where does that even come from? Lemme guess, your mama and kin are part of a bevy of folks bankrolling those dickwads like Jim and Tammy Faye Bakker?"

Bubba lowered his eyes. He fumbled with his rabbit's foot before putting it back into his chest pocket, where it fit snugly.

She shook her head before rolling up the food wrappers and shoving them into her Taco Bell bag. She crumpled up the bag and tossed it on the floorboard, where it joined assorted candy wrappers and other trash. Before she resumed her task of counting money, she apologized.

"I didn't mean to take a shot at your family like that. That wasn't fair."

"I'm the one who should be sorry, Miss Rose." Bubba kept his head down. "That was a cheap shot on my part," Bubba continued. "It's just what some of my kin used to say but that don't make it right."

"So that's what your mama thinks, huh?" Rose asked. She tried to hold a stern expression, but failed. "Tell you what, as long as your mama keeps sending you that cornbread, she's free to say whatever comes to mind."

Bubba looked up. A broad smile spread across his boyishly handsome face.

"Say, ya want me to count the rest?" he asked.

"Nah, don't sweat it," Rose said. "You keep eating."

Rose tallied a very hefty sum of money, one far more than the fifty thousand they were tasked to recover. After forty-five minutes of counting and eating in the Taco Bell parking lot, she and Bubba were off to their usual meeting point: the rest area on I-95 south, about a mile from the Mass border. In their possession was over eighty-two thousand dollars. It was collection money destined for Donnelly, money which would add to his impressive wealth. Except, it was money that was never his in the first place.

A week before Christmas, Rose and Bubba decided to head over to Above the Waves for a few beers. It was one of only three restaurants open in the offseason. Given the unseasonably mild weather and the restaurant's proximity to their hotel, they decided to walk. They had been cooped up in their room for the previous three days as a Nor'easter brought heavy, cold rain and biting winds off the Atlantic. Today, however, marked a temporary reprieve from winter. Another storm was due in two days, and this one was forecast to deliver several inches of snow. But none of that mattered to Rose. She smiled feeling the warmth of the sinking sun as she and Bubba walked up a short flight of wooden stairs leading from the beach to the top of an eight-foot high cement sea wall. As she reached the top, she heard a nearly deafening shout from behind. She spun on her heels and plunged her right hand into her parka, ready to pull her pistol if need be. A few steps behind her, Bubba turned and dove his right hand into his jacket.

What Rose spotted down on the beach was of no threat: a fat man with wild black hair seated Indian-style on a towel. He was a few feet from the wet sand and was facing out to sea. She could make out strands of back hair creeping out from below the neckline of his sweatshirt. She figured he sat there watching a kid on a surfboard wearing a wetsuit, a few hundred feet from the shoreline. He was waiting on the next wave. He didn't have to wait long. A moment later, he lowered himself onto his stomach and turned the nose of his board toward the beach. He began paddling hard as a growing swell approached from behind. As the wave closed in, the back of his surfboard began to rise. As it did, the kid pushed himself up, pulled in his knees and executed a perfect mount. He stayed in a low crouch and, a few seconds later, he was inside the tunnel of the chest-high wave. After watching the flawless mount and perfect balance, the fat man raised his arms, rigorously clapped his hands and shouted.

"Way to go Jimmy! Nice one!"

The kid on the board waved back and smiled, before paddling back out to the break zone to wait on another tasty wave.

Rose's gaze returned to the man seated on the towel. There was something familiar about him. The hair, the sheer size of him. *Kind of resembles that fat guy I pulverized a few weeks ago*, she thought. *The same guy we stuffed into a closet.*

Bubba interrupted her ruminating. "He looks familiar, doesn't he?"

"I was just thinking the same thing."

"That mess of stringy black hair, his size," Bubba said.

Rose nodded, her eyes locked on him. With his attention focused on the surfer, he was oblivious to their presence. "Let's get going. If it is him, we don't need to be around."

Bubba walked up the last few steps and stood next to Rose. The two gave the man a final look before walking onto the large, empty parking lot, which was across the street from their destination. From behind them came another cheer celebrating another ride on an icy wave.

Before reaching for the door leading into Above The Waves, Bubba stopped and turned to face Rose, slipping his hands into his pockets as he did. He appeared deep in thought. Rose frowned.

"Whatever it is, I don't wanna hear it. I want to enjoy this sunny day, have a beer and not think about work," she said. Of course, that last wish was just blown out of the water after seeing that fat slob on the beach.

Bubba leaned in a little closer, even though there was no one around.

"Did it strike you as a little peculiar that we end up at a house where we collect over eighty grand?" Bubba let the question linger before continuing. "And when Donnelly's guy assigned us that mission, all he said was something about fifty grand, but was never specific. We've always been told the exact amount. Then when we dropped off the money, he never asked what we'd collected. That too was a first."

Rose began to feel light-headed, not wanting to hear anything more about yesterday. Bubba wasn't done.

"We've never collected anywhere near eighty grand." Bubba paused for a moment, as if expecting a response from Rose. She offered nothing, so he continued. "I tell ya, something about that mission just doesn't add up. Something that bugs me a whole lot."

She didn't want Bubba to notice her growing anxiety. In an attempt to appear to dismiss his concerns, she casually waved a hand and rolled her eyes.

"Come on, Bubba," Rose said, forcing a smile. "We both knew these missions would be riskier over time. We also knew they'd be more lucrative."

"Yeah, but eighty grand?!" Bubba said in a raised tone, before noticing a look of agitation on her face. "Sorry, I got carried away. You're right. It's probably nothing. It's just that I find it hard—"

Rose cut him off. She had heard enough. "Remember the rules I laid out for you on the day you came parading into our hotel room dripping wet *and late*?"

"Yes, but I don't see how—"

"New rule: when it comes to our future assignments, don't question the purpose. It's always been the same: we get the money and we get the fuck out. We don't question what we're asked to collect nor what we come away with. As long as we collect what we're asked to collect, I don't give a fuck."

His eyes expressed a desire to protest.

"Got it?"

Bubba hung his head and nodded.

"Atta boy. Now grab that door for the lady," Rose said, pointing to herself and smiling. "Then march up those stairs and, when we get to the bar, buy me a beer. Maybe two."

Chapter thirty-four

Two days after cheering on his nephew, who had fearlessly ridden some towering waves on York Beach, Jay Natale, aka the Candy Man, opened his mouth and placed an acid stamp onto the end of his tongue. It was his third in less than thirty minutes. His blood pressure was already elevated and there was visible sweat on his cheeks and forehead. The Candy Man preferred cocaine, usually the same coke he sold. Occasionally, however, he liked a good acid trip.

The acid was just a sampling from folder of 100 which he would later be handing off to a small-time dealer from Sanford, one of a legion who owed his allegiance to Jay's boss, a temperamental, porky Italian who called the shots from Providence. The Candy Man couldn't stand him.

"Fuckin' piece-of-shit Wop. Always barking orders and bitchin' about profits. Damn lazy motherfucker. Prolly never got his own hands dirty," he told the empty kitchen.

Getting that off his chest, he lowered his nose to just a few inches above a short line of coke, closed his left nostril with his index finger and snorted in through his right, as he moved up the line. According to the experts, coke and acid should never be taken together. Cardiac arrest and even death were possible outcomes of the dangerous union of these drugs. But the Candy Man didn't care. He considered himself a seasoned vet, a pro. Not to mention, checking in at close to 300 pounds meant he could absorb a lot more without overly stimulating himself. At least that's how he saw it.

Within seconds of snorting the coke, the feeling of euphoria arrived. It swiftly combined with an acid-induced sensation of weightlessness and drifting. As it did, he leaned back and stared up at the ceiling. Creatures resembling foxes line-danced across the ceiling. They seemed to wink down at him as they did. He thought they were the most talented dancers he had ever seen. As they paraded left-to-right, then right-to-left, they stayed in rhythm, keeping the beat to some melody never recorded nor ever to be heard by a man in his right mind. The foxes multiplied from six to twelve and from twelve to twenty-four. Before they could double in strength again, he felt it necessary to verbalize what he witnessed.

"Look at that. It's that ballroom dance . . . the foxtrot. Get it? It's the foxtrot 'cause there's a bunch of foxes up there," he said dreamily.

He was so focused on the ceiling entertainment that he didn't hear the pop of the front door's lock nor the door creak open. He never heard the footsteps as they approached. Not that any of it would have mattered. It was the outline of a tall, pallid man wearing a Scally cap standing across the table which pulled his attention back to real things, back to something scary.

It took the Candy Man a moment to recognize the man who stood across the kitchen table. As soon as recognition hit him, he knew exactly why the man had come. The Candy Man knew that his life was over. The theft of approximately eighty thousand dollars by the tall, blonde-haired man and his chunky sidekick had brought the hitman to his house. On that fateful day, he had lost a ton of money belonging of that same piece of shit Wop in Providence who called all the shots. The two thieves had bested him, beating the shit of him and cramming him into a closet. The greasy Wop had sent the hitman to collect; there was only one way this encounter was going to end.

In a measured tone, the hitman asked him for the eighty grand.

Stuttering and fidgeting in his chair, no longer under the rapture of coke and acid, the Candy Man concocted a fairytale about a gang of Mexicans, believing that maybe, just maybe, it might earn him a reprieve. However remote the chance of saving his life was, he had to give it a shot.

"A dozen of them . . . little Mexicans scampering here and there . . . they were everywhere," he breathlessly claimed. He was desperate for leniency.

Once again, the hitman asked the question: where was the eighty grand? The Candy Man double-downed on the myth about the dozen scampering Mexicans. The hitman was not impressed and reached into his trench coat, pulling out a pistol. The Candy

Man watched in horror, as the hitman extracted a silencer from a coat pocket and then screwed it onto the pistol's muzzle.

The Candy Man choked up. He offered ways to get the money back, begging for a second chance. Not a word in reply came from the hitman. No shred of his earlier coke-acid high remained. His thoughts turned to his nephew, an award-winning surfer who had a bright future in places like Hawaii, Baja California and Puerto Rico, places far-removed from the misery of a life steeped in crime and violence.

The Candy Man held his hands out in supplication. He knew what was coming, and he knew there would be no mercy. He only hoped it happened fast, as painlessly as possible. By comparison to the beating he had taken from the heavyset woman, instant death would be generous.

The hitman raised the pistol and fired twice. Both slugs punctured holes in the Candy Man's forehead, one above the right eye, the other above the left. The blowback of blood, brains and bone against the refrigerator was impressive. The hitman smiled for a moment and then took out his Polaroid. The boss would want evidence; he always did. He snapped three pictures; one was a spare while the third was for his scrapbook. Chuck Aiello kept memories of each job. He was a sentimental man.

He slipped the Polaroid back inside his jacket and then blew on the silencer to cool it down, before placing it into his coat pocket. The whole affair, the loss of eighty grand and an experienced dealer, could be chalked up as a business write-off, a bad investment in an unreliable dealer who could not keep his nose out of the stuff. You win some and you lose some, Chuck maintained. But you always send a message. He knew that killing the Candy Man was strategic messaging designed to influence the boss's cadre of top dealers: the price of failure was extreme. It was not the total sum that was so appalling. Eighty thousand could be earned back in any number of ways: cut commissions to the bookies; increase the cost of protection to shopkeepers who might not have previously realized the perils of doing business in Rhode Island and Connecticut; generate an inflationary tax for the products and so on. As in any business, losses were to be expected. But for an envelope which Chuck spotted on his way out of the house, the eighty grand would have been exactly that: a loss.

As he was leaving the kitchen, Chuck noticed the envelope poking out from under the refrigerator. He bent down and picked it up. It was open, and there was still a card tucked inside. The return address was Burgaw, North Carolina. The recipient was a Bubba Coslaw, who received his mail through General Delivery in York Beach.

Chuck grinned as he slipped the envelope into his coat and walked outside, zipping it up to combat the December. He had a good idea as to how this would play out. He knew how his employer would respond to what Chuck figured was a clue to the whereabouts of the money. With a return address on the envelope, he would soon be headed to Burgaw. Sure, eighty thousand could be written off, but not when one had a lead as to its recovery. Chuck only hoped it would not interfere with Christmas. He hated the thought of missing the smiles on the faces of his grandchildren. In a dark, stained world filled with violence and despair, Christmas with his grandkids was a beacon of light on a landscape of shadows.

Chapter thirty-five

Patrick Donnelly sat in the Galley Diner, his favorite restaurant in South Boston. Across the table from him was Ira Levin, his consigliore, though Donnelly never referred to him as such. No right-minded Irishman would stoop to use a guinea title. It was bad enough that people mistook him as Italian, with his thick, jet-black hair and aquiline, Roman nose. Outwardly he shrugged off such suggestions, but it irritated him to the core. He was often tempted to ask the observer if they had ever seen a blue-eyed, fair-skinned wop. But he never did. Instead, he would smile and write it off as just another stupid schlub with nothing better to do with his or her time than to make some worthless observation about someone's appearance. Since Donnelly could not order the execution of everyone who aggravated him, he had learned to let many things roll off his back. Being Irish, but not resembling the Lucky Charms-shilling leprechaun, was apparently a bridge too far for simpletons who, in sheer volume, dominated the Earth's population.

With just a week before Christmas and much shopping to be done, the very last place he wanted to be was listening to Levin drone on and on about the left- and right-hand sides of the balance sheet. Levin was both a lawyer and accountant. As such, he could not help himself and his tendency to constantly fret about money.

Donnelly considered lawyers greedy and self-centered. In his experience, the generalizations about lawyers applied. They were the kind of people you wanted to choke to death with your bare hands. Leave the gloves in the car. Enjoy the sensation of crushing the esophagus of some Armani-wearing shitbag lawyer as he begs and pleads through bulging eyes like some trapped animal. Be sure to use your knuckles when you clamp down on the neck, Donnelly had been taught. The use of one's knuckles was more efficient.

Lawyers were a dime a dozen. They were full of braggadocio in a courtroom. They would point and gesture; they would threaten. But all that took place *inside* of a courtroom. Outside the courtroom and without the protection of the state, it was entirely different. When you had them cornered in some stinking public restroom on Castle Island—and what high-society type would be found dead in such a working-class bastion of recreation—they would crumble. It was there that the once-pompous lawyers would come to realize the true balance of power. They became utterly pathetic.

These excuses of men were nothing like Donnelly's father, who grew up dirt-poor in Castlemaine, County Kerry, a place devoid of such sycophantic men. The men of County Kerry acted like real men. They protected their woman, they earned a living, however meager, raised their kids and they faced danger head-on. Not so with lawyers, who paraded around like a bunch of fairies. Whatever happened to the John Waynes? The Audie Murphys? Gone. In their void, an army of greedy, self-serving and duplicitous lawyer waifs. How could you trust them? And while it was true that his very own trusted agent was a lawyer, Ira Levin was not a typical lawyer.

Ira had been his dad's trusted agent after his dad scratched, dug and climbed the subculture ladder, landing at the top of the family, unseating his worthless alcoholic uncle, Michael. Patrick's father trusted Ira. Ira was good with the books, initially serving as only his accountant. Ira never attended the many parties, nor involved himself with a mistress. He never partook in the high life associated with the mob.

Ira and his wife Edna were practicing Jews. They kept the Sabbath and lived virtuous lives. He never drank and never swore. He drove a Dodge K-Car, an ugly, boxy thing on four wheels. He bought his and his wife's clothes off the sales rack at Filene's Basement and paid for everything in cash. Unlike most Jews that Donnelly knew, Ira didn't thirst for riches. His father had compensated him well, which did not change when Patrick assumed the mantle of leadership. On a number of occasions, Patrick offered him more money. But with each offer came a polite refusal.

For a modest income, Ira kept the spreadsheets clean and

provided sound, objective advice. Another plus: Ira possessed an uncanny street instinct, so unusual for a milquetoast guy. Ira lived comfortably on the outskirts of the Donnelly clan, just where he liked it. He figured that to get too close would invite temptation. Of Ira's many talents, however, one stood above the rest: he never opened his mouth. Unless it was to answer a question or offer advice when solicited, Ira remained mum. The fifty-five-year-old was the employee that Patrick Donnelly admired most.

Donnelly stared at his Guinness as Ira continued pouring over an array of spreadsheets, his half-eaten pastrami sandwich was pushed off to the side. He droned on about which reps ("spokes") had settled on time and which were in arrears. One rep, a shifty fella from Braintree, had been unreachable over the past several days. He owed seventy-five thousand and had not made a payment in a month. Seventy-five thousand was budget dust by Donnelly's standards, but a sum that should be acquired nonetheless.

"We have to assume he's on the run. His credit card was used at a gas station in Pittsfield on the twelfth and in Binghamton, New York, the next day," Ira said. He shuffled a few papers and produced a road map, rotating it for Donnelly's reference. "He's not moving very quickly and we can assume he's following the interstate."

Donnelly silently acknowledged; he didn't have to say a word.

When that happened, he went to extremes. It had been years since killing was part of his routine, but he had not outgrown the act altogether. As the family boss, however, his focus was on business growth and managing an ever-expanding crop of wealthy clients.

Donnelly excelled in the sales arena, just as his father had. Persuasive, charming and with energy to spare, few were immune to the charismatic Patrick Donnelly. In recent years, expanding the family business beyond the Boston suburbs had become his sole mission. So, when Levin got around to discussing his grand plans to push into northern New England, Donnelly perked up and rejoined the business meeting. Unfortunately for Donnelly, however, Levin was nowhere close to being finished with the spreadsheets. The fucking things were all over the table.

I'm gonna stab myself in the eye if this goes on much longer, Donnelly thought.

Lifting his apathetic gaze away from Levin, he noticed a young tart making eyes with him from a few tables away. She smiled at him; Donnelly smiled back. He loved women: young or old; short or tall; blonde, brunette or redheaded. He especially loved it when they flirted. And flirt with Donnelly they did. When he flashed his movie-star smile, women swooned. Bagging a dame was never a challenge, nor did it require divulging his personal wealth and power. Rod Stewart once claimed that some guys had all the luck—Donnelly was one of them.

On and on Levin spoke. His words had become like background noise, almost like that piped-in music in a department store. *Sooner or later, he's gonna deliver the bottom line so I can enjoy my sandwich and beer.* But Donnelly knew better. Not convinced the end was in sight, he interceded.

"Ira, my dear friend, I love ya, but you're killing me here." He reached for his corned beef on rye and took a bite. With a mouthful of food, he added, "I've got shopping to do, so let's wrap it up. Let's part company with the minutiae and discuss my expansion plans, eh?"

"Of course, boss, as you wish," Ira shuffled a few of his ledgers, set them aside and found his notes. "Yes, here we are." He pushed his reading glasses up on the bridge of his long nose. "There were two things I wanted to discuss . . ."

More paper shuffling. Donnelly rolled his eyes and took a swig of his Guinness, the only beer he would let touch his lips. He glanced back to the blonde, who sat two tables to his right. He caught her staring at him. She smiled, dipped her head, then rolled her shoulders, playing coy. Donnelly liked it and maintained his gaze. She looked back again, totally ignoring the dweeb wearing a cardigan sweater who sat across the table from her. Donnelly pointed at himself, then to her. Her smile grew, she nodded her head and blushed. Yes, she was interested.

Donnelly craved the pursuit. After the hunt had ended, and always in his favor, it was off to the next challenge. If this one was lucky, she might find herself spending the evening with a forty-year-old multimillionaire. If so, the outcome would be predictable: she would never be Miss Right, but she could be Miss Right Now.

". . . anyway, should I call in a favor from the judge up in New Hampshire or do we—"

"What judge?" Donnelly snapped, drawn back to the conversation from which he had wandered.

"You haven't been listening, have you?" Levin frowned.

"Honestly, no. I was beginning to like it that way." He grinned at the brooding lawyer. He continued, turning more serious. "Unless you're about to tell me it has something to do with that blowhard, Grant?"

"Yes, I am," Levin replied.

Donnelly felt nauseous whenever he heard Judge Grant brought up. The man was a fucking train wreck. He had an ego, a temper and a mistress half his age, whom he flaunted around town. Routinely he displayed poor judgment. Donnelly often wondered why he ever got involved with that self-serving narcissist. It was a gamble, to be sure. His dad had scores of judges on his payroll and used them regularly. Donnelly figured a judge up in New Hampshire could facilitate his push into northern New England. That Judge Grant had aspirations for high office made him all the more useful. But he was prone to mistakes. The last thing Donnelly needed was a high-profile figure like Grant cutting a deal with the Feds if he ever got in a pickle.

"What'd he screw up this time?" Donnelly asked, unamused.

"Nothing, boss," Ira replied. "You're aware of his desire to become the next state Attorney General?"

"Yes, of course." Donnelly took a swig of the dark beer. "Not to get off topic, but how did those hicks up there settle on the state motto anyhow? Ever wonder about that? What kind of message does 'live free or die' send?"

Ira started to sweat. He wiped his forehead with a napkin, and then returned to his notes. His boss rarely digressed into trivial matters. When he did, or when some young lady caught his eye, Ira did his best to bring him back to the business at hand. He continued, this time raising his voice just enough to maintain Donnelly's attention.

"My concern is that, in his quest for office, he undertakes a ruthless campaign of treating every infraction as prison-worthy in order to demonstrate a tough-on-crime stance to the public. If he does that, which I believe he will, it may cut into our bottom line."

"As stupid as Grant is, he knows better than to toss my dealers into the slammer. He and I have had this talk. He knows what's in store for him if he ever considered doing something so stupid."

Levin took a sip of his ginger ale.

"But it's more than just the current dealers up there," Levin explained. "You may have troubles moving some of your talent north. On the demand side, we may see a dip as the more casual clients elect to stay away from the stuff altogether. Stiffer prison sentences, harsher penalties, you know?" Levin shrugged his shoulders and opened his palms, seeking approval.

"I see your point," Patrick said. "What do you recommend?"

"We present him with the classic 'carrot and stick.' He will leave our reps alone or face the consequences. If you jail any of our guys, then not only do we pull support, but we respond in a heavy-handed fashion." Levin took another sip of ginger ale, then burped. "On the flip side, he shields our reps, as he's done for four years, and we up his stipends, a stimulus to jump-start his bid to become the AG."

Donnelly leaned back into the booth's faded blue cushion and rubbed his fingers over his chin. With his eyes cast down on the Formica table, he slowly slid the glass across the table from hand to hand.

"Of those on your payroll, none are as whimsical as the judge. He's a wild card, Patrick."

"You got that right," Donnelly sighed. I knew it was a risk getting involved with him, but I'm sure we can keep him compliant."

When he first considered a prolonged business arrangement with Judge Grant, Donnelly had consulted his trusted agent. Ira asked his boss to take a more analytical, not emotional, approach. Donnelly had and, to this point, it had paid off.

"Be careful not to become too emotional, Patrick. You know it doesn't suit you," Ira said.

Donnelly was confident that he could put that genie back in its bottle if he had to. Or simply kill him. Ira had evidenced no qualms suggesting that Patrick eliminate the judge, if need be. Both Donnelly and Ira hated the judge on a personal level. In the pro column, however, Grant was the odds-on favorite at becoming the next AG, squarely putting New Hampshire in the win column. Even his dad never owned an attorney general, which impressed Ira. After what appeared to Ira to be deep contemplation, his boss spoke.

"Let's go with it." Donnelly finally said. "I'll deliver the message. I want him to know, with no ambiguity, that if he fucks up, I'll be the one to deliver the bad news."

Donnelly ran a hand through his hair. "As you know, I got that prick deeper in my pocket than any of the Boston pols who call 24 Beacon Street home."

Donnelly looked down at his watch.

"Okay, I'm short on time. What else do you have?" He ran a hand through his hair and checked his look in his spoon's reflection.

"It's Rose McDougal and that goofy Southern fellow," Levin pulled a leather dossier from his briefcase, which rested on the seat next to him.

Donnelly appeared confused.

"She's the, you know, the full-sized woman." Ira gestured with his arms.

"Of course, Rose and that hick, Bubba, from North Carolina." Donnelly laughed.

Ira figured his laughter had something to do with the image of the two. Maybe a mental image of the two walking into this very deli. Her cursing, him lumbering in tow.

"What a pair those two must make in public," Ira said. He nearly laughed himself. There was a damn good reason why Ira had suggested the pairing: they gave off the image of ineptitude, the image of two bumbling fools. Of course, this was not the case. They only looked stupid. Bubba's boss, known across south Florida as "Pico the Castrator," had described Bubba as very capable. Ira's own research had revealed the same.

"They've been working together for over six weeks now," Levin began. He shuffled a few pages and readjusted his reading glasses. "They've collected from every one of our delinquents in southern Maine and the Portsmouth area. They've made thirty-two house calls without incident. No cops, no mess. Equally impressive, they've delivered the required sum of money within twenty-four hours of snatching it." Levin removed his spectacles before continuing. "If I may editorialize for a moment, their operation has been exceedingly successful."

"Hmph. Do we have any other reps with a perfect track record?" Donnelly asked.

"At one point, we had this couple. They were good. If I'm not mistaken, this was about six years ago, maybe seven. They had this strange way of—" Ira began.

Donnelly held up a hand. "I got it. No need to continue."

Ira nodded. He knew his boss was not overly interested in details, especially his tendency to deliver excessive detail. *I need to work on that,* Ira thought, and not for the first time in his career. Ira always tried to stick to the highlights, but didn't always succeed. He shook off further ruminating and returned to the business in Maine.

"There's more," Levin said. "You may recall Gambini's guy, Jay Natale, who lived up in Maine? He was the one who cornered the youth market. He was the one who blocked our early attempts at getting a foothold up in Maine."

Donnelly nodded. "Of course, the Candy Man. Another greasy piece of shit like his wop boss, Gambini. Unfortunately, he's been doing a damned good job."

"Well, not that good of a job, Patrick. On your order, Rose

and the redneck snagged just over eighty grand last week from Natale, thinking it was your money they were returning. As an added bonus, Natale was later found dead. And it wasn't our duo. It was an inside hit."

Donnelly smiled. Ira knew his boss appreciated besting his chief competitor.

"Nice. Very nice," Donnelly said.

"Anyway, you recall our offer to Rose?" Ira asked.

"Of course. I made it," Donnelly said. He waved over the waitress, who came hustling. Ira watched as he slipped her a business card and a twenty-dollar bill, instructing her to deliver the card to the "young lass" in the violet sweater. Levin resumed after the waitress departed.

"It was always our intention that if they flourished—maintaining their cover as a married couple—they should be promoted. With Gambini's guy out of the way, there's now a supply issue, one which we can solve immediately."

Ira gently set his papers aside and folded his hands in front of him. He felt a rare sense of pride. He took great satisfaction when his recommendations resulted in profit for his boss, far beyond those envisioned. Infrequent as they were, this was one such occasion when Ira displayed a degree of conceit. Ira Levin would go to the grave as a mild-mannered and measured man, but this was a personal victory. He cracked a smile, something he rarely did in his boss's presence, savoring Donnelly's visible pleasure.

"Well done, Ira. Very well done," Donnelly said, and reached across the table to clap his shoulder. "Send those two what they need to get things going. While you're at it, get them out of that dump they're staying in and put them in a nicer place. When I was a lad, my dad and mum took me to York Beach. We stayed in the same place they're in now. It was a shithole then. I can't imagine it's any nicer today."

Ira watched as Donnelly smile in the direction of the young blonde, who glimpsed over at him as she left with her date.

"I'm on it, boss," Levin replied, as he scribbled notes regarding tasks which rushed to mind as he considered new aliases for Rose and Bubba. ID cards and birth certificates were just two of the documents he would need to generate. No detail could be overlooked.

"Not sure where I'll end up tonight," Donnelly said as he stood up. He winked at Levin and added, "I'll call you with a number when I get there."

With that, he was off.

Chapter thirty-six

On Sunday, December 18, Rose and Bubba received close to fifty grand and a suitcase full of the highest-quality samples of cocaine that Donnelly peddled. The money was for clothing (nice, respectable clothing, they were instructed), better lodging, food and for bribes, in the event they encountered a mix-up with the sort of police who could be paid off. In recognition of their hard work, a Christmas bonus was also included—two thousand bucks each. On Donnelly's orders to find better digs, they moved into the Union Bluff Hotel, which overlooked Short Sands Beach.

The difference in accommodations was most welcomed. With enough cash to afford a junior suite, Bubba and Rose enjoyed their own queen-sized bed and their own chest of drawers. No more sharing of any sort. The room also included a minibar, which featured a stocked cabinet, its contents for sale at a reduced rate. Another perk was a free breakfast every morning. Not some measly continental spread with moldy bread and weak coffee, the Union Bluff offered a full-course meal, leaving nothing to spare: bacon, eggs, sausage, pancakes, waffles, and assorted fruits.

The first few days in the Bluff were spent in quiet study. They needed to learn their new characters, inside and out. They needed to learn social etiquette, no easy task for someone increasingly predisposed to the use of vulgarity like Rose, and not much easier for Bubba. But study and prepare they did. Their first venture would be attending a Christmas party up in New Whitby on December 24 where, they were told, numerous people of power and influence would be in attendance. For the first time in either of their lives, they would learn the importance of the salad and dinner forks and the sequence of using each. First outer, inner last.

Hundreds of miles away, Chuck Aiello knocked on the screen door of a double-wide trailer in Burgaw, North Carolina. He was careful not to knock too hard, lest the Christmas wreath, which hung above a peephole, become dislocated from a coat-hanger hook and fall onto the porch. After a second knock, a woman answered the door. She wore an apron and had her long hair pulled up in a bun. She smiled, identified herself and asked how she could help him. Chuck replied that she probably could, and to her son's benefit. Through the screen door, he could smell the riches of homemade food. Names and pleasantries were exchanged.

"No point continuing this conversation with you standing outside in this chill. You'll catch your death out there. 'Sides, you mentioned my Bubba," the woman drawled. She pushed open the squeaky door for her unexpected guest. Chuck thanked her and stepped inside.

Forty-five minutes and a plate of sweet potato pie later, Chuck was gone, well on his way to the interstate which would take him back home. He spent time inside the house of a man he would never meet, but one he would soon kill. Everything he gathered, from pictures hung on wood-paneled walls to the mother's glowing memories, painted a very clear picture in his mind.

Learning it all through the time-tested sweepstake's winner ploy, he had discovered Bubba had been in Maine since early November. He had written his mama every week. His return address had been general delivery, though she was aware that he had been staying at a motel on the beach. His most recent card, however, talked about moving into the Union Bluff. More than that, Chuck learned Bubba was not operating alone.

He had a partner, a very nice woman who apparently liked to eat as much as Bubba did. As an added bonus, he learned that Bubba's partner drove an old Chevy Impala that Bubba had worked on. The woman told Bubba what to do and what not to do. From what Bubba's mother surmised, this woman was his Amway supervisor. *Poor guy, saddled with another mother*, Chuck thought. Though Chuck was not overly concerned with the female partner, knowing he needed to look out for two, and not one, was good to know. He would have to kill her, too.

The three-day journey to Burgaw had cost Chuck precious time away from his grandkids, but it had proven most fruitful. In the end, he left with all the information he needed to settle the score for his boss, Mr. Carlo Gambini.

Chapter thirty-seven

"Look, Ma, look," Frankie exclaimed as he nearly dove into the front seat from the back of the limo, startling Richie, the chauffeur.

"Look, look! The bridge!"

Frankie flapped his left arm towards the limo's windshield and the road ahead in the direction of another Depression-era bridge which crossed the Piscataqua River, separating New Hampshire and Maine.

"Yes, Frankie. Amazing, isn't it? We'll be at the top soon," Claire said. She grabbed his hand and stroked it gently to settle him down. He was in a fever. She then asked, "Do you know why the bridge is so high?"

He sure did. "So the good-guy ships can sail under and chase the pirates out in the ocean."

"Something like that," his mother replied. Claire looked down at the river as the limo began to ascend the massive steel structure. The cobblestone streets and tidy shops of Portsmouth began to disappear behind them. Just ahead was Maine.

Richie glanced into the rear-view mirror and smiled at Claire and Frankie. Not only an excellent chauffeur, Richie was a kind soul. Without hesitation, he had jumped from the limo to load their bags in trunk. He made sure they had their beverage of choice and were comfortable. He agreed to a quick stop at Dunkin' Donuts, the one Frankie visited daily. Frankie thought his friends, who in his mind included even those who mocked him, would be interested in seeing him in a stretch limo. He thought they might like to see just how cool he really was. Unfortunately for Frankie, the apathetic customer service rep working the counter barely noticed. The fact that President-elect William Cartwright had sent a limo for Frankie and his mother would not have mattered at all to a handful of self-centered eighteen-year-olds who were strictly interested in their next high, their next lay, or enough money to buy a pair of overpriced jeans. Show up in a limo with Axl Rose or Sammy Hagar and you have a different story. Frankie might then have earned their full attention.

As the limousine descended the bridge into Maine, Frankie sat back in his seat. He considered the night ahead. The meeting with the President, something which his mother had said very few people got to do, sounded like fun to him. He liked the thought of wearing a tie and eating whatever he wanted. However, it was not meeting the leader of the free world nor franks and beans served on Chinese porcelain that mattered so much. What mattered most was Santa's visit, the thought of which had Frankie's nerves bundled up in knots.

If he was not at home and in his bed, then how would Santa know where to deliver his presents? Santa might get confused. After all, he had a gazillion kids to visit. What if he went to Nashua, only to find him and his mother gone? Then what? Santa was a busy man and he had a deadline. What if he didn't know that Frankie was in Maine? His letter to Santa was written right after Halloween. It went out in the mail on November 2 with the return address being their apartment in Nashua. Santa would expect him to be home in Nashua, regardless of where one of his helpers—the nice man driving—was taking him. He might think Frankie was trying to be deceitful, which would be grounds for lumps of coal in his stockings. This was not good at all. Santa had two lists: nice and naughty. Lie to Santa and watch where that takes you, he had been told as a child. Terror rose in Frankie's heart.

"Ma, will Santa know where I am tonight? Will he?" His eyes pleading for a yes.

Claire gently took her 32-year-old son's hand as she had done countless times before. She squeezed it gently.

"Frankie, do you remember the Christmas special with the Miser brothers? Heat Miser threw the flames and his brother, Snow Miser, zapped people with icicles?"

Frankie nodded.

"Well, in that special, Mrs. Claus told all of us watching TV that Santa knows what we're doing and whether we've been naughty or nice, right?"

Again, he nodded. His expression was stoic as he seemed to struggle to understand what she was getting at. Claire elaborated.

"If he knows what we're doing at any time of the day, then he knows where we are any time of the day, right?" She looked over at Richie. "Plus, we've got one of Santa's helpers with us right here. Richie will call up to the North Pole and see to it that Santa knows where we are."

That did the trick. Frankie's smile returned.

"Absolutely, ma'am," Richie said. He winked into the rear-view mirror at Frankie.

"He sees everything, huh, Ma?" Frankie asked, his heart rate slowing to a more normal pace. He breathed a sigh of relief. Before long, his attention went back to the interstate traffic. In short order, he spotted an orange license plate with blue lettering.

"Ma. Ma . . . I think it's a New York plate."

Claire looked out and found Frankie's vehicle. "Nice job, son. You're exactly right." She turned to him and smiled. "Listen, you know how it is with Santa. As long as you're asleep before he arrives, then you'll be just fine." She grabbed his forearm in excitement. "And when he shows up at our place here in Maine, I have no doubt that he will help make this Christmas our best yet."

"Really, Ma?" Frankie asked. By asking, Frankie wasn't questioning his mother's integrity. Never did he doubt the veracity of her words. He simply liked hearing good news repeated twice, thrice . . . even ten times.

"Yes, Frankie. I'm one hundred percent sure."

Frankie grinned. That issue put to rest, he returned his gaze to the outside world where tall pine trees zoomed past to the south in the opposite direction of the speeding limo as it trekked toward their exit.

Gazing dreamily on the scenery outside, Claire soaked up the numerous snaking estuaries; wooden rowboats canting to the right or left, caught in the muck by the ebbing tide, its paddles protruding from within; leafless oak trees and dark-green pines pointing above into the milky-blue sky of winter; seagulls drifting lazily in the crisp, cold air. All of it encompassed the landscape tapestry of coastal Maine in winter. Soon, she found her mind traveling back to the past.

York Beach. What a place. What memories . . .

In 1955, Claire Dubois spent the summer of her sophomore year waiting tables at the Goldenrod. From the 1930s on, the Goldenrod dominated York Beach. More than just a restaurant or candy store, it was a destination, a must for visitors. No vacation to York Beach was complete without a Goldenrod breakfast and a box of its world-class taffies for the journey home. Over the course of a typical summer, the Goldenrod served over 20,000 patrons. In the summer of '55, one such patron was an Indiana native named Jack O'Brien. An Air Force bomber mechanic, Jack was stationed at Pease Air Force Base in nearby Portsmouth.

On a Saturday morning in July of that summer, Claire served breakfast to Jack and two of his Air Force buddies. She and Jack made eye contact a few times during the forty-five-minute meal, but Claire thought nothing of it. So, when he and his pals left to stake their claim on the beach for the day, she was surprised to find Jack's phone number scribbled inside a folded napkin.

Growing up under the strict dictates of her father, a proud and traditional native of Quebec who considered protecting the Dubois name his life's mission, Claire never pushed the limits, never gave thought to doing something that might bring shame to the family. Two full years at UNH in Durham had not dented her piety: she remained a virgin. The weight of her father's expectations hung heavy. When she made the decision to call some random fellow, she was stepping far out of her comfort zone.

The brief phone call, which took place a few days later, opened the door to fun and excitement, the likes of which Claire had never experienced. With trips to Fenway Park, whale watching out of Gloucester and a hike to the top of Mt. Washington, the summer of '55 was a magical one. Jack was funny, charming, tall and handsome. He was everything her purist father was not. She fell in love. Within a few weeks, she surrendered her virginity to him. By the end of the summer, she was pregnant. Unbeknownst to her at the time, the man for whom she would bare a child was not fit to settle and not capable of working the boilerplate five-day, forty-hour-a-week routine. Jack O'Brien was a child stuck in a grown up's body.

At first, Jack seemed excited about being a dad, not fully understanding the ramifications on his free-wheeling lifestyle. However, a family was anathema to the limitless adventures which the twenty-three-year-old sergeant so frequently spoke about. For a spell, however, he gave it a go.

He met her parents. His charm had even managed to overcome the disapproval of Claire's father over his daughter's unintended pregnancy. Jack proposed to her on Labor Day, and she accepted. The two were married at an outdoor service in Exeter, New Hampshire in October. The backdrop, a canopy of dazzling reds, brilliant yellows and fiery oranges, presented an idyllic scene. Yet as magical as her wedding day had been, Claire knew somewhere deep in her soul that a lifetime marriage with this carefree man could never be. The birth of their son, Francis Patrick, on April 30 the next year, cemented her premonition.

From the start, both knew there was something wrong with Frankie. The first few doctors chalked up Frankie's unresponsiveness to a lack of sleep; the next crop of doctors blaming his condition on Portsmouth's tarnished drinking water. All of the doctors, however, reassured the young parents that he would grow out of "his funk," promising that his cognitive functioning would eventually resemble that of other normal boys and girls. But nothing of the sort happened. His condition worsened and it became apparent to more and more people.

At age four, Frankie was diagnosed with the harsh, steely label of the day: mental retardation. If in Jack's mind he needed an out, he now had one. As Jack saw it, raising a retarded son meant an end to any semblance of adventure. Before Frankie's fifth birthday, he split, a reassignment to Japan abetting his escape. He left with a bag of clothing, a few pairs of shoes, his favorite suit and some toiletries. He left a note wishing Claire and Frankie well.

Good memories? Not all of them, Claire thought.

"Ma . . . Ma." Frankie tugged on her collar, pulling her attention back to the present.

"Yes, what is it?" Claire felt a bit tired, but she was thankful for the suspension of her journey into the past.

"The sign way back there had a giant red lobster, Ma." He spun back to look outside, straining to make out a deep-green plate screwed onto a passing car. "Ooh . . . ooh . . . look! Vermont, Ma!"

"That's right, Frankie: Vermont has a dark green plate," she replied, turning her head to yawn.

"Have I been here before, Ma?" Frankie asked, squinting as he looked at her and into the setting sun, an angel's halo circling her perfectly styled and recently colored hair.

"Yes, but it's been many years. I took you up here when you were about eleven."

Then Claire laughed loudly, taking Richie by surprise as a memory hit her. It was the memory of Frankie running headlong into the icy water, unaware of its cold sting until it was too late. She remembered his pained shrieks as he sprinted back to the warmth of his towel. As she briskly dried his chilled skin, she remembered him acknowledging her with a thanks and a smile. He told her that he loved her very much and that he would be okay. Raising a mentally challenged child was a struggle. On those rare moments when Frankie seemed to possess full understanding, however, she felt a great peace.

"I love your hair, Ma. It looks good," Frankie said.

"Why thank you, son. You look quite handsome yourself." She ruffled his hair. "I know you will have a great time tonight. And don't worry, Mom will make sure you're under the covers on time."

Frankie grinned.

"Sorry to interrupt, ma'am," Richie said softly. "I wanted to let you know that we're about a half hour away. Would you like me to stop and get you and Frankie anything?"

"Thank you, Richie, but we're fine," she answered. She began trying to comprehend just what lay in store.

She and her son were a couple of hours from a black-tie formal with the nation's president-elect in a mansion on the beach. She had done a little research at the library and came across a few photos of the Cartwright compound. The place was majestic.

This is really happening.

Like much of the last few months, it seemed too good to be true. But it was true, and it was all her son's doing. She watched him as he studied each car that passed with such wonder and awe. The simplest things always managed to intrigue him. Watching him made her smile.

Chapter thirty-eight

Chuck Aiello barely noticed the luminous white limousine in the lane to his right. He passed it without a glance. He had seen his share of limos over the years and frequently rode in his employer's black stretch version. Limos were the toys of the ultra-wealthy, the powerful and the corrupt. Chuck's employer, a first-generation Sicilian, was all three. He ruled Providence's underworld with an iron fist. Chuck respected his boss and was fiercely loyal to the man, but he had no personal desire to acquire such power and wealth. Unlike most goombahs in his profession, money and possessions did not inspire Chuck. Such things were chattels of the superficial, he maintained. Guys like his boss could keep their possessions, their super-egos and armies of ass-kissers. For Chuck, it was his passion to succeed as a "one shot, one kill" assassin which drove him. Of course, the "one shot, one kill" standard didn't always fit. Select jobs required a more audacious display, especially when Gambini needed to send a message.

Chuck thrived on each challenging mission, many of which bestowed grave danger. Preparation was his strong suit; he trained constantly. He was a tall, thin man who walked with a slight lurch. He had grayish skin and sunken cheeks. But he only looked weak. He possessed the stamina and speed of a man half his age. He was nimble and had remarkable reflexes. In mob circles, Chuck was known to have the quickest draw. That he had been successful in his trade for almost thirty years supported this claim.

For his lethal efficiency and unwavering loyalty, Chuck was

well paid. By his own choosing, however, his pay was not what it could have been. He had been presented with numerous opportunities to climb higher in the pecking order, but he never accepted a promotion. Like the Jewish consigliore from a rival family up in Boston, he turned them down. Chuck didn't want to be anywhere near Gambini's inner circle. He was nothing like Gambini's other top hit man: Boris Radic, a Serbian madman. Radic, who had a penchant for torturing his victims before killing them, enjoyed the fine trappings associated with wealth and power. Chuck could not stand the prick. In his unbearable English, Radic was forever boasting about his kills, his torture and the terror he inflicted. Given the choice between a root canal from a blind dentist or five minutes with Radic, Chuck would have sprinted to the dentist's chair, foregoing the Novocain if need be.

Chuck lived a modest lifestyle, choosing a nondescript, two-story colonial house in North Kingston, just outside of Providence, to call home. Like his home, his attire was inconspicuous. He moved through a crowd like a fish in the sea, barely detected. His wife carried herself much the same way. No ostentatious jewelry, no flashy car in the driveway, no mink coat draped over her shoulders. Fran Aiello resembled a librarian, mousy and homely in appearance. Chuck loved her just the way she was. She had delivered two great kids and had been his rock for twenty-eight years. Not once had he strayed.

When not on the job, family was priority. Every Sunday, the grandkids came to the house after church. His wife always laid out a banquet-style dinner spread, with her special desserts closing out each feast. Their four grandkids always arrived teeming with energy. They kept Chuck and Fran on the go: in the living room, up the stairs and out into the spacious backyard. He played catch with them, tossed water balloons with them, took them to Toys 'R Us, Chuck E Cheese, movie theaters and other places which demanded a large dose of patience. Though exhausting, he loved every second with them. Sundays, holidays and vacations spent with his grandchildren brought out his cheerful side. On the job, however, he was an entirely different man.

Business was never personal for Chuck. He remained detached when executing his assignments. Without batting an eye, he would kill a seemingly innocent family if it were his charge. He would mow them down with a hail of bullets to settle a debt or simply send his boss's message. Whatever the mission, discreet or demonstrable, he would accomplish it to the exacting standards his boss desired.

Chuck Aiello signaled his intention and turned into the right lane, a safe distance in front of the limo he had just passed. He removed his sunglasses and placed them on top of a small leather satchel. It was just after three o'clock, and already the sun had sunk low in the western sky below the tops of the soaring pines. It would be dark by the time he arrived at his motel, The Portside on York Beach. He had no intention of spending the night, but would keep his room in the event he needed to clean up before driving the two hours back home to Rhode Island.

Before he got to The Portside, he needed to make a swing past The Union Bluff on York Beach, where his targets were staying. Establishing positive identification of the subject car was compulsory before conducting any vehicle follow. He patted a breast pocket. The sensitive electronics were in place, the ones which he would place under the car's fender.

Chuck slowed the car down to fifty-five. It was widely known that one didn't exceed Maine's speed limits. This was especially true for one traveling with unregistered weapons and sporting an out-of-state license plate.

Chapter thirty-nine

“Ma, look, up ahead. Rhode Island . . . the Ocean State!” He pointed excitedly at a black Cadillac about 200 feet ahead. Its right blinker was on as it left the interstate.

“Yes, Frankie, very good eyes,” Claire said.

“Good job. That’s another, Frankie,” Richie said. He noticed the Cadillac’s operator was wearing a fedora, a wardrobe accouterment which one seldom saw. It was Richie Manzama’s job to notice such things. Doing so ensured he maintained an outstanding situational awareness.

“Not much farther now, Miss O’Brien,” Richie added cheerfully. “About another forty-five miles before our exit.”

Almost there, she thought. She smiled at the prospect of feasting in an elegant dining room and strolling across a polished marble floor. She would wear the formal dress she had purchased a few days earlier. It was the sort of dress that she had never imagined wearing again.

“Thanks, Frankie,” she whispered softly.

Chapter forty

Rose studied her look in the mirror, paying particular attention to the fit in the seat of her dress.

"Not bad, McDougal, not bad at all," she said.

Hours earlier, she was seated at the edge of her bed staring at the dress, grousing about its size and wondering just how the hell she was going to squeeze into such a thing. Yet somehow, she had. A few months earlier, before Y-3's torturous training sessions, she would have never gotten into the lower-cut, sequenced cocktail dress. While she had a long way to go, she was pleased with the progress she had made at getting into better shape. Fitting into a sexy dress was proof positive. *My how times have changed.* Not just in her appearance, but with her status with Donnelly.

As much as she still hated her job, she was officially an up-and-comer in Patrick Donnelly's tribe. No longer just a collection girl, she was destined for the big leagues. In their new role, as modern-day Clampetts who had stumbled into riches, Rose and Bubba represented Donnelly's bridge to an endless supply of affluent Yankee couples. Tonight, they would meet two such couples, with the intention of hooking them with the high-quality samples she and Bubba would be delivering. A little taste to whet their appetites, if you will. From an entry-level appetizer, the goal was to draw the two couples into the hopeless world of hard-core addiction, addicts who paid on time and in full.

Rose turned to the right in her high heels, checking out her ass. The mirror's image supported the marked improvement she could feel. She was nowhere near cover girl material—and knew she never would be—but she was not slovenly. Her butt, once as wide as a canoe, had shrunk. She liked her new look and flashed a smile back at her mirror's equal. She had lost enough weight that she had to part company with a number of her favorite kick-around clothes. Her sweatpants, some of which were once snug, now were big enough to swim in. For some of her T-shirts, it was much the same. Most notable was her pine-green Granite State Paving tee. It was her victory shirt. Its mark of distinction, the product of a drunken fistfight outside Kegler's Den, was a smeared bloodstain which ran from her right shoulder down across her midriff. The stain represented a badge of courage. She had earned it after busting some dude's nose. Only Vic's generosity had allowed her to stay for another beer following the scrap.

Indeed, the threadbare tee had served her well. Surrendering it from her wardrobe had not been easy. She made a mental note to stop by Granite State Paving to purchase a new one when back home in Nashua. *Whenever that might be*, she thought. As for the legendary shirt itself, she thought about framing it, maybe putting a little bronze plaque on the bottom of the frame to commemorate her victory that night. She now had the money to do such things. Framing stuff on the wall and sprucing up her place was something else she would do when back in Nashua. Maybe even finding a new place altogether.

"Whenever that might be," she repeated aloud.

She looked down and checked out her heels.

Like the cocktail dress she proudly modeled, high heels would have never been a part of her attire. The bedroom closets in the rundown apartments of her past had never housed high-heeled shoes, let alone open-toed ones. She never had a need for them. The closest thing to formal footwear she had ever owned was a pair of men's penny loafers, each with nickel-sized holes under the balls of the feet. Her weight would have never supported heels in the past. But now, nearly fifteen pounds lighter, spinning on pointed high heels—while not drilling holes into the floor—was possible.

I might even consider a swimsuit for the summer if, God forbid, we're still stuck up here.

She reached onto the nightstand and grabbed her lipstick. Very carefully, she applied a thin coating of a light red, before dabbing her cheeks with blush and rouge. The full-day "charm school," which Donnelly's protocol officer ran them through, had provided Rose with guidance on how to apply make-up like a woman of dignity and grace. Make-up was to be applied sensibly, accentuating one's best features. In Rose's case, that was her nose. Make-up was not to be applied in slapdash haste, like painting a doghouse.

Rose dabbed on some Poison perfume, all the rage with the young ladies. Perhaps a little too junior a scent for a forty-something, but it was the only perfume that came to mind when she and Bubba visited the outlet malls in Kittery. Bubba said he liked the scent, claiming that it brought out her "sexual appeal." While it was not her intent to elicit such a response, she appreciated his approval. As despicable and heartless as they could be, men could occasionally touch a tender nerve with a well-timed compliment. Bubba had delivered a few of late. There had been nothing awkward about them, nothing suggestive, and he had shown no disrespect. For her part, she just smiled, saying nothing in return. She never told him, but she had come to enjoy his attention.

She checked her new watch, its face rounded with mini-diamonds. It was 3:30. She yelled into the bathroom. "In the god-damned time that you've spent fucking around in there, I could've repainted the Sistine Chapel or learned Polish."

"Sorry, ma'am, I mean, Miss Rose. I'm 'bout finished. Was just spreadin' a little Dapper Dan through these golden locks of mine. Ain't nothing in a can quite like Dapper Dan. Wait until you see my look. Tom Selleck ain't got nothing on this mama's son."

Bubba clicked his tongue against his teeth, making that annoying sound he often made. Rose squirmed.

"Whatever. Just get your ass in gear."

She grimaced and then primped her hair and double-checked the hairpins, which held the tips of her hair off her shoulders.

Like some absurd infomercial, Bubba was forever cutting up and blathering on about some obscure product, like that stupid hair gel he loved so much. Though his speech had become more understandable, she still had to strain to comprehend half the shit he said; North Carolina might as well have been on another planet. Which other state's citizenry "hankered" to put Tabasco all over perfectly-popped popcorn? Or craved pickled eggs nesting in a large jar of some disgusting pink liquid after knocking back a six-pack? Who showered in Old Spice before a big night at some church-hall fish-fry? She remembered picking out his scent from across a restaurant they had visited a few weeks ago. Sweet Jesus, when sitting next to him that night, the stench was overpowering. She was busy recalling some other absurd Bubba fetish when she heard the bathroom door open behind her.

"About damn . . ." Rose started. She turned to face him and left it there. She was caught off-guard. He looked good. Damn good.

"So, Miss Rose. Whatcha think?" Bubba asked. He did his own little spin, far less graceful than hers. "I'm thinkin' I might just buy this jacket."

Why not? Rose thought. It fit him nicely. The additional training and the stricter diet—which meant cutting back on the fried clams he had fallen in love with—had done Bubba wonders. He had not lost the weight she had, but he had shed a few pounds.

"Sure, you do that," Rose said. "It's not like you can't afford it now."

She checked her watch again. The party started at 4:30. She peeked into her purse. The two golden-framed tickets, which Rose had been given at their last money drop were there. Without those, there would be no admittance to tonight's grand event. *Can't lose those. Lose those and Donnelly kills us*, she thought. For perhaps the one-millionth time since she had arrived in Maine, the omnipresent thought occurred to her: God, I hate this damn job.

She craved a drink. If they left now, there would still be time for a cocktail down in the hotel's pub. As instructed, they were to arrive fashionably late, but not too late. The drops needed to be handled with the utmost discretion, which meant sobriety for both her and her "husband," Norton. Sobriety meant making the link-ups before the party got too rowdy. Timing and discretion would determine the outcome: a wealthy client for life or, God forbid, a bust resulting in a lengthy prison term. To be sure, this evening's delicate mission would prove far more challenging than barreling into some unsuspecting, defenseless dope pusher's beach shack.

God, I want a drink.

Her mind wandered into the details of the night's soirée. The hosts were unknown to them, but she was told to expect extreme wealth: velvet curtains, gold fixtures, caviar and champagne, servants, limos, ascot ties and the like. They were told to expect powerful, influential people, the societal upper crust. For all Rose knew, Robin Leach might be on the guest list. And to protect these powerful people meant weapon-wielding men. There would be plenty of security.

High-society parties featured these trigger-happy security types parading around in their cheap suits and dark sunglasses. Ultimately, it didn't matter whose party they were attending. What mattered was not fucking up. Fucking up meant that any escape came down to their ability to evade those same trigger-happy guards. Failure meant getting nabbed with samples of cocaine and doing hard time—make small rocks out of big ones—in some federal prison. As Donnelly put it during their two-minute call earlier, there would be no cavalry riding to the rescue. They were on their own.

Jesus, I need a drink!

Across the room, Bubba dithered and dallied in front of the other full-length mirror, which hung on a closet door. He was struggling to comb down loose strands of bristly, blond hair. Rose studied him for a moment, her patience on the wane. There he stood wearing his trademark goofy grin, showing no observable signs of stress. *Does he have any idea what we're about to do? Does he even understand what no-fail mean?*

His face wore an expression more suited to a young boy embarking on a field trip to the zoo, an outing where there would be rides, drugged-up wild animals, and fried dough and cotton candy around every corner. But nothing about tonight resembled anything of the sort. How could he be so nonchalant? She understood he had been in some tight spots in his past, even some shootouts down in Florida. Still, didn't the magnitude of tonight's mission have him even remotely concerned? Apparently not. He was another Alfred E. Neumann: What, me worry?

Jesus, this guy . . .

And still he dawdled in front of that stupid mirror, now fighting to get his damned cuff links snapped into place.

"Quit fucking with those things." Rose ordered. "Grab your piece. Let's go. I'll help you with those downstairs."

"Yes, my love . . . yes, Miss Busey," Bubba replied, turning to Rose and opening his arms for a hug.

Rose could feel her blood boiling. "You don't want to push my buttons," she warned, then seeing his perfectly innocent face, she relaxed a little. She managed a smile and then wagged a finger at him, giving her best David Banner, the Incredible Hulk's, human side.

"Mr. Busey, you wouldn't want me angry."

"I'm sure I wouldn't, Miss Rose. I was just getting into my character. You know, the whole Mr. and Mrs. Norton Busey thing." Bubba winked at her. "Say, how about that last name. Pretty clever, isn't it?"

Rose lowered her head and breathed in, quietly counting from one to ten and back again.

Bubba walked over to the nightstand by his bed, opened a drawer, and withdrew his Saturday Night Special. With his thumb and index finger, he pulled back the upper receiver. He locked it in place and checked the chamber. It was empty. Next, he reached back into the drawer and fished out a box of .22-caliber bullets. He scooped out a handful. He loaded six into the magazine, dropping the rest back in the box. Before securing the pistol, he rechecked the chamber.

"Always double-check the chamber," he mumbled. He slapped the magazine into the pistol grip and released the lock on the upper receiver. There was a hard metal-on-metal click.

"Easy over there," Rose said, grimacing.

"Sorry, Miss Rose."

Bubba lifted his right leg and placed his foot on the edge of his bed. He slid his pant leg up, slipped the pistol into an ankle holster, and then lowered his foot to the carpeted floor. The tuxedo pants, wider on the bottom, glided easily over the concealed pistol.

Norton Busey had a story line in the event his pistol was discovered, one which Rose could accept. As a Texas oil tycoon, Norton feared for he and his wife's life; their well-being was forever in jeopardy. Without their usual security element in tow, it was his responsibility to keep the two of them safe. A proper Southern gentleman always protected his assets, especially his woman. And should a security guard discover his pistol during a pat-down, and fail to accept Norton's story, then so be it. Being weapon-less just meant having to be more alert.

Bubba spoke, startling her. "Not to worry tonight, my Belle. I've got your back."

"I'm going to beat your ass for that, by the way. Belle? Of all the names you could've picked." Rose jabbed a finger at him. "And what's with this Busey shit? Who, besides you, idolizes an actor who hasn't been sober since grade school?"

"That may be, but he's one nice fella. That nifty car I'm drivin' was a gift from the man himself." Bubba nodded his head and then adjusted his tie.

"Speaking of which, we ought to take the MG tonight. You know, arrive in style." Bubba turned to Rose and smiled. "Of course, nothing against your car, Rose. It's just, you know . . ."

Rose checked her watch again. Now, they were just killing time, jaw jacking. "We've already talked about that. My car is fine. You fixed it, remember? Anyway, you've got five seconds to get outta this room before I kick your nuts up through your mouth."

Bubba carefully extracted his gaudy, white-felt, ten-gallon Stetson from a box on his bed, admired its beauty and then plopped it on his head. He reached for the bedroom door, winking at Rose as he pulled it open. He extended an arm.

"Ladies first."

Belle and Norton smiled as they passed Mrs. Parker, the hotel's proprietor. She stood behind the check-in counter, which was merrily adorned with silver tinsel and a handmade pine wreath. The counter was also topped with two smartly arranged, pint-sized Christmas trees. Nothing lurid or garish. Jane Parker, who was straight up and down like six o'clock, kept her historic hotel modestly decorated in a classic fashion. Like her mother and her mother's mother, who ran the hotel before her, Christmas was her favorite season.

Jane forced a smile at the couple, wearing it only as long as she had to. As they passed her and slipped into the pub, she frowned. There was something about those two that had rubbed her the wrong way from the moment she met them, especially that galoot of a man.

They had been in her hotel for five days and had already worn out their welcome. She watched how they cut up in her quaint pub, treating it like some kind of Texas roadhouse. Belle, who bore no resemblance to her charming name, drank like a sailor on shore leave. Her husband, Norton, was just as bad, often wearing an absurd white cowboy hat, like he was planning a duet with Gene Autry. They flashed their riches around, buying drinks for everyone. They commandeered the jukebox, filling the peace and quiet with crap like Guns and Roses, or Alabama or that other obnoxious Southern band whose name escaped her. They were always asking the bartender to turn it up and always getting the desired response, proving that big tippers got things their way. They did shots of rum and whiskey, they arm-wrestled, they belched, they swore profusely, they played cards, and they shot pool on her antique table while jousting at each other with the cues. They caroused right up until closing, which according to state law was 1:00 a.m., then begged the bartenders for bottles of liquor for the post-party in their ocean-view suite. More often than not, the bartenders would oblige. They would pour the first drink from each bottle. That done, they would then exchange the now-opened bottles of liquor for a substantial tip. Regrettably, there was no law on the books to prevent such free trade.

Jane had never trusted people from south of the Piscataqua River, never mind below the Mason-Dixon Line. How could Americans be so markedly different? Natives of Maine, such as she, were dignified, polished and well-read. Southerners? Simply ludicrous. What with their phony, toothy smiles, their how y'all doings, their sweet potato pie—which, her rigid mother had warned, went straight to one's hips—their cheery greetings and, sweet Jesus, that accent! Could educated people really talk like that? Really sound so dumb? And the partying and carrying on all night; did they have no couth? Who could possibly live to be forty acting like that every night? Especially that woman, that appalling, trashy woman who actually smoked cigars! It was folks like those two who put that hick, President Reynolds, into office. She shook her head in disgust, while turning the page of her *Yankee* magazine.

On the other hand, they had paid their bill in full and in advance: fourteen nights and $1,500 cash, which was about what they had spent in the pub. Their money was warmly received by Jane, even though their evening antics were not. As hard as it was watching those two clowns parading around, she reminded herself that a hotel was a for-profit enterprise. During the off-season, it was nice to have a handsome supply of cash coming in. As the stated purpose of their visit, well, that was another matter altogether.

Just yesterday, the Buseys had inquired about waterfront property, somewhere close by. Norton conjured up some fabrication—of that Jane was certain—about wanting to enjoy "nature's air-conditioning" during the summer. He said he needed an ideal spot to squirrel away some of his newfound oil wealth or something like that. Jane didn't trust his motivations, didn't trust anyone who spoke like he did. Whatever he meant by "newfound wealth," she was sure it was unlawfully acquired.

While she could understand the allure of Maine, she didn't want those two ruffians as neighbors. She suggested they drive a few hours north to Acadia or, better still, Eastport, claiming those two beach communities were about to boom. Hours further north minimized the chance she would ever have to run into them again after they checked out of her hotel. It was bad enough having Massachusetts natives crawling in from cesspools like Malden, but Southerners?

What Jane Parker didn't realize, as she skimmed listlessly through her magazine, was that her wish would come true and a lot sooner than expected. Forty minutes later, she would watch the Buseys leave the hotel, slip into their repulsive Chevy and drive off into the night. It would be the last time she ever saw them.

Rose and Bubba spent a half hour tucked away in a booth in the Union Bluff's largely vacant pub. They had their drinks, but there was no joviality. Tonight, it was all business. They quizzed each other on their covers. Rose had learned everything there was to know about Norton Busey; Bubba had done the same with his wife's cover, the former Belle Reese of Omaha. Rose could not pull off a debutante's Southernese, so she was assigned Midwestern roots.

The story of their newfound wealth was best described in a way the silver screen *Beverly Hillbillies* came upon theirs: pure luck. "I reckon some guys are just plain lucky," he had told the bartender. The pub's bartenders and the patrons alike could care less as to the source of his wealth. As Rose put it, their cover made sense. The real world was not that complex: there were loads of rich idiots. No one would give a shit about how some cowpoke like "Norton Busey" acquired his money. They were too busy enjoying his generosity.

Before leaving on their mission, they settled up with the bartender. They left the warm confines of the pub, stepped into the cold night and walked across the street to the hotel's satellite parking lot where Rose's car sat. If they maintained their cover and didn't trip up, they would do just fine.

Chapter forty-one

Chuck followed Route 1A as it wound through a landscape of mansions, set back off the road by lawns perfectly mowed. Interspersed among the stately homes were smaller cottages and a few trailers. As he passed an RV park, the Atlantic Ocean appeared on his right. He had officially reached York Beach. Gambini's guy up in Ogunquit had given him the news that his evening's targets would be headed to a holiday party of great significance in New Whitby, about fifteen miles up the coast. Bubba and his female partner, who was described as "tall and rather bulky", would be driving a blue and rust-colored Chevy Impala, circa 1975. Worn-out jalopies, like the one he would be tracking, were easy to spot in affluent communities.

Not unlike any of the countless missions undertaken, Chuck would lay low and blend in. Should he get into a pickle, he was told to ask for a Mr. Lujak, who ran security at the site. Lujak would help. Unbeknownst to Chuck at the time, the party would prove to be as momentous an event as any he had attended.

Chuck kept his speed at, or slightly below, the speed limit. The ocean was calm and dark. The sun hung low in the sky. It was setting fast. It would be as dark as a coal miner's ass by quarter to five, not long after he placed the tracking device on Rose's car. Its purpose was to provide the exact location of the rusty shitbox when the two parked. Chuck was no fan of technology and wasn't sure if the fucking thing would work. To be sure, he decided to tail them when they left the party.

After he placed the quarter-sized device, he checked its signal strength from various places within York Beach. Points within two miles signaled strong. Having confirmed the device's effectiveness, he took up his lookout position in front of the Fun-O-Rama, a block away from their hotel. Thirty minutes later, the two stepped out into the night.

The woman, gaudily clad in some sort of a cocktail dress, led the way. Chuck figured it must have taken her a tub of Vaseline to get into that vulgar outfit. Bubba trailed close behind. He sported a cheap tuxedo and an outrageous cowboy hat, which clashed horrifically with his tux. White felt with rhinestones and a brown leather strip adorned the rim. The hat would not have paired well with any outfit. It shone like a beacon. Inside the cabin of his Cadillac, Chuck laughed out loud. He thought about getting out of the car, strolling up behind them, and capping them right in the middle of the parking lot they now stood in. He could chalk it up as a mercy-killing; mercy on those who would not have to bear witness to their fashion atrocities. Then he remembered Gambini's instructions on making at least one attempt at recovering the money, before sending an audacious statement to his nemesis in South Boston.

"This is too much," Chuck said, grinning.

It was dark when Rose and Bubba slipped into her car and drove off. From a safe distance behind, Chuck pulled out and began to follow. The tracking monitor beeped and blinked. Placed within a cup holder, its digital green display measured the distance and cardinal direction of Rose's car as well as the signal strength, which from a few hundred feet away was very strong. He allowed himself to slip back to a mile. The palm-sized device worked like a charm. The pulsing green dot moved steadily north on a map background. Chuck figured that as long as he remained about a mile back, he would be fine. Even if he didn't, he already had directions to the "event of great significance."

Chuck had not a worry in the world, continuing north passing signs that advertised off-season rates for ocean-view hotels on charming Wells Beach. "Breakfast included!" one sign declared. He drove on, the car's cruise control locked at forty-five, barely noticing the billboard clutter. He had no plans to stay in his own room back on York Beach, let alone in some dive on Wells Beach. He would whack the two ham-handed fools, slip away unnoticed and be home before midnight. Doing so would allow plenty of time for him and "Mrs. Claus" to slip into their costumes. On more than a few occasions, the grandkids had expressed their desire to see Santa this year. And by God, what they asked for, they got, especially at Christmas.

Was there a better time to celebrate with family? Chuck wondered.

He switched on a soft-rock station. The pleasing vocals of Phil Collins filled the car. From the cup holder, the green dot on the device silently pulsed on.

It was dark when Rose and Bubba arrived. Rose parked in a makeshift parking area in front of the massive compound. The parking area took up a sizable portion of the front lawn. It was roped-off with cones and set back a good distance from the compound. Unless a guest chose valet, this was where she would park. Reducing any confusion at all, there were four high-powered, yellow sodium floodlights set at each corner. She chose a spot in the corner furthest from the house. On the other side of the rope was a copse of scrub pines, which flanked a cliff overlooking the ocean.

Her Chevy joined a few dozen other parked vehicles, most of which were newer and far prettier than hers. Up a slight incline and about a quarter mile away, the walk to the house would not be easy, but there was no way she would have taken her car up to the valet stand. It would not go over well if their presumptive clients happened to catch her and Bubba getting out of a shitbox like hers. Who could take seriously someone coming out of such an eyesore?

Aside from a handful of what Rose assumed were conservative Yankees, she assessed most to be limousine liberals, the types who lectured incessantly about the fragile ecosystem and how gas-guzzlers like hers were burning holes in the ozone layer, even as they themselves were globetrotting in their private jets. They were the same suckers who, just a decade earlier, were convinced the next Ice Age had Mother Earth in its grips. They were scolding, scholarly types who had all the answers.

Well, if they don't like the look of my car, then they can shell out ten grand from their massive fortunes and buy me a new one.

Rose squinted, looking up into one of the floodlights, as she stepped out into the cold. She opened the back door, reached in and grabbed her purse, another knock-off item she had purchased at one of the outlets. She slipped it over her right shoulder.

"So, I got to thinking," Bubba said, rubbing his chin.

Rose offered him a look of suspicion and rolled her hand signaling him to continue.

"This place looks like it's crawling with security. Much more than what I figured. Ain't no way I'm getting in there with this." Bubba lifted his pant leg flashing his stubby pistol.

Rose looked up to the house and back at Bubba. "No, probably not."

Bubba nodded. He bent down and extracted the gun. Leaning back inside the car, he slipped it under the front seat. He pushed the door closed, then walked around the front of the car to tend to Rose.

"Let me help you on this walk, Missus Busey," he offered with a smile. His ridiculous white hat and white teeth shone abnormally bright.

"Knock the chivalry off," Rose scoffed. "Remember the deal: we hate each other. We're only together for the kids—"

"Oh yes, of course. Just for the kids. Plus, a divorce would clean my clock."

Rose popped his shoulder and smiled. "You bet your ass it would."

They walked slowly up towards the house. Before falling into the security line, the two conducted a final preview of the link-up plans for both of the prospective client-couples. At six they were to meet the "Blacks," a youngish, good-looking couple, they were told. Mrs. Black was a blonde, who would be wearing pink. Fifteen minutes after that link up, they would meet the "Whites." Mr. White was a broad-shouldered Samoan, who would be wearing a navy-blue suit. Mrs. White was black and would be wearing a green dress. Easy enough. Both meetings would take place in the guest bathroom set off from a large family room, which was to be cleared for dancing. The bathroom was coed and large enough to accommodate eight, so as to avoid any suspicion when the four walked in.

Establishing positive identity would begin with Mrs. Busey making an innocuous statement to the missuses, inquiring about other elegant estates in the local area which might be on the market. The misters would reply in the affirmative. Specifically, they'd claim to "know of such a place." That was their cue. Hearing that, the Buseys were to head to the designated bathroom. Sometime thereafter, their prospective clients would join them. Once in the bathroom, the Buseys would casually inquire about real estate agents and pricing, as Norton stealthily slipped them Ziploc bags of high-grade cocaine onto which a Boston-area payphone number was inscribed. After some small talk, they would agree to meeting at an open-house event down in Perkins Cove five days later. At those meetings, the Buseys would bring much larger bags of blow, enough to satisfy the growing clientele which the Whites and Blacks would be expected to supply.

Closer to the estate, Rose noticed small groups of very serious looking men carrying hand-held radios arrayed across the grounds in elements of three. They wore sunglasses and black suits. The three-man groups were spread out along the property's south and east ends, which fronted the rock cliffs leading down to the ocean.

Typical security detail: cheap suits and sunglasses, Rose thought.

"Security here is so tight you'd need a shoehorn to get a dog's flea past these guys." Rose said under her breath.

The burly men paid little mind to her and Bubba. After pat downs, the two were asked to produce their tickets. That done, they were cleared to proceed.

As they stepped onto the brick patio that led to one of the four sliding-glass-door entrances, Rose muttered, "Who the hell lives in this place?"

It wasn't long before she had her answer.

"Belle, you won't believe this," he said excitedly, tugging her arm. "Look! I know that woman."

Rose spun to face him and then spoke through clenched teeth. "Lower your goddamned voice."

"See there? That's Diane Cartwright," Bubba pointed straight ahead.

Rose looked over. She was stunned.

It can't be her. Tell me that's not her. Please let that be a doppelganger.

But there was no mistaking the signature white hair: it was Diane Cartwright. And that meant this party was for that dreaded soul who would be sworn in as president next month. Rose had heard the Cartwrights had a compound somewhere in Maine, but never cared to know where. Of all places, this was it: this mansion on this compound. Thirty feet away, Mrs. Cartwright stood in a reception line, shaking the hands of guests as they entered her home.

This can't be happening.

Rose grabbed Bubba's tuxedo lapel and spun him around to face her. She looked over her shoulder to make sure no one was within immediate earshot before unloading.

"This has gotta be a fucking joke," she growled and then forced a smile. "Tell me you didn't know about this."

They had landed their first sales job at William Cartwright's presidential election celebration and were in line to shake the soon-to-be First Lady's hand. Running at full speed off the edge of the lawn and swan-diving onto the rocks below would be welcome over having to shake her hand. Bubba saw matters in an entirely different light.

"Well, whoop-de-goddamn-doo. We're actually at the president's retreat," Bubba said, bursting with excitement. "And no, my love. I had no idea, but we ought to be polite and go shake her hand."

Rose shot him a dumbfounded look. "You can't be serious. Shake her hand with all those cameras flashing? There's press crawling all over the place. What part of laying low are you having a hard time understanding?"

Bubba frowned and shrugged his shoulders. Rose pulled him out of the reception line and out of earshot.

"Let me guess: you voted for Cartwright?" Rose asked him, then looked around to make sure no one heard her.

"Yes, I did. Absentee ballot, in fact. He was John Reynolds's right-hand man," Bubba replied, then looked at Rose with mild wonder. "You mean you didn't?"

"Hell no, I didn't."

"Well, not to worry, my dear. You know the old saying about how opposites attract. That's why we've stayed together for so long." He offered his arm in a chivalrous gesture. "And because of our delightful kids, of course."

Only begrudgingly, and only because they had an image to portray, did she accept it. She wanted so badly to slug him in the nose. Then, that lingering thought struck her again.

God, I hate my fucking job.

Rose took a deep breath and pulled herself together. She forced a smile and slipped her left arm through his right. "Listen, nothing stupid. No chasing down autographs and acting like some kind of groupie. Got it?"

Avoiding the greeting line, the two walked arm-in-arm toward an alternate entrance where a man wearing a white tuxedo and sporting a Santa hat stood. Cheerfully he slid open a glass door and ushered them in. They opted to forgo the dining room, settling on a cocktail instead. It was 5:15, forty-five minutes before their meeting with the Blacks.

Chapter forty-two

Frankie ate every morsel of food brought to his table and put in front of him, except the steak with a fancy name. He ignored that and asked for franks-and-beans. His request was happily granted. One serving wasn't enough for the hero from Nashua. He requested a second, and then a third, helping. He inhaled all three. With dinner out of the way and his appetite not yet satisfied, his mind turned to dessert. He was told dessert was coming, but not before a series of speeches from men wearing fancy black suits. As good as cake and ice cream sounded, suffering through long-winded speakers uttering words he could not possibly understand did not appeal to him. The only exception would have been Santa Claus as the keynote speaker, but he was busy. Frankie figured he was probably delivering toys to good boys and girls in the Soviet Union. He heard Soviet kids lived a rough life, but Santa loved them, too. Frankie asked his mother if he could be excused.

"Okay, but don't wander too far. Our hosts want to meet us after the fireworks. So, let's make it two hours, okay? If I miss you outside, come back to this table."

"Okay, Ma," he dutifully replied.

He rolled his chair back from the table. He liked chairs with wheels. He wished he had them at home. They would be fun to zip around on in the kitchen. *Only if Ma let me, though.* They would make a great Christmas gift, but it was too late this year. Santa already had his list; he had had it for weeks. Speaking of his hero, soon Santa would be done with the Soviets and then fly west, visiting the good boys and girls in Europe and Africa. If they believed and had been good, they would get presents. If they had been bad, he would leave coal or simply fly over their homes or straw huts.

Frankie walked off into an even larger room, where couples were dancing to music that sounded like stuff he had heard on that show where people wore straw hats and talked with goofy accents. He paid them little attention. He looked down at his new digital Seiko, a gift from Nashua's mayor. It read 5:19. Adding two hours meant that he needed to be back with his mother at 7:19. Only in the past year had he learned to add hours and minutes to the current time in order to determine a later time. To his mother, it was a crowning achievement. To Frankie, it was no big deal. All the kids he hung with at Holman Stadium already knew how. Knowing how to add the time meant no longer missing the first pitch at a Pirates game. In any case, he set out to explore the opulent home.

The fireworks were scheduled to start at 6:30, so he had some time to kill. He could cover a lot of ground, both inside and outside the mansion, in an hour. Frankie had seen homes as big as this on TV. On the TV show, *Dallas*, the rich people lived in grandiose mansions like this. They were never happy and frowned a lot, but they had tons of money and fancy cars. He liked watching *Dallas* with his mother on Friday nights. But *Dallas* paled in comparison to *Doctor Who*, his favorite show. Dr. Who was a good guy, who helped poor people. Dr. Who wore grubby clothes and didn't appear to have much money. But he smiled a lot. By his mother's assessment, the wealthy people on *Dallas* had boatloads of money and still took advantage of poor people in order to make even more money. Since Mom was always right, *Dallas* had gone from one of his top five TV programs to somewhere in the twenties, a ranking which Frankie did not diligently track.

Frankie wandered into a vast kitchen, where a smiling black man whistled as he squeezed red frosting from a tube onto a cake the size of a small couch. He wore one of those funny-looking white hats. Two women cooks, also wearing hats, scurried around carrying trays covered with other dessert treats, setting them under an open window looking out onto the dining room from which Frankie had come. They were too busy to notice him standing near the kitchen's rear entrance. On one side of the cake, there was cursive writing in dark blue frosting which Frankie could not read. The cake looked delicious and he hoped to get some later.

"Hi. My name is Frankie," he announced to the kitchen staff in a loud voice. "That cake is the biggest I've ever seen! I bet it's yummy."

The chef stopped what he was doing and looked up. He squinted to make out the Frankie's facial expression. Initially disturbed that a grown man would simply burst into his kitchen on a night like tonight, the chef quickly established that this was no ordinary fellow.

"Sumpin' ain't right with that boy," he muttered, as he laid the frosting dispenser on a table nearby.

Frankie waved to the man and flashed his characteristic toothy grin. He then checked his watch: 5:23.

"I'm Frankie. I'm here for the party," he announced. "Did you know the fireworks are coming on in . . ." He glanced back at his watch and did some quick math. ". . . in sixty-seven minutes?"

"Hello, Frankie. My name is Lawrence," the cook replied, relaxing his frown. He walked a few steps towards Frankie. "Yes sir, I had heard about those fireworks. I might even sneak out and watch them myself. Mr. Cartwright and the missus always put on a great display."

"After the fireworks, though, I have to meet my mother. That's at 6:49," Frankie stated. He then took a more serious tone. "I don't want to be up and about when Santa comes. That would be bad."

The chef smiled and then, as if telling Frankie a secret, cupped a hand near his mouth. With his free hand, he pointed at his assistants. "Maybe I'll meet you for the fireworks and leave the work to them."

Frankie smiled back, shouted out his goodbye and was off. He walked back into the dancing room where Bing Crosby's "White Christmas" kept the spirits bright. It was a song which Frankie loved. Christmas music always brought him joy. Noticing Frankie grinning cheerfully, a tall woman wearing a sparkling, sequined dress smiled back at him. She was drawing close to a man in a black tuxedo as they danced. Her hands rested on his butt. Frankie blushed. He once remembered seeing boys and girls in ninth grade dance that way. He himself had never done so and was afraid of being too close to a girl. Except for his Ma, girls were trouble. The woman began to turn, but kept her smile locked on Frankie. Still blushing, Frankie turned away and began walking swiftly towards the next room.

As he entered, he stopped and looked around. The next room was equally as lavish, with even more Christmas decorations than the others. Posted in each corner of the room were giant Christmas trees wrapped with strings of popcorn and cranberries, adorned with beautiful ornaments that included battery-operated elves clinking hammers and sawing wood for the purpose of making toys. Each tree was rung with soft, blinking white lights and shimmering tinsel and topped with angels. Under the trees were countless presents, filling any gaps between the hardwood floor and the tree's lowest branches. Many presents were addressed to a "Friend." Some of the other names Frankie made out were William Jr., Jonathan and Diane. By the sheer number, there appeared to be one for all of those who had come for the party. *Am I a Friend?* he wondered. He thought so.

Soaking in the beauty around him, he thought that this had to be the best Christmas party ever, even better than the ones at school where large bags of candy were handed out. Unfortunately, he would eat every piece, which would earn him a serious bellyache, or worse. Tonight, there was no bellyache or upset stomach. Tonight, there was only excitement and joy.

He felt as if he had walked into a dream, a very happy dream like the recurring one where he and his daddy, a man whose name he never remembered, play catch in Holman Stadium under the lights on a warm, summer night. It's the dream when his daddy says he's happy to be back and that he made a mistake leaving. He says he's sorry and hugs Frankie, as the two walk to his car before driving off to get ice-cream sodas. Frankie always woke up sad after those dreams. But tonight could not be a dream, because he never laid down on a bed and under its covers. Then it occurred to him that maybe he forgot that he had gone off to bed.

Did Ma send me to bed? Could I have forgotten?

Panic began to creep in. Was he awake or asleep? He needed to know for sure. The only way to know for sure was to pinch your arm as hard as possible, or so he had heard. In order for it to work, it had to sting like a yellow jacket. That was the only way to know for sure. If it stung like crazy, then you were awake. Frankie chose a tree in the corner and stepped around to the back, hidden from the partygoers. Sufficiently out of view, he pinched off a sizable chunk of skin from the top of his forearm. He rolled his overgrown fingernails into a prime pinching position. All at once, and as hard as he could, he drove the thumb and index finger deep into the stretched skin, sharp fingernails leading the charge. The pain was instant.

He shrieked.

"Ahhh! Okay . . . okay! It hurts! Okay . . . I'm awake!" He dropped his persecuted left arm, shaking and rubbing it furiously with his right hand.

Some of the partygoers heard him and stopped what they

were doing. What they found brought them relief. There was no cause for alarm. It was just some big goofy guy, red-faced with a damp brow, grinning like an idiot from behind a Christmas tree.

"A little too much eggnog, sonny?" an old man asked.

Laughter erupted around him. Frankie laughed, too. He didn't mind them picking on him. He was just happy to be awake. As for the pain, that would go away. He rubbed his arm a bit more. Knowing this was no dream and that fireworks and Santa Claus were in his immediate future had him back on top of the world. Was this the best day ever? Maybe. He smiled back at those who still watched him as he came around from behind the tree.

"Need another drink?" the same man inquired. "You know they're free until midnight."

More laughter followed.

Frankie waved to him. "Hi, my name is Frankie. I have to get back to my ma after the fireworks at 7:19 p.m."

Which reminded him—nervously he looked down at his watch. The green digital display now showed 5:48. "I've got ninety-one minutes left. I better go. Okay, bye."

"Sure, sonny," the man replied. "Listen, come back. Bring your mom. We'll knock back a few free drinks and sing Christmas carols."

Frankie stuck his hand up and waved. As he turned to leave, he noticed a big man standing across the room. He was Frankie's height, which put him among the room's tallest. He wore a black tuxedo like most of the other men. On his head sat an enormous white cowboy hat. It was adorned with a brown leather strap and twinkling jewelry. By a long shot, it was the biggest hat Frankie had ever seen. The big man's back was turned to Frankie as he stood telling a story, waving an arm in an animated fashion to a group of young women who had gathered around him and a tall woman with black hair, who was nestled up against him, presumably his date. She, too, had her back to Frankie.

"Just like the guy on Dallas," Frankie mumbled to himself. "I have to tell him that I love Dallas, even though I don't. If he is an actor from the TV show, then he'll give me an autograph like the important man from Boston who came to see me."

He watched the cowboy man for a moment, drawn to his arm-waving and booming laughter. Then he remembered: the time. Anxiously he checked his watch: 5:51. *Shit,* he thought, nearly saying the bad word out loud. Eighty-eight minutes before his curfew and thirty-nine minutes before the fireworks. If he didn't start heading outside now, he would miss getting the best spot for viewing. If he got out there early enough, he would save a spot for his new friend, the black cook. It occurred to Frankie that the black cook looked a whole lot like the black cook from that scary movie he was not supposed to have watched, but did once when his mother had fallen asleep. In the movie, the black cook gets killed trying to help a family stranded during a blizzard. It was a terrifying movie. It gave him nightmares for months.

Frankie did his best to brush the memory out of his mind by humming "Rudolph the Red-Nosed Reindeer," which was playing in the next room he entered. He decided that he would go outside within thirty minutes, get the best spot and, with any luck, find his new friend, the cook. No matter how long the fireworks show lasted, he would be back inside to find his mom by 7:19, unless she found him outside first. Nothing would cause him to break curfew.

Chapter forty-three

Chuck Aiello followed the green blip on the radar. After a lengthy drive, he found what he was looking for. It sat just off the shoulder along Ocean Avenue, which was consistent with his scribbled directions. A white sign, bordered with orange reflective tape, sat off the edge of the road. The sign bore the word **EVENT** with an arrow pointing toward a dirt road which cut into dense forest. Under the arrow were two smaller words: **INVITATION ONLY.**

Since he had turned off Route 9 and headed north on Ocean Avenue, the Atlantic Ocean, motionless and flat on this clear night, had been visible on his right. The moon splashed white light on the sea. It was beautiful to behold. He made a mental note to bring the missus up sometime. The two could do a little sightseeing. Maybe take the grandkids with them. They loved swimming in the ocean. When the water was not so goddamned cold, that is.

Chuck took the prescribed right and followed the narrow, tree-lined road. The moon's light cast shadows through the bare branches of oaks and maples. The road gradually widened as he drove on. After about a half mile, everything opened up: small buildings, cars, lights and one enormous mansion. This was the place.

In front of him lay a vast grassy field, which had been converted into an improvised parking lot. Orange traffic cones and elevated spotlights marked its confines. Closer to the mansion, the expanse of which Chuck could not have possibly begun to grasp from where he sat, were limousines and other fancy cars parked close to what appeared to be a two-story guest house which, judging by its size, had to have had four or five bedrooms.

If that's just the guest house, what does that tell you about these folks?

To his right sat a boathouse. On its own, the boathouse would have been the lap of luxury in his boyhood neighborhood. It could have comfortably housed families of six or seven in New York's Lower East Side. Chuck figured that the views inside the mansion were breathtaking. Nearly the entire bottom floor was glass windows overlooking the ocean. Adjacent to the mansion, a large patio with scattered fire pits kept the folks outside warm. Even with the distance, Chuck spotted a drink in nearly every hand. He heard laughter and singing.

"This is too close," he told himself.

Chuck shifted the Cadillac into drive, executed a three-point turn and drove back down the tree-lined road and parked about 100 yards from the lawn, where it would be almost impossible to see from the mansion. More importantly, the nose of his car pointed toward Ocean Avenue, his exit route.

He stepped out into the night, shut the door and walked to the back of the car. He popped the trunk and took a look around. Satisfied there was no one near, he reached in and grabbed his black jacket and slipped it on. He took a step into the adjacent tree line and withdrew the silencer from his pants pocket. He then pulled his Heckler VP9 from the trunk and quickly screwed the silencer onto the pistol's barrel. The veteran assassin could generally screw it on in three seconds flat, but this was not his Beretta, not his personal killing machine. This was a throw-away gun, in the parlance of his business. It was registered to a guy who was no longer alive. The gun's serial number had been sanded down. There could be no linkage back to Chuck or the Gambini family.

Chuck slipped the silenced weapon into its holster and gently placed it back in the trunk next to his Polaroid. The gun would stay there until the hit, which he decided to do away from any crowds. He was not about to smuggle a weapon, let alone a high-power, silenced one, through security, which was sure to be plentiful at an estate like this. Gently, he closed the trunk and then patted his coat's breast pocket. Feeling the wad of hundred-dollar bills made him smile. On most hits, he made a point to carry a little hush money, which came in handy during a couple of hasty exits in his past. Before walking up to the mansion, he needed to find the jalopy which had earlier delivered Bubba and his chunky sidekick.

Chuck walked toward the overflow lot, hoping to find the

rattletrap there. He stepped over white engineer tape strung between two of the orange cones. He didn't have to walk far to spot her vehicle. New Hampshire tag 44-G0FU sat polluting a corner of the impressive piece of beach property. The front of the car was parked less than twenty feet from the tree line. Only diffuse light bathed the appalling rust bucket. Chuck grinned, thinking this would be the perfect spot to cut down the two buffoons.

His boss had asked for something audacious. He wanted Chuck to send a clear message to the meddling Irishman in Boston that his foot soldiers should expect no safe harbor up in Maine. A clear message tonight would mean whacking those two in close proximity to a large crowd. Not to mention, it would be near a whole shitload of armed security personnel. That translated into a near impossible escape from the party down to his car, almost a quarter mile away. As audacious as his boss demanded, Chuck's priority was getting out safely after the hit. To that end, Gambini would understand the need for discretion.

The subject mansion, which sat on a small rise, was awash in lights, jammed with partygoers and, judging by the cheap suits and black sunglasses, was protected by a large number of armed personnel. Despite the number, Chuck figured that the guards in this detail would have a devil of a time nabbing a pro like Chuck. Even so, since he had not had the time to conduct a daylight recon, he decided on something inconspicuous. He decided he would make the hits at the fat lady's Chevy, which was a short distance from his own car and only seconds from the dirt road which would take him to freedom.

Chuck walked toward the house and the substantial crowd outside on the patio. It was 5:30. Whatever the business of his two targets, it was sure to conclude early. Wealthy folks, like most of the partygoers most certainly were, didn't rub elbows with the likes of Bubba and his partner. Trashy, ugly folk like those two, as the photos plainly revealed, were amusing for short spells. When you got tired of laughing at them, you sent them back to where they came from. And in the case of these two, back to their shitbox in the overflow parking lot.

Where I'll be waiting.

Chuck grinned as he walked on, wondering who called this magnificent place home. While pondering the thought, he was distracted by a young woman walking in his general direction. As she drew near, he heard her crying and noticed her running makeup. Not wanting to be noticed, she began to circle around Chuck, eyes downcast. Before she could pass, he called out to her.

"Miss, excuse me, miss."

She stopped in her tracks and looked up at Chuck. Initially startled, she seemed to relax in the presence of a tall, homely looking man in a fedora, the type of man who presented no observable threat.

"Yes, sir." She sniffled as she spoke, casting her moist eyes away in shame.

"Sorry to trouble you, but do you know who the hosts are?" He waved a hand toward the mansion. "I was given the address, but no details."

Chuck shrugged his shoulders and smiled, something he rarely did on the job.

The woman wiped her eyes and sniffled. "You mean you really don't know?"

"Nothing about the hosts, no. I got a phone call invite, the address and was supposed to get my invitation mailed, but . . ." Chuck paused, patting his pant pockets. "I never got it in time."

Chuck held his hands out and frowned.

"You're not kidding about not knowing the hosts, are you?" She raised a mock glass in a cheer. "Well then, let me be the first to welcome you to the pre-inauguration party for president-elect Cartwright."

Chuck was stunned, his mouth dropped open. "President-elect? As in Cartwright?"

"You honestly didn't know?" She looked flabbergasted. She mouthed something unintelligible and then stuck a hand into her purse. A moment later, she fished out a ticket. "This was for my date who never came," she said holding up the ticket. "Anyway, I'm leaving. Here, take this. I just wanna forget this night."

Chuck suppressed his delight. His bribe money worked on rent-a-cops, but would never pass muster with the Secret Service. *This is a Godsend*, he thought as he graciously accepted the ticket slipping it into his pants pocket and thanked the young woman.

She wiped her eyes and wished him a good evening, then walked away toward the parking lot. Chuck thought he heard her begin to cry again as she disappeared into the darkness.

"How about that?" he mumbled. The boss wasn't kidding at all when he mentioned a party of "great significance." Chuck Aiello had loved Tom Reynolds and figured he could grow to like Cartwright. Either way, he was a whole lot better than that governor twerp, the very one who was forever digging his little hands into the public treasury and the coffers of businesses, including some of his boss's companies.

If time allowed, Chuck wanted the chance to shake Cartwright's hand. He could always size up a man by his handshake and how he looked you in the eyes. A firm handshake with a steady glance was a sign of trust. If Cartwright could give him that, he would not only thank him for the invite, but give him unconditional support during his tenure as president.

"So far, so good," he mused and then patted his pants pocket.

His targets could not have parked in a more optimal spot to meet their fate. The location meant minimal noise, good cover, and concealment prior to the hit and ready access to an escape. As a bonus, he stood a decent chance of meeting the next president. He stepped onto a stone walkway which led toward the gaily-lit house. Two guards gestured him forward, and gave him a quick pat down, neither asking for a ticket. That done, he was in. Casually he sauntered across the patio and stepped into the mansion through an opened sliding-glass door.

Once inside, he spotted a tuxedoed server holding a tray of martinis and shots of some clear liquor. He flagged him down and took a small glass off his tray. Chuck thanked him, slipping a five-spot into a coat pocket. The man smiled and thanked Chuck, before walking off into another room where the music was louder and people danced. Chuck looked around him. From the paintings on the walls, the opulent furniture, the tasteful Christmas decorations and the professional wait staff, he decided that the Cartwright mansion was as impressive a place as any he had seen. Adding to the home's décor were the scores of rich folks wearing tuxedos and gowns. Chuck was intimately familiar with wealth, but these were not the rich types that he catered to back in Providence. These were the types who either inherited their money or legally earned it. His boss, and those with whom he kept company, had acquired theirs through coercion and blackmail.

Chuck belted down his shot and immediately spat it up. It was not what he expected: it was vodka. He hated vodka. He had hated it since his honeymoon in the Bahamas when an overindulgence of the stuff ruined his new bride's dream of all-night romance.

He set the empty glass down on an end table, wiped his mouth with the cuff of a shirt sleeve and walked into the dancing room, where a DJ dressed like Santa Claus had just selected Frankie Valli and The Four Seasons' "Bye Bye Baby." Chuck scanned the crowd. Six couples spun on the dance floor, while others looked on. It took him no time to spot his targets: the big buffoon and his portly partner-in-crime.

Looking absolutely ridiculous.

The man was impossible to miss with that hat. If he had strapped a flashing beacon to a football helmet and paraded around naked with DOOFUS spray-painted across his pasty body, he would have been no easier to spot in this crowd. His rented tux was two sizes too long and about two or three sizes too tight in the waist. His chunky partner wore a tasteless black evening gown rimmed with rhinestones. The stones on her dress matched the stones twinkling on his offensive hat. An obvious knock-off, she had probably swiped the dress off the sales rack at some discount store. Her hair was sloppily pulled up off her neck, clearly a rush job. If he had not been in such a hurry to kill them, he might have enjoyed just watching them for a few days, purely for sport. Ensuring the whereabouts of the two would be a cinch. On its own, the hat couldn't be missed. Even outside in the dark, it would glow like the burning bush on Mount Sinai.

Fate had tossed Chuck a softball; Santa had just delivered an early Christmas gift. He turned and walked back to the reception hall and found a small bar tucked in a corner. From there, he could monitor everyone entering or leaving. He walked over to the bar for a drink. He needed something to purge the lingering taste of vodka. A beer would do the trick. *Maybe two*. He decided to keep an eye open for William Cartwright as well. Meeting the president-elect and then killing those two boobs would make his time away from the missus on Christmas Eve more bearable.

"Two beers, my friend," Chuck said to the bartender.

The bartender, whose name tag read DENNIS, nodded as Chuck rested an arm on the portable bar. Dennis pulled two bottles of Coors Light and two frosted mugs from a cooler. He poured the beers into the mugs, tilting the mugs as he poured, so as not to create much foam. Chuck lifted one of the mugs, smiled and stuffed a couple of dollars into a glass jar. Dennis thanked him.

"I don't suppose you have a pen I could borrow," Chuck asked Dennis. He hoped for the opportunity to get an autograph from the president-elect.

"Of course," Dennis said, reaching into his jacket.

He pulled out a pen and placed it on a stack of napkins. Chuck thanked him again, then lifted the mug of beer to his lips. He took a long pull. The beer was cold and delicious. Chuck smiled and turned back to the dancing room, where Bubba's ridiculous, detestable hat dominated the scene. It was impossible to miss.

"Merry Christmas to you, Bubba, and to your fat sidekick as well," he muttered.

Few jobs were ever stress-free. He could not remember any he had dared label as too easy, but this had all the makings. He took another long drink. The beer was cold and delicious. His second beer would be just as satisfying.

Both bathroom link-ups went exceedingly well. Within ten minutes, Bubba and Rose had done business with both the Blacks and the Whites. While exchanging casual pleasantries, high-quality samples of cocaine, along with a card, were stealthily traded for business cards within the private confines of the guest restroom. Had another guest been inside one of the stalls, they would not have heard nor seen anything out of the ordinary. The Blacks, who were as white as the driven snow, extended an invitation to a home-viewing taking place three days later in Perkins Cove.

"The place has a spectacular view of the Atlantic," Mr. Black crowed, as Bubba handed him two baggies of blow. Mr. Black dropped the samples into his tuxedo's interior pocket and added, "Just as good as the views you would see here."

The Perkins Cove home was his listing. Though the line of prospects had been growing, he pledged to hold off contract talks until the Buseys had a chance to see it. He was all too happy to help his new friends and was more than willing to work a deal.

It was twelve minutes after six when the Buseys returned to the dance hall. Bubba grabbed a couple of pink-colored drinks from a waiter's tray, and dropped a ten on a vacant spot of the tray. He handed Rose her drink.

"Good job earlier, Mr. Busey," Rose said softly.

"Why, thank you, Mrs. Busey."

They raised their glasses in a toast, then took a sip. Simultaneously they winced. The drink was way too sweet. Bubba took Rose's glass and set both glasses on a wooden table next to a Christmas tree.

"Let's chalk up that drink to trial and error," Bubba offered. "Let me go and fetch a couple of beers."

Bubba was about to wander off to the bar in the next room when the DJ slowed the music down a notch. Ruby and the Romantics' "Our Day Will Come" came on. The song was a classic, one which Bubba had loved as a teen. Unbeknownst to him, so did Rose. He turned to her and, in a moment of bravery, he extended his hand.

"You know, we could set aside our differences for a bit," he smiled, and nodded toward the dance floor, where couples had begun filling in any empty space.

Rose fought off the urge to fire off a snappy comeback. Instead, she relaxed some and then rolled her eyes. "Okay, but don't get any ideas. Remember, we suffer together for the kids. . . and only for the kids."

"Of course," he replied.

"Remember, we're that couple that splits up as soon as the kids go off to college," Rose said, and then feigned a sigh. "A tragedy, yes, but part of life."

"Yes, darling, a tragedy indeed," he sighed briefly and then brightened. "But even miserable couples enjoy flashes of romance."

Once again, her first instinct was to deliver a stinging comeback. Maybe a jab at his massive chompers or that mop of disheveled blond hair or that goofy smile. Once again, however, her instinct had been stymied. They had done well. They deserved to relax and kick back a little. Besides, Bubba looked pretty good. His twin racks of teeth, colossal though they were, shined bright and his hair was neatly combed. His tuxedo was a good fit. As hard as it was to have earlier imagined, the tux gave him airs of sophistication. The only criticism she could offer dealt with that stupid hat. But even the hat served its purpose: it was disarming. Sporting the hat, Bubba played the role of the fool quite convincingly. Who would look at a man wearing something so crude and peg him as a high-profile drug dealer? All that aside, his request for a dance remained unanswered. Rose broke the suspense and took the lead.

"What are you asking me, Mr. Busey?" The sensation of butterflies fluttering in her stomach struck her. She couldn't remember if she had ever felt that way. Before she could let the feeling take hold, she fired a playful zinger at him, at once settling her nerves.

"You gonna ask me to dance or just stand there like some stupid schmuck from . . . where was it I found you? Burgaw?"

Bubba extended a hand. "Yes, Mrs. Busey. That's exactly what I aim to do."

Gently, Bubba pulled Rose near and took the lead. It was her first slow dance. She had chaperoned her share of school dances, but never paid much attention to the kids and their dancing, especially when they held each other close to the music of Prince or Led Zeppelin, whose "Stairway to Heaven" closed out almost every dance she had supervised. What she vaguely recalled, was that they seemed to simply rotate in one spot. Apparently, that was just what Bubba had in mind, she decided. After a few moments of stiff shuffling, she relaxed some. Bubba's hands guided their slow motion. She soon realized that the gentle touch of a man, one who could be trusted, could be a pleasant sensation.

Her scarce occasions of intimacy with men, if they could be labeled as such, had been cold and insensitive. She felt Bubba's hand slide down to the small of her back. Chills ran up her spine and tickled her scalp. She could not remember when she had last been touched so gently. Then a thought occurred to her: was he acting? Was this all just part of the Busey couple ruse which, to this point, they had employed so well? She told herself not to sweat it.

Just go with it, Rose.

Bubba whispered to her. "Mrs. Busey?" His warm breath on her ear was almost stimulating.

"Yes, Norton," Rose answered. She felt light-headed and tingling in her knees, but she kept moving with the music.

"Did you ever dance to this song? I'm bettin' that your senior year was twenty odd years ago, right?"

Rose stopped the sway, gently pushed herself back against his embrace and looked him in the eye. Almost immediately, Bubba appeared regretful.

"Are you teasing me for my age?" she asked.

She tried to appear bothered, but she couldn't. Her smile quickly returned. Bubba breathed easy, pulled her close and resumed their sway.

"I never went to a dance, Norton. Never went to a formal or prom. I was never invited."

Bubba gripped her lower back a little tighter. He made no attempt to slip his hand lower.

"Well, Rose," he whispered as he looked around. The dance floor was crowded, but no one paid much mind to what went on outside of their own lovers' concerto. "Men are just plain stupid sometimes. I'd have asked you in a second."

Rose smiled, though he couldn't see it. She squeezed his left hand tighter.

"Thank you for saying," she said. "That means a lot to me."

Rose slowly rested her head on his shoulder. More than just a dance, the two were enjoying their first moments of true intimacy. Neither had ever experienced such tenderness. And while their feelings could not be described as love, it was beautiful in the moment. Phil Collins's "Against All Odds" followed Ruby and the Romantics, as the two danced on. Lost in the music, the soft tones of nearby conversations and the warmth of their embrace, they were protected from the cold and, for the moment, the danger which lay in wait outside.

Chapter forty-four

Frankie led his mother outside to a picnic table close to a space heater, proudly informing her that he had picked it out just for her. They seated themselves on a wooden bench. The clear night had grown colder since they had arrived and the breeze off the ocean increased the chill. Where they sat, however, the high-powered space heater erased it, the electric coils radiating a blanket of warmth to those gathered near. Staring into the vast black sky, Frankie appeared eager, almost to the point of bursting. Claire gave him a look, but thought nothing of it.

He has his own nuances like anyone else, she thought.

He had a tendency to remind her to not think of him like he was some silly cartoon character, but rather a big boy, one who could be trusted to spend the night at a friend's house or ride his bike to the Pennichuck to fish, privileges he had yet to earn. Of course, it never occurred to Frankie that he didn't have sleepover-caliber friends, nor would he ever. As Claire saw it, the art of the possible—however remote—was good enough for her challenged son. For over thirty years, that alone had served to fuel his child-like curiosity.

Behind them, an older woman wandered onto the patio, holding a server's tray with three steaming mugs. She spotted Claire and Frankie before the two could see her coming. She walked up behind Claire and cleared her throat, catching Claire by surprise.

"I'm sorry, dear. I didn't mean to frighten you," the older woman said, setting the tray down between Claire and Frankie.

"Oh no, you're fine," Claire said. She readjusted herself on the bench. Claire shook her head. "I was caught up with the view when you approached. It's just so . . . so beautiful."

The woman smiled warmly. "You should see it in the summer."

"I can imagine." Claire glanced at the tray and then back to the woman. "Do you work here?"

"You might say that. It sure feels that way. Always picking up after Bill and the kids."

Maybe she's a waitress or a cook?

"I'm sorry. Where are my manners?" Claire stood up to shake her hand and then turned to Frankie. "This is my son, Frankie. I'm Claire. We came up from Nashua. We were invited by the Cartwright family." Claire paused, looking back out over the twinkling Atlantic. "It's so beautiful here. Everyone is so kind."

"Mind if I sit?" the woman asked.

"Of course not. Please do," Claire answered.

The older woman seated herself on the bench across from Claire and Frankie, her back to the ocean. She slipped her hands into her sweater's pockets. The warm glow from the heater illuminated her smile.

"I know who you are," the woman began. "My husband told me all about your son during dinner. He pointed you out. I'd planned to meet you at dinner, but things got a little hectic. Happens sometimes when Bill and I entertain."

"Bill as in William?" Claire looked stunned. "You mean the president?"

"Let's not get ahead of ourselves," Diane added, and then winked. "He's still only president-elect."

"Which makes you the . . ." Claire was shocked and could not continue. The woman who sat with her and her son would soon be the nation's First Lady. Yet here she sat, thinking the woman was one of the hired help.

Diane Cartwright nodded and smiled. "Guilty as charged."

"Oh, wow. I'm sorry I didn't notice . . ." Claire shot up and extended a trembling hand. Diane accepted. Nervously, Claire kept pumping her fist.

"Nonsense. Please sit. Now you're making me nervous." Diane laughed as she gently slowed the handshaking. "You and your son are our guests, and we're happy to have you."

Claire sat back down, composing herself. She begged the topic wouldn't turn to politics.

God, please don't let her ask me who I voted for last month. Please God . . .

"Your son asked me about Santa Claus," Mrs. Cartwright said, nodding toward Frankie. "He asked if there'd be a chance to see Santa tonight."

Claire had hoped to keep the whole Santa business under wraps. She had hoped to get through the visit without having to explain her son's mental challenges. In her customary manner, she opened her mouth to apologize for her thirty-two-year-old son's most bizarre query about an imaginary man who lived at the North Pole and rode around in a sleigh. Before she could, Frankie, who had squirmed in his seat at the mention of Santa, piped up.

"Yeah, Ma, and this nice lady said that . . . she lives here with Mister President so she can make sure Santa shows up during fireworks or even after if I get worried!"

Claire lowered her head into both hands trying to hide her embarrassment. She wanted to crawl under a rock.

Diane Cartwright got up and took a seat between Frankie and Claire. She put an arm around each. Claire lifted her head as Diane spoke.

"Well, it is Christmas Eve. So, I'd say it's as good a night as any for Santa to visit." Diane turned to Frankie. "I'll bet those fireworks will help guide him as he crosses the Atlantic on his way to America."

Frankie's eyes lit up. Claire knew that what Mrs. Cartwright had just said made perfect sense in his world.

"Oh, before I forget, I brought some cocoa." Diane announced. "Let's get to it before it gets cold."

She reached between Frankie and Claire and slid cups closer to the two, before reaching for her own. As she sat down, the first salvo of fireworks blasted into the sky. A white stream of sparks trailed a rocket as it whistled into the night's sky, before exploding in a boom high above the ocean. Oohs and aahs followed. Frankie was beaming ear-to-ear. Diane raised her white cup and proposed a toast to health and prosperity in the coming year. Three cups clinked.

The three sat watching the continual barrage of space-seeking rockets and missiles and explosions of red, green, white and blue over the beach. Behind them, a tall man wearing a fedora, pulled low on his forehead, slipped unnoticed onto the patio. He walked head down, his hands deep in his pant pockets. He walked onto the lawn and out of the light. Flashes from the torrent of fireworks illuminated his back as he disappeared into the darkness.

The song ended and so did their moment of intimacy.

"Thank you, Norton. That was very nice," Rose said. Before

breaking their embrace, she leaned in close and whispered. "Time to go. No point in tempting fate."

Rose looked up to Bubba and smiled. Bubba's response, puzzling and inappropriate, took her by complete surprise.

"Why, I'd love ta, darling!" Bubba exclaimed, pretending to have been propositioned for a little hanky-panky. He stepped back and regarded Rose with delight and fancy. Inexplicably, he declared something completely preposterous. "Only I ain't wearin' them straps tonight. Hot damn, woman, you had me twisted up like a pretzel last time!"

He patted Rose's ass in a playful gesture. Clearly disturbed, nearby couples turned and glowered at them. Rose grabbed Bubba's forearm, pinching him as hard as she could, as she led him away from the crowd. He winced in pain, obediently complying.

"Okay, numb nuts, you made your point," she said through gritted teeth, then looked around before continuing. "Everyone in here thinks we're a couple of dumb-ass hillbillies, no threat to anyone. So, why rub their faces in it?" She poked his right cheek with two fingers, fighting back the urge to wipe that stupid grin off his face. "Besides, we're leaving, remember?"

"Yes'm," Bubba whispered, then tapped his hat and winked.

Rose clenched her fists. She could have knocked his fucking head off. He could not leave well enough alone. He just had to push his luck.

"Come on, darling. Let's get our coats," she instructed, and then grabbed his arm, pinching and twisting harder as she led him to where a man in a tux stood behind a counter. He was taking numbered tags in exchange for jackets, coats and hats.

"Ow . . . ow." Bubba whined like a puppy, prancing on his toes as if walking over hot coals. Unsure of who may be listening, Rose addressed him in softer tones.

"Tell you what, Mr. Busey, if you can behave like an adult for five minutes, the amount of time it'll take us to get to my car, then I'll let you buy me a couple of beers—and not kick your ass—when we get back to the hotel."

Bubba lowered his head.

"Yes, Miss Rose."

Chapter forty-five

Chuck Aiello watched as his targets moved off the dance floor, the chunky woman pulling Bubba, the cowboy hat-toting-lug, by the arm. They walked to the back of a line where folks stood waiting for their jackets. Whether they were going outside to watch the fireworks or leaving the party didn't matter to him; eventually they would leave. When they did, he would be waiting for them by their vehicle.

He grinned and shook his head. Watching the two carry on was like watching that porky mayor, Boss Hogg, and his bumbling sheriff, Rosco, in *The Dukes of Hazzard*. He almost felt bad for them. They had no idea what was coming and no way to stop it. Then again, did any of his victims? If nothing else, killing them would spare the gene pool of their progeny, if sex was something they engaged in. He winced at the thought of them partaking in any form of intimacy.

All told, Chuck was content, the by-product of soothing music, pleasant conversation with Dennis the bartender and a couple of beers. He imagined closing out Christmas Eve back home in Providence enjoying a brandy nightcap, as his wife and twenty-five-year-old son worked on corralling those lovable grandkids into their rooms and under the covers long enough so the adults could get into their costumes: Santa and his two elves. Before slipping on his fedora, Chuck pitched a few bucks into Dennis's tip jar.

He made his way outside, where a crowd had gathered to watch the fireworks. As he stepped onto the patio, the first volley of rockets exploded in the night's sky. If the two left soon, the booms of exploding fireworks would serve as a well-timed commotion, one which would disrupt the pop of his silenced weapon and the muzzle flash.

He whistled a tune as he strode down the lawn in the direction of his car. It was almost seven o'clock. Instinctively, he brushed a hand over his jacket's left breast pocket and felt his fold-out Polaroid camera. Those two buffoons would soon be dead and he would be on Interstate 95 south and headed home, where a glass of brandy, his darling wife and their precious grandkids waited.

Rose and Bubba put on their jackets. Bubba dropped his right hand into a pant pocket, fishing around for the two business cards. It would be quite a stretch explaining to their employer that everything had gone according to plan, but they had lost their contacts' information. Excuses didn't wash in Donnelly's world. Fortunately, he and Rose would not have to consider the consequences of such a colossal fuck-up. Both cards were safely tucked away.

On their way out, Rose grabbed a glass off a server's tray. The drink was clear and on the rocks. She didn't really care what it was. Waiting until they got back to the Union Bluff was not an option; she needed a drink immediately. She would sip it while Bubba drove. Driving them back to the hotel, while she drank, was the least he could do for acting like a moron. *What the hell was he thinking?* Whatever it was, she was going to unload on him back at the hotel.

Bubba's bizarre outburst aside, everything had gone well. Even so, she felt anxious. It all seemed too easy. They had met their contacts, exchanged sample products for phone numbers, and established meetings where larger amounts of product would be exchanged for large sums of money. The end result: four wealthy Americans would draw even more addicts into Donnelly's dystopia. In part, thanks to Rose and Bubba.

It was true that they had begun their role in expanding Donnelly's dependency class, the role they played tonight seemed trivial. Their four contacts would sustain the supply of cocaine; they would do the heavy lifting. But Rose and Bubba? They were merely facilitators. Practically disposable. Replace Rose and Bubba from the lucrative chain of addiction and Donnelly would still get his addicts.

This whole thing doesn't feel right, she thought, as they approached her car.

It all seemed too easy for the bump in pay. This concerned the pragmatic Rose McDougal.

Sure, the money's better, but storing and transporting cocaine? People do long, hard time for that kind of shit.

Bubba interrupted her ruminating.

"Did you enjoy yourself, Mrs. Busey?" Bubba asked, as the thunderous report of an M-80 exploded hundreds of feet above. The boom of the fireworks startled her, causing her to tense up. Another rocket whistled overhead. Seconds later came another deafening blast. Rose looked over to Bubba and noticed his mouth moving as if he was speaking to her. She tilted her head to listen. She heard no words.

"What'd you say?" she asked, as she walked toward the front of her car.

"I asked if you had a good time."

Rose looked him in the eye and then took a sip of her drink. It was straight vodka on the rocks and it was pure fire. She made a face as the liquor slid down her throat and then turned her attention—more like her wrath—back to Bubba. She was shaking; her stomach was in knots. This couldn't wait until they got back to the hotel.

"Listen to me and you listen good," she said, jabbing a finger in his sternum. "You ever pull that stupid shit again in front of a crowd, it won't matter that we're supposedly married. I'll rip your fucking head off. You got that?"

"Which shit?" Bubba took a step back. He tilted his head and held his palms up. He looked thoroughly confused.

"Don't bullshit me. You know what I'm talking about!"

Bubba shook his head, his palms out and mouth open.

"That childish stunt about me tying you up in bed. How I had you twisted like a pretzel. You actually said that in the *President's home.*"

Another volley of fireworks split the sky above. Rose waited for the booms to end before continuing.

"What the hell were you thinking?!" Her eyes darted back and forth. She lowered her voice a bit before continuing. "Bubba, our success, hell, *our lives*, depend on us keeping our heads right. I'm already on pins and needles here."

He hung his head, shaking it as her words sunk in. She was 100 percent right. The night had gone very well, right up to the point when he felt the need to cram his size twelve into his mouth. The couple of slow songs they had enjoyed exposed a different side to his partner. For a few moments, he had made a connection with her, the kind of connection he had never experienced with a female. Then he went and blew it all up.

"I'm sorry. I was an idiot."

"You don't say?" Rose sniped. She dug a hand into her purse and pulled out her keys. "Here, take these. You're driving."

She tossed him the keys. He stuck a hand out to catch them but missed. The keys struck him in the chest, slid down his coat and fell onto the grass below. Another volley of rockets ripped through the evening sky. Deafening booms followed. Rose waited for the silence.

"Driving's the least you can do for being such an idiot," she said.

The cars that had been parked around Rose's were already gone. Though the night was still young, the parking lot was practically empty. *These wealthy Yankees are boring.* She walked around to the passenger side and began taking off her coat. Meanwhile, Bubba fumbled on his knees, cursing the darkness as he fished around for the keys on the grass. Hearing him curse, Rose sighed. She was about to snap at him when she caught a flash to her right, coming from under a pine tree some twenty feet away.

Startled, she spun in the direction of the flash and watched as a tall man, sporting a cap and a dark suit, stepped out from under the shadow of the pine tree, his silenced pistol leading the way. He stopped within a few feet from the front of her car. He said nothing. In spite of her fear, she found herself returning to Bubba's words about the effective range of a pistol; from where he stood, he was well within that range. The man briefly looked at Rose. His face betrayed no emotion. He then turned and settled the pistol's aim on Bubba, who was oblivious to his presence. He was still on his knees fumbling away in a frenzied search for the car keys. He was cursing the dark when, suddenly, he found them.

"Got 'em!" he shouted.

He popped up from below the car and looked over at Rose. Admiring the keys he held in his right hand, he smiled proudly. *We got bigger problems than the keys*, she thought. She shook her head at him and nodded toward the man holding the pistol. Bubba shot her a look of confusion. She gestured again. Bubba slowly turned his head to the left and saw the armed man. His puzzled look jumped to shock and then to almost acceptance. His face said it all: their game was up. Slowly he elevated his hands in the air. Opening them as he did, the keys fell back onto the grass with a soft thud. The armed man finally spoke.

"Good evening. My name is Chuck and I have a question for you both. I will ask you this question only once."

Chapter forty-six

Frankie had grown restless. During the fireworks intermission, his mother and Mrs. Cartwright had begun discussing boring, grown-up stuff. Listening to that kind of drivel was as bad as being forced to eat leftover squash. Yuck! When the topic turned to croquet, he decided it was time to split. He begged his mother for another thirty minutes (and not a minute more, he promised). He checked his watch. If she agreed, 7:30 would be his curfew. Reluctantly she did, with a little encouragement from Mrs. Cartwright. Frankie thanked Mrs. Cartwright for the hot cocoa and promised his mother he would be back on time, assuring her that when he returned, he would be ready for bed. After all, he reminded her, "Santa skips homes where naughty boys and girls try to stay up to meet him." It was a timeless truism.

Frankie walked off the patio, onto the grass and down to a white picket fence, which separated the lush, manicured lawn from a steep cliff that ended in wave-battered rocks. To his left was the fireworks stand, the launching pad for the evening's outdoor entertainment. Three men stood on a large platform, which jutted out over the cliff. One of the men stared suspiciously at Frankie. The intensity of his stare suggested that another step or two closer to the explosives and Frankie would be stopped. Explosives were not toys and only experts could safely handle them, his mother once told him. Frankie never noticed the man's stern visage. Then again, he rarely did. He simply smiled and waved a hand at the three men before walking away.

He had grown tired of the fireworks. Initially spectacular, a drawn-out and earsplitting firework barrage had quickly become annoying. Tonight's second round would feature more of the same. Protracted fireworks displays were like the steady, wailing siren of a fire truck or police car, both of which annoyed Frankie. They always had. Worse still, despite his mother's friend suggesting the fireworks might guide Santa to the USA, exploding fireworks might scare him off altogether. If Santa arrived while fireworks were still exploding in the sky above, he would need to avoid the roof and find a poorly-lit part of the property on which to land, if he could land at all.

Frankie wandered along the fence line, from time to time peering down on the rocky shoreline below. Every so often, a wave would lap gently against the rocks, shimmering under the moonlight. The fence, which formed the boundary between the lawn and the rocks and sea below, stretched into the darkness ahead.

He walked around a slight bend, formed by a small grove of pines. Behind him came three hollow thuds; the show had resumed. Seconds later came three ear-splitting blasts. The landscape of trees, lawn and cars was immediately washed in a bath of white, red and green light. In the brief glow, Frankie made out the outline of three people a few hundred feet ahead. They were standing around a car. By his estimation, their distance away was about the same as from home plate to dead center at Holman Stadium. Though not eager to do so, he considered venturing off in another direction to find the ideal spot from which to watch the rest of the fireworks. But he didn't. He was curious as to what the three people around the car were up to. He maintained the designated course, plodding slowly ahead.

"Where's the money, Bubba? Or should I say, Bubba Sunshine?" Chuck asked.

"I'm not sure I understand, sir. Money? What . . . what money?" Bubba spoke slowly in an apparent attempt to buy time. His eyes shifted to Rose and then back to Chuck.

"Wrong answer, Bubba." He flashed his muzzle on Rose before returning his aim to Bubba's chest. "Let's try again. Where's the fucking money, Bubba?"

"Well, sir . . . I'd like to be more helpful, more . . ."

Chuck cocked back the hammer of his double-action Beretta. He had run out of patience. He was convinced that they had either squandered the money themselves or handed it over to that Irish cocksucker, Donnelly.

Holding his aim, he looked up toward the house one last time to ensure no looky-loos were gazing down. He glanced away a second too long. It provided his would-be victims with a last hope for survival. The 44-year-old assassin, who had never failed his boss, never saw it coming.

This motherfucker plans to kill us.

Rose watched the muzzle of his silenced pistol move from Bubba to her and back to Bubba again. His steely black eyes never blinked. She felt as helpless as a deer, captured by the headlights of a speeding pick-up truck in the middle of a country road in the dark of night. For a moment, she resigned herself to her fate: death. Death was the fate which should have claimed her a few months earlier. The Grim Reaper had arrived and he was not leaving, not without harvesting two fresh souls. She started to accept the fact that it would be a bullet which would end her life, not carbon monoxide. But her acceptance of death was erased when the hit man referred to her as Bubba's "chubby fuck-buddy."

Those three words triggered rage, a burning desire to pulverize the man into dust. It was one thing to show up and carry out a professional hit, but it was an entirely different thing to insult her along the way.

She squeezed her glass of vodka. Every fiber of her being wanted to rip his larynx right out of his throat, wanted to watch him bleed, slowly in an indescribable pain. But how? He owned them; he called the shots. His silenced weapon was the tiebreaker.

That is, until he dropped his guard.

As he turned his attention back on Bubba, she decided to act; it was their last shot at survival. In an instant, she did what she had done in that dark and dirty Manchester alley when she bested those three goons. She called upon an old athletic skill.

Rose hurled the glass of vodka at the armed man. He never saw it coming. Her toss was dead center. The vodka arrived a split second before the glass struck. The liquor splashed across his eyes, blinding him, as the glass struck his left cheek, knocking him backwards a few steps.

"Dammit!" Chuck screamed. "You bitch!"

He bent over, raising his left hand and frantically rubbing his eyes. He shot up fully erect, squinting through scorching eyes. Her perfect pitch had practically blinded him.

Immediately, Bubba fell to the ground, raked his hands through the grass and, as he had done earlier, declared that he had found the keys. Rose watched as he jumped up and lunged for the door handle. His hand trembled as he struggled to find the keyhole in the dark, jabbing the key in a desperate attempt to get it into the slot. Eventually the key found its mark. He unlocked the door, but it wouldn't open.

Chuck's eyes burned like a motherfucker. His blurred vision would not serve him well when it came time to drive away. Fortunately for him, his targets were ten feet away, at most. He raised his weapon to fire as the sky lit up in green and red. A booming thunder followed, as he squeezed the trigger. The bullet left the silenced weapon at 2,500 feet per second and met its mark. Chuck heard a grunt of pain. Squinting, he saw Bubba slump against the car. He then turned his attention to Bubba's partner. Even through blurred vision, he registered fear in her eyes, noticing her watch Bubba slump against the door, sliding to the ground. Chuck rubbed his eyes again and pointed his gun at her.

"I fucking hate vodka, you bitch," he said, then smirked. "Listen, I'm sorry I won't be able to offer you a final meal but, by the looks of it, you haven't missed many."

A smile spread across his face as he raised his muzzle level with her head. As he began to apply pressure on the trigger, he heard grunting and heavy panting coming from his right. Thinking it was Bubba taking his life's last gasps, he never turned to acknowledge the sound. His focus remained locked on Rose; she was the next to die. Suddenly, the grunting and panting, now louder, was joined by a warning.

"You! Nobody . . . hurts . . ."

Chuck spun to the right to address the threat. It was too late.

"What the—?!"

". . . hurts . . . Miss Rose!"

Chuck's pause was all that Frankie needed. He had closed to within two steps when Chuck finally swung his Beretta towards Frankie. He squeezed the trigger just as Frankie's massive fist cleanly struck his nose. A geyser of blood exploded from Chuck's nostrils, while Frankie fell to his knees, his left hand gripping his right arm, which was now warm and wet. Chuck fell backward onto the cold, hard ground, moaning. Tears filled Frankie's eyes. Desperately he searched for Rose. He had been shot.

"Miss Rose . . . oh, Miss Rose . . . it hurts so bad . . . hurts . . . hurts soooo bad."

Frankie begged for Rose to end the pain, but she could barely move. She was still in shock. Her feet felt like cement blocks, her arms like railroad ties. As if in slow motion, she watched Frankie crying and gripping his bleeding arm. From across the car, she heard Bubba groaning. Both had been struck, though Bubba, whose breathing was labored, appeared to be worse off. He had slid down the side of the door to where he was invisible to her. She saw blood smeared against the driver's-side window. She assumed that he had taken a slug somewhere in his torso and would not survive without medical care. Both needed her help . . . immediately. But she was frozen. She might have remained that way had she not seen the beginning of what would have been a most cowardly, despicable act. Fireworks boomed and lit up the sky as Rose overcame shock and sprang into action.

"Miss Rose!" Frankie sobbed. "It hurts . . . so much."

Seizing a chance to strike, to end the infuriating delays, Chuck struggled to a kneeling position before pushing himself up onto his feet. He stepped over to Frankie and aimed the pistol at his head. Chuck squinted to focus and cocked the pistol. But that was as close as he got to snuffing out his assaulter. Before he could squeeze off the night's third round, Rose struck him on the back of the head with her fists locked in a hammering motion. Y-3 and Sergeant First Class Jackson would have been impressed.

A blast of air escaped his lungs. Spittle shot from his contorted mouth. He fell to his knees. But Rose was not finished with him, not by a long shot. She reared back her right foot and kicked him in the teeth. The hitman wheezed. Blood from his mouth joined the trickle from his nostrils. He fell onto his stomach, desperately trying to roll himself onto his back and counterstrike with his VP9.

Before he could, Rose reached down, ripped it from his right hand and hurled it over the cliff. She kicked him a final time, hurried over to Frankie and wedged her left shoulder under his wounded right arm. As gently as she could, she lifted him to his feet, nearly losing her balance and keeling over. He yelped in pain.

"Sorry Frankie, I'm doing my best," she said. "You're gonna be okay."

Rose led Frankie to the backseat of her car instructing him not to lie down but to remain seated upright. She told him that he needed to squeeze his right bicep, where the bullet had struck. She ripped a sleeve off her dress and wrapped it snugly around his wound. Satisfied with her work, she then ripped off the other sleeve and wiped away as much of his blood as possible.

Thankfully, he had only been grazed and appeared to be in no immediate danger. She instructed him to leave the ripped sleeve in place and not to loosen it. She told Frankie to scoot over. She told him that he was going to share the backseat with her friend; he was a "good guy" and would need Frankie's help. Frankie nodded to Rose, appearing to understand his responsibility. That was all Rose needed to see. She smiled at him, then turned her attention to Bubba.

Bubba struggled to speak. His words were unintelligible. Rose crouched low and wrapped her arms around his waist. She felt his thin wisps of air in her ear and saw the spread of scarlet across his shoulder. She kicked off her heels and shimmied her bare feet in the cold grass to get into a lifting position.

"One . . . two . . . three," she said into his ear.

On her third attempt, she lifted his limp body off the ground and inched him toward the back of the car, his feet dragging behind her. As she labored on, the grand finale of the fireworks began. If Santa had had his sights on the Cartwright residence, he would have decided to return later. The sky above was ablaze with green, red and white. The fireworks proved useful, offering just enough light so she could slide him into the backseat. His head and shoulders flopped onto Frankie's lap. With great effort, Rose rolled him onto his back and folded his legs so that she could shut the door. She then leaned in and nudged him further to where his chest and head lay in an elevated position on Frankie's lap. It was time to find out exactly where the bullet had struck. Absent a functioning interior light, she ripped open his shirt and waited for the next flash from the fireworks. It came quick: thirty seconds of thunderous booms and brilliant light.

Immediately, she found where the bullet had struck. The entry wound was a little smaller than a dime. It was square on his shoulder. From the bullet hole, blood slowly seeped, trickling down to his waistline.

"Hang in there," she whispered to Bubba. Then to Frankie: "Try not to move, buddy."

Frankie nodded, his moaning lower in volume.

Rose bound out of the backseat, grabbed the keys from the driver's-side door, and raced around to the back of the car, nearly tripping on Bubba's stupid, fucking hat. She turned and cursed, seeing it there scuffed and soiled. Without thinking, she reached back, grabbed it and tossed it on the backseat floorboard. She slid the key into the trunk. It popped open. She reached inside with both hands and feverishly began tossing out items onto the ground next to her. An empty donut box, a few beer bottles, soda cans and oily rags. All sorts of crap, but not the damned first aid kit.

"Where the hell is that fucking thing?" she cursed.

In a rage, she heaved out the tire jack, almost taking the spare with it. Her shaking hands found more pieces of useless junk, all of which were summarily dispatched onto the Cartwright property. She was about to give up when, at last, her hands found the intended object: the first-aid kit, a small blue metal box with a red cross. She set it on the grass next to her. Without thinking, she leaned down and picked up some of the miscellaneous crap and placed it back where it came from. She slammed the trunk, grabbed the first aid kit off the ground and dashed back to Bubba and Frankie.

"Hang in there, Bubba," she said as she dropped to her knees to render aid. She popped the latches of the first-aid kit and removed gauze and bandage. After ripping three pieces of gauze from their paper packaging, she set them on Bubba's stomach, which had gone nearly motionless. She instructed Frankie to hold the gauze in place as she worked the bandage. She tore the stretchy bandage from its plastic casing, unwound it and handed it to Frankie.

"Frankie, hold this for a sec," she instructed.

Rose stacked the three large gauze pads over Bubba's bullet wound and pressed firmly. Bubba winced as she did.

"It hurts, Miss Rose," he said.

"Good. That means you'll be okay," Rose said. "Frankie, can I count on you to be a big help?"

"Yes, Miss Rose." Frankie answered. His groaning stopped.

"I need you to press down hard on those white pads on Bubba's shoulder." Rose demonstrated. "Don't worry. You'll be helping him. Can you do that, buddy?"

Frankie answered with resolve. "Yes, I can, Miss Rose."

"You can't stop, unless I tell you," Rose said. "We're going on a ride. We'll call your mom as soon as we can, but we need to go now. You and Bubba need a doctor."

Frankie said nothing. He just nodded and gritted his teeth. That was exactly what Rose needed to see. She closed the first-aid kit and set it on the floorboard next to him. She had filled up the tank earlier in the day, so they didn't need fuel. She would stop once, just long enough to make a phone call, maybe two. If need be, she could redress the wound at that time. For now, however, getting far away from the president-elect's mansion was the priority. Rose slid out of the backseat, grabbed her heels and slipped them on. She was about to jump behind the wheel when she remembered the gunman.

She had left him unattended. Perhaps for too long. She lunged into the backseat, fished out her pistol from under the driver's seat and then hustled to the front of the car. What she discovered brought her relief.

There he lay, his head hidden under the car's bumper. He was a threat to no one. He was a wretched mess, unable to lift his head, let alone get to his feet. A few of his teeth were scattered on the ground next to his bloody mouth. He moaned and grunted something about payback, something he was in no position to exact. He had been neutered by the great Rose McDougal.

"Sayonara, shithead," she said. "Have fun with the cops or, worse still, with security. I hear they're just as bad as the police."

Rose spat at his feet before jumping into the car behind the wheel. She cranked the old Chevy. It roared to life on the first turn. Acknowledging the work Bubba had done on her car, she silently thanked him. Rose dropped the transmission into reverse and backed out. She kept the lights off and idled out of the parking area before turning onto the unlit dirt road. Once clear of the house, Rose switched on the headlights and increased speed. She maintained the posted speed limit and stayed within the lines. This was no time for screwing around.

Saving her friends required a plan. Frankie and Bubba needed immediate medical help, especially Bubba. But they could not risk exposure, which meant treatment in a hospital in Maine was out of the question. Bubba and Frankie's condition would invite many questions. Gunshot wounds, and no calls for an ambulance? Undoubtedly, there would be police involvement, which would represent a palpable threat to Donnelly's business, not to mention inevitable incarceration for her and Bubba. There was only one person who could help.

Chapter forty-seven

Two hours after their hasty departure, they were closing in on New Hampshire. The Chevy initially shook in protest to her urging for speed but, eventually, it obeyed. Rose checked the side-view mirrors. She saw no headlights behind them, only a black landscape.

"Good," she mumbled.

Save a brief stop at the tollbooth ahead, the interstate promised fast and easy travel until they had to pick up secondary roads. She eased into the center lane. Lights from the Lexington Plaza toll booth came into view. She turned to check on Bubba and Frankie.

Frankie sat quietly, mumbling something as he gazed outside at the shadowy outlines of pine trees and estuaries. His left hand held the gauze on his right bicep firmly in place. She watched a few seconds longer before turning back to face the empty highway. The tollbooth was now just ahead. She let her foot up off the gas and returned both hands to the wheel, driving as if she were being graded. She looked up into the rear-view mirror to address Frankie.

"Frankie, I need you to do me a favor, okay?"

"Yes, Miss Rose," he replied, pulling his attention anyway from the outside scene.

"I need you to keep your left hand firmly in place, but I also need you to lean your head back and close your eyes like you're sleeping. Think you can do that, buddy?"

"Sure, Miss Rose," he said, smiling. Then, turning serious. "But this is just pretend, right? You don't want Frankie to fall asleep for real. Bubba needs me."

"That's right, buddy, he does. And yes, just pretend to be asleep. This is only make-believe."

Frankie nodded and then glanced down at Bubba. His chest barely rose, noticeable only to someone in close proximity. Bubba inched his head upward in Rose's direction and cracked a smile. He strained to lift higher, but the pain was too much.

"No need to say anything, Bubba. Just lay low," she said.

Bubba grunted something and smiled. Rose returned her attention to the road.

"Thanks, Frankie," she said. She steered the car directly under the single green arrow and only open lane.

Benny frowned as he watched a jalopy of a car approach. Benny liked his job working in a toll booth. Taking coins and singles and returning change was a cinch. With eighteen years on the job, he could retire in another two. But he was a miserable man who didn't see the upshot of enjoying his second retirement and still be under sixty.

"Don't these folks have homes, for crissakes?"

The driver, a sizeable woman from what Benny could gather, slowed to a stop and fished a twenty from her purse. She smiled at Benny as she rolled down her window. Cold air flooded inside his cozy booth. *For the forty-fourth goddamned time tonight*, he thought.

Benny was a sinewy man, who hated the cold. Silently he cursed as he pushed open his window. He looked down and studied the woman. He spotted two men sprawled out in the backseat. Whatever they were up to didn't matter a lick to Benny. *Probably two faggots.* He stuck out a bony hand and looked away from Rose. She and her passengers offended him. His watery eyes maintained a steely gaze on the register in front of him.

"One dollah," he said in perfect Yankee.

A bill was placed in his open palm. He looked down and found a twenty. He wrinkled his face. A twenty meant additional time with his booth window open to the cold and higher likelihood that the woman might want to brag about her Christmas plans or just engage in small talk. As stress-free as his duties were, which was exactly why he had chosen this profession, there was one irrevocable problem: people. Too many wanted to chat. Too many wanted to tell you their plans for the night, the weekend. Their goddamned retirement. He wasn't interested in any of it. Quickly he snatched the change from his cash drawer and shoved nineteen dollars in Rose's direction. Without a word, she grabbed her change from his wrinkled hand and sped off, her smile long gone.

Fifteen minutes later, Rose spotted the lights of the Piscataqua River Bridge. New Hampshire lay on the other end. As she drove, she felt a mix of emotions: anxiety, fear, anger, even anticipation. But now was not the time to dwell on emotion. Her priority was for the two men in the back. In the case of Bubba, that meant infection or worse. He had lost a significant amount of blood. While she didn't believe that a small slug could kill him, she didn't know for sure.

Should've paid better attention during EMT training.

Preventing the loss of a lot of blood meant keeping Frankie focused on his job. She looked in the rear-view mirror. She grinned as she noticed the concentration on Frankie's face, his eyes squeezed tight as his right hand maintained pressure on Bubba. Rose smiled.

"You don't have to play like you're asleep anymore," she said.

Opening his eyes, he flashed his trademark toothy smile. "That was easy, Miss Rose."

Turning serious, she said, "But we're not in the clear yet, buddy. We need to get Bubba to a hospital."

Frankie nodded solemnly before turning his gaze back on the scenery outside.

"Frankie, you've got a big job. Are you ok with that?" she asked.

Again, he nodded. Muscles in his forearm bulged and tendons flexed, as he applied additional pressure on Bubba's shoulder.

"It's going to take an hour to get to the hospital, maybe a bit longer since I'll have to stop to make a phone call," she said. "That's a long time, but I know I can count on you. I know you can do it."

They had begun their ascent over the Piscataqua River, a snaking figure of cold, moonlit water below. Frankie sat motionless, his body stiff. His attention seemed focused on the bridge's steel beams, which rapidly ticked by. Rose wondered what he was thinking, what occupied his mind. Surprising her, he spoke.

"Bubba is my new friend, and he needs my help. Ma will be happy I helped my new friend." Frankie softened his posture. A grin spread across his face. "If Santa was here, he would help, Miss Rose. And . . . and, Miss Rose . . . he's coming tonight, you know."

"Of course he's coming, and of course he'd help," she said, then flashed him a smile in the rear-view mirror. "After all, he is

Santa."

Claire was terrified. Frankie had promised to return by 7:30 and it was now approaching 9:00. Frankie knew that she would worry and he was always mindful of her concerns. He knew his tardiness would trouble her. Whenever he said he would be back at a set time, he had always followed through. What's more, he had never willfully disobeyed her. Her son was as honest as anyone she knew. In thirty-two years, not once had he disobeyed her, which added to her worry. What was more troubling was that he had insisted on being asleep before Santa came. Frankie knew well the risks of being awake when Santa plunged down the chimney or mysteriously appeared through a wall into the living room. Believing the lore about Santa, Frankie would never deliberately jeopardize his opportunity for Christmas-morning bliss.

Claire set the glass of red wine on the table behind her. She and Diane had migrated to wine after Frankie had gone off, and now Claire was feeling lightheaded. The fireworks had ended long ago and the visitors were all but gone. She and Frankie were to spend the night in the main house; Mrs. Cartwright had seen to that. She had just dispatched an assistant to prepare their rooms. Given her growing concern over Frankie, however, the preparation of their guest rooms was the last thing on Claire's mind. She could no longer sit still. She had to get up and do something.

"Mrs. Cartwright . . ."

Diane frowned and set her glass aside and looked into her house hoping to spot Dennis. "Come on, Claire. Call me Diane, or simply Dee."

"I'm sorry. This is just . . . you know, this is kind of strange." Claire blushed. "Maybe I shouldn't be, but I'm worried about Frankie. It's not like him to just wander off and bust his curfew. He never does that, especially with Santa coming."

Claire took a deep breath, then exhaled.

"He should've been here almost two hours ago, Diane." She shrugged her shoulders. "Maybe I'm overreacting. Hell, I don't know."

Diane stood up. As she did, she spotted Dennis, the bartender. He was standing in the threshold of the open glass door, squinting against the patio light.

"Miss Cartwright? Are you out there?" he asked, shielding his eyes.

"Over here, Dennis," she replied. "Here with Claire."

"The president asked me to check up on you."

"That's nice. Anyway, Claire and I are going for a walk. I need you to bring me my special bag. You know the one."

"Right away, ma'am." Dennis darted back into the house.

Claire was not only worried about her son, but also about the burden she was placing on Diane. She felt like a nuisance. *Imagine me tying up the First Lady on Christmas Eve, because I lost track of my son.* She closed her eyes, lowered her head and brought her hands up to her face. Seeming to catch Claire's vibe, Diane put a hand on her shoulder.

"Listen, we're going to find him. Both of us. I can't have you strolling off on your own in the dark. No one knows these grounds better than me. As for the party, Bill can say the remaining 'good nights.'" Diane waved a hand toward the house.

Dennis arrived holding a large bag by the straps. To Claire, it looked like the kind of over-the-shoulder bags she had seen the beatniks toting around during her short stint at the University of New Hampshire.

"Thanks, Dennis," Diane said as she took the bag. "As we're checking things out here, I'd like you to organize a small group to search the house. I don't want anyone to be overly concerned. It's Frankie we're looking for, and he may have wandered back inside. Meantime, Claire and I will search the grounds."

"Yes, ma'am," Dennis said. He started making his way back inside, then paused at the door. "If the president finds out I was okay with the First Lady traipsing off on the dark, he'll have my damned head," he muttered quietly.

But not quietly enough.

"What was that, Dennis?" Diane asked.

"Ma'am, I don't think it's a good idea. Please let me get one of the boys to go with you. I don't feel comfortable with you being . . ." Dennis nodded to the darkness beyond, "out there alone. If the president were to find out, I'd be a dead man walking."

Diane waved a hand at him. "Nonsense. There's nothing to worry about. We'll be fine," she said dismissively. "If Bill says something, remind him that he's still the president-elect. If he still has any issues, tell him to take it up with me later."

"Ma'am, with all due respect, you can't be serious. I'm not about to say anything so reckless—I value my life. And I just can't—sorry, I won't—let you wander off on your own," he shook his head. "If anything were to—"

Diane cut him off. "Ok, fine. But if secret service isn't here . . ." she checked her watch. "in three minutes, then we're going off on our own."

Dennis nodded, then pulled a two-way radio out of his pocket. He thumbed a button, broke the radio's static and mumbled some jargon. He waited a moment. Static broke on the other end and jargon came in reply. "Ma'am, there's someone coming. He'll be here inside of two minutes."

Chapter forty-eight

Rose pulled into a rest area off Highway 101. There were no vehicles, except for a snowplow parked in front of a building labelled MAINTENANCE. Rose checked her watch. It was almost 10:30. By her estimation, they would get to the hospital around 11:30. But to do so, she would have to hustle, minimizing the time associated with this pit stop. She looked back at Frankie, telling him that she needed to check on Bubba and then make a few phone calls. She pushed open her door. She shivered and rubbed her hands before opening the back door.

The car's interior light was busted. A light mounted on a nearby concessions hut cast light toward the car, but it was faint, which made her examination difficult. She twisted her torso left and right, eventually finding a position that provided just enough light to get a good look at Bubba's wound. The wound wasn't as bad as she had imagined. The area around the bullet hole appeared to be drying. Bubba's chest continued to rise and fall in a slow but steady pace. His milky eyes squinted up at her. *Thank God*, she thought. The worst thing would be for him to fall unconscious. He labored to talk, mouthing words which she could barely make out. All she picked up was "thanks."

"No thanks needed." Rose said, then cracked a smile, "but you're picking up the next bar tab."

Bubba worked up a smile and gave her a thumbs up.

Then she remembered Frankie's bullet wound which, albeit a glancing blow, was still a problem.

"How's your arm, Frankie? Any pain?"

Frankie shook his head and twisted his right shoulder so

that she could see. Her ripped-sleeve bandage remained in place. She had tied it tight enough to seal the wound and stop the bleeding, but not so tight as to cut off circulation. She loosened the bandage, allowing Frankie more motion. Had they been there to see her handiwork, Y-3 and Sergeant First Class Jackson would have been pleased.

"No pain? Good." Rose craned her neck to get a closer view. "Looks like the bleeding has stopped. You're going to be just fine, buddy."

Frankie smiled up at her, while keeping his left hand off Bubba's shoulder. "Miss Rose, can you call my ma and tell her I'm okay?"

"Count on it," Rose assured him, then checked her watch again.

I gotta make this fast.

"Frankie, we gotta hustle. Do you need to take a pi—" she caught herself and switched to something more appropriate. "Need to use the toilet? Maybe something to drink? I can get you a soda."

Frankie shook his head. "Ma says soda's bad at night."

Rose shrugged her shoulders. Claire was probably right. Mothers usually were, especially for a guy like Frankie. Plus, Rose didn't have the time, nor energy, to discuss the benefits of caffeine under time-sensitive circumstances which required a sharp focus. Instead, she winked at him, then sprang from the car, slamming her door and running to a bank of pay phones.

It took Diane, Claire and Joe, a Secret Service agent who stood six-foot-six, about ten minutes to search the property immediately surrounding the compound. Moving slowly, the three checked every square inch: around the back and on both sides. Each held a flashlight. They cast beams of light under and behind every bush, into every shrub, under the patio and into every copse of trees. Diane walked to the edge of the property, which butted up against the steep ocean wall, flashing light down on the rocks below.

Thank God, he's not down there, Diane thought.

Unfortunately, however, they had not found any clues as to his whereabouts. Their calls and shouts to him yielded nothing. Now, back on the porch, the place where their search had begun, Claire feared the worst.

"Maybe he just . . . I don't know. Maybe he just ran off." She wrapped her arms around herself appearing to fight back the winter chill. She shook her head. "This is not like my son. Not at all. He knows I'd be worried sick. And on Christmas Eve of all nights!"

Diane took one of Claire's hands.

Claire continued. "What if he's been abducted? I mean, he trusts everyone. He loves everyone, and thinks everyone loves him."

Her eyes pleaded for a contrary reply, which Diane provided.

"I sincerely doubt that anyone who came to the party would've taken him." Diane gripped Claire's hand. "We're going to find him. There's a place we've not checked. Out front down by a wooded area."

Diane Cartwright, the woman who would stand by her husband's side in under a month as he took the oath of office, led Claire in the direction of what had been the makeshift parking lot. The secret service agent, Joe, lagged a few steps behind.

Once teeming with vehicles, the overflow lot was now empty. Diane swept the flashlight to the left and right as they crossed the matted grassy area. Evidence of vehicles, tire treads in the grass and dirt, and a few cigarette butts were all they found. She looked over to Claire and then at Joe, whose gaze was fixed on the darkness ahead.

"Claire, see the dirt road ahead?" Diane asked, pointing her flashlight ahead of them.

It was the entrance to a narrow road which disappeared into a dense thicket of pines and barren oaks. The three walked on.

"Frankie . . . Frankie!" Claire called.

Silence.

"Francis Michael O'Brien!"

Diane reached out for Claire's arm, gently applying pressure. Claire turned to face her. Diane looked serious, intense. She held a finger to her mouth. She gestured to the ground with her flashlight. The shaft of white light revealed an oily rag and what looked like red paint.

She released her grip on Claire's forearm and lowered herself to a knee. She felt Claire leaning over her shoulder. Meanwhile, Joe maintained his watch, his right hand resting on his holstered pistol. Diane dabbed the ground with two fingers and then rubbed her thumb across her finger. She turned to look up to Claire and Joe, aiming the light to the impression of a shoe. Diane was convinced—it wasn't paint; it was blood.

The discovery of blood pointed to the likelihood of foul play. She heard Claire gasp behind her. Diane inched up the flashlight's beam in the direction of the road. She found another footprint. She stood up and took two steps forward, elevating her flashlight as she did. She spotted another footprint and more drops of fresh blood. A few steps further netted more blood spots and footprints. The blood trail and footprints followed a path toward the dirt road ahead. A few steps later, she heard a distant grunting sound. She looked back at Claire and Joe and raised a hand and then placed a finger over her mouth. The two froze in place. Diane took a few steps forward, then stopped. She heard the grunting again, this time louder. Slowly she elevated her flashlight. Less than a hundred feet away was a man, the source of the grunting. Even with the distance, Diane spotted tears and stains on his jacket. He seemed not to notice three of them, as he limped away toward the road.

Margo promised Rose that everything would be in place when she arrived. To keep it discrete, she told Rose to drive around to the back of the hospital. The doctors and administrators were all home and the nursing staff was minimally manned, which was perfect.

Meanwhile, Frankie was holding up well. That was great. Bubba had maintained his breathing and, equally important, remained conscious. He had even coughed out a few words since they had left the rest area. That too was great. However, they had another hour to drive, and she was getting tired. That wasn't great.

Rose pushed the Chevy to sixty miles-per-hour, which exceeded Highway 101's declared speed limit of fifty-five. Normally, she would have had no problem barreling down an empty highway at speeds closer to seventy, or whatever the temperamental Impala would allow, but tonight she could not take that risk. While she doubted the presence of cops on Christmas Eve, she could not take a chance. Not with two gunshot victims in the backseat.

Minus the occasional highway light and home ablaze with Christmas lighting, both of which were few and far between outside of Exeter, the car's headlights represented all the light for as far as Rose could see. She sped past a sign promising another twenty-four miles to Manchester.

"Shit," Rose muttered, and then remembered Frankie behind her. "Sorry buddy. There goes Miss Rose's mouth again, huh?" She looked in the rear-view mirror.

There he sat, that determined look fixed on his face. In his right hand, he held a can of Coke, which he had only reluctantly accepted at the rest area. His left hand kept the right amount of pressure on Bubba's shoulder. Seeing Frankie, so committed to help, filled Rose with a mix of remorse and pride. Here was a grown man with the mind of a seven- or eight-year-old. He had been teased and picked on all his life. Yet when it mattered most, he had stepped up. If the whole experience had been hard on him, it didn't show.

Rose turned back to the road ahead. An old pick-up truck sped past in the eastbound lane. As it passed, black emptiness returned, as far as the eye could see. She pressed a switch on the floorboard with her left foot activating the high beams. Brighter light sliced through the darkness. She switched on her radio. Static blasted through the worn speakers causing her to cringe.

"Sorry, buddy," she said, spinning the dial to cut down volume.

She turned the tuner to the end of the FM band and found 107.3 WAAF. Jethro Tull's "Teacher" was playing. She inched the volume back up, but only a touch. She loved classic rock and Jethro Tull was a favorite. *Good music calls for a cold beer.* But beer was the last thing she needed. Absent a beer, she figured a good smoke would suffice, even the cheap ones. She patted her chest pockets for her Garcia y Vega's, forgetting the fact that she was still in her formal garb.

So what if they were cheap cigars, she thought. Cheap meant you could buy more of them, which was important to someone who was used to living on the brink of poverty.

Rose had always kept a stash of stogies in the old beater. She only hoped they were not in the trunk. That would mean pulling over, and that was not an option. She reached across the cabin and pushed on the glove box, into which she had crammed a lot of stuff. It was amazing the amount of crap one could shove inside a glove box. It reminded her of that time when Sergeant Jackson cracked a joke about soldiers and a Volkswagen.

"How many GIs can you cram into a VW Bug?" he asked.

No one knew, and no one dared to pretend they did. It was always best to let the imposing instructor deliver the punch line to his own jokes.

"One more," he declared.

The same held true for her glove box. And the trunk as well, for that matter. Seemed there was always room to pack in one more piece of useless junk. She checked on the road ahead, then began pounding her right fist against it, demanding that it open. It felt spring-loaded, like it could burst. Because it would. Eventually, the banging served its purpose. The glove box exploded. Out flew candy wrappers, bottle caps, oily napkins, empty boxes of Good and Plenty, plastic spoons, a fork and a Nashua Pirates program. She was about to swear loudly but caught herself.

"Shit," she mumbled. Eyes on the road, she plunged her hand deep inside the glove box. She fished around for a moment and then found what she sought.

Jackpot!

A full box of Garcia y Vegas, stuffed deep inside, lay in wait. Rose pulled it out, swerving the car for a split second as her eyes admired her prize. In fine print on the side of the box, a label read: Best before 26 NOV 1982. She blew it off.

It's not like milk or fish. A stale cigar can't kill you; it just might not taste as good, that's all.

"Sorry about the swerve back there, buddy . . . and those nasty words," she spoke to the rear-view mirror, again forgetting to check her language in front of Frankie. Frankie said nothing.

Why does every goddamn thing I need have to be in the very back or bottom of wherever I'm looking? she wondered. She brushed the thought aside.

"I promise to do a better job with my language," she said and then shrugged her broad shoulders, peering back into the rearview mirror. "Sometimes those words just slip out."

Frankie appeared to wake from a trance.

"It's okay, Miss Rose," Frankie said in a matter-of-fact tone. "My mother says bad words."

"Your mom swears? I have a hard time believing that, but I'll take your word for it," Rose said.

She pressed the car's cigarette lighter and waited for it to pop. The lights of Manchester were now visible in the distance. By her reckoning, they were ten miles away. A moment later, the lighter popped. Rose peeled off the plastic protecting the cigar and placed it in her mouth. She bit on the cigar to hold it in place. She pulled the lighter up to the cigar's tip. After a series of puffs, she had a functioning smoke. To an observer in the backseat, like Frankie, her head would have appeared to be smoldering, as purplish-gray smoke wafted up and away from the tuft of her previously styled, now frizzy black hair. The acrid smoke filled the front of the cabin before rolling into the back.

"Hope this doesn't bother you too much, buddy," she said. "But God knows that Miss Rose needs a cigar."

Frankie frowned. Speaking slowly, he warned: "Ma says smoking is really bad for you."

"She's right," Rose replied.

"Ma says it makes you look older."

"Yup. She's right." Smoke drifted into the backseat. Rose heard Frankie cough softly.

"Ma also says smoking stunts your growth."

"Again, she's ri—." Rose stopped in mid-sentence. She twisted in her seat to look back. "Well, had I known that years ago, I would have started smoking at a much younger age. Too late for me, I'm already a big gal."

She grinned at Frankie, who appeared to fight off his own smile. Rose reckoned that smiling would mean she had won the point, which was something Frankie probably didn't like after having defended his mother's unassailable wisdom. She turned back to the road ahead and then cracked the window a few inches. Instantly the smoke rushed out of the car. In its place came a blast of bitterly cold air.

"Well, your mom's right. I imagine she always is. You know, she's a very good friend." Rose took a long drag on the cigar and waved it towards the road ahead. "Anyway, we're making good time, but we still got a way to go."

She tapped the cigar at the crack of the window. Ashes disappeared into the cold night. A sliver of a moon cast light on the endless tract of white pines that flanked both sides of Highway 101.

Bleeding and sore, the man in a Fedora shuffled on toward the tree-lined driveway. He had reached the opening of the road when Diane called out, splashing her flashlight's beam on him.

"Stop right there!" she demanded. She took a few steps, closing their distance.

He turned around to acknowledge her, shielding his eyes from the light. He grinned, apparently assessing there was no threat from the three behind him. He resumed his walk forward, pushing himself to move faster. Unsure whether he was armed, Diane cautious followed him, maintaining a safe distance.

Fresh drops of blood, the product of what was most certainly a beating, marked his progress. He had crossed the Cartwright property line, still only fifty feet away from Diane and the other two, and nearly disappeared around a curve in the road which lead to Perkins Road.

This far from the house, it was pitch-black. On countless occasions, Diane had asked her husband to install lighting. Each time she nagged, he promised to take care of it, but never followed through. It had become a ritual between the two of them.

"Joe, take care of him," Diane said.

Joe walked ahead and pulled out his pistol from his holster. Pistol aimed chest high, Joe quickened his pace. Diane came up behind Joe, with Claire in tow. Diane kept her flashlight aimed on the man who hobbled on, his feet shuffling on the dirt road. In her left hand, Diane held her pocketbook. It was bulky and she struggled with its weight, but given what lay inside, it was worth the effort.

Now less than ten feet behind the man, Joe gripped his gun in both hands, then shouted.

"Stop right there! Don't take another step."

Claire caught up to Diane. The two ladies stopped a few feet behind Joe. The man turned around, noticing the gun pointed at his chest. He looked up at Joe and squinted in the flashlight's bright light. His face resembled his jacket: bloody, dirty and ragged. Blood and dirt was smeared across his cheeks and nose. His swollen, cracked lips bled. Beyond his cracked lips were four black holes where teeth had once been. His salt-and-pepper hair bore a thick brown-green stripe of matted dirt and grass that ran from his left ear to the crown of his head. Yet despite having received a serious beating, and now held at gunpoint, his face showed no fear. He flashed a glance at Joe, then regarded Diane and Claire with only a mild curiosity. A smirk crept across his face. His smirk seemed to suggest that the man and two women who stood before him represented no threat whatsoever.

"And to think, you'll soon be our First Lady," he said, shielding himself from the bright light.

"Who are you?" Diane asked. Her eyes narrowed. She felt convinced that he had something to do with Frankie's disappearance.

"So, I was leaving your party and I fell. Dark out here. Ought to get some lighting down here," Chuck replied, his voice whistling through gaps in his teeth. "I'm sure you or the president could get someone to get some lights installed." He shrugged his shoulders and grinned, which was more of a leer. "Maybe you get *Lujak* on the job." He over to Joe. "I bet *Lujak* could do the job. I hear *Lujak* is a talented guy."

Joe stared the man down. The agent's eyes gave no emotion. The barrel of his pistol remained locked on his chest. Diane took a step forward next to Joe.

"You were just leaving, huh? I don't buy that bullshit for a second," Diane said. From behind her, she heard Claire gasp. "You didn't fall. You got your butt kicked." She looked up at Joe before turning back to the stranger. "And who's Lujak? There's no Lujak here."

Claire slowly stepped forward next to Diane.

Still full of confidence, the man held out his hands, suggesting 'guilty as charged.'

"Let's try this again," Diane said. "Who are you?"

The man took a small step back and rotated his left shoulder forward, attempting to conceal the movement of his right hand, as it slipped inside his jacket. Diane caught the spike of concentration in the man's eyes. So did Joe. He cocked the hammer of his pistol and stepped forward.

Diane slowly handed the flashlight to Claire. Claire took it. She kept the light aimed at his face.

"That's good, Claire. Don't move," she instructed. Diane thrust a hand into her pocketbook, swiftly retrieving a can of bear spray. She leveled it at his head, about ten feet away.

The man now had two weapons trained on him, one deadly and one incapacitating. Either way, he had been bested; his confidence was gone. He dropped his head and slumped his shoulders. Just the same, Diane had no problem spraying a blast of the burning liquid into his eyes. If his actions were some kind of ruse, a bout of temporary blindness, burning lungs and choking would set him straight.

Claire's wide eyes flicked from Joe's gun to Diane's bear spray.

"You always carry that stuff around?" Claire asked Diane.

Diane kept her eyes on the dirt-stained man. "Wander these grounds after dark, my dear, you never know what you might find."

Diane had run out of patience with the man. "One last time: who are you and what happened tonight?"

Finally, he spoke. His words were interspersed with whistling sounds on account of his missing teeth. "A big man . . . a real big man rushed at me out of the dark," he answered. "He knocked me down. I . . . I don't remember anything after that."

"That had to have been my Frankie. It had to have been," Claire said. She strode toward him. She would have struck him, had Joe stuck out a hand stopping her advance.

"What did you do to my son? What did you do to him, you sonovabitch?!"

Diane closed in on him, getting to within arm's reach. The bear spray was trained on the man's eyes. From this close, a shot of the stuff would blind him for life. The man took a step back and raised his hands to cover his face.

"I don't believe you," Diane said. "None of us do. Time to tell all. And I mean everything."

Olaf rested the phone back in its cradle and sat back down

behind her desk. So much for a quiet Christmas Eve. In short, two men had been shot and one was in bad shape. At least now her suspicions about Rose's business up in Maine were proven true: there was nothing innocent about it. And whatever the business, Olaf was convinced that shady character who had visited Rose's hospital room had something to do with it. Her ruminating was interrupted by her first assistant. Olaf could not stand her.

"Who was that?" Nurse Brenda Clark inquired.

"Wrong number," Olaf shot back.

A tireless busybody, Brenda was a wretched, petty woman who always suspected that her co-workers were up to no good. She constantly badgered Olaf about the other nurses and the "shortcuts" she claimed they were always taking. She wore horn-rimmed glasses, making her appear even more condemnatory. Olaf fantasized about slapping the glasses right off her face. If not for her position as the head RN, she would have done exactly that long ago. Instead of a physical assault, Olaf punished Brenda with tedious tasks.

"Anyway, never mind that. Get up to room 314 and check on Mr. Johnson. Make sure his breathing is still normal." She furrowed her brow, then glared up at Brenda, who stood across Olaf's desk with her arms folded. Olaf continued, "Check his bedpan this time. And while you're up there, check on Boudreau, Gallaudet and Murphy. Check their bedpans, too. Got it?"

Brenda opened her mouth to protest but bit her tongue. She scowled at Olaf, her face twisted in irritation. She then stormed off, huffing away.

Olaf waited until she was at the end of the hallway. As soon as she turned the corner toward the elevators and out of sight, Olaf sprinted in the opposite direction to the stairwell. For an overweight woman, Olaf could move quickly when she needed to. She bolted down a flight of stairs to the first floor, where three of her favorite nurses were working, ones she could trust in this most delicate matter.

Olaf took to get to know all of her nurses but made an extra effort to get to know those she trusted most. For those select few, she met their husbands, boyfriends and children. During her seven years as a head RN, six nurses had earned her total trust. It so happened that three of them were working tonight.

Like Olaf, they were selfless and committed to their patients. They worked double shifts over major holidays so that their co-workers with children could spend time at home. The three nurses embodied the divine qualities of their profession—selfless and nurturing.

Olaf arrived at the first-floor nurses' station where two of the three, Renee and Tricia, sat watching *A Christmas Carol*. Unlike the third floor, only four rooms on the first floor had occupants. Renee and Tricia had just finished visiting each of the four rooms and had finished with their charting. They had some time to kill.

When times were slow and the charting was accomplished, Olaf allowed her nurses a chance to get off their feet. Crossword puzzles, reading, college basketball and movies on TV filled the void. Olaf didn't mind, as long as they made their rounds and kept the doctors happy—and out of her greying hair. What little of it was left, she often lamented.

Renee and Tricia were reliable. They were young and beautiful. More importantly, they were smart. They had rejected repeated advances by countless doctors. Normally, it was the good-looking, oblivious types who Olaf had to worry about. Doctors swam like sharks around such naiveté in search of their next "flavor of the month." When they bagged one, they would coddle them, flaunt them at their country clubs, and make arrangements to align their work shifts so as to maximize their time together. From that point on, Olaf could expect no real work from them.

Those most coveted would be pulled away on "special business," including out-of-town conferences, some of which evolved into long-weekend getaways. Once in the good graces of the doctors, Olaf might not see them for weeks. Sooner or later, however, the fairytale lifestyle would end for the nurses. The doctors would eventually grow tired of them and move on to newer targets. In the end, the dumped nurses were ineffective and of little use to Olaf. Such was not the case with Renee and Tricia. As greenhorns, they steered clear of the predatory doctors and developed into outstanding caregivers.

"Gals, come with me," Rose said. "I've got a job for you."

Renee switched off the TV. She and Tricia stood up and followed Olaf toward the ER. Along the way, Olaf found Donna Sipperly in room 108, her other favorite. Besides Olaf, Donna was perhaps the most talented RN in the hospital. She responded promptly to Olaf's wave from the hallway. She put down the book she was reading to her 93-year-old patient and walked out into the hallway.

"I've got something you're gonna like," Olaf said.

"Better than *The Old Man and The Sea*?" Donna asked.

"Better than A Christmas Carol?" Tricia asked.

"Yes and yes," Olaf answered.

Olaf nodded to her nurses and started walking down the hallway. The three followed closely behind her. Donna exchanged smiles with Renee and Tricia. The three were good friends who played volleyball and surfed together on Hampton Beach. Leading the way, Olaf barged into the ER. As she entered, she came upon a travesty, a serious assault on hospital hygiene: a couple of male orderlies were sitting around a table playing cards and smoking cigarettes. Smoking was a big no-no inside any hospital. Olaf was not amused.

"You gotta be shitting me!" Olaf shouted, placing her hands on her hips. "Smoking in the ER?"

Olaf stormed over and flipped the table, sending it skyward, the cards scattering across the dingy ER floor. The terrified orderlies jumped up from their seats.

"After you pukes finish playing 52 Pickup, you're going to make this damned floor shine. It's going to shine so nicely that I'll be able to see my beautiful face when I gaze down on it."

The orderlies lowered their heads in shame and replied in the affirmative.

"You've got thirty minutes to bring this floor up to my standards," she commanded. "And when you're done in here, you're going to mop and buff the front foyer."

St. Joe's front foyer was a massive, open area, an infinite terrain of tile for the poor soul assigned the task of cleaning and buffing it. It would take the two of them hours to get it done. Which was the point. Olaf needed them out of the way. The fewer snooping eyes, the better. The orderlies scurried around on all fours, picking up cards and cigarette butts.

"Chop-chop, you little brats! I haven't got all night."

Quickly, they bustled. Olaf smirked, gesturing the nurses off to the side and out of earshot of the orderlies.

"Okay, here's the deal. We've got two gunshot-wound victims on the way; one may be serious. I've told the driver to come around to the loading docks. We need the usual kit and we'll need a stretcher. They'll be here in . . ." Olaf checked her watch. "under an hour."

The three nodded.

"Who's the doctor on duty? Is he here?" Olaf asked.

Renee answered, "It's Levesque and, no, he's not."

"Good. Let's keep it that way," Olaf said. "No one else in this hospital is to know what's going on. Absolute discretion, please." Olaf frowned and then looked at the nurses intently. "The driver is a good friend."

Rose slapped herself across the face, awakening her nerve endings and sending a sharp pain message to her brain. The slap left a red imprint across her cheek and hurt like a bastard. Unfortunately, the pain lasted only a minute. Slapping herself did little to shake off the inevitable: she was fading fast. The anxiety related to the night's mission at the Cartwright's; the violent encounter with a would-be assassin; and the dash to escape the scene and get her friends to medical attention had sparked an adrenaline rush. But that rush was long gone.

Rose craved a bed, wanting only to lie down and sleep. For a week if she could. But there was no sleep in her immediate future. Bubba had lost a fair amount of blood; time was not his friend. Thankfully, on account of Frankie's diligence, she assessed Bubba's survival chances as good. At the rest area, the bleeding had slowed. With Frankie's continued pressure on the wound, the bleeding may have stopped altogether, though it was impossible to know from where she sat. Rose could not guarantee anything, and that scared the hell out of her. It scared her to the point that her hands shook. She slid open the car's ashtray and set the cigar down.

What more could this terrifying night send my way? The answer: a growing fatigue, one which threatened her ability to remain awake and the safety of her occupants.

She released her grip on the wheel and shook her arms. She clicked her teeth together and turned her head side to side. Neither did much to combat her drowsiness. Talking to Frankie may have helped, but she didn't want to distract him from his task. She placed her hands back on the steering wheel. The road ahead looked like a journey into an endless sea of black, a sea which appeared to swallow the flickering of ghostly light coming from a distant home. The steady hum of the engine, the gentle roll of the tires was all she heard. The sounds became hypnotic.

"No, Rose. Don't let it happen," she mumbled. "Come on, old girl."

Yes, dear, relax. Give in and come follow me, a soothing voice encouraged.

Soon, Rose's eyelids began to droop. She was powerless to fight it. As her head slumped, her chin traced a slow arc toward her chest. The old car began to drift across the white line, over rumble strips and into the breakdown lane.

Thump . . . thump . . . thump . . . THUMP . . . THUMP . . . THUMP!!

Just in time, Rose snapped to. She shot open her eyes, gasped, and jerked the steering wheel hard to the left, pulling the car so hard that it shot out of the breakdown lane across the double yellow line into the eastbound lane.

"Jesus!" she shouted, and then yanked the steering wheel back to the right, sending the speeding car back across the yellow lines. She hammered the brakes with both feet. The car skidded to a screeching halt. The front half of the car poked into the breakdown lane, while the back of it jutted out into the westbound lane of Highway 101. The smell of burning filled her nostril's.

She had gotten to within six feet of sending the three of them down a shallow embankment and onto a crop of jagged boulders, which the headlights illuminated. She wiped a trail of saliva from her bottom lip, then looked up to the rearview mirror at Frankie. His eyes were bugged out, but his hand remained in place on Bubba's shoulder.

She exhaled deeply. "Oh, God. That was close."

She apologized to Frankie. She drew in a deep breath and immediately exhaled. Her hands shook and her eyes watered. Rubbing her eyes with the palms of her hand, she slowed her breathing down to something closer to normal. She pulled her hands away from her face and shook them out. She then checked the side mirrors.

For as far as she could see, there was no light. She let up on the brake pedal, gently turned the steering wheel to the left and guided the car back into the travel lane. Gradually she increased her speed to sixty-five.

Rose had fallen asleep. While it was only for a few seconds, it didn't matter. A split second more could have done the trick. Had she blown through the breakdown lane, Bubba's life would not have been the only one in peril. As desperate as she was for rest, she knew that there was no time for a power nap nor a quick stop for a cup of joe or a Coke, even if they could find a place open on Christmas Eve. She had to carry on.

Just up ahead was Manchester. Closing in on Manchester meant another twenty minutes before they reached St. Joe's Hospital. Rose reached down and plucked her cigar from the ashtray. She puffed on it. The calming smoke infiltrated her nostrils and chest. The feel of the cigar between her thumb and fingers brought a measure of comfort. She held the smoke for a moment before exhaling and releasing another cloud of gray-purple smoke.

And then, she felt it again. That caressing pull.

She felt her eyes growing heavy. She began stomping her feet in an attempt to get her heart rate up, before remembering the small hole in the floorboard. One mighty stomp could send her foot through the floorboard, slamming it onto the highway. Can you say instant amputee?

How the hell am I supposed to stay awake?

Rolling down the window and allowing a blast of cold air to wake her up would buy some time, but it would be bad for Bubba. Not to mention, an open window for any length of time might be deadly for all three of them. Pinching or biting herself would do no better than another slap across her face. The answer came to her: pain. Not a slap, pinch or bite, the effects of which were short-lived. Rose needed pain that would last. Rose took another puff of her cigar. She was studying its glowing red end when it hit her. A burning pain, the kind of pain which the end of a cigar could deliver, might do the trick. It would certainly get her attention and keep her awake.

"God, this is gonna suck," she mumbled.

Rose looked over to the front passenger seat, where she found her pocketbook resting against a seat cushion coil which protruded through the threadbare vinyl. She didn't want to frighten Frankie any more than she already had. She figured cramming something into her mouth would help suppress the volume of her screaming, which were sure to follow. For all she knew, Frankie's stoic posture was a charade, an attempt to appear in control. He could be hanging by a thread and ready to snap. There was no way to know for sure since he could not communicate like a normal adult. After burning herself, Rose was subject to scream and flail. That kind of response would likely prompt Frankie to lose it himself. In doing so, he would be unable to continue caring for Bubba. Frankie had been through enough already. There was no way the events of the night had not impacted him. The least Rose could do was to minimize the volume of her post-scalding conniption fit.

She reached over to her pocketbook and fished out her compact. It was the only item inside. It would have to do. She could already feel the next wave of drowsiness, a gentle massage tickling the back of her head. She approached another prison-made road sign informing her that Interstate 293 was a half mile ahead. She decided to wait until she was on 293 before she broiled herself. If nothing else, the four-lane interstate would offer her a wider margin of error in the event the burn caused her to swerve madly. She drove on, flexing her hands and occasionally tapping her cheeks. The pain was put off, for another few minutes anyway.

Chapter forty-nine

"Mrs. Cartwright!" Rodney cried. He was panting. "Ma'am . . . are you . . . are you there? Joe, Joe . . . you there?"

He shone the flashlight through the bare trees and ran as fast as he could toward the dirt road and the edge of the Cartwright property. His light swept left and right, up and down. Rodney hated running. He hated anything that had to do with physical exertion. For Mrs. Cartwright, however, he would do anything.

"Mrs. Cartwright? Joe? Every . . . everything . . . okay?" he asked between wheezes.

"Yes, Rodney. I'm here," Diane replied. "Everything's okay. We're all okay."

Rodney ran around the bend of the road and stopped. A short distance ahead, he spotted Mrs. Cartwright and Joe from security. There weren't alone. There were two others with them: a woman and some guy who looked like he had fallen out of a speeding vehicle. Joe held the man at gunpoint. Mrs. Cartwright was pointing something in the face of the disheveled man, something Rodney could not make out.

Oh Lord, what has she gotten herself into this time?

Rodney sighed and then began walking in their direction. He was out of breath. He was a heavyset man who ran for nothing, except the toll of the dinner bell. The half-mile run he had just completed may as well have been a marathon.

Rodney Garrard was in his eighth year as an assistant to Mrs. Cartwright. He loved working for her. She was a generous woman who had a smile for all. When Rodney needed time with his family down in Rhode Island, she never hesitated in approving his leave. But she loved adventure and was always on the go.

That meant trying to keep tabs on her, which was often a challenge. So, when he saw her holding some kind of weapon out in the dark with a member of the Cartwright security detail, he was not surprised.

Rodney walked up to her, Joe and a woman he had seen earlier in the night. He leaned forward and placed his hands on his knees to catch his breath. A few seconds later, he raised himself up, ran his fingers through his hair and adjusted his tie.

"Is everything okay, ma'am?" Rodney asked. He was about to ask her if she needed him to call for backup, then remembered he forgot to take a walkie-talkie. Calling for backup meant running another half mile to get it.

"We've got matters well in hand, Rodney," Mrs. Cartwright replied.

She kept her eyes on the man that Joe held at gunpoint and with whatever she held in her hands. "This man was just about to answer some questions before you arrived." Her eyes narrowed. "Weren't you?"

Then Rodney remembered the phone call he had just received, the reason he had ran the torturous half-mile in the first place.

"Ma'am, I nearly forgot. About fifteen minutes ago a lady phoned. I apologize . . ." He bent forward again, wheezing. "I . . . I ran the property looking for you and your friend."

He gestured to the woman who stood next to Joe. She had to be the one. He turned to her. She looked terrified.

"Ma'am, I believe the lady who called has your son. Is his name Frankie?"

"Who has my son?" the woman asked. Her expression of fear switched to rage, as she turned to face the man under gunpoint. "If you hurt him, in any way, I'll kill you. I swear—"

Rodney interrupted her, his breathing back to normal. "The woman who called said your son is fine. She told me to tell you he's not in danger. They're headed to St. Joe's Hospital in Nashua."

"My son is fine? Who drives to a hospital when everything is fine?" the woman asked, her voice trembling. "And on Christmas Eve, no less."

"It doesn't make sense to me, either," Mrs. Cartwright said. Her stare remained locked on the man.

Rodney studied the man from top to bottom. His pants and jacket were covered in dirt and blood stains. His face was a filthy twisted mess. He spotted a few missing teeth through cracked, bleeding lips. The man wore a Fedora, one which had seen better days. Taken in total, he looked like shit.

"It's obvious, isn't it?" the woman declared. She pointed at the man. "This man, this sleazy piece of shit had something to do with Frankie being taken to a hospital." The fury in her eyes returned as she addressed him. "That man who gave you a serious whipping, was my son!"

She charged at him, her fists clenched, "You son of a bitch!"

She got to the man before Joe could stop her. She grabbed his shirt, jerking him back and forth and releasing him only so as to slap his face before kicking at his shins. Joe pulled her off the him before she could do any real damage.

Rodney watched in shock before realizing what was happening. He snapped out of it and placed his hands on her shoulders, gently pulling her away. He needed to bring some calm into the situation

"Easy now. Easy," he said.

Still looking at the man, Mrs. Cartwright spoke.

"Claire, outside of a little well-deserved satisfaction, pulverizing this creep will do us little good. Whatever information he has, I guarantee we'll get it. In the meantime, getting you to that hospital in Nashua is our priority."

Claire nodded.

Mrs. Cartwright cracked a devilish grin. Then she nodded in the direction of the mansion. "There are a few folks up there who are really good at getting answers. You'll soon find out that stonewalling is not an option."

The man said nothing. His expression remained stoic.

"Rodney, I need you to run back to the house. First, tell Max what's going on down here. He'll send the welcoming committee. Then I'll need you to get us a car."

Us? Rodney thought. There she goes again, off on another adventure.

Rodney's shoulders sagged. He had hoped that his half-mile run would be the last run for a while. *Dammit. That's what I get for forgetting to bring a walkie-talkie*, he silently lamented.

He was tired and ready for a snack, maybe a nice glass of Merlot, but that wasn't in the cards; participating in another Diane Cartwright adventure was. He nodded to his boss and set off, running back to the mansion as fast as his short, chubby legs would take him.

Ten minutes later, two cars arrived. The first was a black sedan, out of which came three large men. Pistols drawn, they signaled Chuck into the backseat. He obeyed. Seated between the husky men, breathing would be difficult. But it would not be nearly as uncomfortable as the experience which awaited him inside the mansion. Right behind the sedan was a red Audi. It was William Jr.'s car, her son who lived in Arizona with his wife. It would be their transportation to Nashua tonight. Behind the wheel sat Rodney, smiling ear-to-ear. Behind Rodney was Clarence, a member of the president-elect's security detail.

"Why doesn't this surprise me?" Diane said, smiling at her loyal assistant. She slipped the bear spray back inside her bag.

"Are you kidding, ma'am? No way I'm going to stay here and miss out on all the fun," Rodney said, as he jumped out of the car to get the doors for the ladies.

Chapter fifty

Rose hammered the gas pedal, leaving Highway 101 and merging onto Interstate 293. The Chevy sputtered and shook, protesting her demands for increased speed. Drumming on the dashboard, her cigar clenched between her teeth, Rose goaded on her old car in an encouraging tone.

"Come on, ole girl . . . one more time. Just one."

Eventually her car stepped it up. The knocking sounds and the belching of black smoke ceased. She smacked the dashboard one final time. That seemed to do the trick and the eight-cylinder engine began to rumble smoothly. They were now within the Manchester city limits.

"Yes! Yes, there you go!" Her smacks turned to lovely pats. "Atta girl."

Rose settled back in her seat, confident that the old car could maintain its speed for the remaining fifteen miles. She sat back comfortably, rolling her cigar between her lips. She eased her head back onto the headrest. That was when it returned, her seductive, deadly guest.

Its lulling embrace crawled, inch by inch, from her lower spine up to her skull. Once again, she was utterly defenseless to its appeal. Her eyelids drooped. Her chin dropped and her tongue began to slide out of her mouth. Her right hand slipped off the wheel and flopped lifelessly onto her lap. As her chin struck her chest, her left hand rolled the steering wheel to the right. The car lurched abruptly. The sudden jerk of the vehicle jolted Rose awake. From behind her, Frankie shouted.

"Miss Roooooose!"

Rose slapped her face and grabbed the steering wheel with

both hands. As she had done earlier, she over-compensated the swerve to the right and jerked the steering wheel to the left, directly towards an 18-wheeler coming up from behind. At the last second, Rose spotted a bright-yellow backhoe riding atop the flatbed. She yanked the wheel back to the right, narrowly avoiding a gruesome ending under the extended flatbed of the speeding truck. Clear of the danger, she quickly scanned right and behind her. No other car to be found. She exhaled a blast of air, offered up a hasty prayer of thanks and then berated herself.

"Shit-shit-shit! Dammit Rose, you dumb bitch."

She heard moaning behind her. She pounded her right thigh in frustration. Through it all, still clenched between her teeth, her cigar had somehow survived. It was indestructible. The twenty-five-cent stogie had survived two dramatic events. Which reminded her. She had business with that cigar, business that could not be put off any longer. She pulled herself together and then, without looking up into the rearview mirror, offered Frankie yet another apology.

"I'm sorry, buddy." She drew in a deep breath. "Is he . . . is Bubba okay? Is his chest is still moving up and down?"

When she heard nothing, she turned around. Frankie lips were trembling, as if he was trying to speak. His face was gray and sweaty. It was clear that he was approaching a breaking point. She could not afford that. She needed him to stay on task for another twenty minutes or so.

"I'm really sorry, buddy. I must've fallen asleep. I promise it won't happen again." She scanned the empty southbound lanes of 293 in the direction of their travel. The 18-wheeler, nearly the night's Grim Reaper, was out of view. She peered up into the rearview mirror.

"Frankie, this is gonna sound crazy, so bear with me." She paused, considering her next words. "I need to hurt myself to stay awake. I know it sounds crazy, but it'll help me stay awake. I need you to be brave and not worry if you hear me scream," she said. *Because I'm going to,* she thought. "You just keep doing your job, okay?"

"Yes, Miss Rose," Frankie said dutifully, and then added, "It's okay if you swerve. Ma does it all the time, too."

"Is that right?" Rose asked.

I doubt quite as recklessly as I am.

"I don't want you to worry, Frankie. This won't last long."

Before jamming the compact into her mouth, Rose offered Frankie a final warning.

"Miss Rose might say more bad words, might even yell them

out. Remember, don't worry. It's only a flash of pain."

Frankie grunted something inaudible. Not that Rose needed his approval to proceed, she only wanted to avoid scaring the bejesus out of him.

With that, she placed the compact in her mouth, biting down just enough so that her teeth held it firm. She selected the impact zone: a chunk of snow-white flesh on the inside of her left arm above the elbow. The nerve endings would be countless and the pain would be off the charts, but any permanent scar would be, for the most part, invisible. She shifted the cigar from her left hand to her right, applying a firm grip on the wheel. Ahead lay an empty stretch of highway, straight as an arrow for at least a mile. No vehicles behind them; the coast was clear. She guided the vehicle into the middle lane. She was as ready as she would ever be. *Let her rip.* Slowly she pushed the burning end of her stubby cigar into her flesh.

Initially she felt very little, just a distant sensation. She drove it deeper into her flesh, wondering if the cigar had any life left at all. Turned out it did.

Like a rushing freight train came the pain. It exploded up her arm and screamed into her head like a banshee. Along with the pain was the hiss of burning flesh. An odor came next, further proof of the cigar's staying power. Registering off the charts, pain impulses raced faster and stronger from the cooked flesh. It was pain unlike any that she had ever experienced. Instinctively her jaw tightened. Her powerful bite crushed the flimsy compact. She dropped the cigar as the make-up container burst between her teeth, most of its contents spraying onto the dashboard; some of the makeup she swallowed. Next, the compact's mirror cracked. Before swallowing them, she had just enough wits left to spit out two sizable shards of glass onto the floorboard, all the while holding the course steady as her land yacht remained in the middle lane. Finally, she screamed.

"Ahhhhhhh!"

She hammered her right fist onto the beaten dashboard in anguish, launching a salvo of profanity while punishing the dash.

"Son-of-a-cocksucker-bitch-fuck-whore-shit-suck-fuck-bitch . . .!"

She cursed until she ran out of breath. As the cursing ceased, she gradually slowed her pounding on the weathered dashboard. She lowered her head, trying to get a grip on herself. Through the whole ordeal, she had somehow maintained a razor-straight run down the middle of 293. Had she waited any longer, she would have lost her chance. As she squinted ahead, she made out the sign for the next exit. It was theirs and it was less than a quarter mile away.

She swung into the right lane and wiped the dampness from her eyes spitting out makeup residue which covered her tongue. She wondered what had become of her cigar. She took a quick look down on the floorboard. There it was, lying lifeless between her feet. Through sheer force, she had flattened it to a stub.

"Well, it did its job," she mumbled.

Rose lowered her speed to thirty-five and turned onto the exit. She peeked up into the rearview mirror and found Frankie looking back at her. Not surprisingly, his eyes were bugged out.

"I warned you," Rose said. She looked down and spat phlegm between her legs onto the floorboard below. "Anyway, it's all good now."

She increased her speed to fifty-five merged into a south-bound lane of the F.E. Everett Turnpike. Nashua was twelve miles away. She shook out her left arm rigorously. A red-yellow ooze of blood and pus had formed. Olaf now had a third patient to treat. But the pain had been worth it; the cigar did the trick. Drowsiness, once omnipotent, had been beaten. She reclaimed the sharp focus that she would need for the remaining miles. The scar stung and her arm throbbed like a mad bastard, but there would be no more napping.

Rose's left arm throbbed like a motherfucker. A quarter-sized hunk of flesh, where the cigar had struck home, was literally cooked. There, the skin was mangled and red. As she examined it, the jellied blood and pus shimmered under the highway lights. It had started to scab on the edges. It was disgusting to behold, and moving her elbow was almost impossible. Turning the steering wheel was agonizing. Unfortunately, that was something she had done several times since getting off the turnpike. The last turn was into the parking lot of St. Joseph Hospital in downtown Nashua. They had made it. It was 10:35.

From the back, Bubba wheezed, coughing out his words in protest. "Stop . . . jerkin' . . . car . . ."

Frankie pressed down harder on his shoulder. Bubba groaned, but his griping ceased.

"Hurts, doesn't it?" Rose asked, snickering. "That's good. Means you're not gonna die. That is, unless you keep bitching about my driving and I'm forced to kick your ass."

She could not be a hundred percent sure, but she was confident that Frankie had stemmed Bubba's bleeding. Had he not, Bubba might be unconscious. Just the same, she was not about to relieve Frankie of his most important task. Not when they were seconds out.

Rose drove around to the back of the hospital, using her right hand as much as possible. Just thinking about her left arm brought on pain, never mind exerting it. As she rounded a large dumpster, she spotted the designated drop-off point. Twin light poles, set in the back corners of the parking lot, illuminated the loading dock, next to which sat another dumpster labeled BFI. She drove past the dock before struggling through a three-point turn, which involved both hands. She fought back the urge to curse. Properly aligned, she backed up to within a few inches of the giant rubber bumpers. She spotted Olaf in her mirror. The red glow of the car's brakes illuminated Olaf's humorless stare as she stood on the edge of the concrete dock, her arms folded. Another nurse, who wore white scrubs, stood behind her. Rose dropped the transmission into park. The Chevy belched out a final remonstration as she switched off the ignition.

Rose raised her eyes up to the sagging ceiling fabric and, for the second time during their race to Nashua, offered up a "thank you." Somehow, they had made it to safety after a night best described as nerve-racking.

"We're here," Rose said quietly. Before getting out, she turned to Frankie. "Don't move yet, buddy. Keep pressure on Bubba's wound, ok?"

Frankie nodded. Rose smiled at him.

"You did really well tonight. Your mother will be proud," Rose said, before stepping out of the car and into the frigid night.

Olaf, whom she had not seen in almost two months, came walking down the steps next to the loading dock. Between two fingers, she held a lit cigarette. A nurse followed behind. As Olaf walked, two other nurses emerged through swinging doors. They hustled down the handicap ramp, steering a stretcher and bringing it up against the side of the car.

Rose smiled in relief as she watched a smile spread across her friend's face. Olaf's eyes appeared moist under the faint light. Tears? Rose wondered. Olaf walked up to her and the two embraced. Their embrace brought Rose a measure of peace. Wrapped in Olaf's arms, for the first time since she had left for Maine, Rose believed things were going to be all right. Olaf released her grip on Rose and pulled back.

"It's good to see you," Olaf said, her right hand firmly on Rose's shoulders. She took a drag of her cigarette and blew the smoke back over her shoulder. Two of the nurses opened the back door to tend to Frankie and Bubba. Olaf released her grip on Rose and walked up to the car. She surveyed the inside. She turned to the nurse who had been standing next to her when Rose arrived.

"Donna, take a look at the entry wound, ok?" Olaf said.

"I'm on it," Donna said.

Olaf turned her attention back to. Rose.

"I only wish it was under other circumstances," she said. "This isn't the reunion that I had in mind."

"I know. It's not the reunion I had in mind either. Anyway, I can't tell you how much I appreciate this," Rose said. She pointed to Frankie, who was helping the two nurses get Bubba onto the stretcher. "By the way, that's Frankie and . . . well, Claire is probably right behind us."

"I remember Frankie," Olaf said, flipping him a wave. She turned back to Rose. Her smile had vanished. "I remember Claire. And when I saw Frankie, I figured this little party might grow."

"Bubba's the one who Frankie was helping on the drive down from Maine. Bubba was my . . ." Rose said, shrugging her shoulders.

"Lemme guess—your business partner." Olaf dropped her cigarette and mashed it out under a heel. Then she leaned in closer to Rose, any sympathy in her eyes was gone. "We'll have plenty of time to catch up. I've got a few questions about your business up in Maine."

Rose cast her gaze elsewhere. Olaf tapped her shoulder and gestured to the car. "But for now, we've got more pressing matters."

Olaf turned to the two nurses near the car. "Tricia and Renee, please bring these two into the rec room. We'll work on them in there." Turning to Donna, she said, "Did you find the entry wound? The slug?"

Donna nodded. "It's in his upper pectoral, but not deep."

With help from Frankie, Tricia and Renee got Bubba out of the back of the car. In the presence of such attractive nurses, Bubba's mood appeared to be on the rise, as Tricia fastened two seatbelts, one across his chest and one across his thighs, despite Bubba's claim that such measures were unnecessary. "Merely a precaution, sweetie," Renee said. The reference to 'sweetie' made him smile. Tricia and Renee backed the stretcher away from the car and pushed him up the ramp.

"Ah, my angels," Bubba offered from his rested position.

Tricia looked down at him. "If you're a good patient, then Santa will bring you ice cream."

"Tell Santa no to the ice cream. I've got something else in

mind," Bubba said, winking. He coughed a little but managed a smile.

Tricia laughed and shook her head, mumbling something about grown men and boys and their many similarities. At the top of the loading dock, Tricia and Renee sped up and Bubba was quickly delivered inside to the warm comforts of St. Joe's. Rose watched as Bubba and the nurses disappeared inside. Then she remembered Frankie, who stood behind Donna.

"He's been shot, too, but it only appears to be a grazing wound," Rose said to Donna.

"Yes, ma'am. I'm fully aware," Donna said, cracking a grin and glancing at Frankie. "He showed me where the bullet grazed his left bicep. I dabbed it with some peroxide, but he didn't wince at all."

Frankie offered his trademark toothy grin and proudly displayed the bandage she had applied.

"The good news with Frankie's wound is that there's no sign of infection and no need for stitches."

"Good work, Donna," Olaf said. "Please bring Frankie in with Bubba. I'll be in shortly."

Frankie looked at Donna, who had so tenderly gone about her duties as she treated him. His gaze suggested a deep admiration. So much so that he could not resist an attempt at charming her as she led him up the ramp.

"I hit the bad guy right in the face . . . yeah! Yeah, and . . . and he shot me, but it didn't really hurt. I got him good. I hit him like Batman on TV. You can even ask Miss Rose!"

"Of course you did," Donna said. She then slipped her right arm under his left arm as they walked. "A tough guy like you, I'm sure you got the best of him."

"Yeah, yeah he was on the ground after I hit him." Frankie grinned, and then got animated. "And then . . . and then Miss Rose raced around the car and kicked the guy in the kisser! He cried and spat out teeth and then she—"

Rose interjected. "Okay, Frankie, I think she gets the idea."

Frankie stopped before they got to the door. He looked confused. "But Miss Rose, you wanted to kill that bad guy. He had a gun and he was gonna—"

"Please drop it." Rose said, cutting him off. "Say, look at the time. It's 11 o'clock! You know what that means, don't you, buddy?"

Frankie's face lit up like a beacon. He looked from Donna to Rose to Olaf and back to Donna, whom he addressed. "Miss Nurse, I got to get inside, lie down and close my eyes. If Santa sees me awake after midnight, I'm in trouble. No presents-no Red Sox jacket-no toys; only coal for Frankie."

Donna frowned. "Well, we can't have that, not for someone as brave as you."

She led Frankie, who blushed like a rose, through the same swinging doors that Bubba had been wheeled moments before. As they walked, Rose overheard Frankie recounting his fearless charge at the "bad guy with a gun and a funny-looking hat." The nurse replied, again referring to Frankie as a hero. Shortly thereafter, their voices disappeared as they walked deeper into the hospital. Rose smiled and shook her head.

That ain't the half of it. He saved our lives tonight. Mine for the second time.

Olaf broke the silence.

"Some scary man with a gun, huh?" she said. "Don't I look forward to our chat. Ought to be real entertaining."

"Yes, of course . . . a chat," Rose said. She lowered her head. "So good to be home."

"I'm sure it is," Olaf said, then whistled. "I'm particularly interested in hearing about this 'bad guy'." Olaf's eyes narrowed, spotting something on her left arm. "And you're gonna tell me all about that, too."

"Tell you about what?"

Olaf grabbed Rose's left arm and twisted it. Rose winced in pain. Olaf pointed to the scar.

"That scar," Olaf said.

"Oh, that? Ha! Nothing to that. Just an accident with a space heater," Rose said, shaking out her left arm. She then tried changing the topic. "So, what's your initial prognosis on Bubba? It didn't look good. We better check on him."

Olaf narrowed her eyes. "I'm not worried about Bubba or Frankie. They'll be fine," she said. She paused and slowed her cadence. "It's you I'm worried about."

"Margo, come on. Gimme a break," Rose protested. "I'm the last person you need to worry about. I've got everything under control. Look, I was able to get those two—"

"A shoot-out on Christmas Eve up in Maine? Call that under control? When you called, where was it you told me you'd been?" Olaf looked around, then dialed down her tone before continuing. "The president-elect's mansion?"

Rose said nothing. She looked away, begging for the inquisition to end. Olaf resumed her reduced-volume rant. But Olaf was not finished.

"An invitation to the president-elect's Christmas party?

Guess you've made the big leagues," Olaf said. She whistled, pretending to be impressed.

"Under control, huh? Two friends of yours have been shot and you call that 'under control'?"

"Listen, I can—"

"You can shut your mouth and listen to me," Olaf shot back. "You told Claire and me that you were off on some sales job, selling books or dictionaries or maybe it was Amway. Whatever it was, it was all bullshit."

"I can explain," Rose said, holding out her hands.

"Oh, you can count on that—you've got plenty of 'splainin' to do, Lucy," Olaf said in her best Desi Arnaz. "And plenty of time to do so."

Rose frowned.

"Follow me," Olaf ordered.

Olaf propped open one of the doors leading into a shadowy hallway.

"Where are we headed?" Rose asked.

"First, to an aid station so I can deal with your little battle wound. After that, to the Doctors' Lounge."

Rose looked down at her left arm. The cigar had left a permanent scar. It still stung like crazy. The promise of the Doctors' Lounge, however, had her feeling a little better. The last time she sat within its grand splendor, she enjoyed an everlasting supply of alcohol and snacks. What with the night's drama and skipping dinner, she felt she could use a drink and something to eat. Anything would suffice.

Chapter fifty-one

Oh, dear God, please. Please *let it be nothing serious,* Claire silently begged.

Diane Cartwright sat in the passenger seat in front of Claire. On a few occasions, Diane had reached back and patted Claire's knee or grasped her hand as a show of support. Meantime, Rodney kept his speed at eighty and his focus on the road ahead. Five minutes after crossing into New Hampshire, he saw a sign for Highway 101 West to Manchester. It was the one he wanted. A mile later, he left the interstate and headed west on 101.

The four-lane highway was practically vacant. In twenty miles, they passed only five cars. Otherwise, the road ahead was a sea of black. Twinkling stars and a splinter of moon offered scant light. At eighty miles an hour, they would reach Manchester in about ten minutes and Nashua in twenty-five. They could not get there quick enough.

"And why the rear entrance?" Claire asked, her voice quivering. "Why tell us to drive around to the back if everything is okay?"

She looked at Diane, and then at Rodney. Their expressions conveyed sympathy. Rodney said something that seemed logical.

"Everything's going to be okay. As for going to the back of the hospital, we can't afford to bring the First Lady in through the front. We need to be discrete."

Diane rested a hand on Claire's arm and gave her a reassuring smile. It did little to squelch Claire's mounting fear, however. Nor did Rodney's assurance that everything was hunky dory.

"No, I don't think everything's okay," Claire said. She looked outside into the dark and began to chew her fingernails.

"You know, the back of the hospital is where they wheel the corpses in and out. Into the basement, through the rear entrance, in the shadows, far away from the cheery receptionists, the paintings on the walls and the clean sheets. That's where hospitals set up temporary morgues."

Someone had once told Claire that was where the orderlies waited for the undertaker's black limo with the white window curtains, the elongated cabin, and some ghoul behind the wheel, a ghoul with long, wispy, thinning, blonde-white hair. She imagined the movie character Beetlejuice.

He would pull up curbside, as she stood helplessly watching. He would float out of the car sneering devilishly, exposing rows of black, filed teeth, extending a white, sinewy hand into which no blood flowed. He would point one of his long fingers at her and then drift around to the back of the hearse, his eyes on her all the while. Gracefully, he would open the back door before turning to her and intoning, with a voice from beyond the grave, that he had "come to collect Frankie."

She didn't remember who had told her all about the undertaker's station wagon. At the time, it was inconsequential, but it mattered now. She recalled the certitude in the person's voice who had told her. The hospital's dead were gathered in the cellar, tucked away from the living above, Claire was told. That made perfect sense to her. With her imagination running at full speed, it all took on a whole new meaning. She needed to stop her runaway thoughts. If she didn't, she'd go mad.

Diane seemed to detect the torment on Claire's face. She reached for her hand.

"Honey, your friend said that your son is fine," Diane firmly. "Have faith."

Rodney interjected in a cheerful tone. "It's almost Christmas, ma'am . . . Mrs. O'Brien."

It took them both a moment to register Rodney's message. When it did, Claire felt a measure of peace. *Maybe things will be okay,* she thought. She lifted her eyes and smiled at Diane, then gently squeezed Rodney's shoulder. Worries about Frankie, and whatever other drama lay in wait, were put on hold for the time being.

Diane gripped Claire's knee and said. "Things will be okay, Claire. You'll see."

With the lights of Manchester looming, they approached another sign. Interstate 293 was just ahead.

"I'll have us there in no time," Rodney said.

From his parked position on the grass infield between the northbound and southbound lanes of Interstate 95, Officer Benjamin King watched as a car approached from the north. It was a cherry red and it was hauling ass. He picked up his radar and aimed it; the radar clocked the vehicle at eighty-three miles per hour.

"Oh lovely. Twenty-eight miles ova' the legal limit means time in the slammah," he said, dropping his 'r' in the customary Yankee fashion.

In fairness to the state trooper, he considered flipping on his lights and giving chase. In the end, he did no such thing. *Why bothah?* he figured. *It's Christmas Eve.*

"Ya don't wanna be getting' outta ya cah in this chill, Bennie," he reminded himself. "Ya know speedin is no'mally inadmissible in a co't of law. 'Sides, by the time ya get onta the ha'dtop, they'll be cleyah outa sight and proly in Na Hampshah."

As an afterthought, he switched off the radar before returning to the Playboy magazine he had been perusing.

If Rose had any notions about a swell time in the doctors' lounge, then she was sorely mistaken. Christmas or not, there would be no gaiety and no glasses clinking. Rose's previous visit to the lounge had been a sampling of the high life, an experience unlike anything she had ever enjoyed before. Save the early moments of painful soul-searching which Olaf inflicted upon her, sitting on the leather couch imbibing on an unending supply of quality booze had been a gas. Tonight, however, Olaf had something else in mind.

As soon as Olaf shut the door, Rose knew she was in for it. Olaf pointed her toward the familiar collection of leather couches and ordered Rose to sit. Rose plopped her rear onto the same cushion which had supported her the last time. She dropped her right arm on the couch's armrest and then, keeping her bandaged left arm elevated, leaned back comfortably.

"How long ago was it that you sat right where you are and bared your soul to me?" Olaf asked.

Rose shrugged her shoulders. *What? Almost four months? You know, so why ask?* she thought to say. She was more interested in some of that fine sipping whiskey. She was on the verge of asking for some when Olaf exploded.

"What in the hell were you doing in Maine? What kind of shit have you gotten yourself into, huh? And what's the story with this Bubba character, besides getting himself shot and nearly killed? She paused to catch her breath before continuing. "And for God's sake, how did you get poor Frankie mixed up in all this?"

"It's not what you think—" Rose began.

"Cut the crap," Olaf snapped. "It's bad enough you wanna go and destroy yourself, but dragging other people into some twisted, personal death wish is over the top."

Rose said nothing. Better to just take the medicine, let it ride and then get the fuck out. Unscathed? No. But, after two months, she still had a key to her apartment at the Dunstable House, which Budzko had said would be available when she needed it. On any other night, she would have stopped to get a bottle on the way home, but not at this hour. Christmas was minutes away.

"Go ahead and sit there in silent defiance. That's your choice." Olaf loomed over her with her arms crossed.

Rose protested, "Now, that ain't fair. I was just about to tell you everything when you cut me off."

Olaf held up a hand and turned around, lowering her head. She began pacing along the back wall, closer to the door.

"Know what? Don't bother," Olaf said, her eyes scouting out a trail of carpet upon which to tread. "Don't tell me a thing. I don't want details . . . don't want names. I don't wanna know about some . . ." Olaf gestured with her fingers making air-quotes, "some 'bad man with a gun.' And I sure don't wanna know the places you've been conducting your illegal business, whatever the hell that entails."

Olaf folded her arms behind her back and looked across the room at Rose.

"I don't wanna be an accessory to any of the crap you've been mixed up in. So, let's hope for the sake of this friendship of ours that my nurses and I aren't involved in something that's gonna bring us any legal problems."

Rose leaned forward in her seat and was about to offer assurances when the door cracked open. It was Donna. She opened the door far enough to peek in.

"Margo, sorry to interrupt. Just so you know, Miss Busybody was looking for you."

Olaf frowned. "Shit. I'd forgotten about her. Where is she?"

"Don't worry," Donna said, leaning further into the office. "I told her that you'd asked me to tell her to go home, to enjoy Christmas with her family."

"She doesn't have a family," Olaf said.

"But she does have eight cats," Donna said. "Anyway, she

was eager to leave. Just to be sure, I watched her leave, hop in her car and drive off."

Olaf walked over to Donna and placed a hand on her shoulder. "You're the best."

"Yeah, right. Bet that's what you tell the others when I'm not around," Donna said smirking. Then, noticing Rose, she added, "I was able to pluck the slug from Bubba's shoulder and patched him up."

"See, that's what I mean: you're the best Now, if you don't mind," Olaf said, shooting a disapproving glance and pointing to Rose, "I need a little alone time with this one."

On her way out, Donna waved to Rose, reminding her not to worry about Bubba. That did little to put Rose at ease. No longer was she worried about Bubba, she was now concerned about herself and how far Olaf planned to take this verbal harangue. Rose waited until Donna left the lounge before speaking.

"Listen, I'm sorry. I know you're pissed off," she said, averting Olaf's glare.

"Oh, I don't think you know just how pissed off I am." Olaf began her way back to Rose's end of the lounge. "You can't possibly know."

"I know I've put you in a pickle, and I truly appreciate all the trouble you've taken to see to our well-being." she looked up and made eye contact with Olaf. She took a breath and then continued. "There's something else I need to tell you, something which might upset you even more."

Olaf walked over and leaned down to within a foot or two of Rose. She folded her arms across her chest.

"Go ahead. Let's have it."

Before Rose could open her mouth, Tricia came barging in. Rose never had the chance to tell Olaf that some of the Cartwrights' company might have been involved in her business up in Maine. Rose could not have possibly imagined what Tricia was about to report. It would not go over well with Olaf.

Tricia was in a frenzy. She strode to the middle of the lounge, clenching her fists, pumping her arms, shaking her shoulders and smiling all the while, her eyes bright with excitement. She acted as if she just won the lottery. When she spoke, she could barely get her words out.

"Okay . . . okay . . . oh my God . . ." Tricia inhaled, and then exhaled, in a failed attempt to control her emotions. Her eyes were wide with excitement. She walked over to Olaf.

"Oh. My. God. Margo, you will never guess who's here!" She tugged on Olaf's sleeve, her words coming out like machine-gun fire. She breathlessly reported that she had just hugged the closest thing to American royalty in the nurses' lounge.

"Royalty, huh?" Olaf asked.

"Oh my God . . . oh my God! Margo, you're not gonna believe it when I tell you!" Tricia brought her hands up to her mouth and began to jump in place.

Olaf turned to Rose and glowered, "You wanna bet."

Chapter fifty-two

Rodney eased the car around to the back. Except for an old beater of a car the size of a small yacht, the parking lot was empty. The old car was backed up against a loading dock. Rodney dropped the transmission into neutral, idling the car toward the loading dock. Eyes scanning to and fro, Claire spotted the parked vehicle. It looked vaguely familiar.

"Rodney, can you stop for just a moment, please?" Claire asked.

He did so. Claire lowered her window to get a better look. *I know that car.*

"Someone out there?" Diane asked.

"No, it's the car. I know that car," Claire said, pointing at an old Chevy. Someone she knew drove around in an ugly clunker that looked a lot like the one across the parking lot. A friend of mine. Someone who always joked about how it backfired whenever it—.

It was Rose's car!

"That's my friend Rose's car. She was the one who called you. That's who has my son!" she said, pointing to the rusted Impala.

Rodney dropped the Audi into first and drove up to the loading dock. As he got close, he noticed a woman wearing all white standing at the edge of the loading dock. He drove the car up next to the Chevy and parked. Before he cut off the engine, Claire bolted outside. She sprinted up a ramp, stumbling and almost falling. Regaining her balance, she ran to the woman in white scrubs.

"Where is my son? Please tell me he's okay," she pleaded.

The cold air burned Claire's lungs. She began to cough. She bent over, trying to catch her breath. The nurse leaned down and wrapped an arm around Claire's waist, helping her up.

"There we go," the nurse said. She held Claire and began guiding her towards the swinging doors leading to the inside.

"Ma'am, your son is just fine."

She led Claire through the doors, out of the cold and into a much warmer place. The nurse looked down at Claire and smiled.

"I'll take you to him and you can see for yourself."

From the outside, Claire heard the sound of car doors opening as the others got out. The nurse kept her arm around Claire as they walked.

"Thank you. Thank you so much," Claire said, looking up at the nurse. A tear stood in Claire's eye. "I can't tell you how worried I've been . . . how terrified."

"It's all going to be okay," the nurse said. She squeezed Claire a little tighter. "I'm Donna. I'm a nurse here at St. Joe's, as if you couldn't tell by the garb."

She smiled, gesturing to her scrubs and nametag.

"And I'm Claire." Claire smiled back. "Known to most as Frankie's mother, or the mother of the hometown hero."

"I'm not at all surprised to hear that, not after what he's told us so far," Donna said.

Claire perked up. "Oh?"

"I think it would be better if he told you, himself," Claire replied. "Based on what he and Bubba have been through, I'd say the hometown hero title is fitting."

Bubba?

Claire didn't have time to give it much thought. She could hear Diane's voice down the hall behind them. Diane and the other two caught up to she and Donna as they came to a set of cipher-locked doors. Donna punched in four numbers. A lock popped and the two doors crept open. All five walked through.

As they walked, Donna turned to greet the others.

"I'm Donna," she said. She was about to lead them into the nurses' lounge where Bubba and Frankie were when she noticed something peculiar about the tall, white-haired lady who had just joined them.

"Nice to meet you, Donna. I'm Diane."

"Ma'am, pardon me saying, but you look familiar," Donna said, concentrating on the woman's gentle face and her ball of bright white hair. The woman who stood in front of her looked like someone she had seen on TV. Maybe it was the poor lighting, but she could have sworn this woman was an actress, and a famous one at that.

"I get that all the time," Diane said dismissively. "So, how are the boys holding up?"

She almost looks like that woman, Maude, from the TV show. But, what would she be doing in Nashua on Christmas? Donna wondered.

Donna suspended her curiosity and answered Diane.

"Those two, well, they're going to be just fine." She gestured to a lighted room three doors down. "You can see for yourself."

She led them to the nurses' lounge, which was nothing like the exquisite doctors' lounge. On the contrary, the door leading into the nurses' lounge was bland. The upper half was almost entirely glass. Across the top of the glass was a simple sign in hand-painted black lettering which read, **NURSES ONLY**. The mood inside the lounge, however, was anything but bland. As she soaked up the scene inside, Claire instantly felt a weight lifted off her shoulders.

There were no beeping and pulsing machines, no steady drip of an IV bag. No brooding doctor, behind a filter mask, checking off the vitals on some pitiless form. No brooding physician's assistant leaning over a critical patient. On the contrary, there was no concern, no looks of worry. It was nothing like she had expected.

The scene inside the nurses' lounge resembled a Christmas party among old friends. Frankie, as animated as ever, was reenacting his assault on the "bad guy with the gun." Running in place, throwing his arms out and wrestling the air, as if Chuck Aiello were still within his grasp, he gave a play-by-play, going so far as to howl in mock pain when an imaginary bullet clipped his bicep. It didn't matter that Renee and Tricia had seen Frankie's reenactment five times, they soaked up every detail, encouraging him on. Only a bandage, wrapped snugly around Frankie's bicep, lent any credence to what would otherwise come across as a far-fetched fiction. When he finished the latest recounting of his story, Tricia jumped up, kissed his cheek and declared him a hero . . . again.

Bubba looked on from his seated position on the couch, a nice improvement from being sprawled out for several hours on Frankie's lap. His expression was one of placidity. The pain pills Renee had given him had dulled the roar in his shoulder. Any bleeding from his wounded right shoulder ended after Donna had removed the slug. The nearly pain-free operation, which took three minutes and involved only a pair of tweezers, had been a success. There was no infection and minimal internal bleeding. Donna considered giving him a pint of blood, but decided not to. For one, he wasn't bad off. Secondly, like most everything else in St. Joe's Hospital, the blood supply was inventoried weekly. The pain, she explained to him, would last a while longer. Not one to overlook a good deed, Bubba had asked Donna to marry him right away, preferably before dawn. The four inside the nurses' lounge laughed, and the laughter helped Bubba forget his own predicament.

Behind Bubba's chair sat a Nativity scene. Peace, in festive bright red and green lettering, was strung across the white-painted wall above the Nativity scene. Someone had remembered to place the baby Jesus in the manger earlier in the day. Hand-carved wooden figures of Mary and Joseph looked down on the Savior-child in wonder. Though yet unseen, equally as awestruck was the foursome outside in the dark hallway.

In a corner behind the Nativity scene was a large TV connected to a VHS player. The TV sat on a serving cart. *It's a Wonderful Life* played on its grainy, black-and-white screen. George Bailey was in a hurry to get home. He had a new lease on life.

So did Claire.

Still in the hallway, she soaked it all in: the festivity, The Nativity scene, the timeless Christmas movie and, above all, the love bestowed upon Frankie. She could not contain herself any longer. She burst into the nurses' lounge and raced right up to her son. She threw the tightest hug around his broad shoulders and then pulled him down so that she could smother him with kisses. The others entered behind her. Cheerful greetings of Merry Christmas and Happy Holidays filled the lounge. Bubba met the future First Lady and then began searching wildly for a pen. He just had to get an autograph. He asked Donna and Tricia for a pen, so that he could get the soon-to-be First Lady's autograph. When Donna realized who she had escorted into the lounge, she nearly fainted. The same with Tricia. All around, acquaintances were made: Renee hugged Rodney; Rodney hugged Bubba. Diane hugged Frankie and Tricia and Renee. Tricia hugged Rodney, who asked if there were any snacks in the lounge. Nothing special, though gingerbread cookies would be warmly received.

For those celebrating inside the nurses' lounge, it would prove to be one of their most memorable Christmases ever. And so it was in St. Joe's Hospital as the clock struck midnight ushering in Christmas. From behind them, George Bailey held his wife close, crying tears of joy. He had saved the Building and

Loan and the town. On a Christmas tree behind him, a bell tinkled. Clarence had earned his wings. There was joy in Bedford Falls and in St. Joe's Hospital. Peace for all.

For all except Rose.

"Take a deep breath, Trish," Olaf instructed.

"Okay, okay . . . I'm better." Tricia did exactly that, then exhaled.

"So, let's try this again. Who exactly is here?" Olaf asked.

Tricia drew in another deep breath and then burst out, her words coming out at machine-gun speed.

"Diane Cartwright is here in this hospital right now!" Tricia's eyes darted back and forth between Olaf to Rose.

Olaf could have sworn she heard Tricia say Diane Cartwright in her gasping declaration. Olaf rubbed her forehead, then spoke slowly, as if talking to a child.

"Okay. Say that one more time. And please say it slowly."

Tricia did her best but seemed incapable of stifling her enthusiasm. "The president-elect's wife, Diane Cartwright is here . . . right here, right now in our hospital!"

"Of course she is," Olaf said, rolling her eyes. "So is Santa. He got here a few minutes ago. Maybe between Cartwright's money and Santa's magic, they can help me with my greying hair and waistline."

"Margo, I swear I'm not making this up. I promise you." Tricia looked her intently.

Olaf saw something in her eyes that troubled her. Whether the president-elect's wife was here or not, Tricia was convinced that she was.

Olaf shook her head and cracked a smile.

"You're shitting me of course, aren't you, Trish?" Olaf shot a look at Rose. "'Cause I'm in no mood for more bullshit."

"No, I'm not dammit! Don't believe me. Come on, Margo. I'll prove it."

Margo lowered her head and rubbed her temples. *What if she wasn't kidding?* Olaf began considering the ramifications of not only treating two gunshot victims, but hosting the nation's First Lady. And on Christmas, no less. She gathered herself before speaking.

"Okay, okay, I believe you, Trish." Olaf looked up to the ceiling, sighed and then spoke aloud, "I've always wanted to meet her, to meet her husband, but God knows, not under these conditions."

Olaf shook her head. Suddenly, like a blinding flash of the

obvious, it occurred to her: Rose's business in Maine; gunshot victims; some big party. It became clear to Olaf that Rose had something to do with Diane Cartwright being in Olaf's hospital.

"I suppose this is the 'something else' you wanted to tell me, something you couldn't do over the phone? You couldn't at least give me fair warning that you were at the president's mansion and that the First Lady might be part of this fucking debacle?"

"Margo, when I stopped to call Claire, I had no idea who'd come with her. You gotta believe me. The First Lady is the last person I'd have expected Claire to drag along."

"No more," Olaf barked. "I thought I wanted to hear what else you had to say, but I don't. I don't have the time for any more of your half-baked bullshit."

Tricia coughed aloud, interrupting the tiff.

"Umm, excuse me. For anyone interested, Mrs. Cartwright is in the lounge with Bubba, Frankie, Frankie's mother and two other men." Tricia smiled, looking at both Olaf and Rose. "So, I figured while everyone's making acquaintances, it might be nice to offer them a few drinks, maybe some food. It is Christmas, after all."

"Yes, of course. Good thinking," Olaf said absently. "I'll join you all shortly."

Olaf was pissed off, but conflicted. As angry as she was, she had pity on Rose. Olaf felt like an upset mother who had to deal with her child's bad behavior, but who also needed to know what was behind the misconduct. Olaf needed to know why, after getting a second chance at life, Rose sought to risk it all again. To be sure, Rose and Bubba had put Frankie, maybe others, in danger. Bringing two gunshot victims to her hospital in the middle of the night put her and her nurses in danger as well. If word of tonight's shenanigans got back to her administrator, Olaf would get canned. Unauthorized medical attention given to gunshot victims in the nurses' lounge with bottles of liquor being passed around? Oh yeah, she would be out the door—in a heartbeat. The same held true for the other three. What's worse, unlike Olaf, they would be totally screwed, as they were years from retirement. It was her friends for whom she was most concerned. For that, Rose would need a verbal kick in the ass.

Despite the risk of losing her job, the ramifications of which she clearly understood the instant Rose called and sought her help, Olaf couldn't say no. Nearly four months earlier, the two hit it off in the doctor's lounge, their friendship cemented over a baring of souls. In the weeks that followed, up to the point when Rose left for Maine, they spoke daily; they bowled and went to bingo; they met for drinks a couple nights a week; they even caught a Patriots game. They carried on as if they had known each other for years. So much so that Olaf swore that she could read Rose's mind. So, when Rose told her that she had landed a temporary sales job up in Maine, a job that would have her out of town for a few months, Olaf had been suspicious. The day Rose left for Maine, she wondered if she would ever see Rose again.

Olaf suspended her ruminating when she looked over and saw that Tricia was still in the lounge. She appeared to be waiting for further instruction.

"Well?" Olaf asked, spreading her arms out.

Tricia flicked her eyes towards the liquor cabinet. A serving cart sat nearby. "You liked my ideas about delivering some refreshments. So, I was thinking the liquor and some of those snacks. You know, the kind worthy of a First Lady?"

Olaf watched as Rose leaned forward in her seat, raising an encouraging smile to Tricia.

What kind of host would fail to adequately welcome someone of Diane Cartwright's stature? Olaf wondered. *After all, it is Christmas Day.*

Olaf now had the First Lady and two recovering patients to think about. It made sense to go down and see them, maybe raise a glass in celebration, make sure that Frankie and Bubba were okay. Wish the First Lady luck as she and the president moved into the White House.

Olaf waved a hand. "Take as much booze as you need. Just leave a little for the docs for when they decide to come back to work."

Rose slapped her knees and stood up. "As much as it pains me, seeing how I didn't vote for Cartwright, I suppose I too should go down and wish our nation's first lady a Merry Christmas."

"Not so fast, McDougal," Olaf said. "Back in your seat."

Tricia hustled to fill up every square inch of space on the wheeled cart with bottles of booze, wine, beer and Coke. She grabbed glasses and bowls, placing them on the bottom tray of the cart. That done, she rushed out, the serving cart leading the way, passing inches from Rose's longing gaze.

"I'll decide when you're free to leave, and it ain't now," Olaf said. She walked over to the door and shut it behind Tricia, emphasizing the point.

Chapter fifty-three

Patrick Donnelly stood in front of a window in his plush tenth-story office at Harbor Point near the JFK Presidential Library and Museum. The window stretched from the floor to the ceiling. It offered a commanding view of the harbor below and Boston's impressive skyline. Donnelly owned a total of five offices across the Boston area; this one was his favorite.

Off to his left was Carson Beach, a black smudge on this moonless night. He swam there as a child. As busy as his dad had been, he always took the time to take him and his older sisters for a swim during summer weekends. The water was indescribably cold, but Patrick cherished those moments when his dad could be someone other than the boss. Seeing the beach from his office always rekindled happy childhood memories. Lately, reminiscing was not the only thing that made his Harbor Point headquarters so treasured.

As far as his eyes could see, from west to north to east, were neighborhoods now under his control. For two generations, the Donnellys ruled South Boston, Dorchester and Roxbury. Over time, he had secured small pockets of Quincy and Braintree. Most recently, he had even carved out a few areas in East Boston and Revere. The Italians had gotten soft.

He looked back down at the harbor. A single light shone from the aft of a yacht that rocked gently on a soft breeze. It was a cold night, not the ideal night for boating. But if you owned a yacht and wanted to celebrate Christmas on Boston Harbor, then chances were you could afford to keep it warm.

"Just don't drink the harbor water," Patrick said, chuckling.

Wasn't it Cartwright who delivered that jab about Boston

Harbor during a debate? Donnelly was pretty sure it was. At any rate, that zinger had created quite a stir.

Totally out of character for one so tame as Cartwright. Reyes really took a blow that night in front of millions of Americans glued to their TV sets.

Many who knew of Donnelly's freewheeling, playboy lifestyle enjoyed hanging out with him for the easy access to a good time. He never minded sharing his bounty of babes, his preferential treatment in the nightclubs, front row seats at Fenway and the Garden. But it all came at a cost to the recipient: a favor, an IOU, or a promise of some other kind in exchange. Favors were the fabric of Boston politics. Part of the reason he respected Reyes was because he never ran in those circles. He and Reyes had never engaged in business, but he struck Donnelly as a guy you could trust, just the same. He might never represent the country on the national stage but, as far as Donnelly was concerned, he was a stand-up guy.

A light tapping on the door disturbed him. It would be Ira Levin. Ira would deliver an update on what had transpired at the Cartwright estate in New Whitby. Donnelly already knew most of what Ira would convey; Donnelly's guy, McElroy, had called Donnelly before calling Ira with a more detailed report. As he always did, Ira would add those finer details, as a detail-oriented guy could be expected to do. As to the bottom line, however, Donnelly was up to speed.

His dad had taught him years ago to trust but verify, even with Ira. Donnelly's dad trusted Ira implicitly, but always devoted another one or two hired hands to help gather facts. 'Trust but verify' when dealing with anyone, especially those whose loyalty was never certain. 'Trust but verify' equated to survival in the crime world.

Another light tapping on the door.

"Come on in, Ira," Donnelly said. He kept his gaze on the boat below, his back to the door. In the window's reflection, he saw the door creep open and Ira take two small steps into the office. Ever the cautious one, that Ira.

"Good evening, boss, and Merry Christmas."

Donnelly said, "And to you, my old friend."

Ira said, "I've brought word."

"Very well," Patrick said. "But tell me, why are you still here? It's Christmas. Certainly, we can postpone business until tomorrow."

"Well, we don't really celebrate Christmas in my family." Ira slumped his shoulders.

"That's right. Happy Hanukkah." Donnelly turned and faced him from across the expansive office. He smiled broadly. "No offense intended."

"None taken, boss."

Donnelly got down to business.

"So, it's the business in Maine?" Donnelly asked.

"It is," Ira replied. He stood erect and pulled a mini-notebook from his breast pocket. Typical Ira Levin, scribbled notes as a hedge against bypassing any of the minutia. He flipped through a few pages, then looked up to Donnelly to speak.

"The bottom line: there's plenty of good news but perhaps a little bad news, or at least disconcerting."

"Somebody spoke to the wrong people?" Patrick asked. He narrowed his gaze.

"No, not so far as we can tell," Ira said. He proceeded to list the many bright spots. "You may be aware that Chuck Aiello was detained by a security element. As one of the additional guards to assist the Cartwright security detail, McElroy was one of the three who brought Aiello back to the house for questioning. When Aiello tried to play dumb as to the nature of his business, McElroy helped Cartwright's crew in taking the necessary—uh—steps to get to the truth."

Donnelly chuckled. During their conversation, McElroy took great delight in telling Donnelly about the "thrashing" that he and the other guard had given Aiello. It would be some time before Aiello would walk upright. More importantly, it would be an even longer time before he was a free man walking anywhere.

Ira continued. "Aiello confessed to discharging his weapon twice and hitting two individuals, one of whom turned out to be Bubba, the other some 'screeching lunatic', as Aiello put it. He claimed that some large woman, whom we know was Rose, took his weapon and tossed it after kicking the 'shit out of him', as McElroy put it."

Donnelly burst out laughing. This was just too much. His imagined being there to see it all unfold. What a twist of rotten luck for the man considered to be New England's most lethal assassin. Donnelly imagined what it must have been like to be knocked on his ass by some screeching madman, pummeled by a woman and then detained before he could make his escape. Bet he never imagined that outcome.

You can't make that shit up, Donnelly silently mused.

"McElroy crept down the side of the lawn and watched as Rose hustled Bubba and the screeching lunatic, both of whom had been hit, into her car. He watched them drive off. No vehicles followed. Meanwhile, Aiello writhed in agony on the lawn." Out of character, Ira smiled coyly. "It's worth pointing out that McElroy believes that he was the only one who saw them leave. He called McDonough, who was in Portsmouth, letting him know that they had left. McDonough drove out to the bridge as they crossed from Maine to New Hampshire. He then trailed them on their trip to Saint Joe's Hospital in Nashua."

"Any chance that Rose and company would've detected McDonough behind them?" Donnelly asked.

"He's certain they didn't. There was very little traffic, so he was able to stay back a few miles," Ira said.

"Hmph." Donnelly turned to look outside at the Boston skyline. He folded his hands behind his back. Ira's story, a product of one of his top soldiers, was consistent with what McElroy had told him. Donnelly liked consistency. "You know, Ira, Rose and her goofy partner . . . what's his name again?"

"Bubba," Ira said.

"Right. Bubba." Donnelly grinned. "You know, those two have exceeded my expectations. Not only did they do what was asked of them, but they escaped alive. Not many who've seen Aiello's pistol can say the same."

"If I may, Patrick, I believe there's more for them within your organization."

"I agree. But what? What to do with those two."

He turned back to face Ira and walked to over his high-backed leather chair. He seated himself comfortably upon one of the many thrones from which he held court. Many an edict had been issued from this particular perch, many involving a decision about life or death. Tonight's decree would be far less momentous. Tonight, with Ira's counsel, he would decide on the future of two employees who had displayed efficiency and loyalty.

Placing his right hand on the desk's blotter, Donnelly began fidgeting with a pen. His wrinkle-free face displayed little emotion. He raised his left hand from below the desk. In it, he held a small tumbler of scotch, two ice cubes clinking as he rested it on the desk.

Ira raised an eyebrow and pointed at his boss's glass of scotch.

"Funny, but I didn't notice that when I came in," Ira said, adding, "I must be getting old." He shook his head before flipping open his notebook to continue with business.

"Anyway, here's what I got from McElroy," he began. He pushed his spectacles up the bridge of his nose. "Rose and Bubba made contact with the two couples. Assurances were made to meet up later this week at an open house, where greater quantities would be exchanged for money." He paused and looked up. "They followed the script to the letter."

"Proof on those assurances?" Donnelly asked.

"McElroy bugged the bathroom where the meetings took place."

Donnelly nodded as he took a sip of scotch. He let the lowland scotch spread its magic across his palate, then rolled a finger, indicating to Ira that he was free to continue.

"Nothing else significant during the party, short of what appeared to be a lovers' spat on the dance floor. Rose promptly resolved that. It was not until they were entering Rose's car that their troubles arose. That was when Aiello emerged from under a tree with his pistol drawn. Words were indistinguishable, McElroy said, but we must assume he was pressing Rose and Bubba for the whereabouts of Gambini's eighty grand."

Donnelly smiled. Four grand had gone back to Rose and Bubba in the form of a bonus. As for the rest of Gambini's money, it had served its purpose in the form of bonuses, sufficient sums of money that would keep his network of pols doing the right thing in the coming year.

Merry Christmas, you motherfuckers.

From some alternate universe, the methodical lawyer droned on, ". . . charged Aiello, drawing his attention from Rose and Bubba. As the screeching lunatic hit him, he managed to fire off a second shot, which occurred during a struggle with the same lunatic. Anyway, the lunatic was hit somewhere on the arm. Nothing serious. Bubba's injuries, on the other hand, appeared to be serious. With Aiello knocked to the ground, Rose sprang from her side of the car and moved to the front, where he lay. She kicked him five or six times. Despite being across the yard, McElroy could hear Aiello's moans. She really tuned him up."

Donnelly sipped his scotch and set the glass down. He remembered meeting Rose in the hospital. There was something about her, something he liked. He had never come across a woman with such gumption. Apparently, she was quite a bruiser.

"It seems we achieved our two stated goals," Ira concluded. He then opened his notebook to a blank page and set it on the edge of his boss's desk. He looked at Donnelly, his pen at the ready.

"I do believe you're right." Donnelly watched the shrinking ice cube melt at the bottom of his glass. A sip of scotch remained. He took it.

"It was always about getting either that madman Boris Radic or Aiello," Ira began. He was uncharacteristically animated. "In this case, Gambini dispatched Aiello. Drawing him out in the open, in pursuit of Gambini's money, was brilliant. Leaving a link to Bubba and Rose, our bait, guaranteed us a chance to nail Aiello. What's more, we didn't even need to use McElroy to take care of Aiello. Anyway, boss, that was a brilliant plan." Ira paused for moment. "If I may editorialize for a moment, I have no doubt that your father would've been impressed." Ira smiled. He removed his spectacles and placed them on the desk in front of him. "More than neutralizing Gambini's go-to guy, you keep the money and maintain plausible deniability with the Gambini family. Aside from McElroy, whom no one in Providence has ever seen, there's nothing linking us to Aiello's detention."

Donnelly leaned back. He was hanging on Ira's words about his father and how proud he would have been. It had long been his idea to draw one of Gambini's top hit men into a trap. Rose and Bubba seemed the perfect tools for the job. Sure, they were loyal but, like most in his army, they were also disposable. In fairness to Chuck Aiello, the two were no match. Yet somehow, they had not only survived, but had bested him. A hard man to please, Donnelly's dad would have been impressed with those two as well. He would have called them a couple of chuckleheads but would have happily invited them up to his bar for a pint and a chance for them to revisit the evening's exploits.

Ira continued.

"Secondly, I believe we have some polished steel on our hands, Patrick." Ira took a moment, appearing to savor Donnelly's smile. He closed with his recommendation, delivered with conviction. "Bottom line: Bubba and Rose are ready for sales positions."

"Is that right?" Patrick leaned forward in his seat. His smile disappeared. He turned serious. "Tell me then, how is a guy who's been shot, and may not have the use of an arm for some time, going to be able to carry out his duties? And please don't tell me about the difference between collections and sales. I get all that. I've done all that."

Ira nodded, acknowledging his boss's concern. "Well, boss, it's true that Bubba may have lost some blood, but McDonough thought he heard laughter as a nurse pushed him on a stretcher into the hospital in Nashua. If nothing else, his spirits seemed good."

"Sure. Probably gonna brush off the gunshot like a bee sting, eh?" Donnelly offered with no shortage of sarcasm.

Ira said nothing. He remained in his stiff posture.

Donnelly noticed that his consigliore's body language suggested an acknowledgment that he had gone too far with his recommendation on what to do with Rose and Bubba. When business was of a most urgent nature, Patrick Donnelly was like any talented CEO. He was fully capable of absorbing vast amounts of information, but he had little time nor patience for conjecture. Only in small quantities was pontificating tolerated, and only when it served a purpose. Donnelly was not merely the playboy with the movie-star looks and a lucky bloodline. He was tough, shrewd and highly intelligent. He was a force, just as his father had been.

When Donnelly smiled again and settled back in his chair, Ira's shoulders slumped from his stand-at-attention mien.

"All told, it's been a very merry Christmas," Donnelly said as he reached into a desk drawer, his right hand invisible to Ira. He pulled out a bottle of Laphroaig, one of the world's finest scotches and refreshed his perspiring glass. With his left hand, he removed a clean glass from a different drawer. Before Ira could object, a glass with two fingers of scotch was pushed across the table. Ira smiled weakly and reached down to retrieve the drink. He thanked his boss, and then Donnelly laid out the way ahead.

"We're going to give them some recoup time. They've been through a lot over the last several weeks." He sipped his scotch and then cast a finger towards Ira's notebook. "Monitor Bubba's condition. I want a full report tomorrow morning. I want word passed to the hospital administrator . . ." Patrick paused and then reversed course, remembering his visit to the hospital. "No, strike that. Not to the administrator. I want word passed to that curmudgeon of a nurse that Bubba and the lunatic fella will have their bills covered. Kindly ask the head nurse to help arrange immediate home health care for those two, if she thinks it's necessary. We need them out of that hospital first thing in the morning. I'm sure the head nurse would agree that their presence in the hospital will only cause her trouble. Since you're here now, pass the word to the nurse tonight and arrange for a tidy sum of money be delivered tomorrow afternoon. Include a few rubles for that nurse as well. She was a big help tonight."

Ira briskly scribbled the instructions.

"I want that same delivery to include Rose and Bubba's Christmas bonuses."

Ira looked up and raised an eyebrow.

"Those two are about as deserving of a Christmas bonus as anybody. Five grand each. Then, get someone else up to Maine to cover the meetings with the Blacks and Whites." Donnelly took another sip and looked back up at Ira. "Keep in mind that Rose and Bubba have already comes to grips with the fact that they should be dead. I'd bet my dollar to your dime that, sooner or later, Rose is going to figure out that there was something else in play when they swiped that eighty grand. She's probably decided that Aiello's appearance wasn't an accident. She's not stupid. For all I know, she's already figured it out. It's my hope that a nice, fat Christmas bonus will keep her mind on other things."

Donnelly paused on that note, gesturing to Ira. "What do you think? Am I missing something?"

"I don't think you are, Patrick. As for Rose, I believe she's smart, and she's clearly loyal. I believe the same holds true with Bubba," Ira said.

Donnelly nodded, validating Ira's assertions. Loyalty meant everything. The world was full of talented, tough and intelligent turncoats, and Donnelly had killed and buried a few in his time. Loyalty superseded a polished tongue, rippling muscles and a high IQ. At the end of the day, you were a hollow executive if you lacked a loyal force at your beck and call.

"Those two have sales potential. I plan to give them an opportunity . . . in time." Donnelly took another sip. "Complementing their loyalty, they're unassuming. What's threatening about some bumbling goofball of a man and a woman who looks like the guy who collects your garbage in the morning?"

Ira nodded. As usual, his boss had a way of painting a picture with few words.

Donnelly continued, "Like I said, we'll give them some time off; Bubba's certainly going to need it. In the off-chance Aiello gets sprung, I don't want them out in the open. Nashua's as good a place as any to lay low. While they recoup, I'll call on Judge Grant to give them cover."

Donnelly took the last of his scotch, allowing Ira a chance to catch up on his scribbles. "I need some time to consider their next assignment. Eventually sales, yes, but maybe something else first. Meantime, I'd just as soon let them think that a return to civilian life lay ahead."

Donnelly stood up and stretched his legs. It was nearly 1:00 a.m., long past bedtime for most, but not for him. Just as soon as they wrapped up their business, Patrick had a date. A redheaded spitfire was waiting back in his Southie condo under the sheets, as he had instructed. Then he remembered Ira mentioning something troubling about the night.

"So, what's this 'not-so-good' news you have?" he asked.

Ira looked uneasy. “It’s Aiello. My concern is how we link him to attempted murder without a gun.”

Donnelly laughed, dismissing Ira’s concern.

“What I would’ve given to seen the look on Aiello’s face as McElroy and Cartwright’s goons tuned him up. If those gorillas did their job right, he may have dropped a dime on his boss. I have to think Gambini, with no knowledge of Aiello’s condition, is sweating it out back in Providence.”

“Any word to pass to Tony, boss? Again, my concern is that they let him go if they can’t find the gun that Rose tossed. While that may seem remote, I’d rather be safe—”

“It’s covered, Ira,” Donnelly said. “Tell McElroy that Cartwright’s thugs needn’t waste their time scrounging for a pistol they’ll never uncover.”

A smile touched the corners of Ira’s mouth.

“They need to get back outside, somewhere near the storm wall. Near that wooden stand used for the fireworks. If they haven’t found it yet, they’ll find what they’re looking for.”

Donnelly grinned as he slipped on his pea coat to leave.

“It’ll be real hard for Aiello to explain away a sniper rifle, one with his prints all over it, one he’d taken on a deer hunt a few weeks ago, lying on the president-elect’s property.”

Chapter fifty-four

Rose sat on the leather couch, her head hung low. She was moping. Filtered through the walls, she heard laughter. She pictured the cheer in the nurses' lounge as a cart loaded with top -shelf spirits arrived. All the gaiety started to piss her off.

Now that's how you celebrate Christmas! You clink glasses. You imbibe. You laugh, even sing. You enjoy the company that surrounds you. What you don't do is sit helpless while a so-called friend berates you over your lifestyle choices, especially ones you had no choice making in the first place! So, I screwed up and got into some trouble. Who hasn't? No one's perfect, and Olaf was no saint herself. Hell, she'd even said as much. Besides, it's not like I had any choice in the matter.

With an idea of where all this was headed, Rose offered what she considered to be a most modest request.

"If I have to sit through your screed, then at least offer me a drink. Consider it a final request," Rose said.

Olaf glared back in silence. Rose pressed the matter. "Margo, you have no idea what we've been through tonight. None at all. The least you can do is to honor my request."

Rose took a more courteous tack. "I mean, it is Christmas after all."

Olaf said nothing as she stood up. She huffed and then whooshed past Rose before she walked out of the doctors' lounge and shut the door behind her. A few minutes later, she was back in the room, toting a box filled with bottles and a few glasses. Rose smiled.

From over her shoulder, Rose heard ice being dropped into

glasses. The slow pour of liquor followed. A splash of some carbonated beverage completed the drinks. Rose licked her chapped lips in anticipation. Olaf appeared next to her, extending a glass filled with a dark liquid, bubbles rising to the surface in place. The lounge lighting was dim, but the drink was a no-doubter: rum and Coke. Not one of Rose's favorites, but it would do.

"To friendship," Rose said, raising her glass high and out in front of her.

Olaf tipped her glass in return, but said nothing.

Rose took a healthy swig, downing half the drink in one swallow. Immediately, she spat it all out, coughing and choking, in a wide spray which rained down on the carpet.

"What the hell!" She coughed some more and spat a little too. "I think you forgot something, Margo . . . a key component . . . like rum."

"I didn't forget a thing," Olaf snapped. She shook her head in mild amusement. "That's your problem, Rose—your drinking. Ever since you left here back in September, it's been fucking up your judgment. Tonight's escapade up in Maine proves my point."

Olaf swung around to the front of the couch, opposite Rose, and took a seat in the exact spot she had sat in their first doctors' lounge come-to-Jesus session.

Rose fired back. "Oh, is that right?" She pointed at Olaf's glass in an attempt to deflect attention. "Bet you didn't screw that one up."

"There you go, Rose. The best defense is a good offense, isn't it? Go ahead, redirect all you want," Olaf said.

"Well, if you think I'm just gonna sit here and get ripped apart and not take up for myself, then you're sorely mistaken," Rose said, her voice trembling in anger.

Olaf took a sip of her whiskey and made a face as she swallowed. She then leaned in as if to respond but said nothing.

Rose continued. "Last time I checked, you didn't have some murderous thug giving you orders, forcing you and your partner into life-and-death situations. No, not Margo Olaf, nurse extraordinaire. Saint Joe's head nurse gets her orders from mild-mannered men with prescription glasses and receding hairlines, men who attend their daughters' dance recitals, mow their lawns on Sunday and . . . and drive fucking minivans or goddamned station wagons." Rose looked away for a moment and ran both hands through her disheveled hair. She pulled up her dress's shoulder straps which had drooped. "Until you walk a few steps in my moccasins, kemo sabe, I'm not interested in your sanctimonious bullshit."

"You forgot a few people, Rose," Olaf said. Her voice was steady and calm. "What about your abusive dad? How about that school department? They really worked you over, too. Let's not leave them out."

"That's right! Thanks for the reminder. Yes, the goddamned school department. After years of loyal service as a sub, they sure did fuck me over."

Rose shot up from the couch, her face red. Sweat had begun to bead on her forehead. She threw back her shoulders, jabbed an index finger into the air, gritting her teeth.

"As for my father, what more needs to be said that hasn't already been said. Point of fact—he ruined my life."

Rose stormed over to the bar. Olaf said nothing. With her back to Olaf, Rose continued her tirade.

"For the record, I don't give a shit if you're judging me or thinking about sending a letter to some asshole judge suggesting that I be committed to the funny farm."

Rose plopped an ice cube into a fresh glass, and then filled it with El Dorado rum. Coke would not be a part of this tipple. "As my partner would say, 'I'm fixin' to drink this here drink down.'"

Rose stomped back towards Olaf, clenching the glass in her right hand. She stopped just in front of Olaf, holding the glass out as if daring her friend to knock it out of her hands.

"Here's a toast," Rose began, her hand and arm beginning to shudder. "To my dad, my dear old dad. May he rot in hell." She swung her arm off to the right, raising it higher. "To Nashua's school department, may it lose the public trust as it continues its reckless journey of filling children's heads with bullshit."

Rose turned symbolically to the left, swinging her arm in that direction and raised her glass. "And to Donnelly, may he live just long enough to pay me for my services before he loses his amazing fucking hair and then dies of some venereal disease."

Her wishes declared, she tilted back her head, opened wide and fired the liquor down her gullet. Not a drop of the pricey rum touched her lips. Unimpressed, Olaf got up and snatched Rose's empty glass on the way back to the bar.

"So, let me see if I got it all right," Olaf said, as she strode to the richly polished bar. "Your dad, a series of lousy relationships in California—let's not forget those—the school department, and some mobster in Boston have all conspired to keep you down?" Olaf turned around and flashed four fingers, counting each finger with the opposite hand. "Did I get that about right?"

Rose looked at Olaf with suspicion, anticipating a "gotcha"

moment. When it didn't come, she shrugged her shoulders and rolled her eyes, attempting to exude an indifference that she could not pull off. She lowered herself to the couch. Her friend, as tough as she had been on her tonight, had summed it up as well as anyone could. It had all begun with her father. Of that, there was no debate. He had led the charge.

It was her father, the abusive, despicable drunkard, who sent her out to face the world, already down in the count, oh-and -two. Two strikes from the jump and no mulligans for Rose McDougal. He had her digging out of the hole he had put her in at a young age. A series of boyfriends through the '60s followed. Each one served to fortify her teenaged failings through her father's specialized barrage of mental abuse. Each failed relationship a reminder of the father she had left across the country, the king abuser himself. Each boyfriend had let her down and proved to be a lying, conniving scumbag.

But for a few years in the Army, the years which followed proved equally as destructive. Compounding setbacks littered her journey through her thirties. The move to Nashua had solved nothing. To this day, she was still unsure about what drew her to Nashua in the first place. Opportunity? The promise of a new job? Years of what she considered faithful service as a damned good teacher had earned her nothing for enduring the unrelenting parental caterwauling and school department handwringing. Rose learned quickly that no student was ever in the wrong. When she needed the school department to resolve an issue, they were nowhere to be found. Part-timers like her were given short shrift. As it happened, the skimpy pay of a substitute afforded one only the most modest of accommodations, hence the last two prison cells she had called home, homes which some hardened criminals might have eschewed. On her meager pay, they were all she could afford.

So, I fucked up and made an unwitting deal with the devil incarnate to deliver boxes of unknown contents. Unknown initially, anyway. As if I ever had a choice.

Though Donnelly paid her well, the money came at a steep cost. She despised being a villain and feared its many associated perils. She was ashamed at the very thought of aiding in the spread of illegal drugs. But with a gun to your head and the very real threat of death, it was damned if you do, dead if you don't. Negotiating with the likes of Patrick Donnelly was pure fantasy. In the end, she had no choice but to do her job as well as she could.

When it came down to cataloging a lifetime of failures, Rose was perfectly content to pass the buck while, at the same time, attempting to justify her own illegal capers. Scapegoating became a natural defense mechanism. Remove the sinister actors in her life, all of whom were men, and who knows what happiness she might have found, what lofty professional status she might have attained. The boiling hostility she felt was therefore justified. So, too, was her newfound abuse of alcohol. Whether Olaf accepted it or not, Rose's massive intake of booze since her attempted suicide was, at least to Rose, therapeutic.

"I guess that's it," Olaf said, slapping her knees. "It'll always be someone else's fault while you remain the helpless bystander, possessing no control of your life."

Olaf's words hung in the air. Rose leaned forward, contemplating a protest, but refrained.

The Christmas celebration continued on in the nurses' lounge. The spirits that Tricia wheeled in had put a celebratory charge into what was already a lively gathering. All except Frankie partook in the consumption of alcohol. Quite content with a ginger ale, he lay stretched out on a long couch watching *A Year Without a Santa Claus*, one of his all-time-favorites and one whose lines he knew by heart. The TV and VCR had come from the AV room, along with an extension cord, allowing the entertainment to be delivered to within arm's reach, just as Frankie liked it. Every so often he would recite the lines of one of the puppet characters. Snow Miser, Mother Nature's flamboyant son, was his favorite. Accompanying the movie was a package of fudge-covered Oreos, into which he periodically dipped his left hand, since his right arm still stung. On most nights, he was allowed three Oreos, but tonight his mother was feeling generous; there would be no limit, she had told him.

Adding to Frankie's delight was his mother's report that Santa himself had been spotted over Nashua. His elation, however, was short-lived. It didn't make sense to him, since he had just come from some place far away. He shot up to a seated position.

"Ma . . . ma, we were in one place and now we're in another. So, how will Santa know where to bring my presents?" he asked. His eyes begged for some good news, something which would wipe away his fear.

He got it.

"Friends in the White House," Diane interjected and then winked at him.

Frankie was, and would for his lifetime, remain a simple man, but he did know about the President of the United States and the power and knowledge inherent in that position. And he sure knew his hero, Santa Claus. As if he didn't have enough reasons to love Santa, he now had another. Despite the crazy turn of events over the last several hours, Santa would still know where to find him. For another year, and another Christmas, Santa would maintain the number one ranking on Frankie's top ten list. It seemed Dr. Who, the witty English time-travelling detective, was destined to remain the runner-up.

As Frankie cheered on Santa and Rudolph, classic Christmas tunes entertained the others. Renee had found a radio in the AV room. The magical Christmases she adored as a child were marked with memories of caroling in her Amherst neighborhood, a true Norman Rockwell community. In her teens, caroling with her parents had become somewhat awkward, but thank God for the liberation of adulthood. At age thirty-two, she could not wait to gather her friends, both new and old, to join in song. Nashua's AM station could be counted on to deliver the Christmas classics. When "Joy to The World" came on, she pulled everyone together and raised her glass as the designated conductor. She led them in a rousing rendition of the timeless American masterpiece.

Bubba tried his hand at singing but sat back down. The nurses had assessed his prognosis as very good, but it would be several weeks before he returned to full strength. Daily rehabilitation would be necessary. For sure, the medical costs would be staggering, but they would be no concern of his. A few minutes earlier, Donna had raced upstairs to take an urgent phone call on Nurse Olaf's behalf. The caller, who wished to remain anonymous, informed her that a man would show up at the hospital before dawn. He would be carrying a considerable amount of money, more than enough to cover the medical bills associated with Bubba's and Frankie's recovery. The one caveat: the caller asked that Bubba and Frankie leave the hospital as soon as possible.

"I'm sure the head nurse would agree that keeping the two in the hospital for long would only invite trouble. For her as well as my boss," the mystery caller added.

Donna didn't need to consult with Olaf on that one. They had stuck their necks out helping Bubba and Frankie. She promised the caller that the two were in good shape and would be leaving soon. The caller informed her that part of the money to be delivered would include Bubba's and Rose's living expenses. In fact, there was already a furnished apartment waiting for Bubba in the Dunstable House, the same place where Rose called home.

The caller closed by adding that there was a little something in it for Donna and the head nurse, provided she kept the transaction a private matter. Donna politely dismissed the gift but assured the man that she and Nurse Olaf would have them out of the hospital as soon as possible.

When Donna informed Bubba about the call, he feigned surprise, claiming he had always wondered what had happened to his wealthy uncle who had "skipped town and moved north without a word."

But Bubba was hardly surprised. Donnelly's ability to effectively manage a far-flung network, one which kept him constantly informed, was impressive. He's good. Really good. Bubba began to accept the fact that, like it or not, his dealings with Donnelly were not finished.

He set aside his drink and thought about his earlier phone call with his mother. Their brief chat was something else that troubled him. True, his mother had said she missed him; said Christmas was not the same without him; and said that she could not wait to see him. That aside, Bubba noted cheer in her voice. Apparently, Bobby Joe Tarleton, who had always been just a friend, was now her boyfriend. *When had that happened?* More than that, they headed to Naples, Florida, in the morning. They had plans to go snorkeling and deep-sea fishing. They would be gone for a week, maybe more. Since they would be leaving early, they needed their sleep, so she had to keep the call short, which was probably appropriate since he was using the First Lady's mobile phone.

The chat with his mom did little to raise Bubba's spirits. On the contrary, he found himself feeling homesick. Bubba could not remember Bobby Joe and his mom being anything more than churchgoing acquaintances. While it irked him on one level, he had always hoped his momma would find a good man. Selfishly, however, he felt left out. Bobby Joe is a decent, God-fearing man, but how had things between he and mom moved so fast? She never mentioned Bobby Joe in any of her letters or phone calls.

Since when did momma learn to snorkel? She never even wanted to go to the lake, let alone the shark-infested Gulf of Mexico. Just how long have I been away?

He pondered the last question, but only briefly. His thoughts turned to Rose.

Renee had informed him that it might be some time before Nurse Margo would be finished with her, whatever "finished with" meant. Bubba knew about Rose's friendship with Margo. He also suspected that Margo, who had stuck her neck out for the three of them tonight, had a few things to say to her about the whole imposition. Being the classy lady she apparently was, she was polite enough to deliver any verbal blows behind closed doors. Bubba only hoped that whatever Rose was taking would not last much longer. For certain, she would need a drink. Which reminded him of his vodka tonic, tucked away behind the couch. He checked to make sure no one was watching. He reached for it and took a quick sip before placing it back.

As the drink slid down his throat, "Auld Lang Syne" came on the radio. He watched as Claire swung her glass high above her head, spilling drops of clear liquid onto the floor while singing off-key. Amongst the lot, she seemed the most buzzed. Bubba tipped his glass in the direction of the doctors' lounge, where Rose was getting worked over. He then frowned and dipped his head before returning his thoughts to Donnelly's vast reach and his momma's Christmas revelation. Both were unsettling. It was easier worrying about Rose than his smitten mother and the Irish mobster. Silently, he wished Rose well. What Bubba could not have seen coming was his own verbal dress-down, which he was about to receive.

Diane Cartwright walked over and stood looming over his shoulder, though Bubba didn't notice right away. It was her feet, appearing in his peripheral vision, which alerted him. He lifted his head, straightened his back and smiled.

"Oh, ma'am. Thanks again for allowing me the use of that phone."

Bubba started to stand but was told that wouldn't be necessary. Diane grabbed a chair nearby and pulled it close. Gone was the holiday joy in her visage. In its place was something else, something he remembered seeing in his younger years. As a child, whenever his mother appeared vexed, he knew he had done wrong and was about to get it. He saw the same look on the First Lady's face. She wasted no time getting to the point.

"I know that whatever business brought you and Rose into my house this evening also brought a man who kills for the mob."

Bubba did not move an inch. He listened.

"I'm not going to ask how you got mixed up with that assassin, and maybe you and Rose don't know."

He kept his mouth shut. A rejoinder would not have been welcomed. Given the First Lady's observation, he figured Donnelly might also have known something about the presence of that hit man. And if Donnelly had known something, then why hadn't he given fair warning to he and Rose, he wondered.

"I could ask what you two were doing under my roof, but I'm not. What I really want to know is what kind of a person—and that would be your friend, Rose—thanks a man for saving her life by recklessly involving him in some kind of scheme to line her own pockets."

Diane inched a little closer. "I could ask any number of questions, but I won't. Not because I'm overly concerned about you and your egotistical partner, but because I care about Frankie and his mother, both of whom, God only knows why, care for your friend, Rose."

Bubba opened his mouth to speak but Diane raised a hand, palm open and facing Bubba. This was exactly like a childhood scolding that preceded a short walk outside to pull a switch, or a trip to his room for a week of incarceration.

"Claire and Frankie have become my friends. I intend to keep in touch with them. In fact, I'm going to invite them to the White House." She raised a finger and then glanced left to right, ensuring there were no prying eyes before delivering her warning.

"Listen to me and listen good. If any harm should fall on those two, then I will track down you and Rose and deal with you myself." She leaned back and flashed a cunning smile. "Of course, I'm not going to have to worry about that, am I?"

Bubba choked out his reply. "No . . . um, no, ma'am."

Diane leaned forward and clapped his knee.

"Great. So, let's forget all that and have a drink." She clapped his knee again, this time harder. "Besides, it's Christmas."

As she stood up and then walked off, Bubba sat immobile, processing her warning. He watched her as she made her way over to join Claire and Rodney, now belting out Burl Ives's rendition of "Rudolph the Red-Nosed Reindeer." In a lifetime, he never could have imagined slow dancing in the president-elect's estate, surviving an assassin's bullet, being threatened by the First Lady while celebrating with her and some new friends in a hospital lounge. *And all in one night.* How wonderfully unexpected the night had been. Bubba didn't dwell on Mrs. Cartwright's words for long. He would do just as she had asked, not only because he respected her, but because Frankie had just saved his ass. For the moment, Bubba put aside his concerns. He looked over at Frankie, entranced with his movie, and smiled at his new friend.

Chapter fifty-five

Rose decided to simply wait it out. Sooner or later, Margo would be called away on business. Sooner or later, she would need to approve an injection or review someone's charts. Sooner or later, she would have to assign work details, see to it that the toilets shined, the floors sparkled and the windows shimmered. So what if it was the wee hours of Christmas morning, there was always work to be done in a hospital. There were patients who needed care, orderlies who needed to be tasked. By Rose's estimation, Olaf had devoted close to three hours preparing for and tending to Bubba and Frankie. Surely other things needed doing. There was no way Olaf could spend the rest of the night with her in this room.

"Just so you know, I got nowhere else to be tonight," Olaf said. "I'm not leaving this room—and neither are you—until I get what I want."

Rose cast a defeated gaze upon Olaf before lowering her head in a shameless attempt to score sympathy. Olaf gave her a disapproving glance, took Rose's glass and set it next to her own empty glass on the coffee table. Olaf got up and walked over to Rose and lowered her considerable posterior onto the cushion next to her. Rose inched further away. She felt trapped. Part of her wanted to get up and run away. She refused to make eye contact, yet could feel Olaf's stare.

While Olaf's stubborn persistence and insistence to unlock the truth only made Rose increasingly agitated, the nurse was still her friend. Just like her first visit to the lounge, eventually Olaf would eventually get what she wanted. That much was apparent to Rose, and maybe it was for the best. Maybe releasing the truth would prove restorative. Whatever the case, inner turmoil would eat her alive if she didn't say something to Olaf.

Rose's face grew flush, her lips began to quiver, and a tear formed in her eye. She decided to open up.

"Don't you see, Margo? Isn't it crystal clear?" Her voice cracked.

Olaf's eyes softened. Her shoulders, once slung back on the offensive, relaxed.

"I've got nothing . . . I've got nobody," Rose said.

Fresh tears formed in her eyes. She wiped a hand across her face smearing her make-up, and then swung in her seat to face Olaf. She pointed a finger into her own chest.

"I've got only myself. There's never been anyone else I can count on. No family, no man, no job, no future. There's no hope."

Olaf reached for Rose's hand, but Rose withdrew. She was not quite ready to play her role in some pity party.

"I rely on me. When I fail, it's on me. Since I was a young girl, it's been me against . . . against the world." Rose sniffled and wiped fresh tears. She silently cursed her waterworks. "I'm tired, Margo. What the hell am I supposed to do?"

Rose continued. "At least with Donnelly, as much as I hate the sonovabitch and that goddamned job, it puts bread on the table. Knock it all you want, but an unemployed substitute teacher has few choices. Just what are my alternatives? Can you name one?"

Rose gave Margo a moment to reply before continuing. "That's what I thought: there are none." She shook her head, wiped her nose, and then continued.

"And alcohol, what you pin on me as my newest failing, has at least comforted me these past few months."

Olaf waited for Rose to finish, and then spoke. Her voice was soft and reassuring.

"I'm sorry that's how it came across. That wasn't my intention. Honestly, I don't keep score." Olaf inched closer. "You're right. For most of your life, it's been just you. I can't fault you for the choices you've made. If the shoe was on the other foot, I'm sure I would've done the same."

She reached for Rose's hand. This time, Rose didn't pull away.

"You're an adult. You're free to do as you please. Please don't take this as a knock against you, but you're free to continue drinking to excess and free to keep working for that mobster," Olaf paused and then leaned in closer. "And you're free to keep convincing yourself that you can't do any better and that you're doomed."

Olaf looked deeply into Rose's moist eyes. Fresh tears traced paths down Rose's cheeks. "You can keep building your own tomb—the demons of your past are the bricks, your self-loathing in the present is the mortar."

"Come what may, I have only myself in the end," Rose said. Her tone was calm.

"But you're wrong. You're so wrong," Olaf said.

She swung her right arm around Rose's shoulders. Rose perked up.

"You've got a lot more than you think. You've got me. You've got Claire. You've got Vic and you've got Flo. Speaking of Flo, can you imagine her reaction if she knew what you'd been up to? Jeez," Olaf chuckled softly. "You've got Bubba, whose life you may have saved tonight. Perhaps above all, you've got Frankie's unwavering respect and admiration."

Rose lifted her chin and looked into Olaf's dark eyes.

"I know what you did for him years ago in that schoolyard. I know how you pulled those bullies off of him. I also know those were the types of bullies who only punched harder when the tears came." Olaf lifted her arm off Rose's shoulder and turned to face her directly. "You put a stop to it, Rose. You not only spared him a vicious beating, but you spared Frankie from another humiliating experience in a childhood marked with too many of them. I'm sure he's never forgotten."

Rose was dumbfounded. "How'd you know about . . . I mean, where'd you hear . . .?"

Olaf shook her head, "It doesn't matter how I know. It speaks to the value other people place on you, Rose."

"I don't get you, Margo. I mean, why do you put so much effort into my happiness? Why bother with a wretch like me? I bring nothing but pain and suffering. Look what I put you and your nurses through tonight. Look at what Frankie got himself drawn into, for crissakes."

"Have you heard anything I've said? You take up for Frankie, and his mother. Who else does that? Who else treats Frankie like a human being? No one. You spend lots of your time with Flo. You bring friendship into her lonely existence, a friendship she craves. It doesn't matter to her whether it's bingo or bowling or just chatting on the phone. It's all time well spent for her. I know this for a fact—she told me." Olaf paused for a moment and pulled a handkerchief from a pocket. She offered it to Rose, who accepted it and dabbed her eyes. "Above all, it was you who carried her through her suffering after her husband died. After the burial, it was you who gave her the strength to get up every morning. One morning at a time, you told her."

"She told you about that?"

"Rose, you've enriched my life in the past few months. You've introduced me to your friends. I now consider Flo and Claire as friends of my own. You've been my own sounding board, my reflecting pool. I see a lot of myself in you, young lady. I cherish you and thank God for our friendship, which I'd like to think is solid."

"But everything I touch . . . all the people I've hurt . . ."

"Does the person I just described sound like someone who has nothing to offer?" Olaf shook her head. "Here's the good news: whatever wrongs you've committed are all in the past. They can be wiped away like a bad dream."

Rose hung onto Olaf's words, words that seemed so familiar.

Chapter fifty-six

On April 10, Nashua shattered a weather record. The mercury soared to a whopping ninety-five degrees. Not only the hottest for that date, it was the hottest ever for the month of April. Even weatherman Al Kaprelian could not have imagined such heat. In July? Perhaps. In April? No way. Certainly not after an inch of snow four days earlier. Al was practically speechless, something unprecedented for the zany weatherman. During WNDS's "Mid-Afternoon Round-Up," with his hands folded and intoning like a mortician, Al took a large swallow of humble pie, wondering how his prediction of eighty degrees could have been so far off. The two anchors somberly nodded. For the time being, summer had supplanted the New England spring. At five in the afternoon, when Rose arrived at Kegler's Den for the party, it was still a blistering ninety-two.

Rose had called Vic a few days earlier and requested a favor. She needed his special touch for a party honoring her friends. Vic was happy to oblige. In honor of the event, he opened his beer garden, which sat outside behind his bar. The garden's umbrella-shaded tables, flanked on three sides by maple trees and rhododendron bushes, provided a most comfortable setting. Four speakers, mounted on fence posts and under plastic shells, piped out the jukebox music from inside. The resplendent beer garden was one of Nashua's best-kept secrets. Other than bowlers from the adjacent Leda Lanes, very few were aware of its existence.

If not for Rose, Vic would have kept it closed until the summer. For her, however, he made a special concession. He went so far as to roll out his twelve-foot-long banquet table, eliciting the assistance of Roger Poisson, one of his regular barstool-boozers, who fussed and griped about the heat as he negotiated his end of the table through the narrow doorway from the bar. Vic might have never told Rose in person, but he had really missed her while she was away. It was good to have her back.

April 10 was the first chance, since the unscheduled gathering on Christmas, that Rose was able to bring the gang together for a celebration; Flo was the only one unable to attend. As Rose reminded Bubba, this would be an opportune time to make good on his pledge to "pick up the tab," a pledge he had made while bleeding in her backseat on Christmas Eve. At least, that was how she chose to remember it. For the group, there was much ground to cover, much to report over the last three months. Many pitchers of beer would be in order. So, too, would food. To that end, Vic prepared a feast, spending several hours barbecuing racks of ribs and cooking his special beans and other fixings.

By 5:30, the whole crew was assembled in the beer garden. Rose got down to business right away. She gave them an assignment, a most simple one. Everyone at the table was to provide a recap of what they had been up to over the last few months. To decide who would lead off, she spun an empty beer bottle on the table. It stopped on Claire.

Claire happily reported that there was now a man in her life, one she had met at work. They had been dating since Valentine's Day. His name was Ricky Gentile and he was thirty-eight, fourteen years younger than she. Of his many charming qualities, nothing mattered as much to her as how warmly he had received Frankie.

Rose could see it in Claire's eyes. She lit up when she said his name.

"And the sex has been mind-blowing?" Rose asked.

The others laughed as Claire faked shock before quickly joining in the laughter.

"Well . . ." Claire looked over at Frankie, who was mesmerized by his handheld Dig Dug video game, and confessed, "yes, of course, . . . there is that."

Then came the invitation to the White House from the First Lady herself. Diane Cartwright had called her inviting her and Frankie down for the Fourth of July celebration. If Frankie liked the Christmas firework display, then he would love this show, Diane promised. They would be her personal guests and would stay in the White House. Ricky was also welcome.

"Ricky actually voted for Cartwright. He'll fit right in!" Claire joked.

Rose held her nose and shook her head, as Bubba glanced at her. To anyone who happened to notice, Bubba looked distant, preoccupied. His mind was someplace else. His face was ashen and there were bags under his eyes. But Rose never noticed and neither did the others. They were too caught up with what Claire had to say. Without a word, Bubba stood up and grabbed the two empty pitchers.

"Anything else while I'm inside?" he asked.

"Since you're offering, yes, there is. A most important task." Rose jabbed a thumb at the speakers behind her. "Please fix the music. Rap music doesn't fly here."

He forced a smile and then walked away. A few minutes later, as Olaf began her recap, The Doors' "Crystal Ship" cut short an obnoxious song about "hos and bros." Before the song ended, Bubba was back with two pitchers of beer.

While Claire had been busy nurturing a relationship, Olaf had been busy at work. Nothing extraordinary, she reported. Her New Year's pledge to cut back on work had gone unfulfilled. Olaf was now working more than ever.

"So, the way I see it, I'll keep doing what I'm doing until I'm dead," she said, before taking a healthy swallow of beer and fanning her shirt. It was still brutally hot, even as the sun dipped below the Monadnock Mountains. The Doors filled the temporary silence before Olaf continued.

"Or until Stanley leaves me for some young Russian eye-candy that he orders from some magazine offering discount brides," Olaf smiled and gestured to Claire. "If that happens, then I'll call Cupid and ask that he set me up with a young hunk like your Ricky."

Rose and Vic laughed. Rose regarded Bubba as he reached for a pitcher. She noticed his pallid complexion. *Probably just a late night out*, she figured. Then she noticed something else: the distance in his eyes. She didn't have much time to dwell on it; Olaf interrupted her train of thought.

"Seriously though," Olaf said looking across the table at Claire, "I'm happy for you, Claire. You deserve the best."

"To Claire," Rose said, raising her glass in a cheer. Around the table, glasses clinked. "If this Ricky screws up, I'll kill him."

"Now that's my partner," Bubba declared, forcing enthusiasm. He stood up and raised his glass. "To Rose: a ball-busting gal whom I cherish so." He looked down at her and winked. He reached across the table and tried to pinch her cheeks, but she slapped his hand away.

"How about I put you in timeout, Gomer," Rose warned.

"Promise? Sounds kinky" Bubba announced. He looked around the table, expecting laughter. Awkward glances greeted him. No one found his proclamation funny. He sat back down across the table from Rose. As soon as he seated himself, Rose applied a swift kick under the table, her toes met his left shin.

She leaned across her beer to rebuke him. Cognizant of Olaf and Claire, who sat close by but were busy chatting about Ricky, Rose kept her voice down.

"What the hell's gotten into you? This some kind of stunt like that shit you pulled back in Maine."

Bubba leaned in over the table. Looking left to right, he wiped the smirk off his face. Rose noticed sweat beading on his forehead and around his collar. It wasn't the heat; it was something else. Bubba looked scared. He opened his mouth to speak.

"Listen, Rose, I think we need to—"

That was as far as he got: the food had arrived. Four bins loaded with fragrant BBQ and all the fixings were placed on the banquet table within arm's reach of all. Pitchers of sweet tea came next, along with another pitcher of beer. A final bin was brought out after the beer. In it were hot dogs, Frankie's favorite. Vic thought it necessary to point this out.

"Ok, guys, I'm not playing favorites here, but I need to mention something," he said gesturing to the aluminum bin which sat in front of Frankie. "This here belongs to the hero. What the hero wants, the hero gets. From what I've been told, that's hot dogs."

Claire looked up at Vic, then at Frankie, and smiled. A tear touched the corner of her eye.

Vic continued, "Now, Mr. Hero, am I right to assume that hot dogs are still somewhere on your top ten list?"

Vic winked at Claire.

Rose and Olaf laughed, while Frankie blushed. Frankie spoke slowly, almost as if he was being graded for clarity.

"Well, Mister Vic, they sure are tonight. Thank you so much!"

Frankie, who had been hungry since noon, peeled back the aluminum cover from the hot dog bin. As he did, a pleasing aroma was released. He dug in and loaded his paper plate high. But before he could tackle his insatiable hunger, he had a story to share, it was his turn. Claire filled in most of the details.

Like his mother, Frankie had also landed a new job, but not before scoring more media fame. Shortly after David Popovich splashed the Telegraph's December 27 front page with the declarative headline:

"NASHUA'S HERO DOES IT AGAIN"

The O'Brien phone began ringing off the hook. It seemed everyone wanted a piece of Frankie, a few minutes more with the hometown hero.

Popovich's story included Chuck Aiello's link to a sniper rifle found on the Cartwright property, the very Mr. Aiello whom Frankie had flattened. That linkage transcended Frankie's rescue of mere commoners: Rose McDougal (yes, the same woman whom he had freed from the jaws of death back in September) and a one Bubba Coslaw, of Burgaw, North Carolina. Popovich made no reference as to why those two were at the Cartwright compound and only token mention of Frankie's invitation. Popovich's established link with the later-discovered sniper rifle was that Frankie's assault on Charles Aiello may well have saved the president-elect's life as well. Overnight, Frankie was back on the TV and radio talk show circuit, a place familiar to him.

Eventually, the media fervor decreased and life was back to something approaching routine. By the end of February, Frankie had convinced his mother that he was ready for a job, ready to do what "big boys do." Looking to parlay his bouts of fame into a job, Frankie applied at fourteen Nashua-area restaurants. Since the Nashua Transit Authority had offered him a free lifetime bus pass, transportation to work would not be an issue. All that was left for him was to get hired. Yet despite his fame, few places showed any interest. Most of the interviewers lost interest as soon as he opened his mouth to speak. Frankie's inability to utter an articulate sentence, or put together a coherent thought, scared away would-be employers. That is, until some well-placed friends stepped in to break the logjam.

Adoring letters from President William Cartwright and Governor Alex Reyes proved more than sufficient for Mr. Ernie Berube, the owner of the Friendly's on Amherst Street. Berube received both letters on March 15. That same day, he called and asked Frankie when he could begin. Right away, Frankie told him. Frankie reported the very next day. He couldn't wait to tell his friends.

"I told him, 'Yes sir . . . I have the Mister Governor's and the Mister President's letters. I said he could keep them and you know what he did? Know what he did? He thanked me so much," Frankie said, laughing, toothy grin and all. Claire added that Berube had the letters framed and mounted above the entrance to the kitchen.

The table broke out in laughter. Bubba clapped Frankie's back and then reached for an empty pitcher.

"Stay put. I got the next one," Rose said. Just as she was about to get up, Vic appeared carrying a tray, upon which another chilled pitcher of beer rested.

As Vic walked back inside, the trees across the parking lot began to sway in a fresh breeze. The trees ringing the beer garden began to vacillate lazily. Somewhere a wind chime tinkled a gentle tune. Despite the evening's heat, Rose shuddered as a chill crawled up her spine. At that moment, she remembered a dream she had of reliving the softball championship game where her grandmother appeared. Maybe it was the brush with death, she wondered. She pushed aside her reflection and nodded over at Bubba. It was his turn to share.

Bubba spoke with no feeling, as if reading the vomit bag on a jetliner. As he put it, little had changed: not much to report. Having Rose to cart him around had been convenient.

"She's been great. You know, she takes me to the store . . . the laundromat, too. Sometimes she'll run me up to that Burger King."

Despite being jobless, money had been no issue. As Bubba put it, a "distant uncle," who had gotten wind of his predicament, had been sending Bubba enough to cover the rent, utilities and groceries.

"Well, good for you, Bubba. Nice to see you coming along." Vic said, as he sat down and rejoined the party.

"And now, the woman of the hour," Vic announced, drumming his fingers on the table.

He clapped Rose on the shoulder. Vic's tap, intended as a love pat, caught Rose, and her mouthful of Budweiser, off-guard. Beer spewed out of her mouth, just missing Olaf's plate of BBQ.

"Sorry about the slap, Rose" Vic said. "Anyway, so I hear you landed a job."

Rose nodded and then took a fresh swallow of beer.

"If that's not enough, the new gig is a lot like my last teaching job: it's safe and it's routine. Which I like. And get this: I'll be supervising a dozen or so hormone-infested little brats, probably some of the same little fuckers I had—"

No sooner did the words escape her mouth than she clapped a hand over it.

"Oops, sorry buddy," she said to Frankie. "That one got away."

"It's okay, Miss Rose. That wasn't as bad as all those words . . .

those *really* bad words you used when you burned yourself in the car and Bubba was hurting really bad and . . . and I helped." Frankie chuckled heartily, before shoveling another mound of food into his mouth.

"Yes, well, I suppose it wasn't." Rose shrugged her shoulders and flashed a crooked smile to Claire.

"This calls for another toast, a very important one," Vic said to the group. He raised a glass and led the toast.

"To Rose McDougal, my friend, who is leaving her free-spirited life to become a tax-paying zombie like the rest of us. Before long, she'll be reading the Sunday paper, clipping coupons, wearing nice dresses, parking between the white lines and, as we just witnessed, excusing herself when using profanity in public."

Vic shook his head in a gesture of mock sorrow and sighed heavily. Claire and Olaf clapped and congratulated him on a brilliant tribute.

Beyond the beer garden, pine trees maintained their dance in the evening breeze. Restless birds, sensing a change in the weather, took flight, skirting across the parking lot to a destination unknown. The wind chime kept in tune.

"Let's hear more about the job, hotshot," Claire said.

"Well, just my luck, this one's cousin . . ." Rose jabbed a finger in Olaf's direction, "hired me as a shift supervisor at the Friendly's where Frankie works." She winked at Frankie whose eyes widened in joy. "Anyway, Margo's cousin owns a bunch of them up in Maine, northern New Hampshire and Vermont. Yup, ole Rose is gonna be wearing a name tag."

Vic craned his neck. "Wait a minute. Is his name Ronnie? If it is, it's gotta be the same guy I'm thinking of. Owns a bunch of restaurants and is kind of a show-boater. He rides around in a limo and parades around with a real bruiser of a guy, a personal security guard or something. I think his name is Scripchek or Cupcheck. It's something like that, right?"

"Yup, that's him. Rochambeau is the show-boater, as you put it," Rose answered. "And I know exactly what you're gonna say: 'How do you trust a guy with a name like Rochambeau?' Well, save your lecture. I'm just happy to have a job." She eyed Bubba and mumbled. "A safe job."

"Yeah, the name Rochambeau doesn't exactly project an image of trust and fair play." Vic laughed and turned to Olaf. "I met your cousin up at a trade show in Concord last fall. He's a flashy guy who likes his entourage, but he's a shrewd businessman. More importantly, he's a good guy, from what I heard. No one had a bad thing to say about him. Said he loved making money, but was a fair broker."

"Let's just hope that business mind was in gear when he bought Friendly's," Rose said.

"Yup, that's my cuz. Always working on making his next million," Olaf said.

There was more laughter. Rose took the final swig from her glass, leaving only a ring of foam around the rim. She stood up. For what seemed like an eternity, she was silent. Then, out of the blue, she released a belch that could have brought down the walls of Jericho. Claire nearly jumped in her seat. Next to her, Frankie burst out laughing.

Having established her ban on decorum, Rose announced, "On that note, I'm gonna go inside and pee. I gotta recycle some of the beer I've drunk."

She got up from the table to make her way inside. Before she got to the door, she heard Claire chime in with her own assault on proper table etiquette. She turned to listen in.

"Ricky says we only borrow the beer we drink." She nodded in self-approval.

Rose nodded, while Vic raised his glass in accord.

Olaf took a shot. "Even though he's almost 60, Stan never tells me he needs to use the men's room. He lets me know that he's 'gotta cop a squirt.'"

Vic and Claire laughed, both saying that was a new one on them. Frankie could not wait to contribute to the juvenile banter.

"I piss, too . . . and . . . and sometimes I forget to shut the door!" Frankie confessed, coughing out his laughter in a fit. Others laughed along.

"Son, was that really necessary?" Claire shook her head, rolling her eyes in mock indignation.

"Okay, everyone done out there?" Rose grinned, standing at the entrance to the bar inside. "I don't wanna be inside and miss out on any stimulating, thought-provoking toilet talk."

She disappeared into the gloomy bar. As she did, Bubba, who had been fidgeting with his fork, shot up from his seat.

"If y'all would excuse me, I need to take a piss myself." He winked at Frankie. "I'll do my best to remember to shut the bathroom door."

He jogged to the entrance which Rose had just used. He walked inside then stopped, allowing his eyes to adjust to the murk. He looked left, then right. She was nowhere to be seen. He spotted Roger Poisson seated at the bar on a stool too high. His legs were crossed and his face was pinched in suspicion.

Bubba called out to him. "Did you see where Rose wandered

off to?"

Poisson scrunched his face even deeper.

Inaudible to Bubba, Poisson muttered, "I don't trust any cretin like you who calls some backwater town down South home." He then jabbed a thumb over his shoulder and scowled.

Bubba offered a "much obliged" and began trotting through the bar toward the entrance to the bowling alley where the restrooms were. He caught the back end of Rose's decaying Granite State Paving softball jersey, **MCDOUGAL 88**, before it disappeared around the corner.

"Rose, stop . . . hold up."

Bubba had waited all day to speak to her alone. What he had to say could not be put off any longer.

As he ran, a new track began on the jukebox. Jefferson Starship's "Miracles," featuring the ranging vocals of a younger Mickey Thomas, drifted from the speakers. Bubba called out again.

"Rose, hold up!"

Rose was just about to enter the ladies' room when she heard Bubba call out. She spun around, immediately detecting the worry on his face.

"What's the matter?" she asked, wariness joining her surprise. She flicked her eyes toward the sign on the door, the door which her left hand pushed open a crack. "You know, I can handle this by myself," she offered.

"He called me this morning."

"He who?" Rose asked. From behind her, the crashing of candlepins preceded an enthusiastic cheer.

"You know who." Bubba's eyes grew wider.

Except she didn't know. Rose had no idea who he was referring to and began to grow impatient.

"Okay, knock off the charades or I'll smack you." Her face was flush. "Just who are you talking about?"

Bubba looked over his shoulders, back towards the bowling alley. Leda Lanes was busy. All but a few lanes were occupied. It was a league night. As busy as it was, however, none of the bowlers or spectators noticed the conversation taking place outside the ladies' room. More candlepins clattered. Another strike.

"I guess I always knew he'd eventually call."

Rose took a step closer. She spoke slowly, as softly as possible. "If you don't tell me who you're talking about, then I'm going to kick you in the goddamned—"

"Donnelly." Bubba cast his eyes to the scuffed tile floor.

"Donnelly called me this morning. Says he's got a job for me."

At once, Rose lost her breath. She felt the color draining from her cheeks.

Bubba looked around again. "He didn't mention your name, and I didn't either, but we both know he ain't taking a 'no' from me. After everything he's done, he knows I owe him."

Rose felt like she could faint where she stood. She gripped the ladies' room doorknob for balance. Candlepins clattered, as if from some distant planet. The cheers that followed came in faded.

"I know I ain't got no business asking you . . ."

Bubba continued to speak, very deliberately. To Rose, however, his words became background noise, like Muzak, that innocuous stuff that drones on in elevators or in a doctor's waiting room. It's music that you never really hear, but you know it's there.

". . . should've expected it, sooner or later, and I 'spose I did. Maybe I hoped . . ."

Rose leaned her shoulder against the bathroom door, convinced that she would faint and maybe vomit, for good measure.

Wouldn't it figure, she thought, *Donnelly coming back to collect.* Coming back to collect his recompense for funding the recovery of one of his soldiers-for-life. She remembered a warning her Gramma had given her as a young girl: get wrapped up with the wrong crowd, Rosey, and see how hard it is to break free.

But this time would be different. She would break free. She had a job, a new life. She had friends who relied on her. Meanwhile, Bubba continued.

". . . but I don't know if I can, you know. It's just . . . just the way he laid it all out, it ain't the type of job for . . ."

Drawn back to the present, Rose pulled herself together and looked at Bubba. She relaxed her shoulders and breathed. For the first time in years, she felt real peace. There would be no recidivism. No more collection calls, no more kicking in doors, no bullets flying. No more perpetual terror. She would not slide into what she once assumed was inevitable: a life of crime and constant danger. She owed that murderous thug nothing. All debts had been paid.

Finally, he asked her what he had been wanting to ask all night: "Will you come with me?"

She placed a hand on his shoulder and stared into his vacant eyes.

"I wish you well, Bubba, God knows I do. But I'm done with Donnelly." She nodded toward the beer garden. "Those people outside—my friends—are what matters now. I'm finished with Donnelly: his drugs, his ego, the guns . . . all his bullshit. I'm out."

She gripped his shoulder and then turned and walked away. Her mind was focused on her friends, not the fear which had dominated her for far too long. She decided she'd share a few more stories and have another beer.

Maybe two, but no more.

Managerial training begins tomorrow. She needs to be focused and fresh.

www.ingramcontent.com/pod-product-compliance
Lightning Source LLC
Chambersburg PA
CBHW060601310726
48982CB00008B/1196/J
* 9 7 8 1 6 2 5 7 0 0 3 5 3 *